Saving GRACE

Michele
Paige
Holmes

Mirror Press

Interior Design by Rachael Anderson
Edited by Annette Lyon, Cassidy Wadsworth and Kelsey Allan
Cover design by Rachael Anderson

Cover Photo Credit: Elizabeth May/Trigger Image
Cover Photo Copyright: Elizabeth May

Published by Mirror Press, LLC
ISBN-10: 1941145264
ISBN-13: 978-1-941145-26-5

To all those seeking forgiveness
or who have yet to forgive–
May you find grace in your life through love,
the greatest power of all.

Other Books by Michele Paige Holmes

Loving Helen: Companion Novella to Saving Grace

Counting Stars

All the Stars in Heaven

My Lucky Stars

Captive Heart

A Timeless Romance Anthology: European Collection

CHAPTER 1

Yorkshire, England—1827

An early-morning mist shrouded the grounds of the Crosby estate as Grace Thatcher slipped out the front doors. For a moment, she stood alone in the chill and darkness, cherishing the silence and freedom where no one could see her. Then, blessing her good fortune at finding such cover, she crept down the wide steps and disappeared into the fog.

She quickly realized her difficulty. Without so much as a candle to guide her, she walked as if blind, hands outstretched, and counted careful steps over the dewy grass separating Lord Crosby's manor from the outbuildings.

One hundred seventy-eight. One hundred seventy-nine. She dared not speak but kept track in her mind, grateful she had taken the time to pace the way the previous evening when the idea for this early-morning conspiracy had first struck. She took a sharp right and extended her leg slowly, foot tapping the ground, searching for the stone steps that led to the bottom of the hill and the stables. When her boot encountered only grass, she realized she hadn't walked as straight as she'd supposed.

No help for it, she thought, dropping to her knees and crawling over the dewy lawn. *Better wet knees than a broken one*. Lord Crosby's stairs were steep and likely slippery at this hour. She'd no desire to begin what was sure to be a trying day by falling down them.

After a few minutes of crawling, her palm struck wet, mossy stone. She started to rise but stopped, listening intently to the sound of labored breathing that was not her own.

Her heart pounded, and she shrank back, though there was nowhere to hide. The dark and mist were her only cover and would not last forever. A little more light or a little less fog, and she would be visible.

Exposed—and alone.

Slowly she reached up and slid a hairpin from her bun.

The breathing grew closer, coming from the bottom of the hill. Someone was climbing the steps. But who? *Or what?*

She waited, hardly daring to breathe, when suddenly a loud sneeze rent the silence. This was followed by a great snort, as if someone were sucking up a cupful of milk through his nose.

Just Harrison. Grace fell backward on the lawn, sagging with relief. *I ought to send him home.*

The countryside did not agree with her servant at all. But as his graying head came into view, his self-sacrifice in aiding her cause did much to warm Grace's heart on that cold morning. Seeing the older man's labored breathing and unusually slow progress, she felt a swell of affection for her driver-turned-footman, turned her general caretaker.

"What are you doing here?" She stood and gave her skirts a shake, then moved closer to better discern his features. "You nearly scared my wits from me, sounding like any number of ravenous creatures who might be about."

"Beg pardon, Miss Thatcher." Harrison snorted again,

then sneezed loudly. "Though it'd take much more'n a little noise to relieve you of your wits. You've a great deal more about you than most young ladies."

"Possibly because I am considerably *older* than most young ladies," Grace said, not the least bothered by the fact that at twenty-four she was decidedly an old maid. And a maid she planned to remain, in spite of her current circumstances: on exhibit for a select number of men who might offer marriage.

Harrison sneezed again, this time bending with the effort.

"You shouldn't be out in this chill," Grace said, drawing her shawl closer. She'd left her cloak at the manor, preferring to have less clothing to hide after her transformation.

"Had to come," he said, a note of concern in his voice. "Are you still set to go through with it?"

"I am." Grace nodded, then hugged her arms beneath the shawl. "I've got to."

"Hmph." Harrison's usual expression could mean any number of things, depending upon the occasion. "Best get it over with then. Take care on the steps."

"It isn't the steps I'm most worried about," Grace said, taking care nonetheless. "It's the riding that has me fearing for my neck."

"You're as fine a rider as any who'll be going out," Harrison reassured her. "And lighter in the saddle too."

"Let us hope so," Grace said. "Were you able to get the stable boy's clothing?"

He shook his head. "No."

Grace's heart fell. Without a disguise, she would never make it to the lawn. She'd never be permitted anywhere near the hunt.

"I've something better," Harrison said, a touch of pride in his voice. "Something the duke himself would have approved of."

At the mention of her grandfather, Grace felt a clutch of sorrow. Were he still alive, she would be acting the part of a gentle-bred lady. Instead, she was being offered up as payment from her father to Lord Crosby.

"I needn't anything fancy to ride," she said. "I'm not proud." *Just desperate to escape this place without an offer of marriage.* "A pair of stable boy's breeches and a horse with a decent gait will do fine."

"Not for you," Harrison said, shaking his head stubbornly. "Your grandfather'd return from the grave to flay me. He'd expect me to do everything in my power to best aid your plan—however peculiar it may be."

They reached the barn doors. He opened one for her, and Grace stepped inside. He followed, closing the door behind them, then taking a minute to light a lantern hanging on a peg inside the door.

Grace rubbed her tired eyes and tried to adjust to her surroundings. Harrison trudged by, sneezing as he passed, and led her to the second-to-the-last stall.

"Go on and look," he said, holding the lantern high, which illuminated his face alight with an expression akin to a child's at Christmas.

Grace peeked over the stall; there was no animal inside, so she swung the door open but stopped before she'd even taken a step. Her eyes were riveted on a scarlet coat, black top hat, and buff breeches, all hanging from nails at the back.

"Oh, Harrison." She breathed out a sigh of utmost gratitude before turning her most radiant smile upon him. "You've outdone yourself. However did you come upon these? Outfitted like this, I shall be able to ride very near Lord Crosby."

"And unseat him when you do." Harrison chuckled. "It would have done you no good to pose as an earth stopper. You wouldn't have been able to get close enough for his lordship to notice."

"He'll notice me now." Grace imagined the expression on pompous Lord Crosby's face after he'd discovered a *woman* riding with him on the hunt. *He'll be furious.*

Best not to be too *close to him when that happens.*

She stepped into the stall for a better look at the huntsman's kit. Her fingers traced the gold buttons fronting the coat. "Specially made buttons for his hunt." She wrinkled her nose at the Crosby seal. "Disgusting. It shall pain me to wear this. The stable boy's clothing, at least, would not have had his crest."

"I wouldn't be sure about that," Harrison said. "Look around. Most everything bears his name or coat of arms. The fox they catch on his land today'll probably have a Crosby brand burned into it already."

Imagining Lord Crosby doing the same to her were she to remain much longer, Grace rubbed her arms briskly, attempting to ward off the cold—and the chilling thought. Since her arrival three days earlier, he had chosen what she ate for each meal. He'd sent specific gowns up for her to wear. He'd instructed her in what to say to other guests during dinner. And in general, he had paraded her around in a manner befitting a child's prized toy. She was to look and act a certain way, with no deviation whatsoever.

Today I am deviating.

Grace snatched the clothing from the wall and began pulling the stall door shut so she could change.

Harrison turned his back to her and walked toward the stable doors. "I'll stand watch."

"And I'll hurry. I still need to become acquainted with the horse I am to ride." Grace quickly discarded the borrowed servant's clothing. She'd had to dress without the help of her lady's maid, so she had nothing cumbersome to worry over.

Men's clothing is so much simpler, she thought as she pulled on the breeches and shirt and buttoned the coat. The latter was large, but that was to be expected. She didn't care, so long as the fit looked decent enough for her to blend in with the others on the hunt.

Her hair was already pinned up, but she took care to tuck any stray wisps into the hat. *No point in revealing my identity before I am ready.*

She exited the barn and turned slowly for Harrison to see. "Well, what do you think?"

His eyes remained averted, refusing to look at her directly. "You're wearing women's boots."

"They'll have to do." Grace shrugged. "I've got to have control of my feet, haven't I?"

"I suppose." Harrison came forward, raising his head slightly. A look of consternation creased his brow. "May I?" He nodded at her poorly tied cravat.

"Please," Grace said. "In addition to your numerous other duties, you may act the part of valet as well."

Harrison frowned. "I'll leave the fussing over clothes to Miranda." But he adjusted the cravat then stepped back.

Grace smiled at him. She took a deep breath, clearing her mind and steadying her resolve for the act she was about to undertake. "I'm ready."

"Ready to catch a fox?"

Grace wrinkled her nose. "Ugh. The poor things. Don't remind me."

"I meant Lord Crosby. We must remove you from his teeth before you're good and stuck. Now, are you ready to catch a *fox*?"

Grace laughed. "Oh yes. And Lord Crosby is the worst kind there is."

The horse Harrison had found was quite remarkable. Grace hadn't had the privilege of riding for close to a year, and her first few minutes—albeit in a saddle and position she was not accustomed to—were sheer joy.

Freedom! Her heart soared, and it was all she could do to not ignore those gathering for the hunt and ride off on her own. But there was her younger sister Helen to think of, so Grace slowed her mount and reined in upon the outskirts of the whippers-in.

Harrison had said she was wearing the clothing of a Baron Davies, one of the youngest participants, who'd suddenly become ill last night. At Harrison's request, Grace had not inquired as to how sick the baron was or how his untimely illness had come about. But she had been assured that after a day spent becoming well-acquainted with a chamber pot, the baron could be expected to make a full recovery.

By then Grace planned to have his clothing safely returned and to be well on her journey away from Lord Crosby's. But for now she hung back, on the fringe of those gathering for the meet. She'd readied herself a full half hour ahead of the others, and from a distance she watched Lord Crosby greet the assembly.

Will he miss Baron Davies on the hunt? She had no idea how close a friendship the two had, but the baron was a guest and had been invited to hunt, which indicated that they were at least on amicable terms.

Not too intimate apparently. Grace watched with relief as Lord Crosby gave the command and the hounds moved off. The party dispersed a little, following the pack at a leisurely pace. Again Grace hung back. She didn't want Crosby to discover her yet.

For the damage to be greatest—for him to be furious enough to be done with me—he needs to realize that I've been here for some time, and that I can ride.

As well as he can, she hoped.

The cries of baying hounds sounded across the field, followed by what Grace thought was a rather lackluster horn. Disappointing. For all of Lord Crosby's hot air, she had expected more.

In spite of the uninspiring call, the riders took off in earnest, Grace among them, moving from the edge to the middle of the pack. The hounds barked louder, indicating they'd caught the fox's scent.

Poor thing. She knew what it was to feel trapped. Thus far she had been fortunate in avoiding capture. Some years before she'd had a close call when her father arranged for her to marry Sir Edmund Crayton, a man known for piracy, and to whom her father owed a great debt. Her skin yet crawled when she reflected upon her one meeting with Crayton, on the way he had openly appraised her, as if she were a delectable morsel he was about to devour. Though he had only touched her arm and face briefly, she'd felt defiled. She'd had to scrub her skin raw and rinse twice in her bath that night before she'd felt clean again. Thankfully, Grandfather's timely arrival in their lives had spared her the actual marriage.

And now? Lord Crosby did not scare her as Crayton had. Possibly because she was older, but more likely because he was a different sort of man. Grace could tell he wasn't interested in her other than as another object to own. Were he to make her his bride, she would be put on display and made to act and look perfect. There would be no affection between them, no mutual respect or friendship. And most certainly, *no freedom.*

After six years at Grandfather's—years free from debt collectors, her father's temper, and worry over providing for Christopher and Helen—Grace could not bear to live without the liberties she'd become used to. She had to free them all from their father, but independence would not be had if she ended up in bondage to another man.

"Tally-ho!"

The shout snapped Grace from her reverie. It was time. *Lord Crosby must recognize me now.* She leaned forward, gripping the reins as the horse obeyed her command and flew across the field. Grace wove in and out of the other riders, her grip and concentration never slacking. She was nearing the head of the group; she could see the back of Lord Crosby's head and how stiffly he perched in the saddle.

As if he is afraid he may muss his hair.

She edged closer, changing her angle until she was but a length behind and riding parallel to him. She dug in her heels, and with a burst of speed, overtook him.

"Glorious day for a hunt, is it not?" she called as she flew past.

As expected, Lord Crosby quickly regained his position as lead. For a minute they rode neck and neck, and Grace dared not take her eyes off the uneven course to look at him. She leaned forward, stretching with the horse as they jumped and cleared a felled tree. Their horses slowed as they neared the pack of baying hounds.

"Miss—Thatcher?" Lord Crosby's voice sounded hesitant.

He does not believe what he is seeing. "Good day, Lord Crosby. Such a fine morning, is it not?"

"It most certainly is not." He glowered at her and reined in. "That is to say, it *was*, until a moment ago when you—you desecrated this noble event with your presence."

"Oh," Grace said, her mouth opening with feigned shock. "Such words, and from a gentleman."

"You speak of words when a *lady* such as yourself appears at a hunt—wearing *breeches*."

"Do not forget my cravat," Grace added, jutting her chin out for him to see. "It is tied splendidly, don't you think?"

The other riders had caught up and were slowing their horses and coming closer to discover the reason for the delay.

Grace took the opportunity to remove her hat and hairpins. She shook her curls out, so they tumbled across her shoulders. "Good day, gentlemen," she said pleasantly. She had no argument with any of them—other than her main objection that they were *men*, and thus prone, with the exception of Grandfather and Harrison, to being a difficulty in a woman's life.

A few returned her greeting with, "Good day." Most looked to Lord Crosby, open curiosity upon their faces, and a few with expressions of shock and outrage as evident as his.

"How dare you." Crosby pointed a finger at Grace and spoke so loudly that those nearby could hear. "How dare you join my hunt."

"Many women hunt," Grace said. *Not that I am fighting for that privilege.*

"Not on my land, they don't. A—away with you," Lord Crosby said, waving her off as if she were a bothersome insect.

"Well." Grace sat straight and tugged on the bottom of her too-large jacket. "If *that* is how you feel."

"It is."

They stared at each other for a long moment, Grace narrowing her eyes in challenge. *Come, Lord Crosby, you can show more anger than that. Be furious with me—so irate that you never wish to see me again.* His face grew crimson, but not with the anger she had expected.

Is he—blushing?

Lord Crosby broke their gaze and looked down, pretending to clear his throat.

His bluster has been but an act. He wants a docile female because he doesn't know what to do with any other kind. I have intimidated him, she realized with some distress.

This turn of events was not good. She didn't want the man cowed into allowing her to stay.

"I *suppose* you would like me to return to my embroidery," she said, in her most disrespectful tone.

"Actually—" Lord Crosby cleared his throat again.

"Yes?" Grace said. *Be harsh now. I know you can.*

"Return to your room and pack your things." His words came out in a rush.

Grace widened her eyes and leaned back, acting as if he had wounded her. The ruse worked; Lord Crosby raised a fist.

"When I return, if you are still in my home . . ." He hesitated, as if scrambling for an appropriate threat.

"You will throw me out without my belongings?" Grace suggested.

"Yes!" He stood in his saddle, towering over her. "That is exactly what I will do."

Grace resisted the urge to laugh. Instead she pursed her lips and wrinkled her brow, doing her best to look thoroughly upset. "I never!"

Never would have believed this could be so simple. Would that I hadn't put up with three days of him first.

She urged her mount forward and threw a last, disdainful glance over her shoulder. *Little wonder Lord Crosby is nearing fifty and not yet wed. He is afraid of women.*

"Farewell gentlemen," she called, perhaps a little too merrily, as her horse broke into a gallop.

For a few wonderful moments, she felt the wind in her hair and the ground moving beneath her as she basked in the glory of her success and newfound freedom.

A step closer to it, at least, she thought as she neared the stables, where she saw Harrison waiting for her. *I must play this out a little longer.*

"Has the fox been caught already?" he asked, coming to help her dismount.

"I was kind; I let him go free," Grace said, smiling to herself.

Harrison's eyes drew together in a perplexed look.

"I shall tell you all about it on our journey," Grace said. "We have been summarily dismissed. It would be best if we are gone before Lord Fox—I mean, Lord Crosby—returns."

"Good," Harrison said, handing her the bundle of her

previously discarded clothing. "Because our next gentleman, Sir Richard Lidgate, is expecting you for dinner."

Grace sighed. It seemed her freedom was short-lived. But if she didn't at least appear to be playing Father's game, it would be Helen who suffered. "Lidgate." She rolled the name around in her mind. It sounded familiar, but she couldn't place it. "How much does Father owe him?"

"Not a red cent," Harrison said.

"Then why—"

"Sir Lidgate is one of the wealthiest men in Yorkshire." Harrison scowled. "He's also had more than his share of women—only now he's looking to settle. His reputation being what it is, he has been unable to procure a bride in the usual fashion."

The victory of shaking off Lord Crosby dimmed considerably with this news. "Lidgate is willing to pay handsomely for a wife?"

Harrison nodded, the look in his eyes having changed to the pity Grace had so often seen there since Grandfather's death. "Your father's line may be of little consequence, but you're the granddaughter of a duke, and him not around to have a say about who you end up with."

And with a father who has no scruples about it.

Harrison would never dare to voice the thought, yet the truth of it was known by all. Grace began walking toward the manor. "Yet again, my status as a lady appears to prove problematic. Perhaps I shall need to take up wearing breeches and riding astride in front of Lidgate. That may dissuade him as well."

"I wouldn't plan on that, Miss Thatcher," Harrison said, falling into step behind her. "Lidgate's not the type who'll be concerned with your behavior, nor your mind. He'll be feasting his eyes, in a manner of speaking."

A blush heated Grace's face. "Harrison," she admonished. "Please."

"I'm sorry, miss." He lowered his head, as if to prove he

was contrite. "Miranda and I thought you should be forewarned."

"Thank you," Grace said. "Please ready the carriage. I shall be but a few minutes." She left Harrison near the base of the stairs and began the climb, the joy from her morning success all but gone.

Before nightfall she would be faced with yet another man, one likely worse than Lord Crosby. A man who wasn't afraid of women, but one she might have every reason to fear.

CHAPTER 2

For the second time in as many days, Grace sat in the mud. Yesterday, it had been an unruly sorrel mare that had dislodged her into a thicket. But just now, feeling rather dazed, half sitting, half lying in the mire, with rain falling steadily through the dark, she could not place the cause of her current circumstance.

"Miss Thatcher, are you all right?" Harrison called to her from somewhere above.

"I am both well enough and *wet* enough," she managed to say before a coughing fit seized her, rattling her entire body and paralyzing her to all but the barest ability to breathe.

"You don't sound well," Harrison said, concern in his voice. "Sit tight—supposing you're sitting, that is—and I'll fetch you shortly."

And take me where? Grace lifted a hand to her aching head, stopping herself just in time when she realized that muck covered her palm. "Harrison," she called through the black. "Where are we? Where is Miranda?"

"Here," Miranda called, sounding somewhat less than *here.*

"We've gone off the road en route to Mr. Preston's," Harrison said. "The carriage tipped, and you with it." Horses' whinnying and the grating of slow-turning wheels confirmed his story.

That explains it, Grace thought, rationalizing that her entire body ached because of the spill from the carriage and not her worsening illness. But who was Mr. Preston, and what on earth had she been going to see him for?

Did Grandfather send me—in the dead of night? Of course not. She stilled, this time crippled by a pain much greater than her persistent cough.

Grandfather could not have sent me because he's—Dead.

I was on my way to see Mr. Preston, the next man in the line of potential suitors, because Father needs money. The only way he knows of to obtain that money is for Helen or me to marry. Grace groaned, wishing she hadn't tried so hard to recollect.

Miranda reached her side. "Are you hurt? Here's my cloak. Put it around you."

"You use it." Grace batted the fabric away. "Cover yourself. I am quite well." It wasn't an entire falsehood. As best she could tell she'd suffered no grave injuries in the fall. The real damage had come during the previous week during that wretched visit to Sir Lidgate's. Grace shuddered, and gooseflesh sprang up along her arms—not from the cold but from fear and tonight's narrow escape.

Harrison slid down the embankment toward them. "Nearly there!"

"What caused the accident?" Grace asked, taking the hand he offered and struggling to her feet. She tested each foot carefully, lest one of her ankles had been twisted in the fall.

"Horse got spooked and took off sudden," Harrison said. "Pulled us clear to the side. The road turned sharp, and afore I knew it, we were tipping."

Miranda took up the tale. "Threw us both against the

door, and that wouldn't have been too bad. But we'd barely stopped when the latch broke, spilling us into this bog."

"Well, I'm right thankful for the muck," Harrison said, his voice grave. "It likely softened your fall considerable. Elsewise, you'd both have been hurt much worse."

"Or—had Father not sold the fine carriage Grandfather left me and forced this miserable one upon us—we mightn't have been hurt at all," Grace grumbled.

Neither Harrison nor Miranda replied. As a lady's maid, Miranda was everything prim and would not deem it proper to share an opinion. Harrison might have, but never around Miranda. Their silence only served to make Grace feel more isolated in some half-class, where servants regarded her as their superior, but her peers did not find her equal.

Dwelling on either her father's shortcomings or her own confused place in the world was of no use, so Grace wiped her muddy hands as best she could and carefully started up the slope. Of more concern was making certain she remained in the world. At the moment, she felt awful enough that her very existence was quite possibly in danger.

My fever is growing worse, Grace concluded as a shiver wracked her. The steady rain intensified to a downpour, plastering her hair to the sides of her face. It did not seem as if things could get much worse, but she well knew they could, were her illness to turn more serious.

Perhaps it is already more serious. She tried to tell herself it wasn't, to ignore the twinge in her chest each time she drew breath.

To her servants, she said drily, "I seem to be developing a rather grand talent for getting thrown out of places." She bent over, coughing again. Both Harrison and Miranda fussed over her, clucking their concern and trying to shield her from the rain.

"Never mind all that," Grace said when her coughing fit had subsided. "I'm right as . . . rain." She attempted a feeble smile, though she doubted either could fully see it or appreciate her effort in the dark. "Please help me back to the carriage. Though I'm loath to see our journey's end, I daresay a visit to Mr. Preston's will be better than this."

"It's not so easy as all that." Harrison held her elbow, steadying her as they made their way across the slippery grass to the road above. "We've a broken wheel, and the carriage is straddling the side of the road. I don't trust it enough to even set you inside to wait out the rain."

"A fine kettle," Miranda scolded Harrison, as if the accident were his fault. "And Miss Thatcher worse yet, out in this cold. She'll catch her death."

"We both know that *isn't* an option," Grace said. Though just now, were it not for Helen, Grace might have thought death would be an improvement over her current situation. She forced back another cough, then pulled her wet traveling cloak tighter. In its current state, it wasn't likely to provide any warmth, but she had to at least feel as if she was doing something to preserve her health.

Because Helen needs me. Grace turned to Harrison, who was slightly more visible now that they'd left the hollow. "What is to be done?"

"We'll have to leave the carriage, but if you're fit for riding, we can find shelter. There are lights not too far distant."

Grace peered in the direction of his outstretched arm. Through the rain she thought she could make out the barest pinprick of light.

"Are you quite certain?" she asked. "Is that still in England? It looks as if it might be across the Channel or on some other continent entirely." In truth it could have been a star in the sky for all she could make out. But her head hurt, so her vision was beginning to blur. "I fear I am *not* fit for riding," she said, swaying dizzily.

Miranda's arm came around her waist, steadying her. "I'll—I'll ride with ye. We'll make out all right."

"Very well, but first I must—sit. Just for a moment." She slid from Miranda's grasp to the muddy road below.

"There, there. Put your head on your knees. Just like that." Harrison helped her into the unladylike, but more comfortable, position. Grace pressed her forehead to her kneecaps, searching for a little relief from the relentless pounding in her head.

Were Lord Crosby to see me now . . . Had she not already ruined her chances with him, seeing her like this certainly would have done it.

Beside her she heard scuffling and grunts as Harrison unharnessed the horses. This was followed by a good deal of complaining from Miranda.

"When's the last time your backside set on a horse?" Harrison asked her.

"When I was a girl at home riding with my pa," Miranda said. "And never you mind how long ago that was."

"Knew it," Harrison muttered. "I'll be riding with Miss Thatcher then. You can break your neck on your own."

Grace heard the sound of a hand meeting horse flesh, and then Miranda gave a little screech as her mount loped away.

"Come along now."

Grace lifted her head to look at Harrison bent in front of her. "Won't do for you to be in the cold any longer than necessary. Let me help you up." He held out his hand.

"Thank you," Grace murmured, though she almost wished he'd leave her here. Any movement was painful, and mounting a horse seemed an impossible task.

Harrison lifted her, carrying her a short distance before gently setting her down, standing this time. He placed one of her hands on the horse. "Steady yourself there, if you'd like. He won't go anywhere."

Grace did as Harrison had suggested, leaning against the animal.

"Stand here a moment while I mount," Harrison said. "Then I'll pull you up."

Grace peered dubiously at the horse. In the moonlight, its tall back was slicked with rain. There seemed no way she'd be able to reach such a height. Harrison stepped onto a before-unseen boulder, reached up, and grabbed the animal's mane, hoisting himself up with far more poise than Grace was certain she'd have.

"Your turn." Harrison leaned over, arm extended. "That's it. Step there. Hold tight . . ."

Grace did as he'd instructed and felt herself slowly rising as he pulled her up. For her part, she did her best to reach as she'd seen Harrison do. After a long minute of awkward struggle on both their parts, she found herself seated side-saddle—minus the saddle—in front of him.

"Whew." Harrison ran a hand across his brow, then wrapped his arms around her so she wouldn't fall.

Miranda called out from the other side of the road. "If the duke had witnessed that painful bit of chivalry, he would have dismissed you on the spot and hired a man thirty years younger."

"He'd be getting but an infant then," Harrison tossed back easily.

Those two. A wan smile curved Grace's lips. It was plain as the nose on her face that they cared for each other, yet the closest they came to admitting it was vying for the worst insult.

Grace leaned back slightly, ever so grateful to close her eyes. "Thank you for keeping me safe," she murmured as she drifted toward sleep.

"Improper if ever I—" Miranda huffed. "If you think to ride up to an estate like that—"

"I think to keep Miss Thatcher alive," Harrison shouted above the clop of the horses' hooves.

"And her things?" Miranda asked. "Are we to leave them behind for whatever beggar happens upon them?"

"Leave them," Grace said, the two words taking every ounce of energy she seemed to possess. At the moment, she didn't care a fig about her garments—new and lovely though some of them were. Miranda's warning about catching her death rang in her pounding head. She felt fever afflicting her now, in spite of the cooling rain. Beneath her soaked clothing, she shivered, and their journey became a wearying kind of torture. Her head lolled against Harrison's shoulder as she flitted in and out of an uneasy sleep.

"At last," Miranda called sometime later, partially lifting the fog from Grace's mind.

She glanced up and noticed that the lights were closer. There weren't many, but they did appear to be coming from an estate large enough that it might be expected to handle unexpected guests—assuming it was a friendly sort of place. In the black of night, the stone walls loomed over them ominously. What little Grace could make of the grounds seemed wild and overgrown, and the whole feel of the dwelling was that of a long-abandoned castle inhabited by spirits of the past.

Before Grace could voice her worry, Miranda began a fit of coughing.

"You're sounding as unwell as I," Grace said. "Remember we're in this together. I could not get on without either of you."

"And we cannot get on without *you*," Harrison said, his voice gruff.

"No worry of that," she assured them, though she felt ill enough that her doubts had grown serious. "I've got Helen to think of. And I'll do whatever is necessary—"

"To keep her safe," all three vowed together.

It took several poundings on the enormous wood and iron doors before someone finally came to open them.

"Excuse me," Harrison said, stepping forward. Grace stood behind him, largely supported by Miranda. He doffed his soaked hat. "Mr. Harrison here, and I've got Miss Grace Thatcher, granddaughter of the Duke of Salisbury, in a terrible state. We've had a carriage accident."

Grace tried to straighten and address the man in the open doorway who held a candelabra, but she hadn't the strength even to confirm Harrison's story.

After studying the trio a moment, the man said, "Come in. Be quick about it. No need to wake the entire household. She's related to a duke, you say?"

"Granddaughter of the late Eugene Durham, Duke of Salisbury." Harrison wasted no time in ushering them into the hall. "This is her maid, Miranda Burke."

"Why are you out on a night like this?" the man demanded. "Oh, but she does look to be in bad shape."

"Thank you," Grace managed, irritated at being discussed as if she weren't present. She lifted her gaze to his for only a moment; it hurt to hold her head up.

"No offence intended, miss," he said. "I'm Mr. Kingsley, Lord Sutherland's butler. You're at Sutherland Hall."

"And extremely grateful to be here," Grace managed. The name was not familiar, and she did not particularly care where they were, so long as it was out of the rain, and so long as she might use a blanket or two. Hopefully those were not as sparse as the lighting seemed to be. Save for Mr. Kingsley's candelabra, the group remained cloaked in darkness. Had she been inclined to be curious about her surroundings, she'd have been unable to discover much.

Footsteps marched swiftly across the floor, and the shadows changed, indicating the arrival of another person, with a candle.

"What's going on?" A woman joined them as a new volley of chills assaulted Grace. She sagged against Miranda and attempted to hold her head up and to greet the newcomer. The housekeeper, she guessed, seeing the bottom of a starched dress and sensible shoes peeking out beneath.

"Miss Thatcher, this is Mrs. James, the head housekeeper." The butler spoke in formalities, as if she were being presented for tea. "Mrs. James, may I present Miss Thatcher, the late Duke of Salisbury's granddaughter, and her staff. Their carriage met with an accident. They are seeking shelter for the night, and Miss Thatcher looks to be in need of a bed immediately."

"Well," Mrs. James said, as much starch in her voice as in her dress. "Of course we can accommodate them, but we've no rooms made up. Wait here while I wake the maids."

Grace bit back a groan of disappointment. But what did it matter if a room was made up when her head was about to burst? The marble floor going in and out of focus looked inviting enough. She felt herself wilting toward it as her coughing renewed again.

"Never mind the maids, Mrs. James," the butler said. "Miss Thatcher may use the blue room."

"But—"

"I'll take full responsibility," he said. "Better to have that on my head than a woman dying in the front hall." Kingsley held his hand out in invitation. "Come now, I'll show you up." He turned away.

Grace took one step, then felt Harrison scoop her into his arms. "Thank you," she murmured when she could breathe once more. "Thank you all. I'm sorry for the trouble."

They followed their host to a wide, curved staircase. Harrison's capable arms carried her up, then deposited her in front of a set of double doors halfway down the hall. The butler pushed them open and bade them enter.

Miranda helped Grace into the dark room, while the butler hurried ahead to light the fire. Grace sank into a comfortable chair, laying her head against the cool fabric. If only someone would throw a blanket over her, she would be content to sleep right here.

"How far is the nearest physician?" Harrison stood in the doorway, twirling his hat in his hands.

"A long piece," the butler said. "You'd best not think of attempting it tonight." He succeeded in lighting the fire, then stood and turned to them. "We're isolated out here. The master's not in residence, so we're short on staff, or I'd send someone."

Another coughing fit seized Grace as Mrs. James entered the room, her worried gaze settling upon her. "We could send for—"

"No," Kingsley's response was swift. "We could not." The housekeeper and butler stared at each other.

"What?" Harrison said, addressing Mrs. James. "*Is* there a physician close?"

"Not a good one," Kingsley said. "And not one welcomed in this house."

"I've brought some night clothes," Mrs. James said, backing down from whatever unspoken argument was between them. "Nothing fancy, but they're clean and dry. The water's heating for her bath."

"No, thank you," Grace said, before Miranda could respond. "Tomorrow is soon enough. All I care for now is a bed." She didn't want the entire household woken on her account.

"But Miss Thatcher—" Miranda protested. "The mud—your hair."

"Will keep," Grace said as firmly as she could.

"It will keep you right into your grave," Miranda muttered. "Then poor Miss Helen . . ."

Grace glanced up at her maid and the housekeeper, both with mouths turned down reproachfully. "Very well," Grace conceded.

Miranda exchanged a look with the housekeeper; Grace knew she wasn't behaving as a lady ought.

As Grandfather would have wished me to.

Mrs. James turned her attention to Miranda and Harrison. "When you're finished here, I've things for the both of you as well, and I can show you to your quarters downstairs."

"Thank you kindly," Harrison said, bestowing one of his rare smiles upon the woman.

Miranda's lips turned down. "I'd best stay here to watch over Miss Thatcher."

"No," Grace said. "You've bullied me into having a bath tonight, but then you're to go to bed. It won't do to have you sick too."

Two maids appeared in the doorway, bleary-eyed and struggling to keep their buckets of steaming water from spilling. These they poured into a tub on the far side of the room, past the fire. When the women left, the butler and Harrison followed, returning a few minutes later with more water, which Miranda pronounced sufficient.

"I'll see Miss Thatcher settled before I come down," Miranda said, turning to the three hovering by the door. "If you'll excuse us now, I need to get her out of her wet things."

The others left, Miranda following them to the door and throwing the bolt behind them. She returned to Grace, still slumped in the chair and unable even to bend enough to remove her mud-caked slippers.

And to think that I once said I didn't require a lady's maid. With some chagrin, Grace recalled a conversation with her grandfather shortly after she'd come to live with him. He'd insisted that she behave as befitted her newly acquired status—by wearing proper clothing and having her own personal maid. At this moment Grace could feel only gratitude; Miranda seemed a godsend.

When the wet stockings had been peeled off and tossed aside, Grace leaned forward so Miranda might reach the back of the gown.

"Soaked to the bone you are. It'll be the death of us both if you get worse." Miranda tugged at the wet sleeves.

"I admit to feeling poorly," Grace murmured. "Sleep"—she yawned—"will do me well."

"Or so we pray." Miranda helped Grace step from her wet gown and underclothes.

Once in the tub, she could no longer keep her eyes opened but leaned her head back, near sleep as Miranda washed her hair. The warm water began to thaw her frozen limbs, and Grace thought the tub even more satisfactory than the chair.

Miranda had other ideas and pushed Grace this way and that, scrubbing and rinsing.

"Oh, let me be," Grace complained as the last bucketful of water—not nearly so warm as the first—cascaded over her head.

"In another minute, miss."

Grace squinted one eye, watching as Miranda reached for the bundle of dry clothing.

Though Grace was positive she couldn't move, Miranda somehow managed to get her from the tub and into the fresh clothes. Grace put an end to her maid's ministering when Miranda produced a comb.

"My head feels as if will explode," Grace protested. "I'm still so cold, and my chest hurts." All of this was true, but she probably shouldn't have told Miranda as much. The poor woman would likely be up worrying for what was left of the night.

"Very well," Miranda said, returning the comb to the dresser. "Let's get you into bed."

Grace leaned on her, then walked the few steps to the massive, canopied bed. Miranda swept back one side of the curtain, revealing a mattress piled high with pillows. "There now. That looks comfortable." She helped Grace climb onto the high bed.

"It's lovely," Grace agreed. "And there's nothing wrong

with me that a little sleep won't fix." She tried and failed at making her voice sound light as she coughed again.

"We'll just see what the doctor says about that tomorrow." Miranda tucked the covers over Grace, who let her head sink into the soft pillow and snuggled under the heavy quilts, vaguely appreciating the fine bed. If only she felt better. In spite of the blankets, another shiver wiggled up her spine. She clenched her teeth to keep them from chattering. Miranda let the curtain fall back into place, and Grace listened as she left the room, closing the door behind her. Only then did Grace give in to her exhaustion and slept at once.

CHAPTER 3

Nicholas Sutherland emerged from his landau and stood on the drive, staring up at the dark night and equally dark and formidable building in front of him.

Home sweet home, he thought wryly, taking in the pile of stone that looked as if it had been abandoned some time ago. *As unwelcoming as ever.*

He hadn't always viewed it this way. When he was a child, the old castle had never seemed gloomy or forbidding, but rather the perfect house for losing one's tutor and avoiding book work, as well as a splendid place for playing Hide and Seek with his sister. Now that he was well beyond his school years, and Elizabeth was gone—Father, too—nothing about the ivy-covered turrets and grey stone appeared splendid at all.

That he'd all but shut up the house and had allowed the gardens to run wild and hadn't kept the walks swept or the hedges trimmed only added to the eeriness and oppressive nature of the place. But perhaps, if ghosts were real and drawn to gloom, Elizabeth and his father felt comfortable haunting here.

"Thank you, Hines. You may go now." Nicholas dismissed the footman who'd accompanied him and waved the driver toward the stables. Alone, he made his way to the front doors, his feet crunching over the slippery gravel drive. He hadn't bothered to have it cared for either, and weeds had sprung up between loose rock, making a treacherous pathway on the dark, wet night.

Nicholas reached the door safely, and, after more than a few minutes and several annoyed raps, the door finally swung open, revealing his rather tired and utterly surprised-looking butler. Nicholas had left his keys, along with most of his clothing and personal items, at the townhouse in London.

"Good evening, Kingsley," Nicholas said, striding into the hall. "You look as if you've seen a ghost. I haven't been gone that long, you know."

"Of course not, milord. It's just that—we weren't expecting you."

"Are you ever?" Nicholas asked, amused. "When is the last time you've known me to keep regular hours or to announce my arrival prior to my appearance?"

"Never," Kingsley said, a subtle undertone of dryness in his voice. "I am most surprised to see you at *this* hour, though. The night has nearly passed. 'Good morn' is almost more fitting than 'Good eve.' You must have traveled the whole night through."

Nicholas eyed Kingsley curiously as the butler hurried to close the door against the cold and rain. The speech was more than Nicholas usually heard from the butler in a month.

"I apologize for my tardiness in greeting you," Kingsley continued. "We were not anticipating your arrival for several days yet."

"So I gathered." Nicholas gave Kingsley one more appraising glance but could find nothing odd in the man's appearance excepting, perhaps, that he was dressed as if it were day, and he seemed more tired than usual.

I really should hire a full staff again. Nicholas looked around the vast, empty foyer. Once the estate had been a lively residence—full of family and, often, friends. Now it seemed little more than a tomb, the resting place he was required to return to after his frequent haunts elsewhere. The house meant little more to him now than quiet sleeping quarters, so he saw no need to spend money or time on its upkeep. It wouldn't matter how much he spent. Nothing could return Sutherland Hall to its former existence.

But the dark circles beneath Kingsley's eyes made Nicholas realize that he ought to consider hiring a little more help at least.

"My business went far better—and quicker—than I had hoped," Nicholas said by way of explanation for his predawn arrival. "And I was loath to stay in London a moment longer than necessary."

"Understandable." Kingsley glanced toward the staircase. "Though I am pleased to hear your endeavors met with success."

"Time will tell." Nicholas turned his back to the butler so the man could remove his traveling cloak. "And now I find myself with an appetite—revenge does make one hungry," he said, only half-jesting. "I suppose it's too early to ask cook to rise?"

"Not at all," Kingsley said, answering almost too quickly. "I believe she could be rather easily persuaded."

Nicholas eyed the butler once more as Kingsley hung up the cloak and retrieved the candelabra he'd set aside on the hall table. He paused, glancing to either side of the entrance hall. "Would you care to wait in your study or in the dining room while I arrange for your breakfast?"

"Neither." Nicholas started toward the staircase.

"There's a great deal of correspondence on your desk," Kingsley said. "Perhaps you might wish to sort through it while cook works her magic."

"Perhaps," Nicholas said vaguely, continuing his stride.

"Though a tray in my room is more what I had in mind."

"I believe there may be some—information—about Mr. Preston among the letters," Kingsley said. "It seems I saw his name on the top of a packet that arrived from London just a few days ago."

"Oh?" Nicholas arched a tired eyebrow. "Very well, then. I'd best have a look." He dearly hoped it was not from any of the solicitors he'd met with at the beginning of this latest trip, almost two months ago. He'd garnered what he'd believed were secure promises from all of them, and he had no desire to discover that any of his plans had gone awry.

Kingsley lit the candelabra in the study, gave a low bow and exited into the hall. Nicholas started toward his desk, feeling put off by papers stacked there. He'd been neglectful of late, and soon he'd have to spend time making things right here, managing the Sutherland holdings as he used to. But for now, the property down the road, the one adjoining the western edge of his land, was of far greater concern.

Looking for any information regarding that property—or more specifically, Mr. Samuel Preston, its owner—Nicholas settled at his desk and sifted through the missives as quickly as possible. He had but a few envelopes remaining when an offending one surfaced. He'd know that handwriting anywhere. A wave of hatred came over him, so intense that Nicholas' jaw clenched, as if holding back his abhorrence. He flipped the envelope over anyway, not the least surprised to see the Preston seal. With fury, he ripped it open.

How dare he?

The gall of the man, writing to him, when he knew Nicholas would love nothing more than to shoot him down in a duel.

He wrested the card free, wishing it were an invitation to duel. *And that I could challenge him.* A scripted card fell onto the desk. Nicholas stared at it in utter disbelief.

Harvest Ball

The Attendance of

Lord Nicholas Sutherland's

Company is requested at Preston Manor

Saturday, the 16th of September

Grand Entry 8:00 pm

He wished to shoot Preston, and here the neighbor was inviting him to a party. *Madness.* But then, the man had never been right from the beginning. *New money at play again,* Nicholas supposed. *What else can it be?*

If Samuel Preston believed that an invitation was the way to mend fences, he was so far out of his mind that shooting the man would be a kindness.

Nicholas tossed the card aside and flipped halfheartedly through the remaining packets without seeing the one to which Kingsley had referred. Irritated over the ball invitation, Nicholas gave up the search, shoving the correspondence aside to be dealt with later. He'd been deprived of his bed most of the past year because of Preston, and he'd be jiggered if he'd allow the man another night. Whatever was on the desk, it could wait until morning.

Feeling somewhat cheered by the prospect of a good meal and his own bed, Nicholas left the study and returned to the faintly lit front hall. He took the stairs two at a time, then made his way down the long, dark corridor at the top, arriving at his bedroom as another yawn overcame him.

He entered the chamber and closed the door, feeling some of the tension of the past weeks leave as he did so. Across the room, a low fire burned in the grate, and Nicholas smiled to himself, once again impressed with Kingsley's efficiency. The man was overworked doing the job of a butler and ten other servants. Someday, when Nicholas planned to stay here for good, he'd change that, but for now, Kingsley and Mrs. James were models of efficiency, keeping the few rooms he used orderly and sterile as he liked them. Nothing was ever out of place. There were never any surprises. Unlike life in London, life at Sutherland Hall was quiet and predictable.

If not quite peaceful—the devil take Preston. Nicholas doubted he'd ever know a moment of tranquility again, and it was entirely the fault of his neighbor.

With his eyes somewhat adjusted to the dim firelight, Nicholas crossed to his favorite chair and sat to remove his shoes and stockings. His valet was still in London and would follow tomorrow; Nicholas's sudden urge to be home had struck late in the afternoon, and he'd had no desire to waste time waiting for his servant.

Upon settling into his chair, Nicholas felt dampness coming through his shirt. Odd. He turned and ran his hand over the plush fabric, to discover it wet. Perhaps in his haste to light the fire, Kingsley had spilled something? Or maybe it had been Mrs. James or one of the maids. *That must be it.* One of them must have tripped in the dark while carrying the pitcher to fill his basin.

No matter. Nicholas removed himself from the chair and in short order had discarded his clothes and located the dressing gown in his armoire. A quick splash of water on his face, and he walked to the far side of the bed, pulled the curtain aside, and climbed in. Though Kingsley would likely be arriving with his tray any minute, the temptation for Nicholas to close his eyes and rest in his own bed while waiting was too much to resist.

He plumped his pillow, lay back, and stretched his arms wide.

And discovered that he was not alone.

CHAPTER 4

Grace came awake at once, aware that something heavy had landed atop her. She reached for the object—*a cat?*—and felt flesh instead of fur. Somehow in that split second, her mind registered that this was not Helen's arm, or Miranda's, but—

"What the deuce?" an angry voice shouted beside her.

Her mouth opened in a scream, but only a pitiful whimper emerged. She shoved whatever—*whomever*—it was off and scooted away, only to reach the edge of the bed and find herself falling and then landing with a sudden, loud thump.

"Who are you?" The angry voice was above her now, and Grace, stunned, breathless, and in pain from her fall, peered up through half-open eyes into a blurred face with a shaggy head of hair hanging over the side of the bed.

Lidgate! He's found a way into my room. She must have forgotten to push the chair beneath the doorknob, and now the overly arduous Sir Lidgate was after her. Grace scrambled to her knees and began crawling away. He caught the hem of her nightgown, pulling her back.

"Let me go!" She breathed in deeply before attempting another scream and this time met with success.

"Come here," Sir Lidgate said. Only it wasn't his voice. "What do you mean by being in my chamber—in my *bed*?"

"*Your* bed?" Grace grabbed a fistful of nightgown and, with a terrible ripping sound, tugged it from his grasp. She stood on shaking legs and peered through the darkness, trying to locate the door.

"Whose did you think it was?" a deadly voice asked, one definitely *not* belonging to Sir Lidgate.

"I—I don't know," Grace chattered as a chill wracked her body. Beneath her feet, the floor was ice cold, and the thin gown did little to provide warmth. She wrapped her arms around her middle and took two steps backward, away from the bed and the stranger rising from it. *Where am I?*

"So you are in the habit of invading unfamiliar beds?"

"No!" she cried, turning her head to and fro but still not seeing a door. *It must be behind me.* She took a giant step back and bumped into a chair.

"Is this some kind of joke? Who sent you?" The man swung his feet—bare, as were his legs, up to his knees, sticking out beneath his robe—over the side of the bed.

Grace turned away, fleeing toward the door she'd correctly guessed to be behind her. She grabbed the handle and pulled, but before the door had fully opened, a large hand closed over hers, slamming the door shut again, then spun her around to face him.

"Not so fast. Not until you've answered my questions."

"Let me go. *Please.*" She wrenched her hand away from his and pushed against his chest, scandalized by the feel of his skin bare beneath his partially open robe. When he did not move, she ducked beneath his arm and scampered out of reach.

He retaliated by moving in front of the doors, blocking her only means of escape. "Who are you?" Anger seemed to vibrate through his entire being.

Before she could answer or ask the same of him, the door flung open, hitting the man on the back of the head and propelling him straight toward her. She shrieked and jumped aside before seeing Harrison, Miranda, and two other, vaguely familiar people standing in the hall.

Her servants appeared tousled, as if they'd been awakened quickly. As Miranda took in Grace and the bare-chested man beside her, her eyes looked as if they were about to pop out of her head.

"Beg pardon, Lord Sutherland." A manservant swept forward into a bow as if he were offering his neck for the guillotine.

"This is going to require a little more than an apology, Kingsley," the robed man—Lord Sutherland—said. "Who is this woman, and what is she doing in my chamber?"

Mr. Kingsley straightened and stepped back. "I can explain—"

"*She* is Grace Thatcher, granddaughter of the Duke of Salisbury," Harrison said, wasting no time moving into the space Kingsley had vacated. "Let her alone at once."

"That is my complete intention," Lord Sutherland said, seeming to take no offense from Harrison's demand. "*After* I discover what she is doing in my room."

"I did not know it was yours," Grace said, shivering again. She looked from Lord Sutherland to the comfort of Miranda's beckoning arms.

"So you say." Lord Sutherland's voice lacked both empathy and trust.

"So it was," Grace retorted. She stepped away from the irritable man before he could trouble her further. Miranda hurried to her side, wrapping a blanket around her and worrying over her like a mother hen.

"Your head is afire," she clucked as she pressed her palm to Grace's forehead. "Burning up she is," Miranda announced to the rest, though Grace very much doubted anyone was listening; Lord Sutherland seemed to be commanding everyone's attention.

He had turned his wrath on Kingsley. "What is the meaning of this? When you said you'd not anticipated my arrival, I didn't know that meant you'd given away my bed. "

"I put Miss Thatcher in your room because none other was made ready," Kingsley explained. "She appeared quite ill, and I did not think it best to make her wait. Had I known you would be home—"

"So this is a common occurrence whilst I'm away?" Lord Sutherland asked. "Who else has slept in the bed I believed to be my own? Do you and Mrs. James play at inn-keeping during my absences?"

"Not at all, milord," Kingsley said, looking properly contrite. "Miss Thatcher is the first, and we had hoped to relocate her before you retired for the night." Kingsley also looked exhausted.

With Miranda's arms supporting her and Lord Sutherland a few feet away, Grace's heartbeat began to calm, and her mind cleared. She remembered their arrival and pieced together how her unfortunate circumstance had come about.

I am the one in the wrong. I was in his *bed.*

She chanced to look up at Lord Sutherland and had the misfortune of meeting his fierce gaze. His eyes were narrowed, lips turned down in a mighty scowl, his whole demeanor fraught with tension as he towered over all of them. Grace felt a chill that had nothing to do with her fever or the cold night, followed by a pang of sympathy for Kingsley, who had only been trying to help.

It remained her duty to step forward and speak up. She summoned her courage and what strength she had left. "I'm afraid—"

Lord Sutherland crossed his arms and looked directly at her.

Very afraid, at the moment.

"— that this is my fault. Our carriage went off the road. We saw your lights and came here, hoping for shelter from the storm. Mr. Kingsley was kind enough to note my poor condition and promptly show me to your room. Please don't take your anger out on him. It is I who've inconvenienced you, and I do apologize."

Lord Sutherland continued to stare. "Why were you out driving on a night like this?"

Grace clutched the blanket tighter, as if trying to wrap herself in protection from his prying eyes. *I'll not recite to him my faults and folly.* If she did, he would likely send her packing at once. She lifted her chin a little and met his intent gaze head on.

"It is a tedious story, one I am not up to telling at the moment. I should greatly appreciate the opportunity to return to bed—another bed," she added hastily. "I *am* unwell." As if to prove her point, a tremor made its way down her spine, and her coughing started up again.

"Yes. I can see that," Lord Sutherland said. "You're rather a mess. I take it you were not even offered a hairbrush. I regret you found our lodging so inhospitable."

Grace's hand went to her tangled hair, and she winced inwardly, wishing she'd made use of the comb offered her earlier.

At last Lord Sutherland looked away, turning his censuring gaze upon his servants. "I imagine my bed is also in poor condition now. Mrs. James, please see that clean sheets are brought up at once. And find somewhere for"—He returned his attention to Grace, searching her face as if that would produce her name— "these people to sleep."

Harrison stiffened and opened his mouth as if to correct Lord Sutherland's address, but Grace shook her head at him. Though she'd done her best to speak as befitting a duke's granddaughter, she had no doubt that she appeared nothing like one at the moment, what with her uncombed hair still damp and flying about her head in who knew what fashion, and only a blanket and a maid's borrowed nightrail covering her. No wonder Lord Sutherland thought so little of her.

"The maids have already been summoned," Mrs. James said, bobbing a slight curtsy. She turned to Grace. "If you'll follow me, please."

Grace did her best to curtsy before taking her leave of Lord Sutherland. As her bare feet padded down the hall, shame washed over her in waves, replacing the fear that had been her companion since she'd been so rudely awoken.

Lord Sutherland had seen her wearing nothing but a nightgown.

And I was in his bed—with him!

She could imagine no greater shame. As she turned to go into the room Mrs. James pointed out, she met the woman's eye and sensed that she, too, was thinking the exact same thing. A new distress swept over Grace as the gravity of her situation set in.

I am ruined.

CHAPTER 5

"Ruined," Grace murmured as Miranda walked her to bed for the second time that night. "What will my father say?"

"Nothing, because he won't be hearing about this." Miranda pulled the blanket from Grace's shoulders. "Goodness," she exclaimed, seeing the long rip Lord Sutherland had made in her nightgown. "No wonder you're trembling. Did this, did he?" Her fingers grabbed the torn fabric trailing to the ground.

Grace nodded, tears of shame building in her eyes as she recalled the dreadful moment. "What was the butler thinking to put me in Lord Sutherland's quarters?"

"I'm sure I haven't the slightest notion." Miranda helped Grace into bed. "But I think he meant well. Servants around here seem to be scarce. They're not prepared for guests, unexpected or otherwise."

"Father will kill me—or Lord Sutherland. Or Lord Sutherland will kill him in a duel when Father loses his temper and challenges him. Oh, Miranda. What a mess."

"Shh now." Miranda tucked in the quilt and smoothed

the top. "Your father needn't find out about this. There aren't many here who'll have to hold their tongues. I'll speak with Mrs. James to see what can be done. I imagine a few words from her will take care of it."

Grace groaned. "I wish we'd never stopped here."

"Can't say as I don't agree," Miranda said. "But bad as it was a bit ago, it's still better than being out in the rain."

"I suppose." Grace found it more difficult to bemoan her circumstances a few minutes later as her head sank into a feather pillow. She ached all over. She was both cold and hot, and she was oh, so tired . . .

Sleep came easily but was not restful. She tossed and turned in the unfamiliar bed, while one troubling scenario after another paraded before her closed eyes, haunting her.

Sir Lidgate had found a way into her room and was after her. She couldn't understand why, when she'd gone to such lengths to dissuade him, even purposely injuring herself in a manner that would lead him to believe she could never produce the heir he so desperately wanted.

Grace rolled onto her side and felt the bruise on her hip proving that the escapade —getting herself thrown from a horse—had not been imagined.

"Go away," she muttered, waving her arms above her, banishing the image of Sir Lidgate and his overly friendly advances.

At last he left. She slept briefly then dreamt again, this time to discover that Lord Crosby had her trapped in his drawing room and was listing all of the qualities he found so important in a wife. His condescending manner and absurd expectations had her seething, and it was all she could do to keep herself from jumping onto the settee and shouting at him. But there were others in the room, men who knew her father, who would report her behavior to him. So she bit her tongue until it nearly bled.

But inside, her mind—she possessed one, contrary to Lord Crosby's belief—was whirring. He didn't really want a wife. He was looking for a trophy or piece of expensive art, something docile and lovely to sit on a shelf and purr for him on occasions he took it down to admire it.

Grace did not wish to be put on a shelf or admired or made to hold her tongue for the rest of her life. She had thoughts and opinions. She was not delicate, but strong and determined.

What more could I have done to dissuade him? Why does he still bother me? He'd asked her to leave after the hunt, hadn't he? Yet his image, complete with grating voice and pompous manner, continued to harass her through the predawn hours.

The nightmares continued, one after the other. Some were products of her imagination, others reenactments of humiliations she'd suffered since her father had so cruelly sent her "out to pasture again," as he put it.

She didn't want to be in the pasture. She wasn't a cow meant for breeding. She didn't want to marry. She'd known a life of freedom, and, if only the inheritance from Grandfather would come through, she and Helen and Christopher would have enough to live on.

If only the new duke hadn't contested the will. And if only they could get Father's gambling under control. Thinking of that, of the list of debts owed that he'd presented to her days after the duke's passing, and especially of Father's solution that Helen be married off to a wealthy man, a feeling of utter hopelessness and desperation came over Grace.

She *had* to marry—and soon—or their father would force Helen to. Helen, who was barely eighteen and shy as a church mouse. Helen, so soft spoken she could rarely be heard. Helen, so exquisitely beautiful that a man like Lidgate would have devoured her instantly.

Grace gave sleep up for good and lay still, contemplating the last several days and the previous night's events, the horror and then the shame of realizing that she'd been in a man's bed—*with him.*

The barest hint of dawn peeked through a seam in the heavy tapestries. She tried to find hope in that tiny ray of light, remembering how her mother had always told her that everything seemed better, brighter in the morning.

The solutions to our troubles oft come with the morning light, she'd said. But Grace could see no solution to her problem. In spite of Miranda's reassurances that the servants would not talk, Grace knew otherwise. She'd spent the better part of six years at her grandfather's house full of servants. She knew how rumor and gossip flew among them, between estates and entire villages, and then spread through London and the ton. It was only a matter of time before the story of her time in Lord Sutherland's bed was well known here and beyond.

Before I am ruined.

Grace tried to recall if she'd ever heard the Sutherland name before last night. Was there any possibility her father knew of him? Not likely, if Lord Sutherland did not frequent London gambling houses, and, given what little she could recall from their arrival last night, she very much doubted that he did.

If so, he is even poorer than Father at winning. For while his residence might be large, Lord Sutherland clearly could not afford to keep it up.

Had he, I would not be in this predicament now, for I should have been properly shown to a guest room. But of course, she had not. *Oh, help me,* Grace prayed.

In addition to worrying about Helen's welfare and Father's debts, she now had to worry over the possibility of a duel. When her father learned of this, he'd be furious. No doubt he'd send Christopher in his stead to face Lord Sutherland.

The only solution Grace could see was to be otherwise

settled before her father learned of it. She would have to quit being so particular about the men he'd chosen as possible suitors. She would have to give up her dream of remaining unwed and living with Helen and Christopher in the country.

I shall have to marry—and quickly now.

And all because of an unfortunate misunderstanding. *Because I was mistakenly in Lord Sutherland's bed. But who will have me?*

No one.

Grace's eyes flew open. *No one* would have her now. *Of course!* Why hadn't she seen it before? This was not a tragedy, but the miracle she'd been hoping for. And all her "problem" would take to blossom into a miracle was a little nudge. A burst of laughter rolled from her lips.

Miranda was at her side in an instant, bending low over the bed, an anxious, concerned, almost motherly look in her eyes.

"Where did you come from?" Grace asked, nonplussed at her maid's sudden appearance. She struggled to sit up, wanting to reassure Miranda she was well and eager to share her sudden inspiration.

"I slept in the chair." Miranda inclined her head toward the far side of the room, which was still in shadow. "I came to check on you shortly after you went to bed the second time, but you were in such a state that I didn't think it right to leave, not with the way you were carrying on and thrashing about."

"Thank you," Grace said, her heart again filled with gratitude toward this woman whom she'd once protested against. Instead of the intrusion into her privacy Grace had feared a lady's maid would be, she'd found Miranda to be the kindest of women, someone who not only looked after Grace's physical comforts but who had proven herself a guide and ally.

Now I must test the strength of our bond. Would Miranda so readily do Grace's bidding at her next request?

"I feel much improved this morning," Grace said cheerily. Indeed, it was true. Her forehead and nightgown were damp with sweat, so her fever must have broken sometime in the night. The chills and persistent headache were gone, and in their place, her mind was calm and focused. She knew exactly what must be done now.

"Your voice isn't right yet," Miranda said. "And your breathing's raspy."

Also true. The vise assaulting her breath still seized in Grace's chest, and her throat was yet sore, but all in all, she did feel far better than the previous evening. To prove it, she pushed back the covers and swung her legs over the side of the bed. Ignoring Miranda's disapproving look, Grace stood and began making her way toward the window to look out at the day. She always enjoyed the morning after a rainstorm, when the world seemed fresh and new. Today, in particular, life seemed alight with possibility.

Grace cleared her throat and began carefully. "As I said before, when word of last night's events gets out, my reputation will be ruined."

"But it won't," Miranda protested. "There's only Mrs. James and the two girls who work here—just them in a place this big—can you imagine?" She shook her head in disbelief. "And I spoke to Mrs. James about it last night. She's instructed the girls, and Mr. Kingsley will see to speaking to the groomsmen. They're none of them to say a word about last night—not if they wish to keep their positions. Mrs. James said they already worry over losing their employment, since Lord Sutherland's been letting the staff go one by one over the past year and a half."

Grace reached the window and pushed the tapestry aside. The view was disappointing—only a neglected, overgrown garden below. A thick carpet of several seasons of leaves covered the ground, making any paths or lawn indiscernible. A mangled twist of rose bushes had only a few long-wilted buds amidst an overabundance of thorns. In spite of last night's rain, everything appeared brown and dull. It was apparent that the gardener had been let go quite some time ago.

"How terrible to have such a grand estate and be unable to maintain it," she said, wondering what misfortune had befallen Lord Sutherland.

"True enough," Miranda said. "But at least you've no need to worry about servants' tongues flapping about last night."

"Oh, but I wish them to." Grace turned from the window to face Miranda, then rushed forward in her eagerness to explain. "Listen to me, please."

The older woman had opened her mouth in protest but closed it now. After a few seconds, Miranda nodded her acquiescence. "As you wish."

"We both know my father is bent on marrying me off," Grace began. "And sooner or later Helen as well. He'll stop at nothing till he's seen the deed done and taken what money he can from it. Helen, with her beauty, is in particular danger."

A pained look flickered through Miranda's eyes; Grace knew her maid had come to care for Helen almost as much as she did. Grace reached out, taking Miranda's hands in hers, imploring her to understand.

"We both know that Helen is far too shy and delicate to be sold off to some unfeeling male. She wouldn't fare well."

"Which leaves the burden on you," Miranda said woefully.

"Unless . . ." Grace began. "Unless something so dreadful happened that neither of us could marry." She hurried on before Miranda could interrupt. "Last night I was found with a man in his bed," she whispered—it was too horrible to speak about it above that.

A sort of choked laugh escaped her lips, but lest

Miranda think she was losing her mind, Grace brought her hands up quickly to cover her mouth. It *was* laughable, really. She'd never even been kissed; turning her cheek to avoid Sir Lidgate's lips did not count.

And now Father is to hear that I've been in a man's bed. She didn't relish the fit of temper that bit of news was likely to cause. She'd have to be certain to warn Helen and Christopher. Perhaps she would be fortunate enough that their father would be taken in for his debts before he found out.

Because if he were able, he would either call on Lord Sutherland or call him out, only to discover that his circumstances were not much improved over their own. She was counting on Lord Sutherland's lack of wealth to protect them both. Her father would be unable to extract any payment for her disgrace, and he would see no monetary benefit in forcing a marriage.

And no one else will be willing to offer for me either. Even Lidgate—with all his talk of my innocence—would not want a bride who has been ruined. I shall be free, and Lord Sutherland will be no worse for it.

"If your father finds out, there could be a duel," Miranda warned.

Grace nodded, already prepared for the argument. During her nightmares, the solution had come to her. "Father is too much a coward to duel. He'll send Christopher."

"And you'd have your own brother die for you?" Miranda said, disapproval puckering her lips.

"Of course not," Grace said, exasperated. "I've spent the past sixteen years of my life keeping that boy out of trouble—no easy task, mind you. Do you think I'd let all that good effort go to waste?" She shook her head as she turned from her maid. "I would never endanger him. I'll post a letter to Christopher today, apprising him of the situation. If Father sends him to confront Lord Sutherland, Christopher will simply go elsewhere. If I am fortunate, Christopher and Helen will both be safely away before Father ever hears of my troubles. Perhaps our inheritance will even be settled by then." Grace spoke brightly, clasping her hands and facing Miranda, who rolled her eyes.

"And perhaps Harrison will quit snorting like a deranged pig."

"Harrison is a dear, suffering so to be here with me," Grace said, defending him. "Would that I could send you both back to London. I worry over Helen at home without me."

"She'll be fine," Miranda said, her tone softening. "You've more need of us right now."

Grace bit her lip. "I fear that I do—more than ever." She'd come to the part of her plan Miranda was least likely to be in favor of.

"Father will be furious. He'll wish he could flay me for such a careless mistake." Grace winced, remembering all too well the times she had felt the sting of a switch. "I'll post a letter to Helen too," Grace said, once again fearing for her sister. "She cannot be home when Father receives the news. But as for me—and what happened here last night—there will be nothing he can do, no way to repair the damage to me, or to Helen, either. Our *family's good name,*" Grace said sarcastically, "will be beyond repair."

"And will you write your father a letter as well?" Miranda asked. "Telling him all that has transpired last night?"

"Oh, no," Grace said. "He'll not hear from me. He will simply . . . hear of it."

For everything to transpire, the servants would have to talk. Grace thoroughly intended that those few scandalous moments be recounted explicitly to the right people and at the right places. She suppressed a shudder as she recalled them: the surprise of Lord Sutherland's arm across her chest, the feel of *his* chest, bare beneath his robe when she'd pushed him away—

"Being in Lord Sutherland's bed is enough to ruin me, and any possibility for Helen as well," Grace reiterated, feeling both determined and delighted. "And if neither of us can marry, Father will simply have to get on another way—without us. And we will be free of him."

"It is what the duke intended all along," Miranda said.

"I know," Grace said. "And it pains me to have to besmirch his good name in ruining mine. But I see no other way. Father will not desist. Not when he believes there is money to be had through us. We must take this opportunity that has befallen us."

"Dear girl." Miranda wrung her hands. "You worry over the reputation of the deceased, when it's your own life you ought to be thinking on. You don't realize what you'd suffer."

"Perhaps not," Grace agreed. "But I can well imagine what I—and Helen—may suffer if I do not take this action." She hugged her arms to her chest. "Thus far I've been fortunate in finding ways out of disagreeable marriages. We both know that that cannot go on forever. What will be Mr. Preston's disposition? Will I be barring my door at night from him as well? Will he wish me to sit demurely at his side and hold my tongue the remainder of my days while he heaps whatever abuses he fancies upon me? Grandfather left me that money so I would not have to marry. I believe he would agree with this decision."

"There must be another way," Miranda implored.

"There isn't," Grace said. "God has given us this oar, and we must use it to make our escape."

Miranda wasn't entirely able to hide her half-horrified, half-shocked look at the mention of Deity.

"I'm sorry," Grace hastened to apologize. "But I feel that

He, too, would want to help me, and so He has. Now it is up to us to do our part."

Miranda took a step back from the bed and shook her head. "I don't want to know what that part is."

"It's quite simple, really." Grace began pacing the floor, taking a minute to think her plan through more thoroughly. She hadn't walked but a few steps when the room blurred before her eyes; she stumbled and nearly fell.

"*My* part ought to be ensuring you stay in bed and get well." Miranda's scolding tone returned.

"A luxury I can ill afford," Grace objected. She leaned on Miranda and steadied herself, waiting for her head to clear. It was discouraging to find she felt faint and weak as she had the previous evening. Shrugging off her discomfort, she straightened to her full height—still shorter than Miranda's—and spoke in her most commanding tone.

"We must make haste to Mr. Preston's as soon as possible. Once there, your task . . ." She paused, catching Miranda's eye and holding it. "Is to gossip."

CHAPTER 6

Grace wrapped her trembling fingers around a cup of hot tea, hoping the warmth would steady them—steady her. Behind her, Miranda deftly wove Grace's hair into an acceptable—if not fashionable—knot at the base of her neck.

"At least your hair's tamed now." Miranda spoke with the satisfaction of accomplishment. Grace knew that, given the state of her hair this morning, after being damp and loose all night, that shaping it into any sort of bun was nothing short of miraculous.

"It does feel better. Thank you." *Most* of her felt quite a bit better after eating a piece of toast and getting dressed in her own clothes. Her chest still hurt, and her hip and back were sore and bruised—either from the fall from Sir Lidgate's horse, the carriage accident, rolling off Lord Sutherland's bed, or, quite probably, the three combined. But all in all, her physical condition was much improved. Her mind, so clear and focused earlier, was another matter entirely; the shaking teacup was evidence of her nerves as she contemplated what they were about to undertake.

Grace gave up any hope of drinking and set the cup back in the saucer before she spilled tea all over her gown, which Harrison had retrieved from their broken-down carriage. "Are we ready, then?" She looked into the glass and caught Miranda's eye once more.

"Lord Sutherland's landau is below. Mr. Kingsley assured us that it would be no problem to use it."

"In the same way it was no problem to make use of Lord Sutherland's bed last night?" A nervous giggle escaped Grace's lips. "Mr. Kingsley knows no such thing about the landau," she guessed. "It seems he takes far too many liberties with his lordship's possessions."

"He may have just cause." Miranda placed a final pin in Grace's hair. "Mrs. James says Lord Sutherland is home not one day of twenty. It's up to her and Mr. Kingsley to keep this place going. Kingsley must make decisions if anything is to be run halfway proper."

"I certainly do not begrudge him his kindness and generosity last night," Grace said sincerely. "If our plans come to fruition, he has done an even kinder turn than he realized."

"I don't know about all that," Miranda said. Contrary to her usual restraint, she'd made her mind known about Grace's scheme. "But don't trouble yourself over using a carriage." Miranda handed Grace her bonnet. "Kingsley said there were several to choose from. It's doubtful Lord Sutherland will miss one."

This was not good news. She didn't want Lord Sutherland to have several carriages or anything else. For her plan to work, he needed to be near destitute.

"Whether he misses it or not, I detest having to borrow anything from him. And I certainly do not want Father to be able to *gain* anything from him." Grace frowned into the mirror as she placed the bonnet upon her head. How she hated being in anyone's debt. It was the very thing she'd both endured and fought against her entire life. "I suppose Mr. Kingsley believes it better that we're gone before Lord Sutherland arises."

"I'd wager you're right," Miranda said.

Grace's fingers stilled on the bonnet strings. "Must you use that term?" She stood abruptly and faced Miranda.

Miranda looked as stricken as Grace felt. "My apologies, Miss Thatcher." Miranda curtsied before crossing the room to pack the valise.

Grace winced at the formality she'd all but begged those in her employ *not* to use. "It's all right," she said, regretful for having given the reprimand. She'd acted as many did toward their servants, but she felt she oughtn't have. Miranda had meant no harm, but Grace could tell that her rebuke had done plenty to injure the tenuous friendship they'd formed since Grandfather's passing. Before then, Grace had had as little interaction with Miranda as possible, but in the months since Grandfather had died, and during the ensuing crisis of her father's debts, Miranda had become much more than a servant. She'd become a friend and confidante.

Miranda's back had stiffened, and the mask of aloofness had descended over her face once more. Her lips pressed together into what Grace was certain would be an extended silence. With one sentence, she had sent Miranda firmly back into her role as her maid.

Grace tried another apology. "You know the term *wager* dredges up many a painful memory for me. But it's none of your doing. I am truly sorry I said anything at all."

"A lady does not apologize to her staff," Miranda pointed out, her tone somewhat stern.

Grace smiled. "*This* lady will apologize as she needs to. I believe my mother named me Grace in the hopes that I would exhibit some."

Miranda did not return her smile, but Grace thought

she might have seen a hint of approval in the older woman's eyes. *No doubt she feels as much a governess as a lady's maid.*

But there wasn't much Grace could do about that at the moment. She was trying her best to find her way in this world so different from the one she'd grown up in. It wasn't easy, and at times, when she thought about her old life, she realized that in some ways, it had been far simpler before the duke had offered her his home and a secure future.

Miranda continued to pack in silence, and Grace crossed to the window, looking out at the unkempt grounds while rehearsing in her mind all that she, Miranda, and Harrison had discussed this morning in a hasty tête-à-tête in the privacy of this room.

"Your wet clothing really ought to be washed before we leave." Miranda held up Grace's still-damp, muddy gown. "I'd intended to see to it this morning."

"No matter," Grace said, privately glad she'd been wearing one of her plainest black mourning frocks, and not one of her newer gowns, for travel. "It's likely ruined. We cannot spare another minute on such frivolities." In part, that was true. The sooner they arrived at Sir Preston's in Lord Sutherland's carriage—something that had been Harrison's idea—the sooner Miranda and Harrison could start spreading the tale that would lead to her ruin. More than that, Grace had a strong desire to avoid another meeting with Lord Sutherland. As she guessed Mr. Kingsley felt the same, she thought it far better if she was gone when the lord awoke.

Miranda held up the borrowed nightgown. "And I don't know what to do about this. The whole side is practically torn out."

"Bring it with us," Grace said. "It's no good to anyone else in that condition, and what better fodder for gossip than actual evidence of the deed?"

Miranda began folding the garment, a distinct frown of disapproval written on her creased lips.

Grace spoke for her, waving her hand in the air as she did. "I know. You still say I haven't the slightest notion of what I am getting myself into."

Miranda gave a tight-lipped nod as she packed the nightgown with Grace's other things.

"Harrison thought my plan brilliant," Grace said.

"Harrison keeps company in the barn," was Miranda's retort. "'Course he'd think well of your idea."

"I imagine the animals might be better company than some I've been forced to suffer lately." Grace recalled Lord Crosby's demeaning comments as she looked out at the garden again. Her eyes strained to follow what she guessed used to be a garden path. Now it was little more than a narrow space winding between thorny bushes and overgrown trees. What had happened to cause Lord Sutherland to let his staff go? And why did he spend so much time away?

She thought of him as he'd been last night—at first savagely demanding to know who she was, then promptly forgetting her name minutes later. He'd been angry, but he'd not tossed her out or even insisted upon knowing why she'd been on a lonely country road in the middle of the night and a storm with just a driver and her maid.

He did not press me at all, Grace realized. And felt immense gratitude for that, and for the role Lord Sutherland was about to play—unknowingly—in her effort to gain her freedom.

I must only endure two days at Mr. Preston's. She reasoned that two days was not so very long. "What do you suppose Mr. Preston will be like?" she asked Miranda, not really expecting an answer.

"Before or after he learns that the woman he'd hoped to court recently spent time in another man's bed?" Miranda had finished packing and stood near the door with Grace's belongings.

"Both." Grace spoke with more courage than she felt. She held her head high and stood a little straighter as she walked past her maid and into the hall. "Let us go then, and see for ourselves."

Grace peered out the carriage at the towering mansion drawing ever closer. The horses turned onto the long, curved drive lined with stately poplars. A hedge of brilliant yellow rosebushes grew along the drive, and beyond these, a lush, green lawn spread endlessly, dotted by an occasional outbuilding and numerous oaks ablaze with fall color.

"Goodness," she said. "Father has outdone himself this time."

As they approached the house, numerous servants exited the front doors to greet them.

All beauty and order here. It was the very antithesis of Lord Sutherland's estate just a short distance away.

"Had we only known we were so close, we could have ridden a little farther last night," Grace said.

"You were in no condition to ride." Miranda sat stiffly in the seat across from Grace, hands folded primly on her lap, and she stared straight ahead at the carriage wall instead of at the scenery.

"True," Grace agreed. "And we shouldn't have had our means of escape so clearly in front of us," she added, again trying to shore up her courage for the damage that was soon to be done to her reputation.

They rolled to a stop, and Grace leaned back into her seat, not wanting to appear over-eager to greet her next would-be suitor. "I cannot imagine how Papa came to know Mr. Preston. And more, how he was able to solicit an invitation for me."

"He didn't." Miranda took up the bag on the seat beside her.

"What?" Grace asked. Outside a footman approached, and the carriage rocked slightly as Harrison climbed down. "Is Mr. Preston not expecting me?" It was one thing to purposely set herself up as fodder for the gossips, but it remained quite another to show up uninvited.

"Oh, he's expecting you, all right." Miranda looked away, but not before Grace caught an abashed expression.

"What aren't you telling me?" Grace pressed, reaching her hand out to touch Miranda's. Outside, she heard the step being pulled down. "Was Mr. Preston forced into it for owing Father money?"

"It's not my place to gossip."

"Nonsense," Grace said. "That's exactly your place. It's what we've come to do, so practice right now. Tell me what you know—*quickly*." She grabbed the door handle and held it fast.

"I don't normally listen in on conversations, you understand," Miranda began. "But this one happened outside, and I was around the corner of the house—"

"Who was talking?" Grace asked, trying to hurry the story along.

"Why, Mr. Preston and your father, of course," Miranda said. "Who else do you think I overheard?"

"No one." Grace waved her gloved hand, urging her to finish.

"Mr. Preston had come to see your father. He'd heard it said that you were to be coming out of mourning early and were looking for a husband."

"*Father* was looking," Grace muttered. She didn't know why she was worried about ruining her reputation. Her father had likely already done a fine job of it. Coming out of mourning early had been scandalous enough, but to advertise so blatantly that he intended for her to marry—The door rattled, and the handle jiggled beneath Grace's hand. "Do go on," she pled.

"Mr. Preston *requested* you as his guest," Miranda whispered. "He told your father that he knew you from previous acquaintance with the duke. He sought you—"

Another tug on the door saw it opened this time. Grace withdrew her hand to her lap, waiting until a footman had extended his and offered assistance. Sending a fleeting glance Miranda's way—*Here we go*—Grace stepped from the carriage.

"Miss Thatcher." A man in a butler's uniform bent low before her. "We were not expecting you until tomorrow, and I am afraid Mr. Preston is away this morning."

"My apologies for our early arrival," Grace said in her most refined voice. "We encountered some difficulties en route and thought it better to impose upon your hospitality an extra day rather than remain at our previous lodging."

"You are most welcome here," the butler said. "I am Mr. Goyle, and this is Mrs. Telford. She will acquaint you with the house and all that you need."

"Would you care to join our other guests in the breakfast room?" Mrs. Telford asked.

"Thank you," Grace said. "But I fear I am still somewhat overwrought from—our travels." From the corner of her eye, she caught Harrison exchanging a covert glance with the servant he'd been speaking to.

So it has started already. No turning back now. Grace felt suddenly ill.

"May I beg leave to rest in my room?" she asked Mrs. Telford. "I'm afraid I did not sleep well last night."

"Of course. Come this way. We'll have your things brought up directly." Grace followed the woman into the mansion, which was modern on many counts compared to

Lord Sutherland's. The floors gleamed, and the light-colored curtains were thrown back, flooding the space with sunshine. Yellow roses, likely from the hedge outside, overflowed from vases on almost every surface. Their scent was sweet and pleasant. A more welcoming room Grace could not imagine.

You are not here to enjoy any of this, she reminded herself. She went through the motions, taking care to hold her gown and walk with poise as they crossed a large hall, ascended a long flight of carpeted stairs, and passed through a corridor lined with paintings. She nodded and thanked Mrs. Telford at all the right moments, then practically sagged against the door in relief when it was closed and she was alone.

Not wanting to wait for Miranda, and especially not wishing to allow her mind the time to think on what was already being said about her in the servants' quarters below, Grace left the door in favor of the inviting bed on the far side of the room. She'd scarcely lain back when her eyes closed and sleep claimed her. This time she did not dream.

CHAPTER 7

Nicholas kept his head bent to the papers in front of him for a good minute after noticing both Mrs. James and Mr. Kingsley hovering in the study doorway. He had not summoned either, so the two of them coming to see him did not bode well.

Are they both here to give their notices? Each would be justified in doing so. Perhaps they'd come together as moral support while facing the ogre. It was a term he'd chanced to overhear some months ago, from one of the few maids still in his employ. After the incident, one *less* maid worked at Sutherland Hall.

Still, he didn't like that the staff considered him a tyrant. He hadn't always been one—a dour, gruff-around-the-edges sort of employer—but it seemed that was the only way he knew how to be anymore. Nicholas used to tell himself that as soon as he'd finished with Preston, he would be better.

Life would be better. But lately, he wasn't sure it ever would.

He set his work aside, looking up at the pair waiting patiently in the doorway. No doubt he'd tried their patience with the way he'd railed at them two nights past, when he'd discovered that woman in his bed. He'd hardly spoken to anyone since. She and her servants had been gone before he'd risen the next day, and now he wished only to put the incident behind him.

He shouldn't have been so hard on Kingsley. Nicholas's conscience pricked, telling him he would never have found the woman in his bed had he employed enough servants to keep up the house—a spare room or two, at least.

"Yes?" he said to his two most trusted servants, inwardly cringing at his brusque tone.

"We have some news that may be of interest to you," Kingsley said. His expression was guarded, as usual, but Nicholas sensed something beneath the blank mask, some worry or concern.

"Has it to do with Preston?" Nicholas asked. Almost anything else didn't interest or concern him these days—even things that ought to.

"Yes," Kingsley said.

"And Miss Thatcher as well," Mrs. James added.

"Who?"

Kingsley and Mrs. James exchanged wary looks. Nicholas propped his elbows on the desk and leaned forward, indeed interested in what his servants had to say.

Had his former brother-in-law become involved with another woman? Nicholas had long suspected it would happen one of these days; Preston was the sort of man possessed with a charming air women seemed to adore.

Elizabeth certainly did. She'd been gone from this earth a scant three years, and it seemed like both yesterday and forever since Nicholas had last seen his sister. Those years had passed slowly. Not a day went by that he didn't miss her. He'd felt the same way—the whole house had—when she'd married Samuel Preston and moved to his neighboring estate. Life at Sutherland Hall had changed then, no longer graced with Elizabeth's presence and the touch of joy she'd brought to everyone and everything around her.

All hope of that joy ever returning had been lost just a year and a half later with her passing, but the echo of her laughter still rang in the halls. Nicholas imagined that he could still hear her playing the pianoforte in the music room. Her garden of roses, though neglected, still carried the sweet, heady scent he would always associate with her.

He hadn't forgotten, or recovered from, the loss. The thought that her husband might be moving on with life only fueled the hatred burning bright in Nicholas's soul. "Who is Miss Thatcher?" he repeated.

Kingsley cleared his throat and tugged at his collar. "The woman who stayed here two nights ago."

That pale, wild-haired thing? Nicholas could not imagine Preston, or any other man, being attracted to her. "What has she to do with Preston?"

"She was headed there the night her carriage broke down," Mrs. James said. "And she is there now. Mr. Preston is hosting a ball this weekend, and she is his particular guest."

"Jolly good for them," Nicholas said darkly, drumming his fingers together. The woman—Miss Thatcher—couldn't hold a torch to Elizabeth, who'd been as rare a beauty as she'd been in spirit. But if Miss Thatcher really was at Preston's, at his particular invite, then *something* about her must have attracted him.

Nicholas told himself he didn't care. Soon enough, no female from here to London would have anything to do with Preston. Once his fortune was gone, he'd lost everything, and had to return to doctoring—Nicholas intended to see to it that the man was barred from that profession as well—Preston would hold no attraction for Miss Thatcher or any other woman.

But for all of Nicholas's efforts to see Preston brought

down, the time was simply not coming fast enough. "I see not what this has to do with me." Nicholas looked at his papers again, searching for the document he'd been reading.

"It has a great deal to do with you, I'm afraid," Mrs. James said. "The story about Miss Thatcher being in your bed has traveled beyond our gates, and Mr. Preston's whole household knows of it. Only Miss Thatcher does not, as she's been shut up in her room at Mr. Preston's, recovering from illness since she arrived yesterday morning."

"Preston believes that the woman he invited to his ball spent the night in my bed?" Nicholas's mouth curved into a near grin. The situation was almost amusing. Almost. There could never be anything truly amusing about Preston. Thoughts of him always circled back to Elizabeth's death and Preston's part in it. "For certain he won't want the girl now."

He supposed he could feel satisfied in that, at least. Preston didn't deserve to find another woman or any sort of happiness, not when he'd been given perfection in Elizabeth and had allowed her to die.

"But he *does* want her yet," Mr. Kingsley said.

Mrs. James nodded. "That was the word at the market this morning, though all the staff and guests, and even Mr. Preston, know what happened."

"What exactly *did* happen?" Nicholas asked. He'd been tired that night, but he was rather certain that his recollection of the events had him and Miss Thatcher in the same proximity of blankets for less than half a minute, during which time he had done nothing to her.

"Oh, it's dreadful." Mrs. James brought a hand to her mouth, as if she couldn't bear to say more. "They say that Miss Thatcher was—was—"

"Taken advantage of by you," Kingsley supplied.

"There's even a torn nightgown been passed around the servant's quarters for all to see," Mrs. James said.

"Ridiculous." Nicholas stood abruptly. *An absurd*

accusation. "I did nothing to her nightgown." But even as he said it, he remembered reaching for the woman, remembered the feel of cloth in his hand and the sound of tearing fabric. "How on earth did it end up at the servants' quarters?"

"Her maid brought it down and asked about thread for mending it," Mrs. James said.

"Is the woman daft?" Nicholas exclaimed. She'd seemed sane enough during their brief encounter that awful night—the night that seemed to be getting worse by the minute.

"I don't understand it either," Mrs. James said. "Miss Thatcher's maid came to see me as soon as Miss Thatcher was settled again. She wanted a guarantee that word of the incident would not get out, lest Miss Thatcher's reputation be ruined."

"Her footman came to see me as well," Kingsley said, his face grim. "Mrs. James and I both assured them that the events of the evening would not go beyond our doorstep."

Nicholas ran a hand through his hair and began pacing behind his desk. "So Miss Thatcher's reputation is in shreds, and *I* am the accused. And truly, Preston doesn't care?"

"So it would seem," Kingsley said.

"Mrs. Telford says he's taken the servants to task for their gossiping and threatened to dismiss the lot," Mrs. James added. "He's planning to dance with Miss Thatcher tonight in hopes of minimizing the damage."

"And what of the damage to me?" Nicholas muttered. He didn't much care what the country neighbors thought of him; he cared even less for the opinion of his peers in London. But his mother would care deeply. She'd had her heart broken enough; he didn't wish to inflict any more wounds.

"Why would Preston still want her?" Nicholas asked, though he guessed the reason easy enough. Samuel Preston might be new money, and he might not set store by many of polite society's rules, but he'd have to be an idiot not to understand that any young, single woman who'd been in another man's bed—for however brief a time—wasn't one he'd want to be involved with. To do so would be to risk everything. Only a man besotted with love would be such a fool.

It had taken time and effort—and marriage to Elizabeth—but eventually, most of Preston's neighbors had accepted him. And, much to Nicholas's frustration, he was becoming well respected and making connections and acquaintances in London. But if what Kingsley and Mrs. James had said was true, Preston stood to lose his precarious standing this very night. His other guests—those who'd heard of the incident, in whatever form it was being bandied about—would shun Miss Thatcher and Preston, in turn, as well.

Nicholas paused, rubbing his hands together almost gleefully. If Preston was to be shunned by the gentry, his business connections would fail. The inheritance he'd come into would last only so long, and the many investments he'd made wouldn't pay off. It might take time, but he could be forced to lose his estate. Then—and only then—could Nicholas live at Sutherland Hall in peace.

Of course, there would be a price. Nicholas considered the outcome for himself. No respectable woman would want him—for a while, at least. But he still had his fortune, and in the end, money always spoke loudest.

Besides, he wasn't looking for a wife just now anyway. He wasn't interested in anything until he'd seen Preston driven out and destroyed—*as he destroyed my family.* All in all, Nicholas deemed the damage to his reputation a small price to pay. Eventually, his part in the "indiscretion" would be forgotten. It was Miss Thatcher and Preston who would not be so fortunate.

"I thank you for the information," he said, dismissing Kingsley and Mrs. James.

Mrs. James nodded and backed out of the doorway, wearing a frown of disapproval. Kingsley, however, made no move and continued staring at him.

"Is there something else?" Nicholas asked.

"I only wondered if there was a particular suit you wished to be pressed," Kingsley said. "I'll advise your valet now, so he has plenty of time."

"Time for what?" Nicholas asked, seating himself at his desk once more.

"To ready your things for the ball tonight." Kingsley spoke as if it were a forgone conclusion that Nicholas would attend. Nothing could have been farther from the truth.

"I am not going anywhere tonight," Nicholas said. "And if I were, the last place would be a ball hosted by Samuel Preston."

"I see. My apologies." Kingsley nodded and turned to go.

"Kingsley, why would you think such a thing?" Nicholas felt both perplexed and bothered by the butler's assumption.

"Nothing—no reason, milord. My mistake."

"Kingsley!" Nicholas's tone was sharper than he'd intended. He tried again. "It was not *nothing*. Did I say or do something to indicate that I wished to go?"

Kingsley hesitated before facing him and answering. "Not at all, milord. I only assumed you would attend because a young lady's honor is in question, as is your own. And both are matters of significance to the Sutherland name."

CHAPTER 8

Dearest Helen and Christopher,

A most unfortunate incident has occurred, but I have determined to take advantage of the circumstance and make the most of it for all of our sakes. However, I must warn you . . .

Grace fastened the clasp of her earring, then lowered her trembling hands—it seemed they'd yet to stop shaking or warm at all in the past two days—and stared at her reflection in the mirror. Her eyes were large and worried, her face pale, but beyond those somewhat usual features, she almost didn't recognize herself.

Gone was her plain bun, and in its place, a riot of curls adorned her head, with a few trailing down either side of her face. A sparkling tiara nestled among the curls, and a matching necklace lay at the base of her throat.

"You've never looked lovelier," Miranda said.

"Nor ever felt quite so treacherous." Grace hadn't thought she'd miss wearing black. In the previous month, her shift to gowns with more of a gray hue had felt like an acceptable improvement. That was shortly before embarking upon this trip, which she now termed "the madness of her father, George."

But after nearly a year of donning only the darkest, plainest clothing, she felt something of a shock to see herself looking fashionable. Tonight she wore an ivory ball gown, with her hair done up and jewels at her neck and dangling from her earlobes, a hint of color on her cheeks and lips. Perhaps Miranda was right that Grace had never looked as lovely as she did right then. But it did not *feel* lovely to be showing extreme disrespect for her late grandfather, who had been so generous to her.

"The duke would understand," Miranda said kindly.

"Would he?" Grace turned to her, once again seeking comfort and reassurance from the older woman. At times like these, she would have given much for a five-minute conversation with her mother. She feared—she *knew*—she treated Miranda as a substitute far too often.

"I believe he'd say that you had your wits about you and are using them."

Grace smiled her gratitude. "That *is* something he would have said. Oh, but how I miss him. How I hope he knows I mean him no disrespect by dressing this way and acting this part. Were it up to me, I should have remained in mourning two years and longer, and I should never have my name known for anything."

"Don't trouble yourself over the gown, at least," Miranda said. "It's a shame to have those fine clothes and never use them. And your father already took you to task for such at Sir Lidgate's."

"*Father.*" Grace gave an indignant flounce and turned to face the glass once more. "His letter only confirmed that he has spies everywhere. I've never felt so tattled upon in my life as I did after that visit. I should very much like to know who told him that I wore my plainest black frock to Sir Lidgate's lavish dinner party. Besides—" She brought a hand to her chest. "I *had* to. It was the only thing keeping me safe from Lidgate's prying eyes and hands."

Miranda let out a snort that sounded suspiciously like laughter. "That you did. And this is what you must wear now *if*"—Miranda leveled a gaze upon her—"you still wish to continue this façade."

"As *if* we have any choice in the matter." Grace shook her head. "No going back. I've no doubt Harrison has already done his job exceedingly well."

"You've no idea." Miranda rolled her eyes. "It appears the man is a natural-born gossip. His tongue has been flapping at both ends since we arrived."

"Wonderful," Grace said. "How perfectly marvelous that everyone here will think the worst of me, that I am a fallen woman . . . that I am no longer marriageable."

Nor is Helen, by association. "All is well," Grace said, her voice stronger, more convinced. *I need only get through this evening.*

Since her arrival yesterday, she'd stayed in her room, partially because she continued to feel poorly, and partly to allow Harrison and Miranda time to spread rumors.

At Miranda's suggestion, instead of accepting Mr. Preston's invitation to dine this evening, she'd begged off, claiming she still wasn't entirely well and needed to reserve her strength for dancing later.

Another half-truth. Her fever had mostly subsided, though she hadn't been up and about enough to test her strength. The more worrisome issue had been her ability to handle herself at an intimate dinner of only twelve or so persons—all of whom, by now, had likely heard of her visit to Nicholas Sutherland's bed.

"It'll be in your nature to want to defend yourself," Miranda had warned when the three of them had met early this morning. "But you can't. Neither deny nor confirm anything. Remain as vague as you can—noncommittal, if confronted."

"It will drive the men mad," Harrison had said.

"And make the women loathe you all the more," Miranda added.

"Sounds like a perfectly delightful evening," Grace had quipped, feeling more unsettled by the minute. *But better than an evening with Sir Lidgate.*

"Take care," Harrison had warned. "Those men you've driven mad will pursue you more than ever, though it won't be marriage they're offering."

Remembering his earlier admonitions, Grace leaned forward, resting her head in her hands and not quite suppressing a groan of dread.

"You're still far too unwell for this," Miranda scolded, but a second later she placed a comforting hand on Grace's shoulder. "You don't have to, you know."

Grace looked up at her. "But I do. For Helen's sake—and mine. We'll have no peace from Father otherwise. Hopefully, he'll be so angry, he'll disown us both."

"If you are fortunate," Miranda said, expressing the same doubt as earlier. Yet it was the encouragement Grace needed.

"You look the part anyhow," Miranda said.

"What do you mean by that?" Grace asked. "Do I look like a woman who would casually share a bed with a man?"

"You look like a woman whom a man would *wish* to share his bed with," Miranda corrected. Then she continued, speaking over Grace's shocked gasp. "And that is important if our exaggerations are to be believed. But it is also important for you to feel beautiful tonight, to stand up and be proud, to act like the granddaughter of a duke—a woman whose reputation matters. No one would fret over a washerwoman's reputation being ruined—it would almost be expected. But the granddaughter of a duke . . ."

"I told you before," Grace said, recalling those first rocky months with Miranda as her maid, "that I am the same person I've always been. Living with Grandfather did not change who I was born to be."

"Do not forget the nobility running through your veins," Miranda advised. "You inherited it from your mother. Whatever you learned at your grandfather's was nothing more than you already were inside. Now sit up straight and look at yourself once more."

Grace obeyed, turning to the mirror. The reflection staring at her was nearly the same as the miniature she kept of her mother.

And what trouble her beauty caused. Grace's heart felt heavy whenever she allowed herself to think about her mother's short life. *Beleaguered by a wastrel husband who wasn't around to care for her during her last days.*

Grace stood abruptly, retrieved her fan from the dressing table, and faced the door. It was better this way, better that no man would ever want her for his wife. She bid goodnight to Miranda and crossed quickly to the door, hesitating only a moment when her hand was upon the knob.

Closing her eyes, she envisioned a quiet country cottage and the three of them—herself and Helen and Christopher—alone in a life of peaceful days and cozy nights, where no debt collectors came calling, and her father could level his rage on them no more.

One night, she told herself. *Just get through this one night, and you'll have your freedom. And this time it will be for good.*

With a smile on her face and all the courage she could muster, Grace turned the knob and left the room.

And took exactly six steps before realizing how unwell she still felt.

A coughing fit seized her, robbing her of breath until the walls spun and she was forced to lean on a side table and close her eyes. She waited for her breath to return and the dizziness to stop, for Miranda to march into the hallway and scold her right back into bed.

And I just might obey, too, Grace thought, taking a peppermint from her reticule and popping it in her mouth. Harrison had brought her a handful of them earlier, and she'd discovered that they had an amazing effect on her coughing, so as to temporarily banish it. She was certain to have minty breath throughout the evening.

That Miranda had not come to haul her to bed seemed odd until Grace heard a similar wracking cough on the other side of the wall.

So she is ill too. Grace had suspected as much and had encouraged Miranda to rest, but of course, Miranda had not been able to, engaged as she had been spreading rumors.

At least she will get the night off now. If not, then on the morrow. Grace would act the part many in her position did—being insistent and bossy, using her authority to order Miranda right back to bed.

When she could finally look and see everything in its proper place, Grace left the support of the side table and made her way to the main hall. She felt hot and cold and shaky all over. It was going to be a very long night.

Thankfully, a sturdy rail ran the length of the third floor hall overlooking the ballroom. She took refuge at the polished banister, leaning against it as she looked down on the splendid, terrifying scene below. Gentlemen swirled ladies about the floor, their gowns flowing out in a blur of colors as their laughter floated upward.

Those not dancing stood in clusters around the edges of the room, some with heads bent together in gossip.

About me, quite possibly. The thought should have made her happy. This whole thing had been her idea—and a good one, too. Only now that her part had arrived, she was blanching at what must be done.

Coward, she scolded herself—but still did not move. She lifted a hand to her forehead and felt warmth. *Dratted fever.* A chill rippled through her body, and Grace glanced at the door at the end of the corridor, grateful it remained closed.

Miranda had not seen her shivering.

I didn't lie to Mr. Preston. I was not well enough to attend dinner. Nor am I well enough to dance. But I must. Grace refused to let her current frailty ruin all of Miranda and Harrison's hard work.

Still she remained where she was, gathering both her nerve and her strength.

On a dais in the corner of the opulent ballroom, a quartet played. For several more minutes, Grace stood at the rail, watching the violinists and listening to the lively melodies. Standing here listening was pleasant; if she only could have remained in the hall all night, she would have been content.

But the time for the fashionable lateness Miranda had suggested would soon be past, so reluctantly, Grace made her way to the second floor and the grand staircase, which led to the ballroom below.

The line of those waiting to be announced at the top of the staircase had grown short. Grace stepped behind the last couple, an elderly man and woman. She hoped very much that they would take a long time to descend the stairs. Every minute that passed before *she* entered was one less she had to endure.

The heavy scent of perfume lingered in the air, and Grace wrinkled her nose with distaste as two women walked by, their falsely high voices grating. In a side room, Grace could just make out a group of men smoking cigars. One of the men laughed, and the unpleasant bark rang through the hall. It was too much—too many people, too much noise, too many scents—and it all combined to make her feel worse than ever.

She looked away, focusing on the room below as the line in front of her shortened. The ballroom was grand, from its gleaming floor to the tasteful paper on the walls and the potted plants tucked into corners. Like the rest of the house, the room seemed full of light, happy.

All of this might have been mine. She thought of Miranda's recounting of the conversation between her father and Mr. Preston.

He'd wanted to meet her. *He wasn't hosting me as a favor to Papa or because of a debt to be collected.*

Why had Mr. Preston wanted to meet her? Grace told herself that it didn't matter anymore; he would want nothing at all to do with her now.

More the better.

Nice home aside, no doubt Mr. Preston was as flawed as all the other men her father had tried to force upon her—notorious rakes or men twice her age, insufferable bores, or domineering and abusive windbags. Whichever Mr. Preston was, she could only be grateful he would have no interest in her now.

I want nothing to do with him—or any man. A grand house could be a prison just as surely as their small cottage had been for her mother. *But no man will ever want me. I am safe.*

A gentleman's name was announced, and he descended the stairs far too quickly for Grace's liking. She stepped forward, her stomach twisting in knots. The couple in front of her, a Lord and Lady Edwards, were announced and began their descent.

Grace paused at the top of the long, sweeping staircase. She gave her name to the servant; his brows arched, then his mouth turned down as he stared at her. Seconds passed before he found her on the list and nodded. Grace's throat felt suddenly tight, and she worked hard to swallow back the hurt. She absolutely could not cry.

It wasn't pity she was seeking, but disgrace. She would be proud and haughty; she'd broken the rules. She wasn't here to make friends; she was here to be shunned.

Grace took a deep breath and waited. As she'd hoped, the elderly Edwards were taking a rather long time to descend.

Searching for something to focus on when it was her turn, Grace looked out to the sea of people below. A few had stopped to acknowledge the approaching couple, but many continued in their conversations. Beyond, on the other side of the room, the dancing went on.

This won't be so bad. Only a few people will be watching me.

One of those caught her attention, smiling up at her in a knowing sort of way, as if—even from that far away—he knew what she was thinking.

Grace tried to pull her gaze from the gentleman standing near the bottom step but couldn't seem to. Neither did he turn away. His smile was broad and genuine, and, like the room that had welcomed her yesterday, he seemed to have a light, pleasant air about him. She watched as he ran up the last few steps to assist and greet the Edwards, to welcome them.

To his home.

Mr. Preston! Oh, no.

The very person she'd dreaded seeing the most was the very one she would encounter first. As she watched him hold his arm out to Lady Edwards, helping her as she shuffled along, Grace felt a pang of regret that she could no longer meet him as her true self—Miss Grace Thatcher, in search of a husband.

Brown hair, without a trace of gray, fell in waves across his forehead. He was tall and lithe, not portly or stooped or twice her age.

He didn't appear the type to be a rake. Indeed, he seemed to be a proper gentleman, albeit a new one, having an inheritance but no title. Instead of joining his own party, he'd stayed behind to personally greet every guest.

Including me.

Their eyes met again, this time with something of more interest and intensity. Grace doubted she would ever be bored in Samuel Preston's presence. Everything about him spoke of vibrancy, happiness, and a genuine love for life. He was looking up at her and smiling, as if he'd been waiting for her arrival all night.

And somehow she knew that though he might have heard the rumors, he had not yet taken them to heart. He was still interested. The realization both delighted and terrified her, and she swayed a little as she stood on the top step.

"Miss Grace Thatcher, granddaughter of Eugene Durham, the late Duke of Salisbury," the servant announced—much louder than she would have liked. At once, nearly all of the activity in the ballroom ceased. Heads turned her way; jaws dropped. Eyes flickered, looking at her with rebuke and expectation. Only the quartet played on, though their tune seemed to flag and the music dropped in volume, as if they, too, did not wish to miss any of the drama.

It took everything Grace had not to turn and flee. As she lifted her skirts and descended the first step, Mr. Preston's welcoming smile turned to a tight-lipped frown.

She'd been wrong. He hadn't realized who she was. He'd likely only been flirting or being a congenial host. *He does not want to meet me, after all.* The thought should have relieved her. Her plan was to be free of *all* men. If making them detest her presence was the only way to accomplish that, so be it.

But the strain on his face pierced her heart. She felt guilt for a deed she hadn't done and wished she could explain her innocence to Mr. Preston, at least.

The thought came again—*All of this might have been mine.* But she felt no sorrow for the loss. *Mr. Preston might have cared for me*, was a much more painful realization.

"Lord Nicholas Sutherland, Earl of Berkely," the servant's voice rang loudly from the top of the stairs.

Audible gasps rippled across the room, Grace's included. Before she could take another step or turn to see if the man whose bed she had mistakenly shared three nights past was really here, she felt his hand on her arm.

"So sorry I'm late. Good of you to wait for me," he said in a voice loud enough for Mr. Preston and those near the bottom of the stairs to hear. Then softer, for her ears only, "Don't worry. Everything will be all right. Just stay by my side."

Without asking permission, he tucked her hand into the crook of his arm and guided her down the stairs toward Mr. Preston. Grace tried to look at him but couldn't. She felt her face flush from embarrassment or fever—or both. She couldn't be sure, and she couldn't find her voice. Inside, she felt like crying.

Her great plan had gone terribly wrong. Instead of facing the gossips alone, she suddenly had two men to deal with. And she very much feared that the one at her side wasn't going away anytime soon.

CHAPTER 9

"Miss Thatcher. It is so good to see you again." Mr. Preston's smile and words seemed sincere, and as he bent to kiss Grace's free hand, she searched her mind for any memory of meeting him.

"I trust you are in better health now than when you arrived." He straightened, his gaze sliding momentarily to Lord Sutherland.

"Yes, thank you," Grace said, feeling herself relax the tiniest bit at his warm welcome. "Your home is lovely, and your staff have been most attentive."

"Preston." Lord Sutherland's voice was tense as he inclined his head toward their host with the barest nod.

"I cannot say that I expected to see you tonight." The smile on Mr. Preston's lips no longer reached his eyes. Grace sensed sadness behind them, and perhaps a wariness, as well.

There is history between these two.

"You sent me an invitation, did you not?" Lord Sutherland asked, reaching into his coat pocket.

Mr. Preston held up a hand. "No need, Nicholas." His voice sounded weary. "It pains me that you thought you needed to bring proof. You know you are always welcome in my home. And if Miss Thatcher is the means of bringing you here at last—" His gaze flitted back to Grace, and this time she thought she read regret in the depths of his brown eyes. "If it is she who has helped to breach your censure, then I thank her heartily for it."

"Temporary, at best," Lord Sutherland muttered.

Grace looked from one man to the other as an awkward silence ensued. Mr. Preston studied them in a curious way; Lord Sutherland's mouth had turned down. Grace had the feeling that he wanted to say more but was somewhat taken aback by their host's generous speech.

"The orchestra is starting a new piece," Mr. Preston said. "Miss Thatcher, will you do me the honor?" He held out his arm and inclined his head toward the dance floor.

"Of course." Grace slid her hand from Lord Sutherland's arm and took up Mr. Preston's, walking away from her unwanted escort without so much as a backward glance. It was rude of her, but she'd recovered enough from her initial shock that she was beginning to feel furious at his intrusion.

What a mess. She did not want everything to be all right, and she most certainly would not stay by Mr. Sutherland's side.

What did he mean by that, anyway? It wasn't as if anything could be done to remedy her situation now no matter how much she might wish it so. The thought came with no little regret as she walked at Mr. Preston's side. He greeted everyone they passed and smiled down at her as if having her at his side were the most delightful of situations. He led her to the center of the floor, where they turned to face each other.

"I have imagined this moment for quite some time," Mr. Preston whispered conspiratorially before stepping back, separating them to a more respectable distance.

"Oh—you have?" A ridiculous response, but what else

was she to say? *The truth, of course.* Nothing else would do. She was in enough of a predicament already, and the last thing she needed was to encourage any man's affections. Especially one whose attention she might actually enjoy. "I must confess that I've no idea where we've met before."

"We haven't," he said, a mischievous twinkle in his eye.

"Oh." *Is that all I can say? He'll think me a dimwit.* "But you said—"

"That it was so good to *see* you again," Mr. Preston clarified. "Though you don't know me, I rather feel as if I am acquainted with you. For the last few years, my box at the theater has been near your grandfather's. Many a time I have watched as you wheeled him into his box and attended to him. He seemed most fortunate to have you and your siblings to care for him so."

"It was he who cared for us." Inwardly, Grace sighed with relief, grateful she had not forgotten making Mr. Preston's acquaintance. Somehow she didn't think she would have forgotten, had she met him before tonight. Something about him seemed utterly *unforgettable*. An aura of happiness filled the air about him, as if he was unaffected by life's cares, which weighed so many down, herself included. "So—we haven't ever actually spoken before today?"

"We have not," Mr. Preston confirmed. "Though as I said, I have for some time felt as though I know you. Watching you with your grandfather was oft more touching than watching the stage. You obviously loved him a great deal and did all you could to see to his comfort and care."

"I do—I did." Their eyes met, and to her dismay, Grace found hers filling with tears. She looked quickly away and was further distressed to see that the set that had formed around them was quite large.

So many people to face, and I am in trouble already. She was not at all comfortable with the way Mr. Preston made her feel—as if he were an old friend she might confide in.

He is making me feel.

That was the problem. None of the other men her father had sent her to meet had made her anything but furious or frightened. Mr. Preston had dredged up far more—and better—emotions simply by smiling at her.

The music began, and Grace blinked away moisture in her eyes. She turned to Mr. Preston once more and held the sides of her gown as she sank into a curtsy to match his bow. They stepped forward, met in the middle, and turned 'round to meet again.

"I do thank you for rescuing me from Lord Sutherland." She forced herself to mention him—and her shame—again.

Mr. Preston frowned. "Has he hurt you in any way?"

His concern touched her. How lovely it would have been if he'd have come to her rescue earlier—first at Sir Lidgate's and then at Sutherland Hall. She shook her head as they parted. "I am unharmed. Though I am certain you have heard the rumors." She whirled away before he could answer, then wound in and out of the set.

"The rumors are very troubling and quite serious," Mr. Preston said, as soon as they were paired again. "I've been worried for you."

"For me?" When had anyone—other than Grandfather, and perhaps Miranda or Harrison—ever worried about her? "I am quite all right." Grace tried to recall Miranda's and Harrison's advice.

Be vague. Noncommittal. They'd certainly been right about her wanting to tell the truth. She wanted nothing more than to explain her innocence to Mr. Preston. Instead, she changed the subject.

"I feel at an extreme disadvantage, never having observed you—as you have me—before tonight. As I did not have opportunity to properly make your acquaintance during dinner, will you tell me of yourself?"

Mr. Preston looked taken aback by the abrupt change of topic, but after a moment's hesitation, and another rotation of partners, he answered. "I have lived here for five years—the best years of my life. Before that, I studied medicine. When I inherited, I left London and retired here."

"Do you prefer the country to London?" Grace asked, hoping—for some reason—he did.

"I prefer it immensely," Mr. Preston said. "I return to London as little as possible. I find everything far better in the country. Or perhaps it is only that I am far more suited to this life than to life in the city."

"I quite agree," Grace said. "The country is a vast improvement over London." She felt herself smiling as they drew close again and he turned her around. His touch was light, barely there at all, but it *touched her*, nevertheless.

If Mr. Preston noticed that she was flustered, he did not show it. Nor did he return to the topic of her disgrace. "You miss your grandfather," he said upon their next meeting at the center.

Grace nodded. "Terribly. My years with him were the best of my life."

"I am sorry for your loss," Mr. Preston said with such sincerity that Grace felt a tiny portion of her heart opening. She struggled to contain it, lest the floodgate of sorrow she'd been holding in these many months come pouring out.

They met for three times more, during which they both were silent. Grace grappled with her thoughts and emotions, trying to get both under control—no simple task with the way Mr. Preston watched her, ever attentive, a thoughtful expression crinkling the corners of his eyes. At last the dance ended, and she was never more grateful and regretful for such a thing to be done.

"Thank you," Grace murmured, curtsying once more. Though the steps had been light and shouldn't have been the least taxing, she felt weary. Her head ached, and she felt desperate to find a cool drink and a seat in which to sit and make use of her fan.

It wasn't to be.

She'd barely risen from her curtsy and started for the side of the hall when she felt a hand upon her back. She turned quickly, looking into Lord Sutherland's shoulder as he led her—with a far too familiar touch—back to the center of the floor.

More fodder for the gossips, Grace told herself, resisting the urge to turn around and wrest his arm away.

On the floor again, she was trapped, surrounded by other couples vying for a close position to the biggest pot of gossip to be had for miles around. Reluctantly, she faced her new partner. Lord Sutherland was slightly taller than Mr. Preston and his build more formidable. His light hair was tamed this evening, far from the shaggy mane that had half-covered his face that night in his bedroom. Blue eyes that might have been considered striking—were they not filled with such frost—glared at her. His smile was overly bright.

"What happened to staying close by me tonight?"

"The last time we met was a bit *too* close for my comfort," Grace said, keeping her chin high.

Lord Sutherland's eyes widened. "Touché."

She didn't care if he thought her clever. She didn't want him to think anything about her. She wished only that he would go away and let her handle being ruined on her own.

"What is your relationship with Preston?" he asked.

It was on the tip of Grace's tongue to tell the truth—that she had no relationship with Mr. Preston—but found herself being curt instead. "That is none of your concern."

Lord Sutherland's eyes narrowed in evident displeasure. "I think perhaps it *is*. Since rumor has it—" He paused, waiting until the dance had begun and they met at the center, where he whispered so only she could hear. "They say I have taken advantage of you."

Grace felt her face heat. What a vile man to whisper such words to her here, in the middle of a dance floor packed with people.

"At the very least"—Lord Sutherland's fingers seemed to burn into her arm as they turned around—"it ought to be your concern. By associating with Mr. Preston, you threaten his tenuous social standing."

"And what of your standing?" Grace asked. "Are you not concerned as well?" His manner annoyed her. "Should *you* be dancing with me?"

He ignored her question. "Dance with Preston again, and I promise that after tonight, his neighbors and associates will no longer hold him in any sort of regard. In short, Miss Thatcher, *he* will be looked down upon as well."

Grace met Lord Sutherland's gaze and could see that he spoke truth. What she did not understand was *why*. And why was he not at least equally concerned about his own standing?

Perhaps he feels some guilt, she mused, remembering the way he'd treated her that night—not allowing her to leave his room, trapping her against the door, and standing close.

She knew her face was blushing. "What do you suggest?" she asked before they split again. From the corner of her eye, she watched as he moved through the set, bestowing the fiercest of gazes upon each successive partner.

The neighbors will not look down upon him, she realized. *They will be too frightened.*

She strongly suspected that anyone who knew Lord Sutherland dared not besmirch his reputation. In the brief moments she'd spent in his company, she'd found him nothing but imposing and intimidating. If he treated acquaintances this way, she could only imagine how he must conduct himself around strangers. Though his peers might speak of his involvement in the affair behind closed doors, they would likely dare not let their feelings on the subject be known in public.

He is a lord, after all. And though he might have fallen on difficult financial times—his estate being run down as it was—no doubt his title still carried weight here. *He is a mean lord,* Grace concluded. *Too mean to be bullied by others or trifled with.*

And I have trifled. As he rejoined her, she felt a moment of panic. His piercing gaze seemed to see past her bravado. His grip on her hand was too tight; he swung her too close. His arm was strong around her. His hand lingered at her waist. A new and terrible worry awakened inside of her.

What if he expects—what if he believes that since such a rumor is known . . .

She didn't allow herself to finish the thought but instead sent a fleeting smile at Mr. Preston as she whirled past him. There was no equality when comparing the two partners. Everything about Mr. Preston showed him to be a true gentleman, one so kind and generous that his neighbors would be only too happy to pounce on his misfortunate choice of guests and dance partners.

On the other hand, Lord Sutherland need not worry over repercussions from his supposed misconduct. She guessed that no one would dare cross him, no matter what he was rumored to have done.

An unjust world, Grace thought, for not the first time, though it was the first time she had considered such from a point of view other than her own. Given her choice of dance partners, she knew whom she would have chosen.

Alas, women cannot choose.

"I suggest you leave," Lord Sutherland said as they passed each other. "At once."

"Is that why you came?" Grace asked. "To tell me to leave, so Mr. Preston's reputation does not suffer?" She couldn't imagine that was truly Lord Sutherland's reasoning. He did not seem like a man who would be troubled by the plight of one inconsequential woman. Nor did he seem particularly fond of his neighbor.

"I came because—" He faltered. "Because it was the right thing to do."

Right for whom?

For him.

She pushed aside a twinge of guilt for involving him. Perhaps Lord Sutherland *was* concerned about his own reputation. Perhaps there was a young lady in his life. Maybe he was courting someone or was even betrothed. Maybe he'd been about to make a brilliant match with a woman whose dowry would enable him to keep his estate.

In which case, Grace should have either pitied him or felt regret for his unwitting part in her scheme. Instead she could only think that she'd done the woman a favor.

"I'm afraid I cannot leave," she said, though she couldn't deny she felt concern for Mr. Preston. He seemed to be a decent sort of man, and she didn't wish her own troubles to tarnish him in any way. She'd have to take Lord Sutherland's advice by avoiding her host.

"Foolish woman," Lord Sutherland muttered under his breath. Then, in an urgent whisper when they drew close again, he added, "It is the only hope I see of saving your reputation. You must claim illness and retire to your room at once. Tomorrow, first thing, return home."

"How will that change a thing?" Grace suspected that he wanted her to leave for other reasons as well, but aside from his reputation, she couldn't fathom what they might be.

"When you're gone, I'll do my best to refute the rumors. I'll let it be known what really happened that night."

"And you believe that will change matters?" Grace could scarce believe his naiveté.

He nodded. They parted to rotate round the set again. Grace moved stiffly through the other partners, steeling herself against both curious and cold looks directed her way. When she returned to be Lord Sutherland's match, it was almost with relief.

"I'll let it be known," he said, "that while a guest in my house, and as a very ill young woman, you wandered out of your bed and tripped. You fell and tore your nightdress. And

I, in the presence of servants, carried you back to bed." His hand caught her waist, and they turned around.

"But that isn't what happened," she whispered.

"*Nor* did what is being spoken about now," he said. "Which half-truth would you rather claim? Goodness, woman, it's almost as if you want to be ruined."

If you only knew, she thought and felt grateful that he did not. She could well imagine his fury were her plot to be discovered. At the least he'd think her mad.

"It would have been better if you'd stayed at my side to concur and then to take your leave without dancing," he said. "But as you've danced with Preston, and since he's watching your every move with intent, we've no choice but to have you leave now."

We've? When had they formed an alliance? And Mr. Preston was watching her—*with intent?* Grace glanced his direction and caught his eye. Something akin to hope flickered inside her. She looked away, tamping the happy feeling down. After tonight she would never see Mr. Preston again. There was no reason to hope for anything regarding him other than that no harm came to him because she'd been his guest.

"The dance will end," Lord Sutherland said. "We'll make our way to Preston, and you'll make your excuses."

She bristled against his commanding tone and turned her head away before he could finish. He caught her a little too quickly when they came forward next.

"Preston will summon a servant to take you to your room," he continued. "After you've left, I'll suggest that a physician be called and let it be known how ill you've been. At least you've had the presence of mind to stay in your room the last two days. That should help."

She didn't believe for a minute that it would. Lord or not, the man was obviously unaware of the delicacies involving a lady's reputation. Even *he* could not have that much sway around here.

Could he?

Grace dismissed the twinge of uncertainty. *Lord Sutherland will not disturb my plan. He'll not threaten my peace.* As she wove through the set, the walls spun for a moment, and she felt beads of sweat upon her brow. The room was crowded and warm. She was doing too much; she *was* unwell. Retreating to the safety and rest of her room did sound lovely.

I cannot.

"—a worse scandal if you dance with anyone else," Lord Sutherland was saying as she joined him again. She grasped onto his words, determined to dance with as many different partners as she could tonight. *To seal my disgrace most thoroughly.*

But first she needed a drink and another peppermint, a moment or two with her fan. The dance was overheating her terribly; it was becoming difficult to breathe. Any second now, she would find herself coughing again.

Grace considered asking Lord Sutherland to accompany her out on the balcony. It would give the gossips plenty to talk about, and the cool air might restore her enough that she could continue on. Just now, feeling as ill as she did, she wasn't at all certain she could.

The quartet struck a final note, and it was all Grace could do not to sag against Lord Sutherland with relief.

"Good. You look ill," he said, staring down at her, revulsion upon his face.

Grace felt the sting of insult. For all the pains she'd taken with her appearance, he'd found nothing in her the least desirable or worthy of praise.

Nor do I wish him to, she silently scolded herself. *But to be told I look poorly . . .*

He steered her toward Mr. Preston, and she hadn't the strength to do more than protest his grip on her arm. "You are hurting me," she said loud enough that several heads nearby turned.

"You're unwell again," Lord Sutherland proclaimed, his voice equally loud. "We must get you to bed—" His mouth snapped shut, and he had the audacity to look abashed as the closest women shot looks of horror in their direction.

Had she not felt so ill, and had she not been the recipient of horrified stares, Grace might have laughed. Instead she felt the sting of tears behind her eyes. "A poor choice of words, milord," she couldn't resist saying when they'd moved past the crush of disapproving glares.

"It was. My apology."

His words took her off guard, as did the wave of black that blurred her vision when she tilted her head to look up at him. Grace's arm fell limp at her side, and her knees buckled as she heard Mr. Preston's exclamation.

"What have you done to her?"

Lord Sutherland's answer and the room were lost as she fell backward and her mind succumbed to the dark.

CHAPTER 10

"What have you done?" Preston repeated, his voice ringing with accusation.

"Nothing. She's fainted, is all." Nicholas looked down at Miss Thatcher, wilted in his arms like a neglected garden flower. He'd only just managed to catch her. "Get back," he barked at the encroaching crowd. "Give her some air."

It was hot—stifling—suddenly. If he'd had a free hand, he would have been tugging at his cravat. Those nearest when Miss Thatcher had collapsed moved in, crushing the space around them to almost nothing.

Nicholas glanced at the floor—a poor place to lay Miss Thatcher, yet there wasn't a closer alternative. He looked over the heads of those around him. Chairs were scattered about the ballroom, but nothing more substantial. Obviously, guests were not expected to faint.

But Miss Thatcher was not just any guest. She was here at Preston's particular invitation, Nicholas remembered as Preston pushed his way forward and tried to take her from him.

"Leave off," Nicholas ordered. "You think pulling on her will cause her to wake? Someone get smelling salts."

A few ladies left, but most of the crowd drew closer. By now, word of the crisis had traveled across the room, and the musicians ceased playing. Those who had been dancing were closing in too, eager to see what had caused the stir.

"I only meant to take Miss Thatcher upstairs," Preston said, leveling a gaze upon Nicholas. "Her maid can attend to her in her room. We can summon a physician as well, if necessary."

"*Now* you'll summon a physician?" Nicholas bit out. *Miss Thatcher is more deserving than my sister was?* Were his hands free, he would have punched Preston. With Miss Thatcher in his arms, he had no choice but to control his temper.

"Yes, if that is what you suggest," Preston said. "Let's get Miss Thatcher out of the ballroom first. She's been unwell since her arrival. She should rest."

Precisely the plan Nicholas had outlined to her not five minutes earlier, but he found himself at odds with the idea—or with the one presenting it, at least.

"Here are the salts! Let me through. I've got the salts." A stout, gray-haired woman, who wore a gown that closely resembled a peacock's tail, waved a bottle over her head and made her way through to them. Nicholas recognized her as Lady Ellis, a neighbor to the north, and one of the more prolific gossips in the county.

Of course she'd find a way to the center of things.

"Thank you," Preston said before Nicholas could tell her to go away. Preston opened the bottle and held it beneath Miss Thatcher's nose. For several seconds, she did nothing. Then at once she stirred, turning her head aside as if the odor pained her. She began to cough and burrowed her face into Nicholas's chest.

Worse by the minute. Nicholas fumed inwardly, wishing he'd never set foot in Preston's house but left Miss Thatcher alone to manage her own troubles. But when he looked upon his charge and she struggled to breathe, an unexpected surge of protectiveness caught him off guard. He tilted her up. "Get some water."

"Miss Thatcher." Preston patted her cheek.

Nicholas pulled back, moving her out of reach. "Slapping her won't help her breathe," he said, knowing perfectly well his neighbor's intent.

"She's burning up," Preston said. "We've got to get her upstairs."

"No." At Nicholas's edict, heads snapped to attention. "No," he said more quietly, though no less stern. "She's coming with me."

Preston stepped forward and placed a hand on Miss Thatcher's arm. "She is a guest in my home and, therefore, my responsibility."

Nicholas shook his head, the old hatred flaring to life at words he'd heard before.

In this very house. From Preston.

Elizabeth should not have been Preston's responsibility. Miss Thatcher could not be Preston's responsibility.

"No," Nicholas repeated, his voice even softer, more deadly. He wouldn't make the same mistake twice. His eyes locked on Preston's. "The last time I left a woman in your care, she died." A flood of gasps rippled across the room. Preston looked as if he had been struck, but quickly he straightened and withdrew his hand from Miss Thatcher's arm.

"You've had your chance," Nicholas said. "She comes with me."

CHAPTER 11

Nicholas reached forward, rapping on the front wall of the carriage. "Take care!" he shouted to the driver above.

In answer, the landau seemed to rock even more, making it difficult to keep Miss Thatcher safely upon the seat. The road was poor here—mostly his fault, as he'd failed to maintain his portion of the once well-traveled thoroughfare between Preston's estate and his own.

Miss Thatcher moaned faintly, as if the motion pained her, but her eyes remained closed, her limbs limp on the seat beside him. Nicholas did his best to keep her balanced there, as comfortable as possible. He hadn't planned on having a passenger for his return ride, especially one so ill as to not be coherent.

"A poor choice," he mumbled, referring to far more than the badly maintained road. He looked over at Miss Thatcher, her face barely visible in the moonlight filtering through the window. He still couldn't believe she was here with him, on her way to Sutherland Hall, and that he'd taken her so boldly from Preston.

If it had been anywhere or anyone else . . . It wouldn't

have mattered. He could have left her there, could have walked away, any guilt over her situation absolved. But to leave Miss Thatcher there tonight might have been a death sentence. What were the chances that Preston really would have summoned a physician?

And if he had . . . At the least allowing Miss Thatcher to remain in Preston's care would have been giving Preston what he wanted.

Thwarting Preston's desires had been a reason for taking her too. Nicholas wasn't certain which motivation for taking her had been greater. Did he truly care about Miss Thatcher's health? Or had the opportunity to take something—or someone—from Preston been too great to resist?

Does it matter? He wasted no more time examining his motives. Whatever they were, Miss Thatcher was sure to benefit. She'd be well cared for at Sutherland Hall. He'd have to see to that now. Holding her in his arms after she'd fainted, and taking her alone in his carriage ensured there would be no repairing the damage to her reputation. No, he would have to see that she was provided for. He wondered absently if she wouldn't mind going to Scotland. It might be far enough away that she could start anew. He could set her up in a little cottage there and forget the whole incident.

Couldn't he?

The carriage jostled again, and her head slid from his shoulder, where he'd propped it carefully at the beginning of their ride. He caught her once more and shifted his arm around her, pulling her close to keep her from falling off the seat.

Her breathing was shallow, labored, and laced with coughing every minute or so. Her hair had come loose, so her tiara listed to the side. Curls had sprung from their pins and fell across her face in long, silken strands. With his free hand, Nicholas attempted to brush them aside, but as he touched her cheek, his fingers stilled.

Preston was right. She was burning with fever.

Why didn't I notice earlier that she is really ill? The answer pricked his conscience. He'd been too busy ordering her around, telling her what must be done to mend their predicament.

And now I've made it that much worse. For both of us.

Her skin was soft. He brushed his hand across her cheek, his fingers lingering longer than needed to push her curls aside. It had been a very long time since he'd touched anyone, and it was a strange, yet not unwelcome, sensation.

He'd first noticed the feeling when he'd caught her waist at the beginning of the dance. And again when their hands had touched during a turn.

Preston had noticed too. He'd had an undisguised look of desire in his eyes while dancing with Miss Thatcher, and while Nicholas hadn't seen her return that look, he had watched her wariness melt away during those minutes. He'd seen her fleeting smile and their easy conversation.

None of which he had experienced while dancing with her. No smile had been forthcoming. She'd expressed no gratitude for his coming to her aid.

Because she felt ill?

Nicholas told himself this was the reason. It wasn't because she was smitten by Preston's charm, and even if she had been, that door was closed forever now. By taking Miss Thatcher home, Nicholas had claimed her as his own. He'd announced as much at the ball, taking responsibility in front of the entire assembly. And while he might not want Miss Thatcher, at least he'd seen to it that Preston could not have her.

Well worth the inconvenience of a day or two. The expense of providing for her did not matter much. They would agree on a sum, determine where to send her, and it would be done.

The carriage rolled to a stop, and the door opened.

Nicholas lifted Miss Thatcher with ease, light baggage that she was.

But baggage, nonetheless. He carried her to the house, calling loudly for Kingsley as the driver hurried ahead to open the door.

"Fetch Mrs. James," Nicholas ordered when Kingsley appeared. "Miss Thatcher will be staying with us again tonight."

"I'm right here." The housekeeper appeared, shoes marching briskly across the polished floor. "What has happened?"

"She collapsed at Preston's. I couldn't leave her there." He owed his servants no explanation but wanted them to understand.

Kingsley nodded as if he did.

"And her servants?" Mrs. James asked as the trio headed up stairs. "They'll be staying as well, I presume?"

Nicholas shook his head. In his haste to leave, he hadn't thought of them. Miss Thatcher's maid would still be at Preston's and of no use to her there.

Of no use at all, the way she carried on about that nightgown and caused so much trouble.

"Her servants will not be joining us," Nicholas said decisively. "They are not to be allowed in this house. Is that understood?"

"Who is to care for her if her maid is not allowed to join us?" Mrs. James asked.

"It doesn't matter," Nicholas said. "Assign one of ours. Hire a new one if you wish. I do not think Miss Thatcher will be here long."

Mrs. James paused at the top of the stairs. "The yellow room would be best, I think. Aside from yours and the dowagers', it is the most recently cleaned."

"I would prefer not to use my sister's room. Find another," Nicholas said.

Mrs. James's lips pressed into a thin line, but she

nodded. "This way, then. We'll just have to make up the bed around her."

"Do what you must with regards to beds." Nicholas followed Kingsley and Mrs. James to the far end of the hall. "Only see that this time she does not end up in mine."

CHAPTER 12

The physician straightened and stepped back from the bed. He removed the stethoscope from his ears and turned to address Nicholas, who stood in the doorway, as far removed from the scene as possible.

"Pneumonia, and a serious case of it, I'm afraid." The physician tucked the stethoscope into his black bag and snapped it shut.

More complications. Nicholas fumed inwardly. He'd be saddled with Miss Thatcher even longer. *Would that I had not taken her home with me. Better yet, would that I'd never set foot at Preston's ball to begin with.*

"How long, do you think?" Nicholas asked. *How many days must I suffer such inconvenience?*

It had been a difficult night with Miss Thatcher under his roof. She'd slept poorly, crying out more than once about someone named Helen. When not in the throes of a nightmare, she'd coughed, and he'd endured more of that than he'd thought to hear in a lifetime. Though today her breathing was so labored that he doubted she'd be able to cough or speak, let alone cry out for some time.

Time that will be spent in my house, disturbing what little peace I have.

"It all depends," the physician said, rubbing his chin thoughtfully. "She may still pull out of it. She's very weak, but I have a feeling she's stronger than she looks. All the same, I'd notify her family."

"Are you saying she may *die*?" Nicholas glanced at Miss Thatcher, tiny and pale beneath the mahogany headboard and thick feather quilt. He hadn't realized—

"That is exactly what I have been saying," the physician said, seemingly put off by Nicholas's ignorance. "Did you not just ask me how long she has?"

"I meant—" Nicholas broke off, knowing he couldn't tell the man that he'd been thinking only of how long he had to house Miss Thatcher.

"I've given instructions to your housekeeper and left some medicines," the physician continued, speaking as he moved toward Nicholas at the door. "They'll help to clear the phlegm—especially important with her breathing. Beyond that, there is nothing more to be done but let nature run its course."

"That is the best you can do?" Nicholas demanded, retaining his position and blocking entrance to the hall. "You're just going to leave her to die?"

"I am leaving her in your care," the physician corrected. "Whether or not she lives will be largely dependent upon that care. I suggest you hire an attentive maid."

"I hired *you*." Nicholas crossed his arms and looked down on the man, a full head shorter. He didn't want to hear that Miss Thatcher might stay here for days or even weeks. He didn't want to hire another maid. He wished her to be well now, and then to be gone—from both his home and his life. And though rational thought told him this was not possible, he'd expected it anyway. He was used to getting what he wanted, the exception being anything to do with Preston.

This is his fault as well.

"I have done all I can," the physician said. "I had heard

you were a harsh man, Lord Sutherland. But I'd not realized the extent of your severity. To be angry with a patient while she lies ill—"

"I am not angry with *her*." Nicholas stepped aside. "Good day, doctor." He used the breach of title with intent. Nothing about the physician had seemed to Nicholas worthy of that distinction.

Kingsley showed the man out, leaving Nicholas with Miss Thatcher. He lingered in the doorway, reluctant to leave her, lest her coughing begin again. Though should it, he'd no idea what to do.

The curtains were closed and the room near dark save for a few candles burning on the bed table. The chamber smelled of sickness and medicine, and when he closed his eyes, he heard her labored breathing.

She may die. Guilt assailed him, and he crossed the room, close to the bed. He gave the bell pull a tug, calling for Mrs. James or one of the other maids.

When a minute had passed and no one appeared, he drew in a breath and stepped closer. Taking one of the candlesticks from the table, Nicholas leaned over the bed, examining Miss Thatcher's pale face, watching the steady rise and fall of the coverlet.

Her hair was in disarray, as it had been the night of their misfortunate encounter in his bed chamber. This was only the second time he'd seen such untamed locks, but he found them tempting to touch, nearly irresistible, spilling as they did across the crisp, white pillows.

Her face was appealing as well. At the ball, he'd thought her best feature to be her eyes: large and expressive and flashing with anger during their dance. But now he noticed the delicate set of her face and the way her lips had a slight curve even as she slept. Was she so prone to smiling, then, that her lips were naturally shaped that way?

What would it have been like to be Preston last night, to have been the recipient of her smile? Nicholas didn't know.

She'd only favored him with scowls. If she lived, he wanted—just once—to find out.

"You must live." His tone was purposefully stern, and he willed Miss Thatcher to hear and act upon his words.

He tried to guess her age but could not. Tiny lines on her forehead and near the sides of her eyes had him judging her as slightly older than most of the young ladies he encountered during the season. But she also appeared too young to be near the age of many of the married women he knew.

Young enough, yet older than most women in her situation. Old enough to be married, but single. *A spinster.*

The hint at sympathy he'd felt vanished amidst a new possibility and unwelcome suspicion. What if she hadn't come to his bed by accident? What if Miss Thatcher had purposefully set out to catch him—and he had played right into her hand?

He returned the candle to the table and stepped back from the bed. A glance over his shoulder told him he was still alone. He must stay a little longer.

If she were to die, everything would be much simpler. Nicholas hated that he'd grown callous enough to entertain such a thought. But it was a truth nonetheless. He wouldn't have to provide for her. There would be no question of being trapped. The gossip would fade away.

He knew that truth well enough. How quickly everyone but their family had forgotten Elizabeth. Even Preston seemed to be moving on with his life, forgetting the lonely grave at the top of the hill behind the church. Elizabeth had always loved to climb hills. She'd thought the view worth the effort of getting to the top, the ability to see far beyond one's limited space a thing to be treasured. He and Preston had agreed upon the location, at least. They had stood on either side of her one last time and laid her to rest.

How deep would Preston's grief run if Miss Thatcher were not to recover? Nicholas wondered. Certainly no one could blame him if she were to perish. It was not his fault that she'd shown up on his doorstep in the middle of a dark, stormy night.

Where had she come from, anyway? What had been so urgent that it had sent her traveling so late and without adequate protection?

Nicholas knew very little about Miss Thatcher, and if he were to do as the physician suggested by contacting her family, he'd best set to discovering who she was and where she'd come from. And then he'd see to it that she lived, if for no other reason than that he had dozens of black marks on his character already. He'd turned into something ugly and dark since Elizabeth's death—a fiend who lived for little more than destroying his former brother-in-law.

But to have this young lady's death on my conscience as well . . .

She was young enough and pretty enough, and he could send her far enough away, that she might yet have a life before her. *Everyone need not be as miserable as I am.*

Footsteps sounded behind him, and Nicholas turned to find not Mrs. James but Kingsley entering the room.

"Mrs. James asked me to send her apologies. She'll send one of the maids shortly. I shall stand guard until then."

"We are not protecting a vault of treasure," Nicholas scoffed. "Only seeing to it that Miss Thatcher continues to breathe."

"Yes, milord." Kingsley stepped aside so Nicholas could exit.

"When you've finished here," Nicholas said, "I'd like you to locate one of the men from the village to do an errand for me. I need to discover what Miss Thatcher was doing the night she came here—why she was out so late and practically alone."

"Of course," Kingsley said. "Erastus Jasper is your man. Knows everyone in these parts and has an ear for that sort of thing."

"Good," Nicholas said. "Find out where she's come from and who her people are. We don't even know her entire name," he realized. He'd heard it announced at Preston's ball but had been too concerned over what he needed to do and say to pay any heed to details like that.

"Her name is Grace," Kingsley said. "Miss Grace Thatcher, granddaughter of Eugene Durham, the Seventh Duke of Salisbury."

"Very well." *An appropriate name for one in such need of Heaven's blessings.* Nicholas cast a final look at the bed and their patient. "Inconvenient this, to be sure, but we must do our best, Kingsley. The new priority, so long as she is under this roof, is saving Miss Thatcher."

Saving Grace.

CHAPTER 13

Nicholas brushed a fallen leaf from his shoulder as he walked in the twilight, Erastus Jasper at his side. "Tell me what you have discovered, my good man."

"You mightn't think me good once I've shared it with you," Jasper said, his cheeky grin in place.

The look, more than his words, stirred unease in Nicholas's gut, reminding him of the one other time he'd used the man's sleuthing services. Four and a half years earlier, he'd had Jasper investigate their new neighbor, Samuel Preston. Jasper hadn't uncovered anything distressing; to that point, Preston had lived a respectable, if not boring, life.

And look what disaster ensued anyway.

Nicholas braced himself for the worst. "Let's have it, then. It's not you I'm concerned with liking."

Jasper nodded. "You're wanting to know if the little miss who caught you is worth the trouble."

A frown creased Nicholas's lips. Perhaps he should have taken the time to contact one of his solicitors in London. "My reasons matter not. Tell me what you have learned."

"At your service." Jasper doffed his cap and pulled from

it a dirty, rolled-up piece of paper. This he handed to Nicholas. "Notes," he said. "In case I forget anything. I can't read it myself, but Kingsley wrote it all down for me while I was waiting."

"Splendid," Nicholas muttered, then supposed he should feel grateful that if Jasper had to confide in someone, it was with a person already familiar with the sordid details. He stuffed the paper in his pocket to be read later, though Kingsley, with his flawless memory, would no doubt prove to be an even better reference.

"Your lady is twenty-four years old. She's the oldest of three—has a younger sister and brother. Her father is a Mr. George Thatcher, known just about everywhere for his excessive gambling."

"They are wealthy, then," Nicholas said, feeling slightly relieved. He'd been thinking the worst of the woman upstairs in his house, surmising that she'd arranged the whole thing to gain a portion of the Sutherland purse. But if she had her own money—

"Poor as church mice," Jasper corrected. "Old George hasn't had much luck the past few years, and it seems he'd do almost anything to secure a bit of fortune." Jasper held up one hand, rubbing his thumb and fingers together.

"Even involving his daughter in a scheme to trap a fortune?" Nicholas mused.

"Even that," Jasper said. "But don't feel too poorly about it. You were not her first attempt."

"Tell me," Nicholas said, though he didn't really want to hear it. He thought back to the night he'd discovered her in his room and then later in the hall, the way Miss Thatcher had come forward, defending Kingsley—a servant she barely knew.

Kingsley couldn't be involved in this. *Could he? Of course not.*

Nicholas banished the absurd thought. Miss Thatcher had appeared ill even then.

Bad luck for her that now she truly is ill. Just rewards if ever he'd heard of them. Maybe he should have left her at Preston's, and *he* would have taken ill too.

"She first visited Lord Damien Crosby of Whitby," Jasper went on. "His servants say he showed interest in Miss Thatcher until she gave herself away for who she truly is—not a proper lady, I mean." Jasper turned his head, glancing at Nicholas, as if to see how he was taking the news.

"Go on," Nicholas urged, wishing Jasper were more direct. He'd forgotten how the man had infuriated him the first time around. "Why do you say she is not a lady?"

"Miss Thatcher showed up for a *hunt*."

Nicholas shrugged. "Some women enjoy hunting."

"Not wearing breeches and riding astride." Jasper's chest puffed out importantly as if, instead of scandal, he'd uncovered a rare jewel.

Nicholas tried but was unable to pair the lady whose delicate, gloved hand he'd taken at the top of the stairs with the image of an undisciplined hoyden wearing men's trousers and sitting astride a horse. He grimaced at the unsettling image.

"I am guessing that incident ended Miss Thatcher's prospects with Lord Crosby," Nicholas said.

Jasper nodded. "He asked her to leave."

Nicholas put his hands in his pockets to ward off the chill as they continued down the drive. It was a cool night to be out walking, but he hadn't wanted to visit with Jasper in his study or even in the drawing room. Though the man was good at what he did, Nicholas didn't trust him not to be sleuthing for someone else at the same time. The less Jasper knew of Sutherland Hall, the better. He could not risk Preston discovering any of his business dealings.

The night air was also good for clarity of mind, something Nicholas desperately needed. His thoughts had run the gamut in regards to Miss Thatcher, and he very much wanted to see them settled on one point permanently.

With this news, it appeared it would be a very low point on the scale.

"I don't suppose she came here next," Nicholas said.

"Nope." Jasper's grin was back. Nicholas wanted to wipe it from his face. He saw nothing amusing in this conversation. "Miss Thatcher left Crosby and traveled directly to Sir Richard Lidgate's home."

"Lidgate." Nicholas knew of the man. *An impossible rake*, he'd once overheard Elizabeth and her friend call him.

"There's the rub," Jasper said. "Lidgate's a *reformed* rake. He's actively searching for a wife—and word has it that he wants an heir before he gets much older."

"Why ever did Miss Thatcher not solicit him then?" Nicholas asked.

"She did. Stayed there four *whole* days."

And nights. Nicholas could well guess what Jasper was implying. With Lidgate's reputation, no respectable woman would stay one night in his house. The only kind of women Nicholas had ever seen in Lidgate's company were those adept at flirting, lonely widows, or the unhappily married who believed there was something to be gained from their endeavors. In the past, that would have meant one thing.

Currently? It was difficult to believe Lidgate to be *that* reformed. Nicholas had seen him in action on more than one occasion, and numerous times with women hanging off either arm.

Once more Nicholas tried to place Miss Thatcher in that role but could not. Yet she must have been if she'd stayed at that house and attempted to win Lidgate over for a permanent situation.

"Why did she leave? What went wrong?" Nicholas asked.

"The third morning, they were out for a ride," Jasper said. "Miss Thatcher took a jump too high for the horse. Her mount threw her, and she was hurt something terrible."

"When was this?" Nicholas hadn't noticed any sort of

injury with Miss Thatcher. She'd danced well enough at the ball, especially considering how ill she was.

"Two days before she arrived at your place. Lidgate had a physician attend to her, and the man told him Miss Thatcher wasn't likely to bear children."

Nicholas's mouth gaped. "From being thrown by a horse."

Jasper shrugged. "Just repeating what I was told."

"By whom?" Nicholas asked. Perhaps Jasper was not as reliable as he was reputed to be.

"The physician," Jasper said. "Spoke to him myself yesterday. The man said he'd never seen bruising like that before."

"Oh." Nicholas marched on in silence. He found this news disturbing, though it shouldn't have been. It wasn't as if he expected Miss Thatcher to bear *his* children. He reflected on the way he'd handled her that night in his room and felt more than a twinge of guilt. Not only had she been ill, but injured, as well, and likely scared. Yet he'd behaved as the injured one, lashing out and demanding answers. Given the trauma she'd recently endured, his behavior had undoubtedly made things worse for her.

They reached the bottom of the drive and turned back. "I assume Lidgate sent her packing too," Nicholas said.

Jasper shook his head. "There's the strange thing. Miss Thatcher left of her own accord in the middle of the night—"

"And ended up with a broken carriage," Nicholas fumed. *And in my bed.* "Why?" If she'd been on her way to see Preston, why not continue on a little farther? Unless . . .

Preston!

Nicholas's hands clenched. These past three years, he'd done his best to destroy Preston. Some of his ventures had met with success, and Preston had lost money—once in excess of £15,000. It had to have hurt. Yet never once had Preston retaliated.

Until now?

Always Preston had remained cordial, going so far as to extend invitations whenever he hosted a dinner, ball, or other event. Never had Nicholas accepted any of them. He'd never so much as set a toe on Preston's property.

"Until three days ago."

"Excuse me?" Jasper looked at him strangely, and Nicholas realized he must have spoken the thought.

"Nothing," he muttered, unwilling to share his hunch with anyone. He'd been made a fool of already; no one need know the extent of his stupidity. He removed an envelope from his coat and handed it to Jasper. "Thank you. You've been most helpful."

Jasper's eyes lit up as he opened the envelope. "Thank you, Lord Sutherland. I can find out more, if you'd like. I'd only a few days this time, but I could—"

"I've learned quite enough," Nicholas said, cutting him off. Knowing and suspecting what he did now, he intended to have one of his solicitors in London delve more fully into Miss Thatcher's past.

Jasper thanked him again and took his leave, and Nicholas was left alone to walk up his deserted drive in the chilly fall evening. A leaf floated down from a maple above, and Nicholas caught it, turning the golden stem in his fingers.

Elizabeth had loved this time of year. She'd loved these trees and the burst of color they sent forth every autumn. As with her roses, a leaf like this was a great treasure. He couldn't count the number of them she'd pressed inside books. Once in every great while, he still stumbled across a book in the library that held one of her preciously preserved petals or plants.

Yet we were unable to preserve her life.

A familiar bitterness rose in his throat, and Nicholas longed for the past in a way he almost never did. He wished he were fourteen again and Elizabeth twelve. They were out on this lawn beneath these trees, throwing fall leaves at one another while their father cheered them on and Mother scolded their mischievousness.

There had been life at Sutherland Hall then. Parties for every season, presents beneath the great tree at Christmas. Family picnics and riding. Not a week had passed during his growing up years that he and Elizabeth didn't roam the surrounding hills together.

It had been an idyllic existence. But now, before he'd fully appreciated what he'd had, it was gone. Not only would he and Mother never get that life back, but there was also nothing in his future to ever replace those happy times. Two of the most important people in his life were gone forever, and the world offered him no solace for their loss.

Only the possibility of revenge—of extracting payment from the one responsible—brought him any measure of satisfaction.

Nicholas let go of the leaf and watched it sway as it fell to the ground. He lifted his boot and stomped on it, grinding the heel until the already fragile foliage crumbled beneath his weight.

He would crush Preston and anyone else involved with him—Miss Thatcher included.

As he walked, Nicholas reviewed the sequence of events at the ball. Preston's greeting Miss Thatcher as if they were long acquainted, Preston dancing with her first, and the easy manner in which they conversed. Miss Thatcher's becoming suddenly ill.

An idea I gave her?

Miss Thatcher fainting. And finally, Preston's uninspiring efforts to keep her at his home.

The more he thought on it, the more Nicholas became convinced that he'd been unwittingly caught up in some scheme of theirs.

It will not work, he vowed. He would send the trouser-wearing, husband-seeking, scheming woman packing the moment she was well enough to stand.

And he would not feel the least bit of guilt about it either. The matter settled, Nicholas returned to the house and retired to his room. As he passed Miss Thatcher's door and heard her coughing, he remembered the doctor's warning. *She might die.*

He decided he would not let her. She would not be freed from this predicament so easily. He would make certain she lived, if only so both she and Preston might pay.

"How bad is it?" Nicholas asked his butler. "Are some in the crowd carrying pitchforks and threatening to break down the door?" He braced his hands on the desk, preparing himself for the worst. Kingsley's face, white and drawn before the study doors he'd hastily closed, indicated that Nicholas was about to hear that very thing.

Likely no less than I deserve, he thought ruefully. For as long as Nicholas could remember, and likely as long as Sutherland men had run this estate, tradition had been that the first Tuesday of each month was set aside for meeting with tenants. During the last few years of his father's life, Nicholas had made the rounds a time or two with his father. But that had been long ago, the last instance being the Tuesday after his father's death, when instead of going to visit the tenants to inquire about their needs, Nicholas had invited them to the house to pay their respects to the former Earl.

That had been twenty-two long months ago, and ever since, Nicholas had seen to it that he was never home on the first Tuesday of the month. Until now. He glanced toward the doors, eyes flitting upward, as if he could see through them to the rooms above. He wouldn't have been home today were it not for the ailing woman presently sleeping in one of his guestrooms. He might have muttered a curse about it—or about her—had it not seemed entirely unholy to curse one already hovering near death.

But since she was here—and he was too—there seemed no point in avoiding the necessary. So he'd invited his tenants to meet with him today.

"How bad?" Nicholas repeated, expecting an answer now that Kingsley had been given a good, long minute to think on it.

The butler's face grew thoughtful, the lines on his forehead bunching as his graying brows drew together. "Do you recall the plum puddings Mrs. Hancock used to make at Christmas?"

"Used to?" Nicholas asked, disappointed to think that one of his favorite treats from childhood had disappeared.

Kingsley frowned. "She hasn't made them these two Christmases past. Not since you said there was to be no more celebrating."

"I didn't mean forever." Nicholas cleared his throat uncomfortably. He vaguely remembered saying something like that, but then, his father had died shortly before Christmas, and they had all still been mourning Elizabeth, as well. It wouldn't have been proper to celebrate the season then.

And the Christmas after that he'd spent in London with his mother. The atmosphere between them had been strained, the whole affair quiet and solemn. But he'd never considered that the holiday had passed the same way at Sutherland Hall. He hadn't intended that, hadn't intended for what used to be good and right—for all the people here—to be stopped with Elizabeth's and his father's passings.

Though I cease to enjoy life, they needn't.

"It was not my intention for cook's famous Christmas pudding to be gone forever. Be sure to tell her I wish it reinstated next holiday."

"As you wish." Kingsley nodded.

"But what has that to do with today?" Nicholas asked. "Have one of the tenants come to complain—all these months later—about my lack of generosity at Christmas?"

"I could not say, milord. Only that whatever their complaints be, they are sure to be many. I've not seen a crowd like this since Mrs. Hancock's puddings were distributed at Christmas."

"That *is* bad." Nicholas drummed his fingers on the desk.

It was a good analogy. He well remembered the line of tenants outside the kitchen, eagerly awaiting the once-a-year treat.

"Would you like me to . . . stay?" Kingsley offered—rather bravely, Nicholas thought.

"Kind of you, but no," Nicholas said. "I believe I'll need you most manning the doors out front. I shall have to bear myself up. After all, this is my own doing." His father's agent had quit months ago, furious with Nicholas over what he'd termed "an extreme lack of leadership and authority that would make your father roll over in his grave."

Likely true, Nicholas reflected, feeling no little amount of shame.

But he was making a start, wasn't he? He'd invited his tenants here today, believing it would be the simplest and most efficient way to begin catching up on long-neglected matters. He could have spent the day visiting with some of the people—but whom to choose had become a delicate situation. Worried it might be seen as favoritism if he spent time with some families, then left again for months before meeting with others, he'd decided instead to offer the opportunity of visiting to anyone who wished. Here. Today.

Perhaps that had been a poor idea, Nicholas thought as

he glanced out the window at the line curving around the house.

"Good luck to you, milord." Kingsley backed out the door, nodding as he went—whether in sympathy or simply as a farewell, Nicholas could not tell.

"Give me a moment more, and then send the first one in." Nicholas tugged at his cravat, feeling the noose of guilt tightening around his neck. Being away so much, it had been easy to forget all that went on here. But now that he'd been back a short while . . .

I'm beginning to see what a proper mess I've made of everything. No wonder Mother refused to stay.

Preparing for an onslaught of the irate, he removed a ledger from the desk, opened it, and readied a quill and ink beside. He also took out his father's record book. A good portion of those coming today would be after money for this or that improvement, or some other such item they felt entitled to by virtue of living on and producing goods upon his land. Most would be justified in their requests, and he had no qualms about providing funds to keep crops growing, animals breeding, and wool spinning as it should. He had ample rent money and could afford to return a portion of it to its origins.

For those few whom money would not satisfy, a decanter of brandy and a few snifters stood at the ready on the sideboard—a tactic he'd learned from his father. Remembering the previous Lord Sutherland's diplomacy, Nicholas felt the beginnings of a smile curve his lips. His father would have been appalled at the state things had come to, but he would have had a jolly good time setting them right. He'd always loved a good challenge, especially one involving his uncanny ability to win anyone over.

"We shall see if I have any of the old man in me at all," Nicholas said somewhat good-naturedly, and he felt slightly better than he had all morning. "We shall see."

Kingsley stepped inside the study doors and shut them behind him, leaving one Myra Lane, wife of Joseph, whose sheep had not been reproducing at a satisfactory rate, alone to find her own way out.

"Dare I hope that everyone else has grown tired of waiting, and we are finished?" Nicholas eyed the longcase clock on the far side of the room. A half hour had not yet passed since it had chimed eleven. He had no reason to hope that he'd managed to see almost two years' worth of troubled tenants in two hours. No reason, but a strong wish.

I am tired of hearing of mutton and mules.

Kingsley shook his head. "Nor is the midday meal quite prepared."

"Oh," Nicholas said, all hope deflated now that Kingsley had denied his second choice—a hearty meal and a few minutes' solitude.

"A Mr. George Thatcher is here to see you," Kingsley continued. "He is most insistent that it cannot wait."

Nicholas looked up from the column he'd been totaling. "I don't recall any Thatchers living here. Have we let land to new families in my absence?"

Have I been that *neglectful?*

For the hundredth time this morning, during which he'd heard tales of a collapsed roof, diseased animals, and struggling crops, he berated himself for his disregard.

"Mr. Thatcher is not a tenant. He has come inquiring about his daughter."

"I hoped I knew our tenants surnames. Surely I cannot be expected to know each of their childr—" Nicholas's confusion turned to clarity. His eyes shifted to the ceiling. "*Her* father."

Kingsley nodded. "Come from London. He insists he must see you."

"Well, this *is* splendid news."

Anything but, more like.

Nicholas leaned back in his chair. "Dare we hope he has come to take her home?"

Jasper's report on George Thatcher still rang fresh in Nicholas's mind. *Poor as church mice . . . has had no luck . . . would do anything . . .*

"I find it doubtful that *she* is what he has come to take," Kingsley said. "For the past thirty minutes, he has been perusing the hall, examining the paintings and furniture, and attempting to see into other rooms." Kingsley glanced over his shoulder. "When I asked him to cease his explorations, he did not take it well. He appears to be predisposed of a bad temperament."

"I see." And Nicholas did—that his day was about to become even more unpleasant. "Likely she could not be moved anyhow," he added offhandedly and began to ponder how to avoid being burdened by playing host to her father as well. "I suppose he'll want to be nearby while she is recovering?"

"He has not asked to see her. Only to see . . . 'the rake who ruined his daughter.'"

Nicholas rubbed his temple, feeling the building of a headache behind his eyes. He hadn't considered that Miss Thatcher's father might come. Apparently the man wasn't too poor to travel.

If news of this scandal has reached London already . . .

Likely her father would have an arsenal of questions, none of them pleasant.

Or perhaps just an arsenal.

"Shall I show him in?"

"Not yet," Nicholas said. "I've enough people upset with me already—people who live and work on Sutherland land—and I must think of them first."

That was true enough, though he also wished for more time to consider his meeting with Miss Thatcher's father.

"Politely explain to the man that this is not the best day for calling. Perhaps he might return tomorrow."

"Very well." Kingsley retreated once more. A few moments later, Nicholas welcomed three women whose chief complaint was that he was not producing enough laundry for them to wash in order to support their families.

"When the ladies used to live here, we had work aplenty," the first explained, a plain woman dressed in gray from the hairs on her head to the toes of her weathered boots.

"And with guests and parties the former earl—may he rest in peace—used to host," the second added, "we'd even have some extra wash now and then." Nicholas's gaze shifted to her, a stout woman with crossed arms and a stern face.

The first, less-threatening woman, spoke again. "But now we're not earning enough to buy necessaries. My daughter, barely fourteen, has gone away to Lancashire to work. First time in four generations our family has moved off this land. I miss her terrible, but unless something changes, more of the family will have to follow."

"What is it you wish me to do?" Nicholas asked. "I can bring back neither my sister nor my father—or their clothing."

"But your mother might stay again," the stout one said, giving him a look that would have made a lesser man shrink in disgrace. He read all that it implied: *If you weren't such a lout and took care of the place, your mother would come home.*

"If you were to stay," she continued, "and if you were to hire more staff again, we'd have the wash from them, too. And with more staff, you could have guests, and they would lead to—"

"More laundry," Nicholas said. "I see. But I'm afraid I cannot supply what you need. Sutherland Hall will never be as it has been. Those grand times are—unfortunately for all of us—in the past."

"They don't have to be, milord," a timid voice spoke up. Gray Woman and Stern Face parted, and a third woman stepped forward from her place after being nearly hidden behind them. Her eyes, bright and hopeful, sought out Nicholas's with a look that was part sympathy, part encouragement. Her face wasn't lined as the others', and rich, dark hair peeked from beneath her bonnet. With her slight build, he had a difficult time imagining her bent over a washtub.

"You are right," she continued. "Life here shall never be the same as when your father and sister were alive. But the future can yet be bright. When my Thomas died, I thought life was over, but after a time, I saw that it didn't have to be. If you'll but open your heart to new possibilities—"

"I'd prefer to open my pocketbook," Nicholas said curtly. *What do these women know of my life?* "If you'll tell me what sum you were paid before, I shall see that it continues, regardless of the volume of clothing you wash. We wish you, and your families, to continue to live as you have previously."

The three women exchanged uneasy glances.

"It's kind of you Lord Sutherland, but it isn't right—getting paid when we've not done the work," Gray Woman said.

Nicholas wondered if the woman realized that she had just described a good portion of the peerage—himself included, at times. "Nevertheless, that is the best I can do—for now," he added as an afterthought when their expressions remained set. "You are correct in saying that the future may yet bring things we do not now anticipate. Until then, let me allow your daughters to remain at home with their families."

The Sutherland fortune can well afford it, he could have said. *Especially now.* Not only had the laundry dwindled to almost nothing, but general expenditures the last eighteen months had as well. He'd spent precious little maintaining the estate. Since Elizabeth's passing, not a single dinner party or ball had been hosted here. Today he could afford to be generous with his tenants.

In the end, the matter was settled somewhat satisfactorily—or so he told himself—and the women left. But before the door had closed behind them, it swung open once more, the heavy oak flying backward toward the wall, saved from collision by Kingsley's quick arm.

Beside him, a disheveled-looking man burst into the room, hat askew, eyes blazing.

"What is the meaning of this?" Nicholas asked, rising from his chair. He could guess well enough and was not surprised at his butler's apologetic introduction.

Mr. Thatcher had arrived.

"Mr. Thatcher insists he has come from London and cannot"—Kingsley cast a disdainful glance at their unwelcome guest—"'fritter away the day waiting to see his *lord—ship*.'" Kingsley spoke the last with a drawl exuding disdain.

"Well, now." Mr. Thatcher righted his hat and tugged an obviously too-small and somewhat worn waistcoat over his stomach. "I don't suppose I said it like that."

"I rather suppose you did," Nicholas said.

Even had Kingsley not been the epitome of honesty and truthfulness to the point of—at times—annoyance, Nicholas would have been certain of Mr. Thatcher's tone and the meaning behind it. It was as he'd suspected earlier; Thatcher was not here to express gratitude for the care of his daughter. Indeed, his face was red with anger, his bulbous nose a glowing beacon of the fury boiling beneath the surface.

"That's no way to treat a caller, that's what," Mr. Thatcher said. "Make a man wait all day to see his daughter."

"Oh?" Nicholas arched a brow. "If only you'd said so in the first place." He looked from Mr. Thatcher's uncomfortable expression to Kingsley, still standing near the doorway and poised for action. "Please ring for Mrs. James and ask her to escort Mr. Thatcher to his daughter's room." Nicholas noted the time on the clock. "I believe the physician will be here within the hour. He can explain your daughter's condition in detail. I regret to inform you that it is very serious."

"Perhaps I was hasty." Mr. Thatcher made a point of clearing his throat, as if he imagined something were caught there, though clearly there was not. "My own health has been poor of late. It mightn't be a good idea to get near Grace, lest I fall ill as well."

"She hasn't got the pox," Nicholas said. Miss Thatcher's fair face came to mind, and he pondered what a tragedy the pox would have been. "She's suffering from pneumonia, a result, so the physician says, of being a long time out in the damp night air." Nicholas waited for Miss Thatcher's father to take his leave to go upstairs, his distaste for the man growing each second. He again turned his attention to his ever-patient butler. "How many tenants are still waiting to see me?"

"Enough to warrant your attention until this evening." Kingsley said without taking time to consider or consult the crowd outside.

Nicholas walked around the desk toward Mr. Thatcher who was—albeit rather subtly—taking stock of the room.

And a fine room it is, Nicholas mused with both a touch of pride and an inkling of discomfort. This was one of the few areas of his home that he'd properly cared for since his father's death—mostly because it had belonged to his father. From the large mahogany desk with walnut inlays, to the wall of coordinating shelves and the impressive volumes they held, to the marble-top side table and the set of gilt wood chairs before the fire, everything about the room bespoke opulence.

Unlike his guest, whose shoddy clothing and filthy boots indicated that his circumstances were somewhat less fortunate. Not a crime, but Thatcher's eyes had a greedy sparkle about them and were taking in every detail in a very suspect manner.

"That's a fine painting you've got there," he said, eyeing the large canvas of a countryside landscape hanging above the fireplace. "Pretty piece of land, that."

"Yes," Nicholas replied, without sharing that the land portrayed in the painting was the northernmost tip of the Sutherland property. "I realize you've been waiting the better part of the morning, but I'm afraid it could not be helped. Your arrival today is unfortunate in its timing; it coincides with the day set aside for my tenants to visit. I've been away a long time, and some of them have waited several months to speak with me."

Mr. Thatcher's lip curled in a sneer, and he gave a forced laugh. "Oh to be so important that the masses flock to see you."

"I assure you, there is no glory in discussing leaky roofs, aged animals, and an extreme lack of—laundry." Nicholas spoke calmly, though inside he was beginning to feel as irritated as his guest appeared. He extended his hand toward the door, nodding curtly. "Kingsley will show you out."

"Not until we're through, he won't," Mr. Thatcher huffed.

"We are finished," Nicholas said. "If you wish to see your daughter, Mrs. James will take you up." He turned away from his unwelcome caller.

"You know who I am here to see—and you know why." Thatcher's tone had changed from hasty anger to one carrying a more subtle, understated threat.

Ignoring it, Nicholas thought of his father's patience and tried to find some of his own. "I have been *away*," he explained once more. "And there are many matters I must attend to."

"There is only *one* matter I am concerned with," Mr.

Thatcher said. "If you wish me to discuss it in front of your servants and tenants, I will happily oblige."

It isn't anything they've not heard already. But feeding gossip fires would only make the matter worse. Nicholas wondered warily what it would take to appease Mr. Thatcher. Clearly, seeing his daughter to reassure himself that she was well *wasn't* his priority.

"You have five minutes," Nicholas said. "I suggest you speak quickly." He looked at Kingsley. "You may go now. Please tell cook that I wish refreshment provided for those still waiting. Whatever she has on hand will be fine. Send her my apologies and the promise of a half day off for her trouble." No use getting on the cook's bad side for all this. Good, familiar food was about the only pleasure still afforded him at Sutherland Hall, and he intended to keep it.

As soon as Kingsley had gone, Nicholas swept his arm toward the leather chairs before the fire. "Shall we sit?" He'd have liked to have requested his noon meal, but he'd looked forward to a few moments of reflection all morning, and he doubted he'd have them dining with Mr. Thatcher.

"Thank you," the latter said gruffly, taking the closest seat.

Nicholas went to the sideboard, poured Mr. Thatcher a generous drink, and handed it to him. "What can I do for you?" Nicholas asked in the most patient tone he could muster, as he sat in the opposite chair.

"It's not me you'd best be doing for," Thatcher said, as agitated as ever, and downing his brandy at an alarming rate. He wiped his mouth with the back of his hand. "You've ruined my daughter, and you'd best be prepared to pay for it."

Ah . . . Perhaps this was a matter that could be solved quickly with money. But he needn't make it too easy.

"I've done nothing of the sort," Nicholas protested. "Indeed her life is in danger, but that is not my doing." He considered Mr. Thatcher for a few seconds, then leaned forward in his chair. "Wouldn't you like to see her?" He asked in earnest, not from a desire to be rid of his guest.

He allowed himself to think of Miss Thatcher—Grace—not unlike Elizabeth, who'd been only a few years beyond girlhood. He recalled the way his father had described sitting at Elizabeth's side as she drew her last breaths, how he'd been there to hold her hand.

As was Preston. The unbidden bitter thought forced its way to the front of his mind.

"I told you, I've not been well myself," Mr. Thatcher said, lifting his glass to his lips only to find it empty.

Nicholas did not offer to refill it. "Your daughter is *gravely* ill," he said. "I've brought in the best physician, and she has constant care, but I fear it may not be enough."

"On your head, then!" Mr. Thatcher suddenly roared. He jumped from his chair, his demeanor threatening as he stared down at his host.

Nicholas maintained his casual posture. "It was *your* poorly maintained carriage that caused the accident and sent her spending hours outdoors in the chill of night."

"And it was *you*"—Mr. Thatcher pointed a pudgy finger at him—"who climbed in her bed and shocked her so that she cannot recover."

"I did no such thing." This time Nicholas rose and enjoyed the height that allowed him to look down on Thatcher. "You ought not believe everything you hear."

"I've proof." Thatcher wagged a finger at him again.

Nicholas quirked an eyebrow. "Have you? Were you here that night as well? To see her suffering from a fever so great that my servant believed her life to be in immediate danger?"

"You were in her *bed*," Thatcher repeated. "You practically tore her nightgown off."

Nicholas suppressed a groan. *That again.* "Actually, she was in *my* bed. Perhaps I ought to take you to task for raising a daughter who is like to scare a tired man half to death."

Weary of both Mr. Thatcher and their conversation, he returned to his desk. He closed both the ledger and record book and put each in their respective drawers. Whether or not money would resolve the current situation, he felt no inclination to use it on one as unpleasant and accusatory as Mr. Thatcher.

"I have a letter here." Thatcher took a folded paper from his coat pocket and followed Nicholas across the room. "From a Mr. Samuel Preston, detailing the evening you were with Grace at his house. According to him, you escorted her in, danced with her, then removed her against Mr. Preston's will from his residence."

"That is one viewpoint of the events that night," Nicholas said.

"Do you deny it?" Thatcher wiped his arm across his brow, though the room was not overly warm. "After all, Grace is here. That seems proof enough."

"I am certain that, for you, it is," Nicholas said. That her father was so intimately acquainted with his former brother-in-law, so as to believe his every word, only soured Nicholas more. "However, I see things differently.

"Your daughter's reputation was in question," he continued. "In the space of a day and a half, her servants spread the story of our mishap so thoroughly as to completely ruin her. I stepped in to stop that. I showed up at Preston's ball so she would not have to face the gossips alone, and I did my best to both nullify the rumors and cast doubt on those speaking them. Though the unfortunate incident was neither my fault nor my doing, I felt inclined to come to her rescue."

Would that I'd not been so inclined. Nicholas looked pointedly at Mr. Thatcher, whose mouth was busy moving about, as if searching for the right words. "When your daughter fainted at the ball, I deemed it my responsibility to see that she was cared for, so I removed her from Mr.

Preston's home. It has been my unfortunate experience that the ill do not fare well under his care."

"Her health was none of your concern."

"As it seems to be none of yours." Nicholas's eyes narrowed. He was starting to understand why Miss Thatcher had been so earnest in seeking a husband. If the alternative was to live with her father, it was amazing she'd endured this long.

Instead of looking abashed as he ought at the accusation of not caring a fig for his daughter's welfare, Mr. Thatcher brought his fist down on the desk. The color in his face brightened to a beet red. "Preston was to *marry* her."

"*If* that is the case, he did not tell me so and did not act in a manner befitting one betrothed."

Had Preston been planning to marry again? The scoundrel. Nicholas pushed aside the memory of the admiring look in Preston's eyes when he'd danced with Miss Thatcher and instead focused on Preston's lack of resistance at having the young lady removed from his home.

Her father acted as if he'd not heard a word Nicholas had said. "And now, because of you, my Grace's prospects are ruined."

"If Preston will not have her, I suggest she travel elsewhere, where her reputation will not precede her. She might go abroad, perhaps to Scotland," Nicholas added, remembering his own musings in the carriage while traveling home with her. He was still somewhat willing to assist in financing such a move, but he did not say so to George Thatcher. In only a few minutes, the man had proven himself so entirely disagreeable that any generosity Nicholas would have felt inclined to give had rapidly disappeared.

"Beyond providing her with a physician, there is nothing I can do to right whatever wrongs you *incorrectly* believe I have done to your daughter," Nicholas said. "Now if you'll excuse me, I must insist on getting back to my work.

As you may have noticed when you arrived, several others wait to conference with me."

"They can wait a little longer," Mr. Thatcher said. "Nothing has been resolved between us, and I'll not leave until it has. And don't go setting that old butler of yours on me again. I'll take him out this time, that's what I'll do."

"I strongly advise that you not so much as even consider touching Mr. Kingsley unless you intend to end up in Newgate," Nicholas said icily. "I have done far more than is required of me, offering the best care to your daughter while she ails. It is not in my power to restore Mr. Preston's intentions, though I advise that if he is so fickle-minded as to take seriously the gossip of a couple of servants—who ought to be dismissed—he is not one you'd wish your daughter saddled with."

"And I suppose you are," Mr. Thatcher said.

Nicholas stared at him shrewdly. "I am not presently in search of a wife." He reached for the cord beside his desk and pulled it, ringing for Kingsley. They were done here, whether Mr. Thatcher wished it or not.

"*You* have certainly acted as one looking for a wife," Thatcher said. "Following Grace to Preston's ball, escorting her there, dancing with her—"

"I have already explained my actions."

Thatcher pretended not to have heard him. "Insisting upon bringing her back to your home, where she lies, unchaperoned."

"I can assure you that either the maid I hired to attend her or my housekeeper is at her side at all times."

"I must insist, Lord Sutherland, that you make right this situation by marrying my daughter."

"She is in no condition to marry." *Nor am I.* Nicholas wondered that he had not seen through Thatcher's scheme at once. But he was delusional if he thought to pull it off. No influence in all of England could persuade him to marry the woman upstairs.

A gleam arose in Mr. Thatcher's eyes. "Preston said you would refuse." He shook the letter in the air. "So I am to warn you that your lack of concern will be viewed by certain parties as—a challenge."

No influence except that one. Nicholas drew in a breath. Thatcher had to be bluffing. It was impossible that Preston would challenge him. He'd promised Elizabeth. *They'd* promised, both at her bedside. Nicholas did not doubt for one minute that his sister would come back to haunt him if he killed her husband in a duel. *No matter how deserving he is. No matter how much I'd like to.*

"Certain parties?" he repeated. "Yourself, you mean? You'd challenge me over your daughter's honor, yet you won't go to the effort of going upstairs to see her?" Nicholas smiled obligingly. "Forgive me if I don't trust the sincerity of your threat."

Thatcher puffed up his chest as he crushed the paper in his fist. "Not I. Though I would if necessary," he added hastily. "You've wronged Preston as well—brought shame to his household by your actions. He—he'll stand in for me."

"I happen to know from experience that he is no longer the dueling type." *And if he is—if he's gone back on his promise to Elizabeth—I ought to shoot him for that.* Nicholas withdrew his record book from the drawer, almost eager to be back to the business of counting sheep and repairing roofs.

"He warned me you'd say that." Thatcher thrust the wrinkled letter onto the desk. Nicholas took it, recognizing Preston's handwriting.

. . . Nicholas Sutherland is a coward and will refuse to marry your daughter—no matter how he has wronged her. When challenged, he will likely refuse, using his sister as an excuse . . .

Nicholas placed the letter on the desk. He would have liked nothing better than to shoot Preston down, and the man well knew it. He also knew that Nicholas could not do it, that to do so would mean breaking the promise he'd made to Elizabeth. It would be showing that he hadn't loved her as much as Preston—though he had. Nicholas had a whole life with her; their ties were made of blood. She'd been his best friend, the joy of their father's life. The cause of his untimely death.

If I meet Preston in a duel—regardless of the outcome—I'll be the cause of Mother's grief.

Nicholas cringed at the thought. He'd caused his mother a fair amount of pain already the past two years. Being here, being home again, he was just starting to realize how much. Assuming there really was a challenge, it had, at the very least, the potential to ruin both their lives.

One of us dead. The other in prison. And Mother to suffer through it all.

He could not do it; Mother had already lost her husband and daughter.

And her son. He cringed inwardly, confronted with the truth. He'd been little help and no comfort to her these two years. *I won't do worse by destroying the Sutherland name. Even though declining Preston's challenge may well mean the destruction of my future.*

"For reasons you cannot possibly understand, Preston is correct. I cannot meet him in a duel—though I should very much like to—and it *is* partly because of my sister, because of a promise made long ago. I believe very much in honoring promises." Nicholas paused, leveling his eyes on Thatcher. "And so I give you one now. If Preston will not have her . . ." With an insurmountable will, Nicholas spoke his next words. "*I* will marry your daughter."

Kingsley chose that moment to open the study doors. Thatcher turned to face him, wearing a nasty smile. "Congratulate your employer. He is to be married."

Kingsley's gaze flew to Nicholas.

"Yes," Nicholas said, with a brief, pained nod. "When

Miss Thatcher has recovered"—*If she recovers*—"it is likely that we shall be wed."

"Just to be certain," George Thatcher said, "to make all around here aware, lest anything *unfortunate* should befall Grace between now and then—I should like the banns posted this Sunday."

"There is no need of that," Nicholas said. "I can afford a license, and a special one at that, if needed."

"Good to know, good to know." Thatcher stood and looked around the study once more. "I had wondered, though *this* room seems nice enough. Place could definitely use a woman's touch."

"Do not count on your daughter residing here," Nicholas said.

Do not count on this being anything close to a real marriage.

"I have a townhome in London where she will be more comfortable."

"I still wish the banns to be published *here.* After all, we wouldn't want anyone thinking you'd misused her."

"Perhaps we will," Nicholas said wryly. *Elizabeth wouldn't haunt me for defending myself, would she?*

"You gave your word," Thatcher said.

"So I have," Nicholas said, his tone solemn. "And you may be assured that I will keep it."

"We have a few other things to be settled." Thatcher rubbed his hands together as if warming to his task.

Nicholas frowned, wavering between having him thrown out and being impressed by his effrontery.

"Grace has a younger sister also ripe for marriage, and with the rumors flying, her prospects have dimmed considerably."

"You wish me to marry both of your daughters?" Nicholas barely managed to keep his mouth from twitching.

"Of course not," Thatcher snapped. "But I expect to be

compensated for lost income—for having to support her until this whole affair with Grace dies down."

"I see," Nicholas said, and he did, more clearly than ever, what a conniving family he'd become entangled with. But just now, he didn't much care. He only wanted Mr. Thatcher out of his study, off his property, and as far away as possible—preferably forever. Nicholas forced a smile. "What is it going to cost me to be rid of you?" he asked bluntly.

Sometime later, when he was at last alone and having his moment of solitude, he wrote the events of the previous hour in his record book.

I am faced with the choice of giving Samuel Preston what he wants or being married to a woman I neither care for nor am acquainted with. Her father is abhorrent, and I harbor little hope that she will be any better. A most impossible situation.

CHAPTER 16

Grace opened her eyes to a dim and dreary world. Save for the single ray of light slanting through the space between the floor-length drapes, she might have thought it was night. But she watched the narrow beam for some time, trying, without success, to recognize her surroundings as she studied the dust particles dancing about.

She'd attempted—several times before, it seemed—to pull herself from sleep, but each time, the effort had been too much. She recalled someone spooning broth into her mouth and being forced to swallow a nasty-tasting medicine. She remembered hushed voices and her own incessant coughing and struggles for breath. But beyond those few recollections, her situation remained a mystery.

She blinked once, staring at the rich velvet of the canopy above her; it was not at all familiar. She turned her head aside to the paper on the walls. The pattern wasn't Grandfather's, but she couldn't imagine where else she might be. The bed was too large and comfortable, the coverlet too luxurious, her surroundings far too grand to be home.

She coughed, and an unfamiliar woman crossed the room and peered at her. "Awake, are you?" she asked, leaning close. She was young, a sprinkling of freckles across her nose and bright red braids tucked under her mobcap, making her look barely beyond childhood.

"Water, please," Grace managed. Her request was granted, and Grace leaned her head forward, gulping the liquid down as fast as her parched throat would allow. "Where am I?" she asked after she'd drained the cup. She leaned back against the pillows, exhausted from the simple effort of sitting. "And where is Miranda, my maid?"

"You are at Sutherland Hall, miss. And I don't know any Miranda. I was hired on a week ago to look after you."

Grace gasped. *A whole week!* "I've been here that long?"

"Longer, miss," the maid said. "At least a week before that, I believe. Lord Sutherland had the idea to send for me only when it appeared you would be staying."

The rest of the maid's words began to sink in, followed by alarm. "Why am I at Sutherland Hall?"

"I don't rightly know, miss." The maid's face mirrored the concern Grace knew must be on her own. "You've had pneumonia, and for a while, it seemed—" Her face flushed red. "Never mind. I didn't say that."

"You said nothing," Grace agreed, though she guessed easily enough.

I've been gravely ill—perhaps to the point of death—for at least two weeks. Panic rose within her. Much could have happened during that time. Father might have been sent to debtor's prison. At the least, he'd likely grown impatient and might have sent Helen off as a prospective bride. She could be in trouble too, forced to entertain Sir Lidgate's attentions or worse.

Grace leaned forward again, this time sitting up all the way. "Miranda is my maid. I *must* find her—and Harrison, my driver. They'll know what happened. I shouldn't be here. I must be on my way as soon as possible."

"I don't think so, miss." The young maid backed away, in the direction of the door.

"Wait," Grace called, reaching a hand out. "What is your name?"

"Jenny," the girl said. "Stay right there. I'll be back. I'll get Mrs. James. She'll be able to talk sense into you."

There was no time for talking. As soon as Jenny had left, Grace flung off the covers. On shaky legs, she moved to the door and clicked the lock into place. Then she set about searching for something to wear. She needed to leave. *This very hour.*

Her body shuddered, and the coughing began again. She collapsed in a chair near the fire, a single tear trailing from her eye as she fought for breath. The door handle jiggled; shouts came from the hall. A moment later, a key turned in the lock, and Jenny rushed in, followed by Mrs. James.

"Oooh!" Jenny wailed, as she spied the empty bed. "I told you she was bent on leaving."

"Miss Thatcher is right here." Mrs. James marched to the chair and reached down, sliding her arms beneath Grace's. "Come along. Back to bed with you."

Grace allowed them to lift her onto the mattress and tuck her in. She winced as Mrs. James spooned some horrid medicine into her mouth. "Please. I must leave."

"You must *rest*," Mrs. James corrected.

"But Helen—" The coughing started again, and Grace fought for breath until she was exhausted. Her eyes closed, and her breathing finally steadied.

I am too weak.

"That's better," Mrs. James said and turned as if to leave the room.

Grace reached for her, catching her sleeve. "Tell Miranda to go to Helen."

The housekeeper's brows rose quizzically. "Your maid is not here. Jenny is caring for you now. Lord Sutherland has hired her for that very purpose. Quite generous of him, considering the manner in which you came to be a resident of Sutherland Hall."

Grace pressed herself against the wall beside the slightly ajar double doors. She wasn't hoping to avoid being seen—little worry of that, the foyer was empty. There seemed to be the same lack of servants now as on her first visit to Sutherland Hall. But the wall lent her support as she worked to steady her breathing and calm her rapidly beating heart, neither of which she could blame entirely on her recent illness.

For the past three days, after persuading Jenny that she was well enough to dress, Grace had attempted to leave her room. At last, this afternoon when Jenny went for her tea, Grace had met with success.

Terse voices came from the other side of the doors—rather, *one* terse voice. Lord Sutherland's rose and fell sharply, and the few words she made out only added to her worry.

"Expense of such . . . ridiculous demands . . . penniless."

She had far too much experience with those sort of words and with the moods her father had been in on the occasions he'd shouted such phrases at her—as if their financial ruin were Grace's fault.

What awful luck to discover a similar circumstance in Lord Sutherland and Sutherland Hall. Had she known as much, Grace wouldn't have stopped here that stormy night. She most certainly would not be here now. She was not yet certain why she remained, her maid being uninformed, and Mrs. James being unwilling to speak of it beyond a few words, all hinting at some fault with Grace.

She is mistaken. I expressed no desire to return. I did not want to. Especially knowing of Mr. Preston's pleasant disposition as I do now.

As they had several times over the recent days, her thoughts strayed to Mr. Preston and their brief encounter at his ball. She'd felt hope during those few minutes that he'd danced with her. Hope and then regret of the action she'd taken to destroy her reputation.

Which will be no better now that I've been alone at Sutherland Hall these many days. Grace pulled her thoughts back to the present and her current predicament. She had to speak to Lord Sutherland to discover where her servants were. Then she would make arrangements to leave as quickly as possible.

One of the doors swung open, and an older, harried-looking man exited the room. Straying hairs combed over the top of his near-bald head flopped in the breeze created as he practically ran across the foyer. His case swung in one hand as swift steps carried him toward the front doors. His other hand reached for the hat and coat that Mr. Kingsley—who appeared out of nowhere—held out. These the man snatched without breaking his stride and was through the doors and down the outer steps in a matter of seconds.

Apparently she was not the only one in a hurry to be gone from this place.

Grace glanced toward the study and then toward Mr. Kingsley again, who was shutting the doors behind the hastily exited visitor. She needed to confront Lord Sutherland before her courage failed altogether, but she also wanted the opportunity to thank his servant for his kindness to a stranger that dark and stormy night, which had been near three weeks ago as best she could tell.

Knowing she might never have another opportunity to do so, Grace crossed the foyer. Kingsley watched her approach with what seemed to be a wary eye.

And who could blame him? She'd witnessed the tongue lashing he'd received for his charity. He might have suffered even worse later.

"Miss Thatcher, do you require something?" he asked as she drew closer. "Is it wise for you to be up so soon?"

"Soon?" Grace smiled. "I've been abed more these past weeks than the sum total of the rest of my life. It would be the sin of idleness to return."

"May I assist you with something?" Kingsley looked toward Lord Sutherland's study. Grace followed his gaze, guessing that he didn't wish to be caught conversing with her.

"I only wished to apologize and to thank you," she said. "I'm sorry my untimely arrival has caused you hardship, but I thank you ever so much for your generosity that night. Had you turned us away, I might not be here today."

But I might have been at Samuel Preston's.

Kingsley frowned. "Lord Sutherland has made me very much aware of that. To accept your gratitude would only prove to him that it was done on purpose." He gave a slight bow. "Good day, miss."

As Grace watched Kingsley walk away, a well of hurt rose up in her throat. *How could someone refuse to accept an expression of gratitude?* She'd been in earnest, yet for some reason her thanks had upset him. The back of her eyes stung, so she blinked quickly, trying to push aside his rejection.

Her feelings subdued, she retraced her steps until she stood before the study doors. The room was quiet now save for the slight scratching of a quill making its way across a page. Grace bit her lip.

Perhaps this is not the best time. From experience, she knew that presenting a man with a request when his mood was already foul was unlikely to produce the desired result. And she did need to convince Lord Sutherland of one more thing—to provide her with transport from his estate.

She'd considered making her request of Kingsley, but now her guilt had multiplied over the trouble—apparently far more than she'd realized—she'd caused him already. She wouldn't put him out yet again.

Grace closed her eyes and leaned her forehead against the wall, once more going over what she must say to Lord Sutherland and how she must say it. Cowering in front of the man would gain her nothing; he'd already made it clear how little he respected her. At least at the ball, they'd made somewhat civil conversation when she'd stood up to him. That was the approach she must take today. She would be confident in her request, and he would see the wisdom of it.

Standing straight, she smoothed the front of her dress, then walked to the doors. One of them stood ajar, but the other, partially closed door, she knocked on.

"Come in!" Lord Sutherland barked. "It's about time, Kingsley. What took so long?"

"It is not Kingsley come to see you, but I." Grace felt foolish for stating the obvious, but Lord Sutherland's dropped jaw demanded that she say something.

"What are you doing here?" His eyes narrowed in obvious displeasure as he tapped his fingers upon the desk.

"I came to ask the same thing." Grace raised her head in determination. "Why am I at Sutherland Hall once more, and how is it that my servants are not here with me? My last recollection is of your rather insistent demand that I make my exit from Mr. Preston's ball. And now I find myself here." She held her hands out.

"You've been ill." Lord Sutherland set the pen in its inkwell. "Pneumonia. I've gone to no small expense on your behalf."

"I thank you, but—why?" Beneath her gown, Grace felt her heart thumping wildly. *He is so angry.* "Why did you not leave me at Mr. Preston's?"

"A question I've asked myself more than once," Lord Sutherland said, his eyes boring into hers. "But at the time, I could not, in good conscience, do so." He broke their gaze, staring down at his papers again. "You do not look entirely well yet. I suggest you return to your room, and we'll have this discussion another time."

Grace made no move to go. She had no intention of being dismissed. She very much wanted to know why he'd felt he couldn't leave her in Mr. Preston's care. She guessed it had more to do with the past between the two men than it did with her, and she hadn't the time or inclination to involve herself in that affair—whatever it was.

"I should like a carriage to be made ready," she said, attempting to match his commanding tone. "I appreciate your attentiveness, and I shall leave an address to which you may send the list of expenses you incurred on my behalf." She'd have to take care that Father didn't discover the bill. She'd have to pay it from the inheritance, further delaying her plans to take Helen and Christopher away, but there was no help for it. For whatever absurd reason, and no matter how much she disliked the man, Lord Sutherland had seen to her care. He would have to be compensated.

"You want a carriage?" He leaned back in his chair. His brows rose, and an almost amused look crossed his face. "You feel well enough to go out?"

"I am well enough to *leave.*" Her foot gave an angry tap on the floor. For all her outward bravado, Grace felt desperate to make her exit. Cold sweat dotted her forehead, and her legs trembled from standing so long. She was not well—or *that* well, at least.

Returning to her room was likely a sound suggestion, but she had to escape this place. She needed to find Miranda and Harrison, to make sure Helen was all right, and to discover what Father was up to now.

While her thoughts spun, Lord Sutherland rose from his chair. He came around the front of his desk and stood before her. "As my—*betrothed*"—he spat the word out bitterly—"you will go nowhere unless I direct you to."

Grace felt her face pale. "What?" Her voice was barely above a whisper. "What have you done?" *My betrothed. My* betrothed. My *betrothed.*

"What have *I* done?" Lord Sutherland's laugh was sinister. "Samuel Preston posed the very same question the night you fainted in my arms. What a coincidence." He pivoted away, walking two steps. "I think not."

"It is no concern of mine what you think," Grace said, doing her best not to retreat, in spite of her trembling. "I've no intention of marrying you."

He turned again, coming toward her once more. "You should have thought of that before you stayed, uninvited, in my home."

"It is not my fault your servants put me in the wrong room," Grace said, her voice rising in pitch to match his.

"But it *was* your fault that *your* servants gossiped about it." Lord Sutherland stopped before her, glaring down at the top of her head. "Do you deny that you told them to do so?"

Grace drew in a sharp breath. *How does he know?* She stared at Lord Sutherland's chest, heaving with anger. Her admission would only make matters worse.

"Do you deny it?" he asked again, his voice deceptively quiet.

Grace closed her eyes. *I must tell him the truth.* She said a silent prayer for courage, then lifted her face to his. "No, I do not."

Something in Lord Sutherland's countenance seemed to shift. His eyes, though glittering with anger, had seemed almost hopeful. But with her admission, bitter disappointment twisted his mouth.

"I can explain," she began, more desperate for him to understand than she'd longed for Mr. Preston to know of her innocence. "I did tell my servants to speak of it, but not for the reasons you think."

"You can stop the pretense now, Miss Thatcher. It was your intention all along to trap a husband, and along the way, you found a way to make the game amusing."

"No!" Grace exclaimed, shaking her head. "You've got it all wrong."

"Do I?" Lord Sutherland's brows arched. He took a step closer, forcing her back until her leg bumped the chair behind her.

"Sit," he ordered.

Grace obeyed, dropping into the chair. It was that or collapse again, and she very much doubted he would catch her a second time. She pressed her trembling hands to her stomach, sick with worry.

"Did you or did you not agree to your father's scheme to go on a trip for the sole purpose of finding a husband?"

Another truth he will take all wrong.

"Yes," Grace whispered. She looked at her lap, blinking back tears and feeling too ashamed to meet Lord Sutherland's gaze.

"Then I see nothing more to discuss."

She lifted her head and stared at him. "You haven't heard it all. You don't understand."

"Oh, but I have, and I do." Lord Sutherland's voice was mocking. He leaned forward, hands braced on either side of the chair, so his face was near hers. "Before coming here, you spent time at both Lord Crosby's estate and Sir Lidgate's manor."

Somehow he has *heard it all.*

"Yes," she said meekly—miserably.

"And neither offered marriage. They both rejected you."

Grace hesitated, unsure how to respond. She had little hope that anything she said could change his view of her. *But I must try.*

"I did not wish to marry either man," she explained. "So I—"

"So you were *relieved* when neither would have you." Lord Sutherland's voice dripped with sarcasm and disbelief. His eyes narrowed, and his mouth twisted with scorn. "How convenient. But then perhaps you were most looking forward to your next suitor. You were to be a guest at Mr. Preston's—his *particular* guest—at a ball. Unlike the other men to whom your father was indebted, Preston sought you out."

Had I only known, Grace thought for the hundredth time. *Had I known of Mr. Preston's disposition, I would not be in this mess.*

"The only question I have," Lord Sutherland continued, "is why you stopped here the night your carriage broke down. Why not continue a little longer to Preston's?" He straightened and took a step back from her chair.

"I should think that is obvious." Grace sat up and met his gaze. "I was ill. Surely you are convinced of that, seeing how I've been unable to remove myself from bed these past weeks."

"But you *knew* Preston," Lord Sutherland argued. "Why not go to him for assistance? His property adjoins mine. Had you stayed on the road, you would have had but another quarter hour of travel."

"I didn't know him," Grace said. "We never met until the night of his ball."

Lord Sutherland's eyes narrowed once more. "Honesty better becomes you, Miss Thatcher. And I warn you, I will abide no less."

Grace pushed herself out of the chair and stood before him. "I *am* being honest."

"Then why did Preston greet you at his ball as if you were old friends? I believe his exact words were, 'It is so good to see you again.'"

"Because he had *seen* me before," Grace said. "Our boxes at the theatre were close, and . . ." Her voice trailed off under Lord Sutherland's knowing stare.

He leaned back against his desk, arms folded. "Do go on. Explain to me how it is that you do not know each other."

Her eyes smarted again, and she balled her hands into fists. *No matter what I say, he will not believe me.* Every word she spoke only seemed to entangle her more.

"You do recall his greeting, I see," Lord Sutherland observed.

"Yes." Grace sighed, weary of the word. "But you do not know the whole of it."

"I am sure I do not," Lord Sutherland said. "Though I can guess easily enough. Preston thought to use you to get at me. He hoped to goad me into a duel, and had I agreed, I would have found myself lured into a trap and in prison soon after."

"No!" Grace said, astonished by such a preposterous scenario. "I had really never seen—never *spoken* to"—she amended, lest, in some odd quirk of fate, Lord Sutherland had somehow been at the theatre too and seen her and Mr. Preston in the same vicinity. "I'd never spoken to Mr. Preston until that night."

"Correspondence, then," Lord Sutherland suggested. "Equally effective for sabotage." He pushed off the desk, towering over her once more. "Do you have any idea of the trouble you've caused me? The predicament I find myself in because I came to your rescue, because I tried to save your reputation?"

"Forgive me, milord," Grace said in her own mocking tone. "For not falling at your feet and expressing my undying gratitude." She stepped closer to him, tilting her head back to look up at him, pushing aside her fear in place of anger. "Before you rode off on your charger to come to my rescue, did it never once occur to you that I might not *want* to be saved?"

"Not once." Lord Sutherland's gaze didn't leave hers. The hard look in his eyes didn't soften in the least. "It had not occurred to me that you were in league with Preston. I had not yet realized that I'd *been had.* Believe me, Miss Thatcher, if I'd suspected at all, I would have left you to your troubles, and perhaps Preston would be stuck with you now instead."

"You needn't marry me," Grace said. "I've no such expectation. It was never my intent to involve you in my father's plan. For that, I apologize."

"You do not deny involvement in Preston's scheme?" Nicholas asked.

"No," Grace said, rather loudly. "Because there was—*is*—no scheme."

"Maybe Preston did not tell you the whole of it," Lord Sutherland said, as much to himself as to her.

"Mr. Preston said nothing beyond a few pleasantries when we danced. My only crime is in agreeing to my father's folly and going on this trip in the first place."

"Ah, your father," Lord Sutherland drawled in a bitter tone. "A pleasant man. Can't say as I've ever been quite as entertained as the morning I spent with him."

Grace felt as if a large, sharp stone had dropped to the bottom of her stomach. "Father? Was he—he came here?" She looked to and fro, lest her father jump out at her.

"Ten days ago," Lord Sutherland confirmed.

Grace's hands flew to her throat. "Oh no."

Lord Sutherland nodded. "I was given the generous choice of dueling your Mr. Preston or marrying you. Oh, do not look so frightened," he snapped. "I could easily kill Preston and should have enjoyed doing so immensely, but I am not a fool. He'd ensnare me in a thrice. More importantly, I am a man of my word and gave it to another some time ago that I would never harm a hair on Preston's head. So you see my predicament."

Our predicament, Grace thought, trying to steady her racing heart. No one was to die over her; that was something. "I will talk to my father," she said. "If you'll allow your carriage to take me home, I promise to right the matter with him."

"It's a bit late for that," Lord Sutherland stated.

"Why?" Grace asked. "Have you gone and done the deed while I slept? Did another stand in as proxy for me?"

He gave a short, harsh laugh. "No. But the entire countryside knows of your supposed indiscretion, and no doubt your father and those servants of yours are busy spreading it about London, as well."

"That is my difficulty to bear, not yours." Grace looked him directly in the eye so he might see the truth of her words. "I am prepared to suffer the consequences to my reputation."

"And what of mine?" Lord Sutherland asked. "How shall I be looked upon by my peers and associates for ruining a young lady and sending her packing?"

"I did not think it would matter to you," Grace said, then cringed at the harsh look he gave.

"No. You did not *think*—particularly about my mother. She will be here in a few days' time, and no doubt she shall have an earful for both of us."

"Oh." This subdued her a bit. Grace frowned in contemplation of what must be done. There had to be a way out for *both* of them. Lord Sutherland had made it abundantly clear that he wished a marriage between them as little as she did.

"Then there is the matter of your sister," he said.

"Helen? What has happened?" Grace bit her lip as she looked up at him.

"Nothing that I am aware of. Nor is anything likely to, according to your father, as you and your servants have so thoroughly ruined both of your possibilities."

"Oh." Grace sagged against the chair in relief.

Lord Sutherland quirked an eyebrow. "This pleases you?"

Here we go again. She chose her words with care. "I am much relieved that Helen will not be forced to marry. She is young—delicate. I worry for her. I fear her sweet nature would greatly suffer beneath—" Her eyes flickered upward to him.

"One so overbearing as myself?" Lord Sutherland suggested.

"Yes," Grace agreed—too readily. *Darn that word again.* She hoped to never say it another time in her life. *Though I shall have to at least once—before a priest.*

She dared another look at Lord Sutherland. He was indeed overbearing and of a temper and—

"No need to worry over your sister. I have paid your father handsomely for his losses seeing as he cannot sell her off as well."

—And generous. Equal waves of guilt and shame assailed Grace. From what little she'd seen of the Sutherland estate, it did not appear that Lord Sutherland had extra funds to dispense of. What must he think of her, having met her father and believing, as he did, that she'd been a willing accomplice to this entire scheme? Though she did not care for Lord Sutherland, she also did not want him believing the worst of her.

"Thank you for that." She met his eyes briefly but saw no welcoming light there. Like Kingsley, he would not accept her gratitude, instead reading it as false.

"You will have ample time to show your thanks in the future." His eyes perused her for a long moment before he looked away. "For now, I suggest you return to your room and continue recuperating. I have not spent a small fortune on the physician to have you become unwell again."

Feeling ill-used, Grace wrapped her arms around her middle and turned to go, eager to escape Lord Sutherland's presence.

A temporary escape. I am indebted to him. I am trapped.

A swell of panic rose inside her, bringing to mind another time, long ago, when she'd been in a similar predicament. Her betrothal to Sir Edmund Crayton, and her worries over what their marriage would bring, had been more than frightening. But then, at least, she'd had the hope that he would leave her often. That he and his pirates would take to the sea frequently.

And then Grandfather rescued me.

She had no such hope now. She'd had her one miracle, a few worry-free years of happiness. Here she was caught beneath Lord Sutherland's fist for the duration of their betrothal, and for a lifetime beyond. When she thought of that, she wanted to cry. To have enjoyed freedom and have it taken away was almost worse than not having known it at all. And now she would be here, alone. She longed for Helen's company but would never dare subject her sister to Lord Sutherland's temper. If only there was someone else she might turn to for help in reasoning all this through, or in finding a way out. Then her situation might be bearable.

If I had a friend—

Grace stopped in the doorway and turned around suddenly, facing Lord Sutherland seated at his desk once more. "I should like my maid to join me," she informed him with as much authority as she dared. "Her name is Miranda. She was with me at—"

"I am well aware of your servants' names and their capabilities for ruining lives." Lord Sutherland looked up from his work. "They are not welcome here. Furthermore, if I were you, I should send word of that at once. I am not under the same constraints with them as I am with Preston, and should either of your servants venture onto my property—" He opened a lower drawer and pulled out a revolver. "I would not be averse to taking them out for the trouble they have caused me."

Grace stared at the pistol, her fear transitioning to anger once again. She'd spent a lifetime being threatened and bullied by her father and his creditors, and she had no intention of continuing the pattern here. Helen, at least, was safe now.

So it doesn't matter if something happens to me.

She stepped back into the room, standing squarely

before the desk. "Perhaps you should rid yourself of the problem right now," she challenged. "Just shoot me and be done with it. Then you can go about your way unencumbered."

A brief flash of what might have been admiration flickered in Lord Sutherland's gaze. He set the revolver aside but made no move to put it back in the drawer. "You are the Duke of Salisbury's granddaughter—and were well received during your time with him in London, I hear. Were I to dispose of you so readily, there would likely be repercussions. I've no desire to trade one problem for another, particularly when the first, at least, promises something in return for my trouble."

Grace felt a blush staining her cheeks at his insinuation and berated herself for it. "I have promised you nothing." Whatever attraction Lord Sutherland might hold for other women, she felt none of it. He was arrogant and domineering, threatening and—far too close, as he rose from his chair and leaned over the desk.

"Get out." He pointed to the door. "I'll summon you when I wish to see you next."

"And I'll come only if I want to," she countered, turning away and walking sedately toward the door. When she passed through it, she grabbed the handle and pulled, slamming it behind her with unnecessary force. Only then did she allow herself to move quickly, practically running across the entry as the previous visitor had done. Kingsley was not there to open the front doors for her, but she exited them anyway, running onto the drive and as far away from her *betrothed* as possible.

CHAPTER 17

Grace stumbled on the loose gravel of the drive, her slippers not being the sort appropriate for an afternoon walk, and the drive having been long unattended. A short distance from the house, she turned into what must once have been a lovely garden. Several seasons' worth of leaves and debris covered the brick paths, and trees and bushes grew in disarray, their previous forms indiscernible. None of that mattered. Grace knew only that her surroundings were as dismal as the man within the towering edifice behind her and that, from now on, she wished to avoid him at all costs.

Even if that meant being out in the weather unprepared and alone in a place that was altogether eerie. She lifted her face to the sky and the low-lying clouds. Rain threatened but had not yet come. The thought of returning to her room was stifling. Being shut up there, worrying about when a summons from Lord Sutherland might occur, held no appeal.

Suppressing a shiver that was part nerves, part cold, Grace wrapped her arms around herself and persisted in discovering where the mostly obscured path might lead. With care, she watched her footing and found herself ducking this way and that to avoid overgrown bramble. After a time, and with more than a few scratches to her person, the house behind her grew distant.

She reached a stone wall of significant height and was faced with the choice of heading one direction or the other along it. With tired feet and lungs burning from overuse so soon after her illness, she chose to rest instead and plopped onto an iron bench near the wall.

As she sat, the reality and severity of her circumstances returned to the front of her mind with sudden force. *I am betrothed to the loathsome man. He has given Father his word and even paid to compensate for Helen. And when shall I even see her again now? I shall never be able to escape with Christopher and Helen to the country.* Grace's throat constricted, and this time she could not stop the well of tears that surfaced and began to spill over. Leaning forward, she brought her hands to her face and cried in earnest, weeping out all the fear and anger she'd barely managed to contain during her confrontation with Lord Sutherland.

How will I ever get out of this? He will own me. Her tears flowed freely, and her shoulders shook from the depths of her sorrow.

The lightest touch fell upon her back, and Grace sat up, alert and wary of what creature might have joined her. She looked up and saw not a bird or insect, as she had expected, but a—man.

She screamed and jumped up, and the man leaning over the wall nearly lost his balance, his arm extended toward her, a coat dangling from his fingers.

"No harm meant," he said, grasping the top of the fence with his free hand and trying to right himself.

Grace widened her eyes at the familiar voice. She stepped closer again and looked up at the face that went with it. "Mr. Preston?"

His smile was the same as she remembered from the brief time at his ball and the many times he'd been in her dreams since.

"Whatever are you doing?" she asked, clasping her hands together in front of her.

"Attempting, somewhat clumsily, I admit, to lay this coat across your shoulders so you do not catch another chill." He held the garment out to her, and Grace stepped forward to take it.

"Thank you."

"I hear you have been quite unwell," Mr. Preston said. "I cannot think that being out in the cold without a proper wrap is a good idea."

"I am better now." Grace pushed her arms through the overlarge sleeves and felt immediate warmth. "You have given me *your* coat," she said, looking up at him, coatless and still perched on the wall, this time more casually now that he'd regained his balance and was relieved of his burden.

"It looks far better on you." He grinned down at her.

"Will you lend me your hand as well?" Grace asked, holding hers out to him.

Mr. Preston looked surprised but took her outstretched hand in his. Grace held on for support as she put one foot and then the other upon the bench and stood facing him. "There. That is better."

Mr. Preston did not immediately release her but looked at her a long moment—not as Lord Sutherland had, as if appraising an item he had purchased—but in a most concerned and caring sort of way.

"You have been unwell in more ways than one," Mr. Preston observed.

Reluctantly, Grace withdrew her hand and tucked it into the warm pocket of his coat. With the material pulled tight around her, she relished its comfort and felt warmed by it in more ways than one. "I am fair enough," she answered.

"*That* is easy for anyone to see," Mr. Preston said, a

teasing glimmer in his eye. "But I heard you crying. You are unhappy."

Grace nodded, then looked down, lest he spy the tears gathering in her eyes again. "Only today did I discover how dire my circumstances are." Her voice shook. "I am betrothed to Lord Sutherland."

"This does not please you?" Mr. Preston asked.

Grace shook her head. "Nor does it please him."

"Has he hurt you in any way?" Mr. Preston asked. He reached across the wall, touching her shoulder lightly.

Grace lifted her face to his. "No." She managed a tremulous smile. "He is rather fearsome to look at, but so far his bark only alarms."

"He'd best not bite you," Mr. Preston growled, with less than his usual good humor. "I must confess that I am aware of your situation."

"As I have just described," Grace said, nonplussed that he considered the need to admit the very thing she had just told him.

"Beyond that," Mr. Preston explained, "when Lord Sutherland took you from my house, your servants were left behind. Before releasing them, I interviewed each most thoroughly and am in full knowledge of the plan the three of you devised before coming to my home."

Grace hung her head, ashamed for the second time that day by her rash and foolish idea and the disaster that had ensued. "I am sorry." *More so than you can imagine.*

"As am I," Mr. Preston said. "I'd every intention of courting you, Miss Thatcher. And now that seems to be impossible."

"I thank you for the compliment," Grace said. "I wish—I had not acted so rashly. Please understand that I had no reason to believe you any different from the other men my father had arranged for me to meet. I was desperate to escape a marriage to any of them—to anyone." She dared look at him again and saw only understanding in his gaze. How much easier it was to explain her reasons to Mr. Preston. If only Lord Sutherland would have let her get a word in edgewise, she might have told him as much as well.

"And now you find yourself betrothed to the worst of them all," Mr. Preston said, a knowing look in his eye.

"So it would seem." Grace sighed heavily.

"Take heart," he said. "Things are not always what they appear to be. Lord Sutherland may not be as terrible as you imagine."

"It is not mere imagination," Grace said. "I've witnessed his wrath firsthand. He despises me and feels I have deliberately trapped him. He even accused me of scheming with you."

"Then you shall have to convince him otherwise."

"How?" Grace asked.

Mr. Preston looked at her peculiarly, as if truly considering her question. "To begin with—and please do not take this incorrectly—it might behoove you to look your best when around him. You are lovely right now, with your tear-stained face and wearing my atrociously large coat. But around Nicholas—Lord Sutherland—I would suggest taking pains with your appearance. Many a fair lady has won over her man with beauty."

"I've no wish to win him over," Grace muttered.

Mr. Preston smiled. "Then I predict that you and Nicholas will yet have many a battle."

"You are on a first name basis with His Lordship?" Grace asked, thinking more on that than his advice.

It was Mr. Preston's turn to sigh. "In the past, yes. Nicholas is—was—my brother-in-law. His sister was my wife."

Grace stared at him. "You were married?" An inane question when he'd just told her as much, but she hadn't imagined him married. He hadn't mentioned it at the ball, and if he'd wanted to court her, he had to be in want of a wife. She'd never considered that he might have had one before.

"Elizabeth died three years ago." The sorrow in Mr. Preston's eyes deepened, and he looked beyond Grace, toward some point in the past that she was not privy to. "Elizabeth was Lord Sutherland's younger sister, and their family was very close. After her death, her father became ill and never recovered. I've heard it said he died of a broken heart."

"I am so terribly sorry." Grace fought the impulse to reach out a comforting hand. "I had no idea . . ."

Mr. Preston smiled, though this time there was a hint of sadness instead of merriment in his eyes. "It would seem that you, too, are acquainted with the sting of death. In talking with your servants, I discovered that you've lost not only your grandfather, but your mother, as well."

"I was very young when she died," Grace said. "In truth, I almost think Grandfather's passing hurt more—or perhaps it is just that his death is fresher in memory."

"'As time him hurts, time doth him cure,'" Mr. Preston quoted.

"Chaucer." Her face brightened. "Dare I hope that you are a lover of poetry, Mr. Preston?"

"Samuel," he said. "If we are to be friends—and I hope we are—then you must call me by my Christian name. And yes, I enjoy poetry. Elizabeth did as well. We spent many an hour in this garden reading poetry together."

The same sense of hope she'd felt at Mr. Preston's ball filled Grace now. Had she not wished for a friend an hour ago? And here she'd been given her very heart's desire.

Almost. Her true desire would have been to go back in time and undo her horrible mistake and thereby be free to be courted by Mr. Preston—by Samuel.

"You may call me Grace."

Their exchange of given names felt intimate. A niggling of guilt struck somewhere deep in her mind. She wasn't about to call Lord Sutherland by his Christian name, and she had no desire for him to know hers. Yet it was to him she was promised.

But there is no law against friendship, she argued with her conscience. There was no reason she could not have a conversation with another man. She and Samuel were not technically even on the same property.

He was watching her now, a curious look on his face as if he knew the gamut of her thoughts. "I assure you, we will be proper. I vow to stay on my side of the fence. If Nicholas were to discover me on his property, he might be pushed beyond the promise he gave his sister not to murder me."

"I am fairly certain he would shoot me first," Grace said. "I could see that he wanted to, when we spoke earlier."

Instead of seeming concerned, Samuel chuckled. "No doubt he will want to do so a time or two more before the two of you are finished being at odds with each other. Do not worry over it. If Nicholas Sutherland is one thing, it is a gentleman—one who is careful with his possessions. Now that you are well and truly in his care, he will not harm you."

"I do not wish to be a possession." Grace frowned.

"I should hope not," Samuel said. "Which is why you must make an effort with him."

Grace gave him a wry smile. "And I am to rely upon my beauty in that endeavor."

"I would not suggest it," Samuel said. "I merely mentioned it as a place to start. You might try talking to Nicholas as you are talking with me."

"Impossible," Grace said. "I attempted as much earlier, and everything I said he took wrong, and he would not let me explain myself. My words and intent were so twisted as to convince me that there is no hope of gaining his respect or understanding."

"There is always hope," Samuel said. He caught her eye, and the look he gave her filled her once again—with hope, and with longing. *For something I cannot have.*

"I never thought to marry," Grace said. "And so I have not devoted any time at all to the art of capturing a man's attention. I wouldn't know the first thing to do."

"No art is required," Mr. Preston assured. "Simply be yourself. There is no chance of success if you cannot be who you truly are. That was what attracted me to Elizabeth. She was vivacious and full of joy. She did not particularly care what others thought of her. So much so that she took a chance on me."

"As would any sensible young lady," Grace said.

Preston shook his head. "Not so. You forget that I have no title. And money without a title is viewed by most as sorely lacking."

"Poor Lord Sutherland," Grace said, without a trace of sympathy in her voice. "I have neither title nor money, and here he is stuck with me."

"So it would seem," Samuel said with a wry grin. "That I should have been so fortunate."

And I, Grace thought dismally. "What a strange and honest conversation we are having Mr. Preston—Samuel."

"There is nothing wrong with admitting what one has wanted but cannot have. Nor do I see it as wrong to accept what is possible in its place instead. We shall be friends, then?" He stuck out his hand as if to strike a bargain.

"We were friends already, from the moment of our first meeting." Grace shook his hand, then pulled hers away quickly. The warmth his offered was tempting in too many ways. "I should go." She glanced at the sky, which was darker now than when they had begun talking.

"You should," Samuel agreed. "Were Nicholas to discover you here, it would not go well for either of us."

"May I beg a favor of you?" Grace asked. He was kindness in every sense of the word, and furthermore, she felt she could trust him.

"Anything," Samuel said.

"I must get a letter to my siblings and to Miranda and Harrison," Grace explained. "But I fear attempting to send any from Lord Sutherland's home. His servants are not amiable, and he is already highly suspicious of me."

"Can you bring your letters here tomorrow?" Samuel asked.

"I think so," Grace said. "I shall do my best to come at about this same time—when my new maid goes downstairs to take tea with the other servants."

"Until tomorrow, then," Samuel said, smiling at her in a way that not only warmed her but made her troubles seem surmountable.

Grace shrugged out of his coat and handed it to him.

"Come if you can," Samuel said. "You need only sit on that same bench, and I will find you."

Grace accepted his hand as she stepped down.

"Remember what I said," he urged as she turned to go. "You will have to put forth some effort to get past Lord Sutherland's gruff side."

"Has he another side?" Grace quipped. "I hadn't noticed. All I know about the man is that he is surly and quick to judge."

"Perhaps you are the one being quick to judge," Samuel suggested.

His words stung. Grace looked up at him in surprise. "You don't know what he said to me."

"And you do not know the measure of his sorrow." Samuel's words were gentle, as if to soften the rebuke. "All that I am saying is consider thinking of him less harshly. Not everyone handles their losses as well as you and I have. For Nicholas, they have been devastating, and he has yet to recover."

"How have you recovered?" Grace asked. "From losing your wife?"

"I loved Elizabeth dearly," Samuel said. "I still do. But life must and will continue, with or without my participation in it. And I know Elizabeth would very much wish the former."

"Nicholas—Lord Sutherland—does not feel the same?" Grace asked, striving to understand. She really didn't want to be at odds with the man. Their earlier exchange had been agonizing. Not only did she suffer from his rebukes, but she felt guilty over her own behavior as well. It was not in her character to use biting words and demands.

"He is still grieving," Samuel said. "Time has not healed for him but has stood still, and the pain has become worse every day, until he is raw from its constancy."

"But why?" Grace asked. "What is so different—"

"That is for you to discover," Samuel said with that same melancholy smile half curving his lips as it had when he'd first spoken of his wife. "Perhaps you will be the one to lift him from it."

His words distressed her. She didn't need the burden of another to care for and worry over. She'd spent her life in that pursuit. *And look where it has landed me.*

"Hurry now," Samuel admonished. "If I don't see you tomorrow, I may worry that I kept you out here too long and that you've become ill again. I'd be tempted to test Lord Sutherland's patience by checking in on you."

"Don't worry," Grace called. "I'll be fine." She willed the words to ring as true in her heart as in her head as she retraced her steps down the path.

I will be fine.

She did not know exactly how or when it would happen, but she took comfort in Samuel's words. They warmed her as much as his coat had, and with newfound courage, she made her way back to Sutherland Hall.

CHAPTER 18

"Goodness, miss, you gave me a start." Jenny placed one hand over her heart and the other across her brow as she stepped back from the door Grace had just entered. "Thank the heavens you're back."

Grace headed toward the chair closest to the fireplace in her room, seeking both rest and warmth as quickly as possible. The walk back through the garden had seemed far longer than her walk to it. She felt close to exhaustion and chilled to the bone.

"Oh no, miss. Don't sit. Please." Jenny stepped in front of Grace, blocking her way. "His Lordship requested you join him for dinner. We've just minutes until you're expected." She wrung her hands. "Whatever will we do?"

"I shall go to dinner, that's what." Grace stepped around the maid and sank into the chair, reasoning that a minute or two of rest was better than none.

"But your hair, miss—and your dress."

Grace glanced at her skirt. It was damp from the rain and might have been a little dirty from her walk, but in the firelight, she couldn't tell. Her slippers were all but ruined with mud, but at least those could be changed before dinner. "My dress and hair shall have to do. I was not expecting a *summons.*" She spoke the word bitterly. "So soon."

The clock in the hall began chiming the hour; Grace leaned her head back and groaned. Behind her, Jenny continued to fret.

"If you'd like, I can go down to tell his lordship you are ill."

It was a tempting offer, but Grace remembered his insistence on complete honesty—a principle she believed in keeping anyway. *And look what deviating from it has cost me.* She had herself, at least in part, to blame for her predicament, and dishonesty would only make the situation worse.

"Thank you, Jenny. But I will go down." She leaned forward, bracing her hands on the sides of the chair and forcing herself to abandon its comfort. "I'll explain that I hadn't time to dress for dinner. I am certain Lord Sutherland will understand." She wasn't certain at all, but her young maid looked near to hysterics, and Grace thought one of them, at least, ought to be relieved.

She left the room and made her way down the hall to the curved staircase. Peering over the railing, she contemplated which of the doors below might lead to the dining room. As if in answer to her question, Kingsley, holding a large, covered platter, exited one door, walked across the foyer, and entered another. Grace felt her stomach grumble and her step lighten as she followed him. If nothing else, she was ready to eat something more substantial than broth and bread.

Upon entering the chamber, which she had correctly guessed to be the dining room, Grace found Lord Sutherland already seated at the end of the long table. A second place was set beside him to the right, and Grace walked directly there, careful to keep her step even and her manner subdued.

Kingsley's eyes widened with alarm as he held out her

chair, and for a moment Grace thought that perhaps her maid had been mistaken and she wasn't to be here at all.

"You are late," Lord Sutherland said, turning to look at her.

Grace settled into her chair and met his gaze, which was as disconcerting as Kingsley's.

"What have you done to yourself?" Lord Sutherland demanded, looking her up and down, much as he'd done earlier in his office.

"I have been walking in your gardens and only just returned." Grace followed his gaze to a before-unnoticed smudge on her sleeve. "I did not expect you to summon me for dinner with no time for me to change."

He looked up at the ceiling as if supplicating aid from on high. "You were out in this weather?"

"It was not raining then—much," she added meekly. Only during the last several minutes of her walk back had the drops begun to fall.

"Do you not realize that you have been close to *death*?"

"Do you not realize you are shouting?" she returned with her own, raised voice.

"In this instance, I think shouting is warranted." He placed both fists upon the table. "So help me, Miss Thatcher. If I've brought you back from the brink of death only for you to become ill again, this time through your own stupidity—"

"You do not blame me for my last illness?" she asked, astounded at such a possibility.

"Of course not." Lord Sutherland lowered his voice and slowly unclenched his fists. "I blame your father for being so careless as to send his daughter to meet a pack of wolves with naught but an ancient carriage and two servants not intelligent enough to hold their tongues."

"Oh." Grace looked down at her plate, thoroughly taken aback. That he found her father's choice of suitors comparable to a pack of wolves, and that he did not blame her for this awful predicament in its entirety, brought a little hope.

"You may serve dinner now, Kingsley," Lord Sutherland said.

Grace sat with her hands in her lap as Kingsley served them both. She graciously accepted each offering, thanking him every time, though he did not acknowledge her beyond the barest nod. Grace sighed inwardly, guessing it would take much work to win him over now.

In the meantime, she vowed a new start with his master. Samuel's admonitions rang in her mind, and Grace promised herself that from this moment, the meal would be pleasant. Though she would have preferred to dine alone in her room, she could not deny the appeal of the aromas wafting from her plate, and she could not entirely ignore the man beside her, watching her carefully.

"You may eat now," he said as Kingsley exited, leaving them alone.

"Thank you," Grace said. "It smells delicious. You must have a very good cook." She hoped discussing food was deemed appropriate at Sutherland Hall. During her time at her grandfather's home, she had learned that not all rules of etiquette applied equally at all levels of society. What one person might deem proper dinner conversation, another might find overly rude.

"I am very fortunate in my cook," Nicholas said. "She has been with our family since I was quite young."

Relieved at his agreeable answer, Grace forged ahead. "Will you tell me about your childhood here?" she asked, as desirous to have a conversation that did not revolve around their predicament as to learn about his sister.

"Some other time, perhaps," he said curtly.

Grace had no response, so she sipped her soup delicately and focused on using the manners instilled in her while living with her grandfather.

After a time, Lord Sutherland cleared his throat. "About our meeting earlier . . ."

Grace ceased studying her bowl and looked up at him.

"I—" He frowned suddenly, then leaned closer. "You have leaves in your hair. Come here."

He might have offered to assist me instead of ordering me about, Grace thought. Nevertheless, she leaned forward.

He reached toward her, hesitant at first, then focused his gaze above her face as he began pulling bits of leaves from her hair.

"Your garden is somewhat overgrown," Grace said by way of explanation. "But it is lovely, nonetheless—or it was clearly lovely once."

"My sister thought so as well." His touch was surprisingly gentle, and Grace closed her eyes, patiently sitting beneath his ministrations.

The room grew silent, and Grace feared he might hear her heartbeat, increasing as it was at his nearness and touch. She told herself she was only frightened, as she had been when at Sir Lidgate's when he'd been near. But she was not entirely able to convince herself.

Lord Sutherland's touch did not seem improper, and his intent was not self-serving or gratifying in any way. Unless the removal of leaves from a woman's hair was somehow pleasurable to him, a possibility she very much doubted.

He gently turned her head. "This side now." His fingers carefully parted her hair, extracting the offending leaves. She dared open one eye and watched the growing pile on the table.

Embarrassment burned across her cheeks. "I didn't realize—what a mess I must be."

"I have seen your hair look better," he agreed. "Then again, I have also seen it worse."

Grace turned to look at him, her eyes flashing.

A corner of his mouth quirked into a near smile. "You looked rather wild that night . . ."

When you discovered me in your bed. She felt a sudden urge to laugh. She remembered going to bed without so much as brushing her wet hair and well knew how she must have looked upon waking. A strangled sort of sound burst from her lips before her hand came up to cover her mouth.

"No offense meant," he said, misinterpreting her look.

"None taken." She laughed again and this time could not cover it up.

Lord Sutherland leaned away, contemplating her with an expression that suggested she'd gone mad.

"You looked funny too," Grace said, after another round of giggles, after which she calmed herself enough to speak. "At first I thought a feline had jumped in the bed, but then you spoke and scared me half to death."

"A *cat*." Lord Sutherland's mouth twisted with apparent disgust. "If you must compare me to an animal, at least choose a worthy one."

The lines around his eyes softened ever so slightly as he looked at her. Grace lifted her glass, took a long drink, then set it back once more and calmed herself.

What must he think of me, leaves in my hair and bursting into laughter at dinner?

"A few more, if I may?" Lord Sutherland said, indicating her hair again. Grace leaned forward, and his fingers resumed their work. The desire to laugh subsided, and she closed her eyes, fearing his touch for entirely different reasons than she had feared Sir Lidgate's.

"There," Lord Sutherland said at last.

Grace raised her head again. A long piece of her hair still rested in his hand, and he watched as she sat back and it slid from his fingers.

"Your hair is very soft," he observed. "And pretty."

"Thank you." Grace was held captive beneath his stare.

"See that from now on, it is kept *up*."

His stern command snapped her from the trance he'd caused. She pushed her chair back and stood, not caring if doing so was rude of her. “Good night, Lord Sutherland. Pray, do not summon me tomorrow. I feel the need to rest.”

She turned and left before he could say or do another thing to disturb her already overwrought nerves.

CHAPTER 19

My Dearest Helen and Christopher,

I have made a grave error, which has landed me in a bit of a predicament . . .

The news from London was good and should have made Nicholas happy. After the debacle at Preston's ball, one of the guests, as well as an investor and potential partner in his mercantile, had withdrawn support, leaving Preston short on goods he'd promised would be ready to ship overseas this month. In turn, the captain of the ship he'd chartered was angry, demanding payment in advance equal to the sales of a full cargo, which Preston no longer had.

Nicholas rubbed his eyes and tossed the letter from his solicitor aside, pleased with its contents, yet not as satisfied as he felt he ought to be. This was only the beginning. Preston would be faced with other problems because of this loss, and his reputation would suffer. More suppliers would likely lose confidence and withdraw their business. This was, quite possibly, the beginning of the end to Preston's ventures as a merchant, one of the outcomes Nicholas had desired for his neighbor for a very long time.

Yet at this moment, the news did nothing but give him a headache.

Nicholas rose from his desk and wandered into the foyer in search of Miss Thatcher. He had not seen her at all today but had heard from her maid that she had not been in her room when the afternoon tea was delivered. The woman needed to eat, but she'd also left dinner early the night before, had not come down for breakfast, and had returned her tray mostly untouched. If starving herself was her latest plan at rebellion, he would not have it.

Neither would he tolerate her running about in the cold. He could not imagine Miss Thatcher actually wandering the gardens again; it was raining.

Given both her physical and emotional states at dinner the previous evening, he wasn't certain what to expect other than constant upheaval. She was the most unpredictable woman he'd ever known: standing up for Kingsley, declining assistance in salvaging her reputation at Preston's ball.

Asking me to shoot her.

The latter in particular was disturbing. Did the woman care so little for her life that she would throw it aside?

Or is the possibility of marriage to me so loathsome?

Either way, Nicholas felt that something had to be done about the situation. He'd planned to handle it at dinner—to apprise Miss Thatcher that there might be a way out of their betrothal, and to judge her reaction to the news that Samuel Preston might yet court her.

If Preston will not have her, I will marry your daughter.

Nicholas had thought himself rather shrewd when making that promise to Miss Thatcher's father. At the time, he'd surmised that it would be to his advantage to pretend that he would keep Miss Thatcher, to make Preston squirm for a bit. It was certain Preston's interest in Miss Thatcher was sincere—no one who'd seen them dancing together and seen the look in Preston's eyes could mistake his interest.

At the least they were good friends. *Having plotted*

together against me. No matter what Miss Thatcher denies. Nicholas was certain they had agreed upon this scheme together, and he wanted both to suffer for it. Then, after a period of misery for each, he would foist the troublesome woman off on Preston. They deserved each other.

In his mind, it had seemed so simple. But after the scene in his study yesterday, he was not so certain. Having Miss Thatcher around for any length of time seemed a poor idea. Giving Preston what he wanted did not appeal to him either. Which was the lesser of two evils? And what if Preston's plan all along was to have Miss Thatcher here?

In my house, driving me mad? And mad I'll be in no time.

There would be no peace with her around. She was sure of herself, confident, and full of life. All qualities Elizabeth had possessed.

And just the kind of woman I don't want around.

The reminder was too painful.

He'd done his best to tamp down Miss Thatcher's spirit yesterday and, conversely, had hated himself every time he'd managed to do so, even a bit. Each time, she had sprung back with remarkable strength.

Such resiliency was another characteristic he did not wish to admire, and one that Preston, assuredly, already did.

The devil take him.

Nicholas stepped into the parlor but did not find Miss Thatcher. He left the room, still in pursuit and still in a quandary about what to do with her.

Throughout her illness, and particularly after her father's visit, Nicholas had envisioned ways in which he might make her pay for her deceit. The lies she had encouraged her servants to tell had caused him to be in this tight spot, so a lie or two aimed Miss Thatcher's direction was easily justified.

Or so he'd told himself.

In his study yesterday, he'd sought to scare her a little,

to set her on edge and have her experience some of the worry he'd had while her health had been fragile and he'd not known whether he wished her to die or to live, while he'd wondered what was to become of them both if she did recover.

He'd wanted her to feel as ill-used as he did, so he'd set his sights upon her as only a man as coarse as Lidgate might have. But Nicholas regretted it. The glimpse of fear in her eyes before she'd left, and the way she'd wrapped her arms around herself protectively, had made him feel like the greatest cad. He owed her an apology and the assurance that he would not take advantage of their circumstance—no matter how tempting doing so might be.

And therein lay the other difficulty with handing her over to Preston—this one more hard put. If Miss Thatcher had been ugly—or at the least, gaunt and sickly from her bout with pneumonia—then Nicholas would have been quite happy to send her away. But the woman who had appeared in his study yesterday, while somewhat thin and pale from illness, was no less striking than the one he'd escorted into Preston's ball.

Showing up at dinner as she had—with her cheeks rosy from being outdoors, her hair tumbling about her shoulders—was enough to test his resolve not to touch her or in any way give in to the attraction he felt. And then he imagined Preston's hands instead of his own entangled in her curls . . .

And so the dilemma grew.

I have given my word. Either Preston marries her, or—I do.

Words Nicholas was in no hurry at all to speak.

He peered into the dining room in case she'd wandered there, but he found it empty. He crossed to the ballroom, only to find it vacant. No sounds came from the music room, but he decided to check there anyway.

At the least, he needed to see to Miss Thatcher's welfare while she was here. And he would call a truce. What was done was done, and there was no sense in continuing to make her pay for it, if for no other reason than that it would make his life equally miserable.

Going after Preston required effort; Nicholas hadn't the strength to turn his talons toward Miss Thatcher as well. Beyond that, he found that he did not want to hurt her. What she had done still vexed him, and would for some time, but having met her father, and knowing the suitors she'd been presented with, Nicholas could not entirely blame her for her rash and desperate actions.

Perhaps, in time, the situation would work itself out—she would simply go away, with no one the worse for it.

Nicholas frowned; that idea was even poorer than his former mistake of leaving his tenants unchecked for nearly two years. Avoidance of an issue was not the answer—though she appeared to be doing a splendid job avoiding him.

The music room was also empty, Elizabeth's pianoforte still covered as it had been since her death, the chairs untouched since that last assembly so long ago.

He considered going upstairs to check the hall of portraits when he remembered something he'd read in the solicitor's report about Miss Thatcher and her family. When the siblings had gone to live with the old duke, he had taken it upon himself to further their education. And while much had been lacking, he'd been pleasantly surprised to discover that each of the children could read quite well. Miss Thatcher herself had taught the younger two, after the duke's daughter—Grace's mother—had taught her.

Perhaps she was in the library. He wondered that he hadn't thought to look there earlier.

His hunch proved right; he found Miss Thatcher there, curled up in a window seat, a book open on her lap as she pressed her face to the leaded window panes and watched the rain sheeting against the glass.

She turned to look at him as he entered the room, and her lips formed a tentative smile. He could tell she was attempting to assess his mood, with no luck. When her smile ceased and she began nibbling on her lip, he forced the corners of his mouth up in hopes that she would not flee before him.

Her shoulders relaxed, but she made no move to rise and greet him, instead tracking his progress with wary eyes as he crossed the room. Nicholas settled in the chair nearest her.

"You did not eat this afternoon." To his own ears, he sounded stern, as if scolding a little child.

"I had an apple." She held up the core as evidence. "I'm sorry if my lack of appetite displeases you. Oft when I am reading, I forget myself, my surroundings, even the time—and the need to eat."

Nicholas cleared his throat, attempting a tone less harsh. "What are you reading?"

"Chaucer." She turned the spine so that he might see. "You've a wonderful library," she added. "I hope it is all right if I make use of it."

"A far better use of time than acquiring leaves for your hair." His words came out stiffly, though he'd intended them to be humorous.

"Do you enjoy reading, milord?" Sitting up, she turned to better face him.

"I used to," Nicholas said, recalling rainy afternoons, not unlike this one, when he and Elizabeth had sprawled on the library floor, reading to each other or listening to the deep timbre of their father's voice as he shared a story. "Now I find I have time only for reading correspondence."

"How unfortunate for you," Miss Thatcher said, her voice full of sympathy. "I have found that a good book can cure almost any ailment."

"How so?" Nicholas leaned forward, eager to hear such sage—and absurd—wisdom.

"Well," she began, clutching the volume of poetry to her chest. "On a day like today, when the world seems entirely dreary, one can read of other places full of sunshine and beauty and imagine himself there. Or—" Her eyes alight, she scooted closer to the edge of the seat and leaned forward, warming to her topic. "If one's life is dull, he can immerse himself in adventure—fighting alongside the knights of the Round Table, slaying Cyclops with Odysseus, or leading an army against the traitor Macbeth."

Nicholas's brows rose in consternation. "This is what you aspire to?"

"Reading is not about aspiring to anything," Miss Thatcher explained. "It is about *enjoying.* Did you ever wish to be someone—or somewhere—else? Have you never dreamed? Hasn't a book ever made you *feel* something other than what you are at that very moment?"

He considered before giving his answer. "Not since I was a child. Are stories and imagination not for the young?"

"Of course," she said. "But why can those grown not enjoy them as well? Why should I not thrill at a beautiful poem or fear as I imagine the Trojans drawing near? Why should I not paint a picture in my mind from the description of a sunrise over the ocean or know what it is to hear a lover's whispered endearments?"

Nicholas's frown deepened at the conclusion of her impassioned speech. Could he have found himself betrothed to a woman any more different than he? She spoke of adventure and poetry and romance and obviously longed for a life filled with such things. He knew only the weight of responsibility and grief and revenge. Even if he had wanted their match to work, there could be no meeting in the middle that he could tell. Theirs was no ideal pairing.

But with Preston . . . she would find much happiness. As would he with her.

Nicholas pushed the thought away quickly. The last thing he wanted was to give the man a gift like that, like the remarkable woman sitting before him.

What other choice do I have?

Miss Thatcher's gaze had turned downcast, and silently she resumed her position at the window, staring out at the pouring rain. Nicholas realized that she'd probably taken his silence as a reprimand, though he hadn't intended it that way. He'd come in search of her to set right their discussion yesterday, but instead he'd upset her, likely because he didn't swoon over books the way she did.

"Just like Elizabeth," he muttered, then realized what he'd said and wished to take the words back. *No one* was like his sister. No one could ever be as good as she'd been, as full of life, as giving and loving.

But it was possible, he reluctantly admitted, that Grace loved books and stories the way Elizabeth had. Grace appreciated them and allowed them to brighten her life.

And it will need brightening here, if she is to stay for any length of time.

Nicholas left his chair and went to retrieve a book from one of the shelves. He didn't particularly care which one. He hadn't come to read and needed only a few minutes to decide how to best approach Miss Thatcher, now that they'd started off wrong again.

Women. He studied this one, engrossed in her book, her lips upturned and a dimple in her cheek that he hadn't noticed before.

Her hair was swept up today in an appropriate, if not fashionable, knot. He doubted that the new maid he'd brought in for her—the washerwoman's daughter who'd been retrieved from Lancashire—knew much about doing hair. She was too young to have been a lady's maid before, so he couldn't expect her to be able to assist Miss Thatcher with the latest styles. Yet he couldn't abide Miss Thatcher wearing her hair down, either. Aside from the fact that no grown women that he knew of wore her hair down, seeing Grace's curls was a temptation he could not trust himself to resist. And resist he must—every last circumstance involving Miss Grace Thatcher.

He would simply have to hire someone else if he wished to see her hair done properly. A dreary prospect. He'd no desire to interview for a new servant. He realized quite suddenly that he would need a few. His mother would soon arrive and see the state of the grounds and house—and probably become apoplectic. He'd need more maids, a footman or two at the least, and someone to care for the gardens . . .

He would have to stay a while to begin to set things right. All because of the woman before him.

Miss Thatcher must have felt his stare, because her attention finally left her book and she turned to regard him. "Was there something you wanted?" she asked. "The way you are staring at me is quite rude."

Nicholas worked to keep a smile at bay. Only one other woman had ever been so direct with him—and she had been family. *I don't want a reminder of Elizabeth around,* he told himself again. But he was pleased that despite his threats of yesterday, Miss Thatcher did not seem to overly fear him.

"You flatter yourself, Miss Thatcher. I was only looking out the window—a great deal of which you are blocking—and imagining the grounds as they were in better days."

"Are there not several windows in this room, all of which look outside to your overgrown yard?" She swung her legs over the side of the seat and stood, moving past so quickly that her skirt snapped at his trousers. She chose a seat in the very center of the room and plopped into it, promptly returning her nose to the book.

Nicholas chuckled. He couldn't seem to help himself. Her ire was entertaining. He found in Miss Thatcher a venerable opponent. If nothing else, she was a great distraction to the usual drudgery of life. If he was honest with himself, he had to admit that he had grown tired of trips to London. His relentless pursuit of Preston was wearisome. And though he was beginning to see its fruition, the satisfaction he'd expected to feel was not there.

In comparison, sparring with Miss Thatcher was proving to be more amusement than he'd had in some time. *If I can keep her here a while, and if Preston somehow learns of my enchantment . . .*

The idea held appeal. Perhaps his greatest tool at getting to Preston was right before him. He need only discover how to use it to his best advantage.

Nicholas abandoned any pretense of reading and crossed the room once more, this time to a table before the fire. He glanced at the cards placed there and was struck with sudden inspiration.

"Might I interest you in a game of whist, Miss Thatcher?"

"No." She did not even look up.

"Your outright refusal displeases me," Nicholas said, irked that she had so quickly dismissed his cordial request.

"As does your ignorance of literature, disappoint me." She gave him a brief, pert smile.

"I am not ignorant," Nicholas said, his voice raised defensively and sounding the very thing. "I am well read."

"But you do not *enjoy* reading." Miss Thatcher stood and set her book aside. "So I must conclude that you do not gather the meaning intended from these great works acquired in your library." She sighed heavily. "'Tis a sin, really."

He scoffed. "I would not speak of sins, were I you—after spending four nights at Sir Lidgate's home, as you did." He regretted the words the instant they left his mouth.

Miss Thatcher's eyes darkened in a way he had not yet witnessed. No blush of modesty stained her cheeks, and she did not look away from him. Instead, she walked closer, arms down, hands clenched at her sides.

"Lidgate is a monster. Had I known as much, I would never have gone to his home—no matter what—" Her voice caught. "—my father's woes." Her hands shook.

"Every minute I was there, my virtue was in danger. I wore my cloak indoors, pretending a chill, to be covered from his prying eyes. I moved furniture in front of my bedroom door at night to keep him out. I even purposely fell from a horse so he would believe me injured and leave me alone."

"You were injured, weren't you? And did he not leave you alone?" Nicholas asked quietly, his own hands clenching, itching to find their way around Lidgate's neck.

Miss Thatcher looked at him a long moment but did not respond.

"Honesty," Nicholas said quietly. "We are betrothed. I have a right to know if—"

"My virtue is quite intact." Her face stained pink with the confession. "If you do not believe me, find the doctor who came to Sir Lidgate's house. Though I suffered only bruises, he agreed to tell Sir Lidgate that the fall had most likely rendered me unable to bear children." She looked away. "I paid him to say it."

"You paid . . ."

Miss Thatcher nodded. "Quite handsomely. It took the remainder of my funds and some of Miranda's and Harrison's salaries too."

Nicholas walked to the fireplace and brought a hand to his mouth as he leaned against the mantel, considering her words. It was a tale considerably different from what he'd been led to believe. Yet her embarrassment while telling it rang true.

"What was Lidgate's reaction upon receiving the news that you could not produce an heir?" Nicholas knew; he'd learned that much from the solicitor: He hadn't offered for her.

And I threw it back at her yesterday.

Miss Thatcher was looking at him again. Her cheeks had returned to their normal color, and when she spoke, there was a coolness to her voice as well. "When Sir Lidgate was told I could not bear his child, he no longer wanted me for his wife."

"So you left—and came here?" Nicholas asked.

"Yes." She nodded and looked back at her book, then over to the door, as if deciding which escape to choose.

Something about her story didn't fit. Nicholas felt certain he was missing something—an important piece of information. "Did Lidgate throw you out?" he asked. "The very night of your injury?"

Miss Thatcher sighed wearily. "He did not."

"Then why your arrival here in the dead of night?" This was it. And it had to tie back to Miss Thatcher's plotting with Preston. *I have her now.*

"Shortly before ten o'clock in the evening, I left with my maid, Miranda. We walked to the road. Harrison, my driver, met us there with the coach."

"But *why*?" Nicholas pressed. "Had you planned a meeting with Preston?"

"No." Miss Thatcher's brow drew together as if she was entirely perplexed by the suggestion. "I have already explained; I did not know Mr. Preston, though I was attempting to travel to his home that night."

"But he changed plans on you, didn't he?" Nicholas walked toward her, wagging a finger, ready to pounce now that he had her caught in the trap.

She lifted her head and stared at him straight on. "The only *change* was Lidgate's desire for me as his wife. Unfortunately his other desires did not alter. He offered me a position as his mistress. He planned to come to my room at midnight to introduce me to my 'duties.' And so, I fled."

Nicholas muttered a word not fit for her ears and turned away, already plotting the various methods he might use to murder Lidgate should the man ever darken his doorstep or any other place Nicholas happened to be.

And what of me? Have I been much better to her than Lidgate? He wanted to think that he had, but his conscience told him otherwise.

The way I appraised her in the study, the accusations I've made—at least some are true, aren't they? But the way I shouted at her and detained her that night in my room . . .

If she'd just come from Lidgate's, it was little wonder she had been so terrified that night.

Nicholas raked a hand through his hair, more distraught than he'd believed he could be at Miss Thatcher's misfortune. *And at my poor conduct. At Lidgate's behavior.*

But what if Miss Thatcher was not being entirely truthful? What if they'd been more than attempts on Lidgate's part? He couldn't blame her for not revealing everything. What if she *had* been ill used by Lidgate? What would a woman who was already compromised have to lose by leaving Lidgate and going elsewhere?

Nothing. And she would have everything to gain in any man even slightly better than Lidgate. Perhaps this was where Preston came in. Perhaps she had fled to him and told him everything, and then, together, they had found a way to foist the blame elsewhere. To turn the deed to their advantage.

Instead of feeling furious at the possibility, Nicholas felt a surge of sympathy for Miss Thatcher and anger on her behalf.

"What are you thinking?" she asked. "I've never seen so many emotions cross a person's face so quickly. It is making me a little dizzy."

"Do not faint on me again," Nicholas warned. "Or we shall be right back where we started, with you waking and asking what I have done, when in truth, I've done nothing at all."

"Nor have I, milord. Though I believe I yet read censure in your eyes."

"I wasn't thinking of you," Nicholas said. "But of Lidgate. Of what I'll—"

"He did not touch me." She stood and walked forward until she was quite close; Nicholas could have reached out and easily touched her. "Believe me—please." It was the most pleading tone he had ever heard from her. "I left before he could hurt me and later arrived at your doorstep, a muddy mess and quite ill, but all in all, much better off than I would have been."

"Until we met later that night," Nicholas said.

She nodded, and he caught her slight flinch at the memory.

"A rather bad beginning," Nicholas summed up.

"The worst," she agreed.

He swallowed uneasily, aware of her nearness and uncertain what he should do or say, though somehow an apology seemed in order. "Perhaps we should begin our acquaintance anew."

She looked up at him through her long, dark lashes. "A new beginning?"

"I believe so." He tugged at his cravat, aware that the room had grown very warm, though the fire burned low. "I will leave and return again to make an introduction."

She smiled, amused. "Truly?"

"Yes." He would have rather left and not returned, retreating to the safety of his study, where he might sort out his confusion. But he could think of no other way to begin to right the many wrongs he had done her other than to go back—as much as were possible—and begin anew.

Nicholas gave a slight bow and left the room, feeling her eyes following him. In the hall, he waited a moment, wondering what on earth he might say when he returned.

This charade is quite possibly my worst idea yet.

With a deep breath, he returned to the library and, with resolute steps, marched toward Miss Thatcher seated exactly as she had been the first time he'd entered, her face pressed to the windowpane, the open book in her lap. He stopped before her and cleared his throat. She turned to him, her hazel eyes sparkling with amusement.

This is ridiculous. I *must look ridiculous.*

"Miss Thatcher." He bowed before her. She rose and extended her hand. He took it, pressing his lips just above her knuckles, noting that her skin was not as smooth as that of most well-bred ladies.

She must have noticed his distraction, for she tugged her hand away and tucked it, with the other, behind her back. "Lord Sutherland, it is a pleasure to make your acquaintance." She curtsied.

He'd expected mirth but heard only sincerity in her voice. "And yours," Nicholas said, finding that he meant it. He turned sideways and inclined his head toward the card table. "Might I pry you from your book and convince you to join me in a game of whist?"

She shook her head. "No, thank you."

He frowned. "This is a new beginning, remember?" He spoke from the side of his mouth through clenched teeth, as if that somehow did not count as part of their new dialogue.

"I have an aversion to card games of any sort," she explained. "They have been at the root of many of my troubles."

"Ahh," Nicholas said, understanding—somewhat. He could have argued that it was her father's lack of self-control that was the root of her troubles, but he did not wish to start another argument. Already he could see that this arrangement of pleasantness was much preferred. "Chess, perhaps?" he suggested, suddenly loath to leave her company.

Her face lit up. "Oh yes. Grandfather and I used to play."

He extended his arm and escorted her to the board. As he held out her chair and she seated herself, the thought came to Nicholas that he had not yet mentioned that there was a possible way out of their betrothal. This would be the perfect time to discuss it—while they were being civil.

He imagined Preston seated across from her instead, being the recipient of more than just her fleeting and wary smiles. Knowing his former brother-in-law as he did, Nicholas guessed that it would take very little for Preston to take Miss Thatcher back.

All the more reason to keep her here a week or two, Nicholas reasoned. He was no longer certain of Miss Thatcher's involvement in a plot against him, but that didn't mean he liked Preston any more.

I should let him wonder, let him suffer, knowing she is here. There would be time enough later to be free of the betrothal. Nicholas told himself he would begin the process when his mother arrived. *But until then—*

He admired the head of dark hair bent over the chessboard.

Until then, he would enjoy a break from his usual labors.

CHAPTER 20

My Dearest Grace,

Christopher has gone to London again to meet with the solicitor about the inheritance, and Miranda and Harrison are taking very good care of me. It is you we are all worried over. So it pains me to make this request—yet I must. Will you do your best to endure your circumstance at Sutherland Hall a little longer? Father's anger will not abate, but if he believes your Lord Sutherland to still be a possible source for income, then I am yet safe . . .

"I shall lose my mind if I don't find something more to do here." Grace balanced her toes on the edge of the bench, then braced her hands on the stone fence and pushed off, swaying upright then leaning forward to push off the wall again as had been her habit the past several minutes.

Samuel looked down on her from his seat on the wall above. "You do realize that if you fall off that bench and break your leg, I'll have the difficult choice of leaving you here to suffer or facing the wrath of your betrothed and admitting to our trysts."

"Don't call them that." Grace ceased her rocking and looked up at him. "This is not a tryst. You and I are but friends."

"So I am reminded every time we part," Samuel grumbled.

Grace jumped off the bench and began walking away from it. "If this is too difficult, I will not come anymore. I can find another way to post Helen's letters."

"No." Samuel's answer was immediate and nearly as sharp as some of Lord Sutherland's replies. Though coming from Samuel, the tone affected her more.

"What is wrong with you today?" Grace returned to stand before him, leaning back so she might better see his expression. "Are you not the one who has been encouraging me to make the most of my circumstance, to try to be on good terms with Lord Sutherland?"

Samuel gave another one-syllable response. "Aye." He drew his knee up to his chest and set his chin upon it, brooding. "Perhaps I was too generous in my original advice. Can you not make the man despise you—cause him to throw you out of his house so you come running to mine?"

"And have Father throw Helen to the nearest shark?" Grace asked. "No, thank you. You realize that I must stay here—for now," she added softly at his forlorn expression.

Grace turned away so he could not guess her own conflicted emotions. There were times—like these when they met at the wall and talked—when she knew she wished for release from her betrothal and the chance to be courted in earnest by the one she found so pleasing to be with.

But there were other times with Lord Sutherland when she felt almost content with her lot and wished she need not find a way out of it. She wondered what would happen if she allowed herself to have feelings for him instead of always keeping her guard up and harboring secret plans of departure in the back of her mind.

Much had served to soften her heart toward him: Late

nights spent facing each other across the chessboard. Discussions at dinner revolving around her daily reading. Their differing opinions on selections they had both read. And the small kindnesses he showed—be that offering her the last piece of bread, extending his arm to her as they went down the stairs, or even his displays of anger at past wrongs done to her.

But it was her heart she needed most to protect.

Lately she had started worrying over Lord Sutherland's heart, as well. She feared that he needed her, though he did not yet realize it. Samuel had suggested as much at their first meeting. She had not wanted to hear it then; she did not want to think about it now.

Or about Samuel, either. He would have been so easy to love. *And he would have taken care with my heart.* He was the first man she had ever known whom she might have trusted it with. But she hadn't that luxury. As soon as possible, she needed to take Helen and Christopher away.

"Don't leave," Samuel said. "I'm sorry." He swung his legs down on her side of the wall and leaned forward as if he meant to jump down.

Only then did Grace realize how far she had strayed from the wall. She moved closer to it—to him—shaking her finger. "You stay on your side, remember?"

"Bossy today, aren't we?" But his usual smile was back in place, and he leaned to his side once more. "Let's see, before my burst of selfish melancholy, we were searching out ways for you to avoid death by boredom or madness from such."

"Yes," Grace said, relieved that the Samuel she had come to know these past two weeks was returned. She did not think she could abide the other. Having one man in her life given to moodiness was plenty.

"Have you considered stitchery?" Samuel asked. "I hear it is all the rage, and the most prestigious ladies do it."

Grace held out her hands. "Too many years of hard

work in these for them to be suitable for delicate embroidery. Though I shouldn't mind making a new dress."

"There you have it," Samuel said. "Just tell Nicholas you'd like to sew a dress, and see what he does. I'll bet you'll be busy in no time—at the dressmaker's. It would not be befitting the status of any Sutherland woman to make her own clothing."

Grace frowned. "I am not a Sutherland." *Yet.* The panic that came over her whenever she dwelt on the possibility of actually marrying Lord Sutherland reared its head. She pushed it firmly to the back of her mind. Christopher and the solicitor would soon have everything resolved with the inheritance. In the meantime, Lord Sutherland had not mentioned another word about their betrothal, and while she could not hope that he had forgotten, until he brought it up again, she was doing her best to pretend it did not exist.

"I do not want him to purchase anything for me—not a dress, or even fabric to make one. He's already spent enough to protect Helen."

"I'll pay for it," Samuel said.

Grace rolled her eyes. "Can you imagine Lord Sutherland's expression when he compliments me on my dress and I tell him, 'This gown is courtesy of Mr. Preston.' You'd hear his shouting all the way in your drawing room."

"Does he still yell a lot?" Samuel asked, his eyes darkening with the concern Grace found so endearing.

"Not so much," she said. "We are learning to tolerate each other and which topics to avoid."

"And does he compliment you on your gowns?" Samuel persisted.

"Yes." Grace smiled wistfully as she recalled Lord Sutherland's lingering gaze the night before, when he had met her on the stairs to escort her to dinner. She hadn't mistaken the approval in his eyes. And never once since that first awful afternoon in his study had he looked at her inappropriately or in any fashion resembling the way Sir

Lidgate had. His compliments were sincere and plentiful. She felt beautiful in his presence, but never in a way that was degrading. Equally sincere and frequent were his compliments on her observations from the books she read and on her strategy when, on the rare occasion, she bested him at chess.

Though she did not see Lord Sutherland much during the day, their time together each evening had evolved into something pleasant.

Not unlike my afternoons in the garden with Samuel, she realized with some discomfort.

"You are lost in thought," Samuel said. "Apparently his compliments leave you much to contemplate." He sounded wistful again, and a glance upward confirmed that he was having difficulty keeping his usual good nature about him.

"Tell me more about Elizabeth," Grace said.

His wife had become a favorite topic for them—a *safe* topic. Personal, but not in such a way as to endanger their fast-formed friendship, propelling it toward something more. Grace could tell that it did Samuel good to speak of Elizabeth, and learning about her helped Grace understand both Samuel and Lord Sutherland. "What would she have done on a day like today?"

"Many things," Samuel said. "Today is her birthday. You should be aware that Nicholas will likely be in a mood."

When is he not?

"As are you," Grace said, then regretted her words at once. "I *am* sorry. You've every right to be sad, especially today." She wished Samuel had told her the reason for his melancholy sooner.

"But not every day," Samuel said with a glance over his shoulder. "In many ways life has been good to me. I meant what I told you at the ball—my time here has been the happiest of my life, sorrows notwithstanding."

"What has made it so happy?" Grace urged. "What did you and Elizabeth do for amusement?"

Samuel gave her a rather pointed look, followed by a smirk.

"Oh." Grace turned away with a flounce of her skirts. "What did *she* do for amusement *before* she married you?"

He laughed. "I did not say a word, yet you assume the worst of me."

She faced him once again, hands on her hips. "You did not need to say anything. I know the look of a scoundrel when I see one."

"I am wounded," Samuel cried, clutching his chest. "And guilty," he admitted, hanging his head, but not before Grace caught sight of another roguish grin.

"And *I* am waiting for an answer."

Samuel stroked his chin thoughtfully. "What did Elizabeth do? A bit of everything, I suppose. She and Nicholas rode all over these hills nearly every day—even after we married, she went with him. And she played the pianoforte with such passion that at times I expected it to come crashing through the floor." Samuel grinned with the memory. "And, of course, there was her garden." His hand stretched out, sweeping the air before him. "The ruin of which you see here. How I wish that Nicholas had kept it up. I have Elizabeth's yellow roses, but they are nothing to the grandeur this place used to hold."

Samuel's gaze turned distant, or perhaps inward, and Grace recognized this as one of those times that silence between them was best. For all the three years that had passed since Elizabeth's death, and for all that Samuel preached about living life to its fullest as his wife would have wanted, Grace could see that he still suffered.

At times like these, she wanted to reach out to him, to be the one to comfort, to fill the emptiness in his heart.

But I cannot.

Into the silence came another sound, so gradual that at first Grace was not certain she had heard correctly. But it came again—a child's voice, sweet and innocent and filled with infectious laughter.

"Do you hear that?" She dared to break their silent reverie, guessing it would be broken soon by the approaching voices. There were two now—the child's and what sounded to be a distraught nanny calling the little one back.

"I must go," Samuel said, swinging his legs to the opposite side of the fence.

"Why?" Grace asked. "Who is it?"

A peculiar expression flitted across his face, giving Grace the impression that he was engaged in an internal debate. The child's voice grew closer so that Grace could make the words out.

"Daddy! I want to be up there too, Daddy."

Grace gasped. "You have—"

A silent plea emerged from the depths of Samuel's eyes, and sudden understanding dawned on Grace.

"He does not know," she whispered. "Lord Sutherland does not know that he . . . is an uncle."

"Please, don't tell him," Samuel pled. "Not for my sake, but for Beth's."

"Of course," Grace said, still reeling with his secret herself. "I give you my word. I will not tell Lord Sutherland of your daughter."

CHAPTER 21

Dearest Helen,

How I miss you. My days here are terribly lonely . . .

No doubt a rusted saw was not the best implement for pruning rosebushes and cutting back overgrown trees. But it was all Grace could find, so she set to work, determined to be done with her idleness and boredom and to become strong once more. And, most importantly, to do something good for both Lord Sutherland and Mr. Preston, both of whom she believed would benefit from the garden being cared for again.

Not that she knew much about caring for a garden.

The meager patch of ground beneath the wash line at their house in London had never yielded much, blocked from the sun by the clothing strung there as it had been most of the time. One summer or two, she'd tried to grow a few vegetables but had eventually given up, knowing that her time was better spent doing the washing and ironing that brought the needed money to purchase their food.

Beyond trimming the dead branches and tidying the

paths, Grace could not think of what else Elizabeth's garden would need. She hoped Lord Sutherland's library might provide an answer, and when she'd finished with the wild-growing rosebushes along the drive, she intended to search for a book on the care of flowers and shrubs.

With vigor, she set to cutting back the most brittle branches, those obviously long dead, those poking out at odd angles, the ones most liable to catch the clothes of one walking by. Working this way and that, climbing on top of a crate she'd discovered the saw in, and bending beneath the lowest branches, Grace pruned the first bush until she deemed it acceptable. She stepped onto the drive to admire her work just as a carriage turned onto it.

Grace moved out of the way, lest the carriage bear one of Lord Sutherland's important and impatient visitors from the city. They were oft in a hurry to arrive and in even a greater hurry to leave again. Though many had to travel a great distance, none stayed long at Sutherland Hall.

She took up the broom she'd brought with her, also found in the shed behind the kitchen, and swept cuttings as the carriage passed. Grace was surprised to see the Sutherland crest on its polished side, but it took two more strokes of the broom before she realized the significance.

"Oh no." Her sweeping ceased, and she turned to the front of the house, where Kingsley, Mrs. James, and Lord Sutherland were just gathering to greet their visitor.

Not a visitor at all. How could I have forgotten that Lord Sutherland's mother was to arrive this week? Illness had delayed the dowager from her original date of arrival—a reprieve Grace had been most grateful for. Becoming accustomed to Lord Sutherland had been difficult enough. The thought of facing his mother was even more daunting.

Grace did her best to shrink into the shadow of a nearby tree—difficult, as it had already shed the majority of its leaves for winter. The carriage stopped, but with its back facing her, she could not see who emerged.

And for the moment, at least, they cannot see me.

Grace hoped the carriage would remain in place long enough for Lord Sutherland and the others to go in. Perhaps then she could go inside to her room, unnoticed, so she might change to a more appropriate gown and make herself presentable.

She had planned to meet with Samuel, to learn more of his daughter, but her curiosity would have to wait. No doubt she would be expected to sit at tea and make polite conversation throughout the afternoon.

"What a bother." Grace crouched behind the tree to wait. She hugged her arms as the chill of the day crept over her. She hadn't noticed it while working, but no doubt Lord Sutherland would flay her if he caught her outside without a cloak.

Minutes dragged by, until at last the landau moved off in the direction of the carriage house. The front steps were empty, the party having gone inside.

Grace tucked the broom and saw behind the tree, reasoning that they were no worse off there than where she'd found them, and hurried up the drive.

She pulled the front door open by degrees, grimacing with every squeak of the hinges. When the opening was just wide enough for her to slip through, she peered inside and felt vast relief at seeing the entry deserted. After slipping inside, she shut the door behind her as quietly as possible, then glanced at the staircase and caught her anxious maid, who was hopping up and down at the top, beckoning for her to come.

Grace held a finger to her lips and tiptoed across the marble floor. She was just placing her foot on the bottom stair when the parlor door opened and voices emerged from within. She did not turn around, but kept her face forward and began a resolute march up the stairs.

"Goodness, Nicholas, who is that?" The high-pitched, unfamiliar voice echoed across the foyer. "Since when do you allow the servants to go traipsing about, looking so disheveled? Have you dismissed the laundresses as well?"

"No, Mother." Lord Sutherland's sigh might have been her own. "Miss Thatcher, come here please."

Grace hung her head in defeat, wishing for all the world she'd chosen any other day to trim the bushes, or any other task to start on.

Why couldn't I have been reading demurely in the library? Or studying the portraits on the walls—or playing whist, even. Anything *but this.*

Slowly, she turned around, smoothing the front of her soiled dress—the one that had been stained with mud the night of the carriage accident and was not suitable for any situation save working in the garden. Grace snatched the kerchief from her head, preferring to risk Lord Sutherland's wrath over having her hair unbound over the humiliation of it being up in a rag.

She retraced her steps down the stairs as Lord Sutherland and his mother drew closer. Kingsley lingered nearby, and Grace was stunned to detect a hint of sympathy in his eyes. For her, or for the dowager, who was now presented with a pitiful excuse for a future daughter-in-law?

Grace forced her eyes to meet the woman's and found an almost mirrored image of Lord Sutherland staring back at her. Deep pools of blue, brimming with displeasure, looked her over, top to bottom. In comparison to Grace's untamed curls and soiled gown, every last hair on the dowager's head lay placidly in place, and her dress had as much starch as if she'd just stepped into it—an impossibility, as the woman had been traveling.

I am in a great deal of trouble. Rather than risk lowering the dowager's opinion of her further by anything she might say, Grace simply curtsied.

Lord Sutherland provided the words—and ample meaning in his tone. "Mother, may I present my intended, Miss *Grace* Thatcher."

CHAPTER 22

"Truly, Nicholas, I cannot understand how you agreed to such a ridiculous demand." His mother had started on him as soon as dinner was over and Grace had left them to retire early, pleading a headache. His gaze strayed through the open drawing room doors and to the base of the staircase. For multiple reasons he wished he could follow.

No doubt her headache was real; his certainly was. Mother and her incessant harping tended to have that effect on people. She was always so serious and stern about everything.

Much like me, he'd realized during dinner when Grace had so kindly pointed out that she recognized where he got many of his best qualities from. He wasn't sure *best* was the appropriate word.

"And I don't see why you—" His mother's berating continued, and, with years of practice, Nicholas effectively ignored her, trusting that he could chime in with an appropriate response when there was a lull in her speech.

Had she always been this way? He quickly concluded that she had. He would have sworn that she and Father—a personality most opposite his mother—had been a good match. She'd kept his mischief in check; he'd lightened her seriousness. Somehow the marriage had worked famously, because Nicholas could not recall any discord in their home during his childhood.

But with Father gone, the tone of their home had changed. With sudden and disturbing clarity, Nicholas realized that Father and Elizabeth had been the light in their home, while he and Mother had tended toward the dark. Left on their own, he imagined they'd flounder in the black for the remainder of their lives.

Unless . . . He oughtn't even entertain the thought. Miss Thatcher was no more a permanent fixture here than the leaves falling from the trees outside. She might last a season or two—until he determined how to best use her against Preston—but then she would be gone, and whatever light she'd brought with her as well.

"How could you agree to marry her, Nicholas?" his mother repeated. "Whatever were you thinking?"

"It was quite simple, Mother." Nicholas jumped into the conversation. "It was that or break my oath to Elizabeth that I would never shoot Preston. He called me out over the girl."

Not the complete truth, but close enough. Nicholas didn't trust his mother to see his view, to understand why he hadn't—why he still couldn't—simply put Miss Thatcher in a carriage and send her over to Preston.

"I don't believe it." The dowager leaned forward in her seat, giving a little stomp to her foot, putting Nicholas in mind of another lady who'd also stomped her foot at him in his study a few weeks earlier.

"I'd not have believed it possible either," Nicholas said. "But I've got it in writing, if you don't believe me. I'd know Preston's hand anywhere, and his words were true enough."

"But you refused to duel?" his mother asked.

"What else could I do?" Nicholas said. "Believe me, I was more than tempted to accept. Only the thought of you,

Mother, and what it might do to you were I to spend the remainder of my days in Newgate—or worse—restrained me."

"You seem overly confident that you would have bested him," she observed, relaxing in her chair once more. "Preston is quite a good shot too, you know."

"Are you trying to tempt me?" Nicholas asked. "I can change my mind yet."

"But you won't." A slight smile lifted the corners of her usually stern mouth. "You loved your sister too much to do that."

She was right, and they both knew it. Even greater than his respect and concern for his mother was the fact that he had given his word. And though Elizabeth was no longer around to see that he kept it, Nicholas intended to honor her by doing just that.

"I might have a way out of the betrothal," Nicholas mentioned casually as he crossed the room, leaving the view of the staircase. He settled in the chair opposite his mother. "I agreed to marry Miss Thatcher *only* if Preston will not have her. According to her father, Preston made an offer."

"Can he be persuaded to take her still?" his mother asked.

Nicholas shrugged. He leaned back in his chair, one leg thrown over the other as if he did not care one way or the other. In truth, he found he was beginning to care a great deal. The longer Miss Thatcher remained, the more he came to know her, the less he wanted Preston to have any part of her at all. "I've not heard a word from him on the matter—aside from the letter calling me out. But knowing of Preston's forgiving manner, I have to imagine he would, especially considering that there was no actual harm to her virtue that night in my bedroom."

Pity that, he thought, his gaze sliding to the doors once more.

"But you've not encouraged anything between the two of them?" his mother asked.

"No." Nicholas's look darkened to match hers. "It is asking a lot of me, to hand over to Preston something that will benefit him."

"Bah." His mother waved her hand dismissively. "What is there to benefit from? Let her shame *him* by running around in a ruined gown and kerchief with dirt on her face. I cannot see that you would be doing him any favors at all by letting him have her."

"Then you are not seeing clearly." Nicholas said. His mother turned her sights on him, her piercing gaze seeing past the facade he'd worked to maintain since her arrival.

"You care for her," she said, mouth hanging open with the last word.

"Not at all," Nicholas said, working hard to banish the image of Grace standing on the stairs, pulling the kerchief from her hair and freeing her chestnut curls to tumble across her shoulders and halfway down her back. He forced his thoughts from her hair to her face, smudged with dirt. And to his dismay, he found his mouth lifting in a smile.

"You *do*," his mother said, seeing right through him. She scooted forward on her chair. "Nicholas, my boy, this is serious. Something must be done at once. This—Miss Thatcher—is the last woman you should marry."

He let her words settle and knock some sense into him. She was right, of course. He did not wish to marry. He wished to destroy Preston, something he'd had trouble focusing on of late.

"What do you propose?" he asked, truly directing his attention to his mother for the first time all evening. "I cannot just hand her over to Preston. Despite what you have seen, Miss Thatcher has her merits. I've no doubt she could make him very happy."

And I don't want him happy. I want him as miserable as I am.

It was a startling revelation. Nicholas had never acknowledged his thoughts so precisely, but he realized how true they were, and how likely it was that he would never know their success. From the first day after Elizabeth's death, Preston had seemed almost stoic in his determination to press forward. Had Nicholas not witnessed Preston's grief firsthand at Elizabeth's deathbed and on two occasions at her grave, he would not have been believed the man had been saddened by his loss at all. Preston was yet of a happy disposition, and he seemed inclined to retain it no matter that death had stolen that which was most precious to him.

He will never be miserable like I am, though I might take everything from him. What would the loss of Preston's income or estate mean, compared to the loss of his wife? *Very little,* Nicholas realized, and his own despair deepened.

"Nicholas? Nicholas, have you been listening? Have you heard a word I've said?" His mother had moved to the sofa beside his chair, and her hand was placed over his arm lovingly. He could not mistake the concern in her eyes. "You are not well," she said. "Miss Thatcher has bewitched you. Look at you—unable to even have a proper conversation."

He patted his mother's hand. "I am well enough, Mother." Better than he had been for some time, if he was being honest. "What do you suggest I do?" This time, he vowed to keep his attention on her.

"You are determined to not give her to Preston?"

Nicholas considered for a long moment. "I do not think I can," he said. "To see the man with more of happiness when . . ."

"When we are both so miserable," she said.

"Yes," Nicholas agreed. "We *are* both miserable, Mother. Why is that? Can nothing be done about it?"

"Of course." She smiled, but her eyes remained dark. Nicholas felt sad to see it. Father had been her light. He doubted very much that anyone or anything could replace it for her. "Now then." Her lips pursed in concentration. "If you do not want Preston to have her, and you have given your word, then our only solution is for Miss Thatcher to cry off."

"She won't," Nicholas predicted. "You've not met her father. Any situation will be better for her than returning to him."

"You give up too easily," Mother countered. She stood and crossed the room to the bell pull, then gave it a tug.

Less than a minute later, Kingsley appeared. He'd been close by, no doubt, knowing the dowager's demands as he did.

"Please pour out for us. The sherry, I think," Mother said.

"Of course, milady." Kingsley bowed and walked to the sideboard to do her bidding.

Nicholas realized he needed to hire more servants, and fast, now that his mother was in residence. Demanding as she was, she'd have both Kingsley and Mrs. James worn clear through with exhaustion in no time at all.

Kingsley placed their drinks on a tray and brought them over. Mother stood to take hers, and Nicholas followed suit.

"We must make life so miserable for Miss Thatcher that she leaves of her own accord. Whether or not she returns to her father is her own concern." Mother raised her glass. "To sending Miss Thatcher packing."

Nicholas lifted his glass, and the crystal clinked together briefly. His mother brought the drink to her lips, draining it quickly. But Nicholas turned away, lost in thought, and did not drink at all.

CHAPTER 23

My Dearest Grace,

Christopher writes that he has made little headway in our case. The courts are so terribly slow, and we are so unimportant. I beg of you, be patient a little longer. Stay at Sutherland Hall . . .

Exactly five minutes before the hour, Grace left her room. She walked down the hall and began descending the stairs, her trepidation growing with each step. If she'd thought the situation strained between her and Lord Sutherland before, it felt ten times worse now that his mother had arrived. The prospect of facing the dowager again—and her firestorm of criticism—was only slightly better, or perhaps slightly worse, than the idea of facing a dragon.

Grace imagined the dowager's sour face on a dragon's body, complete with green scales and belching fire. The image brought a smile just as she entered the dining room.

"Good morning," she said pleasantly, as if there were no

other place in the world she'd rather be or people she'd rather be with.

"Good—morning." Lord Sutherland's response was stilted.

Grace could tell her cheery greeting had caught him off guard. Mornings, she had noticed, were not the best for him. It seemed almost as if it took the whole of each day for his temperament to mellow into the cordiality they enjoyed each evening.

And then we start all over again the next day. She sighed inwardly, weary already for the effort of the day.

The dowager, of course, said nothing by way of greeting but deigned to glance up from her plate of eggs.

They did not wait for me. Grace felt the intended slight. Though she knew she'd arrived for breakfast on time, Lord Sutherland and his mother had decided to eat earlier.

Without me.

She pretended not to notice and graciously accepted the platters Kingsley brought to her. Now that the dowager was in residence, serving oneself breakfast from the sideboard was, apparently, no longer acceptable. Grace knew she wasn't the only one suffering from the older woman's presence. The staff had to be more overworked than ever. Yet, oddly, there seemed to be a bounce in Kingsley's step. When he leaned over to pour her juice, she almost thought he had a bit of a merry twinkle in his eyes. And he'd taken to acknowledging her and even given her a brief smile—once.

"Did you sleep well?" Lord Sutherland asked.

Grace nodded. *Leave it to him to wait to address me just when I've a mouthful of toast.*

"Quite," she managed after forcing the bite down too quickly.

"Good." He looked directly at her. "Then I thought we might take a ride around the estate today. If you're to be mistress of Sutherland Hall, you ought to know the land and people living here."

"I should like that very much," Grace said, half-wondering if this was another ploy to scare her off. Lady Sutherland had certainly taken pains to do so since her arrival. But she and Lord Sutherland did not understand that no matter what attempts they made at making Grace miserable, they would not meet with success.

Not yet, anyway. I cannot *leave. No matter how much I may wish to.* Helen's safety depended upon it.

"Will we be riding or taking a carriage?"

"*You* ride?" The dowager peered down her long nose.

"Yes," Grace said, struggling to keep her tone light. "Grandfather taught me—or, rather, saw to it that I had lessons when I came to live with him."

"That must have been lovely." The dowager's words rang as false as her smile. "To go from a life of poverty and hard labor to wealth and luxury, overnight. You are a fortunate girl, indeed."

"I was *most* fortunate that Grandfather found me," Grace readily agreed, earning another look of surprise from Lord Sutherland. "And it *was* wonderful," she continued, meeting the dowager's stare. "To go from a house where I was seen as a burden, where my only value was as a possession to be sold off, to live in a home where I was appreciated and loved—I suspect that may be the only time in my life I shall ever enjoy such an experience." She pushed her chair back and stood before Kingsley could cross the room to assist her. "If you'll excuse me, I fear I've lost my appetite." She turned to Lord Sutherland. "Shall I change into my riding habit, or—"

"The curricle will do today," he said, his tone even more brusque than usual.

Grace cringed, upset with herself for inciting his bad temper so early in the day. If only she had kept hers, but it seemed an impossible feat around his mother.

And now as punishment, I shall have to endure his bad temper for hours. She pressed her lips together and nodded.

"I shall await you outside." Before either could protest her rude departure, she turned and walked from the room.

She'd just entered the foyer when Lord Sutherland's scolding words reached her ears.

"You shouldn't have chided her like that, Mother."

Grace stifled a shocked gasp. And though the remainder of the conversation was lost to her as she marched briskly across the marble floor, she felt the tiniest catch in her heart.

He defended me.

Perhaps things were not as hopeless as they seemed.

"Our closest tenants are a ways out," Nicholas said, snapping the reins. Obediently, the horses began a slow trot down the drive, lined this morning with workers busy pulling weeds and hoeing gravel back into place.

Didn't want Miss Thatcher attempting that next, he'd reasoned as an excuse for why he was bothering to clean up the lane. Neither did he wish her attacking his sister's roses as she had last week. He'd employed a dozen gardeners to see that she'd never have reason to again.

"I suggest we use the time before us to become better acquainted."

Miss Thatcher looked sideways at him, as if she didn't at all believe he was in earnest.

Why should she? Nicholas acknowledged. *I've been nothing but curt with her since Mother's arrival.* He tried again. "As we are betrothed, I believe it prudent we know about each other—our backgrounds and upbringing at the least."

Miss Thatcher coughed into her hand. "Really, Lord Sutherland? I am quite certain you know all about me that you wish to know—probably *more* than you wish."

"None of which I've heard from you." He glanced at her, his gaze lingering on her face a second longer than necessary. *How much better were she plain,* he thought for probably the twentieth time. Instead, each day they were together, the more he became aware of her beauty.

When he'd first taken a place at her side at Preston's ball and she'd looked up at him, he'd scarcely believed Miss Thatcher to be the same woman he'd discovered in his room. Her wide, shocked eyes had looked the same—albeit brighter than he'd remembered—but all else seemed changed, from her fitted gown and pink cheeks to the tempting curls adorning her head. To put it mildly, he'd been stunned.

And he'd known at once what Preston found so attractive.

It had been easier than Nicholas had thought to take her hand and claim her as his own—for the evening, anyway. He certainly hadn't planned on what had come after. But moments like this, with her sweet scent and those pouting lips so close, he almost didn't regret their situation.

Almost.

As if she was aware of his thoughts, Miss Thatcher shrank away, practically hugging the far side of the buggy. "What do you wish to know?"

"Tell me of your family," Nicholas said, his attention again directed to the road, where it had best stay. *It wouldn't do to have an accident—with the carriage or otherwise. That's what started this whole mess.*

Sometime during the past weeks, he'd come to believe that Miss Thatcher had spoken the truth about not knowing Preston and had not, in fact, plotted with him at all. Her presence at Sutherland Hall had been completely by accident, and then, at the insistence of her father. The initial anger Nicholas had felt toward her had dimmed considerably.

"Tell me where you've lived and traveled. What your life was like before and after you met your grandfather." His questions were sincere; her comment at breakfast had piqued his interest.

He hadn't intended on having this conversation when he'd asked Miss Thatcher to go driving this morning. He'd hoped, at his mother's suggestion, to show her just how out of her element she would be here. How much better it would be for her to return to her father, and for both of them to forget that this whole thing had ever happened. His mother believed that if Grace saw the difficulty of her life here, saw that she could never be accepted—even by his own tenants—that she couldn't handle the responsibilities of being mistress over such an estate, then this little charade would soon be over.

But just now, for a few short hours, Nicholas didn't want to think about any of that. He wanted to know the woman next to him for who she really was. Which, he'd begun to realize, wasn't at all who he'd believed her to be.

"You've already had the misfortune to meet my father." Miss Thatcher spoke as if she had a bitter taste in her mouth. "I cannot imagine you wish to know more of him."

"No," Nicholas agreed. "I cannot say that I do. But what of your mother—the duke's daughter?"

"She never lived as a duke's daughter when I knew her," Miss Thatcher said. "She was a mother who loved her children unfailingly, who did all she could for them in spite of our wretched circumstances."

"She is deceased?" Nicholas knew as much already. It had been in the solicitor's report.

"She died when I was eight." Miss Thatcher stared straight ahead, her voice devoid of emotion. "Consumption, the doctor said, but I always thought she died of a broken heart. My grandfather had been against the match and threatened to disown her if she went through with it. But my mother loved my father—don't ask me why," she said, glancing at Nicholas. "They ran away and were married. Grandfather was furious and refused to give them a penny. After that happened Father suddenly failed to return her affection. He marched Mother off to the nearest slum, and they took up residence there."

"And still your grandfather did not intervene?" Nicholas asked uncomfortably. He could well imagine the man's wrath against George Thatcher, but wouldn't his heart have softened toward his daughter? Would he have held a grudge, knowing how it hurt his only child?

"He never attempted to find Mother," Miss Thatcher said. "He did not even know of her death. It wasn't until many years later—after he'd become quite ill himself and experienced a change of heart—that he determined to find her."

"And found you instead," Nicholas said.

"Yes." Miss Thatcher smiled, likely recalling one of her few good memories. "I was eighteen."

She survived ten years with only her father for support. "But what did you do after your mother's death?" Nicholas asked, trying to push aside the image of an eight-year-old girl weeping over her dead mother. "How did you manage without her?" From what he'd seen of George Thatcher, he could not imagine the man had been a particularly attentive parent.

"I did what she asked me to," Miss Thatcher said, sitting a little taller in the seat. "I promised Mother that I would take care of my younger siblings, Helen and Christopher, and so I have. So I *am*," she said pointedly, this time more than glancing his way. "It is the *only* reason I agreed to my father's scheme of finding a husband. It was the only way to protect Helen."

"So you do admit it *was* a scheme?" Nicholas didn't intend to sound angry, but he knew she'd think it of him.

"I never said it wasn't." Miss Thatcher turned in the seat, facing him. "I only said that *you* were not a part of it. Blame your involvement on a stormy night or a broken carriage wheel or . . . on me." She sighed. "I speak the truth when I say that I am as regretful as you are of our situation."

He knew she was being truthful, and it bothered him. No doubt she wished she'd ended up with Preston. The thought rankled, as did the fact that Miss Thatcher didn't appreciate her circumstances, did not realize how fortunate she was

Fortunate to have landed in my bed.

He was not a monster like Lidgate. Since that first stormy afternoon in his study, Nicholas had treated her with respect. She was safe and well cared for. And if they did marry, she could have anything she wanted, any luxury life afforded, and yet—

She loathes me.

Nicholas very much wanted to know why and suspected it all circled back to her father. "What did your father do after your mother died?" he asked, steering the subject away from the present and purposefully softening his tone.

"The same thing he's always done," Miss Thatcher said, turning away from Nicholas again. "He gambled."

"But his profess—"

She gave a harsh laugh. "Gambling *is* his profession. Or so he's always said. He's never worked long elsewhere."

Nicholas arched a brow, disbelieving. "And he was able to support a family on his winnings?"

"Of course not," she scoffed. "Mother supported us. And when she died, *I* did."

How was on the tip of Nicholas's tongue, but he dared not ask. Miss Thatcher had proclaimed her virtue, yet there were limited ways a woman could support herself in this world, none of them pleasant. A sick feeling formed in Nicholas's stomach. He didn't want to think of Miss Thatcher's being involved in those sort of things.

And from age eight.

"Mother was a washerwoman," she said, not sounding the least bit ashamed by the admission.

Relief surged through Nicholas. "Perfectly respectable," he heard himself say and meant it wholeheartedly.

Miss Thatcher nodded. "Mother taught me how to do laundry—how to wash and hang the clothes, how to iron and fold. As she grew more ill, I did more of the work. I made the deliveries, too, so that when she died there wasn't much change. I didn't tell her customers that she was gone. I was afraid of losing their business."

"Did any of them find out?" Nicholas asked, thinking it was doubtful that she would have lost their business, though likely some would have tried to cheat a little girl. He didn't much care for the image of an eight-year-old bent over a washtub all day either, but it was far better than what he'd initially imagined.

"Not a one," Miss Thatcher said, a touch of pride in her voice. "I kept them all and even took on a few more as the years went by. It was enough that we survived."

"Your brother and sister helped as well, I hope," Nicholas said.

A smile that was both part joyful and half-wistful curved her lips. "Christopher was three and Helen two when Mother died. I was delighted if they stayed out of the fire and didn't muss the folded sheets," Miss Thatcher mused. "Of course, they helped when they grew older, but I wanted them to experience childhood, as well—something I—"

"Never had," Nicholas guessed.

She nodded. He looked over at her, and their eyes met. Hers held no sorrow or bitterness. He felt both on her behalf.

"It wasn't fair of your mother to leave you with such a burden. You were so young."

"Who else should she have left it with?" Miss Thatcher asked. Then she continued quickly, as if she didn't expect him to answer. "It was the best thing she could have done for me. Caring for Helen and Christopher became my purpose. It left me precious little time to grieve, and it fueled my desire to live; it made my work not so wearisome. In giving Mother my promise to care for them, *I* received a gift. I learned what it is to love someone so much that you would do anything for them. And in loving like that, I did more than merely survive. We had joy and love in our home."

For a long minute, Nicholas said nothing; he couldn't. He'd never felt more dumbfounded in his life. "But you were *eight*," he repeated. "Just a child yourself."

Miss Thatcher smiled at him again, and it lit up her whole face. Clearly he'd found something she liked to talk about. "My birthday was a month after she died. Then I was nine."

"*Nine*," he scoffed. "Still far too young for that kind of responsibility."

"Just as Mother was far too young to die." Miss Thatcher's smile faded. "But she taught me much in the few years we had together. She knew children need love. And that our father had none to give. But she also understood that I was old enough to give love—and, in doing so, could also receive it from Helen and Christopher."

Nicholas flicked the reins, urging the horses on faster. All this talk of love made him uncomfortable. As did Miss Thatcher's nonchalant attitude about what had to have been a terribly difficult life.

"What you did is admirable. Tell me more," he said, his voice gruff for reasons entirely foreign to him.

Warmed to her topic, Miss Thatcher rambled on as they drove. She told of cold winters when they were out of coal and she would pile not only every quilt they owned to keep warm, but all of the laundry she'd taken in as well.

"Wasn't that clever and resourceful of me?" she asked. "You've no idea how heavy women's ball gowns can be. I've no doubt that the weight of Mrs. Mackenzie's silk and petticoats saved us from freezing more than a time or two."

He gave her a sideways glance and when he caught her grin, found himself smiling. It was funny, sort of, imagining eight—no, nine-year-old Grace—heaping dresses upon a bed so she and her siblings would stay warm.

"I take it your customers never found out how their laundry was aired," Nicholas said.

"Of course not." Her lips smoothed into a serious line.

"Go on," he encouraged. This was the most entertainment he'd had in quite some time, though he didn't feel it appropriate to say so. It didn't feel right to be entertained by stories of such hardship.

When she spoke of their meager suppers and how they'd learned to survive on two meals a day, he was no longer amused.

"I simply hadn't the time to cook more than twice," she said. "As it was, I felt as if I cooked—boiling laundry—the whole day through. Our food went further if we rationed it anyway. Helen and Christopher never complained. We ate breakfast late and supper early and went to bed as soon as the work was done. We'd lie in bed, and I'd tell them stories of Camelot, of faraway castles and princesses and dragons and knights—the same stories Mother used to tell. It was our favorite time of day."

A strange lump had formed in Nicholas's throat. He felt angry when he thought of the way his mother had driven Miss Thatcher away from the breakfast table before she'd taken two bites. She was too thin, and no wonder, growing up as she had. The pneumonia hadn't helped either.

"And did you always have enough to eat two daily meals? Did your father never once help to put food on the table?"

"Oh, he did," she assured him. "He just didn't realize it." Her mischievous grin returned. "Often I'd lie awake, waiting for him to come home—sometimes he didn't, you see—so I'd bar the door at last before going to sleep myself. But on nights when he came home merry—singing and staggering and the lot—I knew he'd had 'a good pull,' as he called it."

Nicholas slowed the horses, guiding them toward the first of his tenants' homes.

"On those nights," Miss Thatcher continued, "when I

was certain Father was sound asleep, I went into his room and searched his coat. I never took much, lest he find out, but often it was enough extra that I could buy a fresh meat pie for the children. Once, near Christmas, I bought them each a peppermint stick. We had to be so very careful that Father never saw them, or he'd have suspected." She lifted a hand, waving to the people gathering to watch as the buggy approached the first cottage. "Look, they've come out to greet us. How pleasant."

"They've come to tell me their woes," Nicholas corrected. "They rent the land, so I'm expected to fix their problems—every last one. Finish your story," he added, wishing they hadn't traveled quite so fast.

"There isn't much more to tell," she said. "I always had to spend the money from laundry before I came home. At first I tried saving a little, but Father discovered it and took it all. I managed to convince him that it was money Mother had saved, but I never did try to hide any from him again. I'd catch him searching every so often, and we needed every penny I earned." She sighed contentedly. "What a lovely spot this is. How fortunate your tenants are."

Nicholas knew many tenants felt otherwise about living on Sutherland land—at least, since his father's death—but he agreed with Miss Thatcher about the landscape. He'd always thought the fields and farmland were beautiful, especially this time of year.

As he stopped the carriage, he noted the wary looks of those gathered in the yard. He raised a hand in greeting, but his movements were stiff, his arm unsure, whereas Miss Thatcher's wave had seemed natural. He'd not told anyone they were coming, and with the way he'd handled matters the past couple of years, he couldn't blame them for not welcoming him.

Perhaps Miss Thatcher will ease the way.

It was an odd thought to have when he and Mother had

plotted this outing for Miss Thatcher's failure. But she was already proving them wrong.

"Hello," she called, climbing from the carriage before Nicholas had made his way around to assist her. She began eagerly shaking hands and asking the names of everyone, from an elderly man leaning heavily on a pitchfork to the toddler tugging at her skirt.

Nicholas hung back, reluctant to intrude. *Utter nonsense. This is my land, and these are my tenants.*

He couldn't deny the echo of truth; he felt uncomfortable as he watched her interacting with the tenants.

She could be a part of this.

She exclaimed over the size of a squash, bent for a closer look at a row of flowers growing along the side of the cottage, and took a fussy baby from a weary-looking mother. Miss Thatcher had a way with people.

Not unlike Elizabeth.

Miss Thatcher would do well here. If circumstances were different, if they had not been forced to each other's company . . .

Would she have caught my interest? Could she have cared for me?

Both were questions he would do well to forget. He watched as she continued to greet his tenants, walking among them and chatting with far more animation than she had done over breakfast this morning.

Contrary to his mother's prediction that she would fail, Miss Thatcher seemed to instinctively know what to say and do. She had a certain poise and—well, a *grace*—about her. Too late, he realized that this expedition had been a poor idea. It would only serve to complicate matters.

The people have accepted her already.

CHAPTER 24

Nicholas couldn't help smiling as they drove away from their last stop. It was long past midday—when he'd thought they'd be done—and they'd visited but half the farms he'd intended, but he felt as if he'd accomplished a good day's work.

And I enjoyed it as well. He wondered absently if Mother had often done these rounds with his father, and if so, how she'd been regarded. Somehow he doubted she'd been as warmly received.

Likely why Mother continues to suggest I find a steward to see to the managing of the tenants. Perhaps I should hire Miss Thatcher. His grin widened at the thought.

"What are you thinking?" she asked. "You look far too smug to trust," she added, leaning away to the far side of the carriage, where she'd made sure to sit this morning.

It hadn't escaped his notice that throughout the day, she'd gradually sat closer to him and had ceased looking as if he might attack at any moment. During the course of their visits, the frost between them, which had shown signs of melting at different occasions, had progressed to a full thaw, one he hoped might be permanent.

"I'm thinking that I may not need to hire a steward if you'll always accompany me on my tours of the estate. The tenants have never been as friendly to me as they were today, and I know it's because of you."

Miss Thatcher shrugged. "They recognize me as one of their own."

"You're the granddaughter of a duke," he reminded her.

"And daughter of a washerwoman," she countered. "I may fit in among the common folk, but we both know I will never fit in your society. I'll never be able to accompany you anywhere without causing your reputation harm."

Nicholas found that this bothered him. And not because he particularly cared what others thought. "I never go anywhere," he said. "So you needn't worry yourself about that."

She gave him an appreciative smile, though her eyes appeared sad, and he experienced a queer tug at his heart that he'd been fighting throughout the day.

"But you used to go out," she said. "You used to be home only one day out of twenty."

"Who told you that?" he asked, the familiar edge returned to his voice. He willed it away and wondered how long it would take him to reverse the habit of being curt with everyone.

Miss Thatcher refused to answer.

"The places I went to were no places for a lady."

"Oh?" She brought a gloved hand to her chin. "I see."

"You don't," he said. "Not at all." It frustrated him that she would infer the worst. "I did not mean *those* types of establishments. I was referring to solicitors' offices and the like. Tedious at best."

"Then why did you spend so much time there?"

It was a good question, considering that no one had forced him to do any such thing and that there had been no financial gain from those many meetings. On the contrary, they'd caused him to neglect his home and his own affairs.

"I was trying to—right a wrong." Even as he spoke the words, he knew them to be false. Destroying Preston wouldn't bring Elizabeth back. "No. I was seeking to avenge a wrong."

"And have you?" Miss Thatcher asked. "Was your quest successful?"

"Time will tell," Nicholas said. "Time and a few more trips to London, I suppose."

"Perhaps I could join you on one of those trips," she said. "With a proper chaperone, of course," she added hastily. "I, too, have a solicitor I need to meet with, a Mr. Littleton."

"I've heard of him," Nicholas said, curious about what dealings she might have with the man.

"He handled Grandfather's estate." Grace did not offer explanation beyond that, but her brow furrowed as if she were considering something. They drove in silence for a minute, when she turned to him suddenly. "May I trust you, Lord Sutherland?"

He'd thought he was through being taken aback by her. Apparently not. "Have I given you any reason to distrust me—lately?" he asked.

She frowned as she studied him. "Well yes, actually. At times, like today, I feel as if we are almost friends. But at others—when we are with your mother, for example—I feel you would like nothing more than to be rid of me. Does that sort of duplicity seem trustworthy to you?"

"No," he answered in a surly tone. She'd pinpointed him exactly. He had been wavering, his thoughts and feelings about her confused. He grimaced, disgusted with his behavior and irritated that she felt unable to trust him.

"Nevertheless," he continued, "I am a man of my word. If there is something you need help with, I will do what I can to assist."

She nodded, then looked away. The curricle rolled on, and Nicholas didn't know whether he ought to drive faster or slower, whether he should put an end to the unsettled feelings or should prolong them by taking the long road, or whether he even wanted her to divulge what was troubling her.

"Well?" he said, after at least a minute or two had passed and his curiosity got the better of him.

She glanced at him, batting those long eyelashes in mock innocence. "Yes?"

"What is this situation you would like to trust me with?"

She smiled. "I have not yet decided if it would be wise to tell you."

"I see." He snapped the reins, deciding a faster end to the torture would be preferred.

She hung to the side of the curricle as they picked up speed. "It could affect you as well."

"In that case, you should definitely tell me," Nicholas said. "You should have told me already."

"I tried." Miss Thatcher frowned, as if remembering something unpleasant.

"When?" Nicholas asked.

"That first day in your study. When you refused to believe anything at all that I said." Her voice held no censure, yet he felt rebuked, all the same.

"Have I not apologized for my behavior that day?"

"Yes," she said. "But I was never offered a chance to speak the truths I wished to."

Nicholas slowed the team. "You may speak them now. Tell me anything you wish, and I will listen. You have my undivided attention." He pulled back on the reins and guided the horses to stop at a sunny spot on the side of the road.

Miss Thatcher clasped her hands in her lap. "Do you promise that you will not be angry?"

"No. That would be ridiculous. How can you expect me

to judge my reaction to something when I do not yet know the circumstance?"

"Complete honesty," she said, giving him a tremulous smile.

Perplexed, he stared at her. "What?"

"That is what you told me was expected that first day in your study. It is what you have given with your answer just now." She took a deep breath. "And it is what I shall endeavor to tell you now."

He nodded, glad that she planned to continue, yet bracing himself to be upset by whatever it was she was about to reveal. *About Preston?*

"My brother, Christopher, has been in London, meeting with Mr. Littleton. Grandfather left us a small inheritance, you see."

"Is your brother attempting to take it all?" Nicholas asked, his uncharitable thoughts toward Preston transferring to this Christopher.

"Oh no," Grace said. "He is attempting to secure it for us children. You see, the new Duke feels that the entailment entitled him to the entire estate, that it was not within the bounds of the law for Grandfather to leave us anything at all."

"It is possible that he is correct," Nicholas said. "Isn't the estate quite large? Is there some reason the new heir feels the need to retain all of the funds?" He had not been acquainted with Miss Thatcher's grandfather personally, but the man's wealth was widely known. As the seventh duke in the line, his holdings were vast.

Miss Thatcher looked down at her lap. "The new duke wishes to keep the money from us because he thinks to marry my sister."

The girl could do worse than marrying a duke, especially considering her father. "And that is a problem because . . ."

"It's terrible," Miss Thatcher said. Nicholas was surprised to see her eyes filling with tears. "The man is selfish and cruel, and Helen would be miserable with him."

Nicholas was beginning to understand. "So he hopes that by withholding your funds, he can force her to marriage."

Miss Thatcher nodded. "My sister is barely eighteen. Not so young, I know, but Helen is overly shy. She fainted at the first dance after her coming out."

"Sounds familiar," Nicholas muttered.

She ignored the reference. "We never could persuade her to attend another ball. She was too frightened, and she is terrified of the new duke."

Nicholas leaned back against the seat, considering the dilemma. "Your father knows nothing of this?"

"No," she confided. "Otherwise, he'd have sold Helen to the new duke in a thrice. Our inheritance is likewise a secret."

"Else there would be no inheritance left," Nicholas surmised.

She nodded. "But if we can continue to keep our father from learning of it, and if the law is on our side, and if the matter is settled in our favor . . ."

Did she realize the amount of ifs she'd described? Or the rather slim prospect that all would turn out as she hoped?

"If the settlement is released to us," she continued, hope evident in the animated use of her hands and in the light in her eyes, "I plan to take Christopher and Helen far away. We could live simply on what Grandfather left us and live in peace. That was what we intended all along. But now . . . if you will let me go." She met his eyes as she added the last.

That was what he wanted, wasn't it? What he and Mother had been discussing in earnest almost every night—how to be rid of Miss Thatcher.

"Why are you here now?" Nicholas asked.

"I am buying time," she admitted. "I'd hoped the issue of our inheritance would be resolved by now. I agreed to go on this trip my father arranged in an effort to give the matter more time to get settled, and to protect Helen. Father wanted to send her, but I persuaded him to send me instead."

As always, her concerns circled back to her siblings. Nicholas found himself admiring her for it. Maybe there was something to her mother's wisdom after all that the way of happiness lay in caring for another—or whatever pleasant feeling it was he'd enjoyed this afternoon—because he suddenly very much wanted to care for Miss Thatcher, or to at least provide the security she and her siblings longed for. It pleased him to think of doing that for them.

Of thwarting their father.

Nicholas recalled how he'd initially judged Grace, pegging her as a fortune hunter out to catch a husband, when in reality, she had wanted nothing to do with him or any other man.

If you will let me go . . . I am buying time.

Buying time so neither she nor her sister would marry a man of their father's choosing.

Yet wasn't such the plight of nearly every young lady? If not, was letting one's daughter marry for love any better? He thought of his parents' reluctant acceptance of Elizabeth's choice in Mr. Preston.

And look where that led. Nicholas frowned, irritated that thoughts of Preston had again intruded his day. In this moment that so much seemed to depend on. *If I agree to help Miss Thatcher, if I release her . . .* It was the honorable thing to do, the *only* thing to do, yet a part of Nicholas regretted that he must.

"Your face is as dark as a storm cloud," Grace said. "You are angry about the money. That you didn't know about it."

"No." Nicholas looked at her. "I am not upset with you, either."

But she'd used a fine analogy; the feelings raging inside

him felt like a violent storm brewing. He started to say that she would be angry if she had lost both her sister and father because of one man's carelessness, or if she had been duped into an engagement that was not to last, but he got no further than, "You—" when he realized how foolish he was and had been.

She had lost her mother and had endured more hardship than he ever would, yet she hadn't let any of those things darken her soul. And she had not deceived him on purpose.

She tried to tell me that very first day.

"Why are you not bitter?" he asked, genuinely curious. "Why are you not awash in despair over your lot?" If anyone had reason to be angry with the world, Miss Thatcher did.

"I do have my dark moments." She sighed heavily, likely recalling some of them.

Nicholas wondered how many of those moments he was responsible for. *Several, since she has been here,* his guilty conscience told him.

"But today—" Miss Thatcher paused, her teeth worrying her lower lip, something he'd noted her doing when she was overly nervous or agitated, as she had been the day she'd confronted him in his study.

What has she to be anxious about now? Their conversation this afternoon had been pleasant enough for him, anyway.

"I will not tell your father of the money," he assured her. "And I would be happy to meet with Mr. Littleton myself to see if the matter might be quickly settled. And when it is—" He imagined her standing in the hall, bidding him farewell, and felt a strange tug at his heart. "When it is, you may go."

Gratitude filled her eyes, and she smiled at him—the prettiest smile he'd seen from her yet. *One like she might have given Preston.*

It looked as if he would not need to foist her off to him now. If Miss Thatcher truly wished to go far away with her siblings, then Preston would not get her either. The thought brought little satisfaction. He might not have to marry Miss Thatcher or give her up to Preston, and she would be able to provide for herself. But she would be gone from Sutherland Hall. No longer would he have their evenings in the library to look forward to. No more would he wonder what each day would bring, what new mischief or temptations she might present.

This realization did not sit well with him. Nor did admitting to himself that he really didn't want her to leave. He didn't want today to end. The hours had flown, with the time spent in her company having been more enjoyable than any time he could think of for the past few years.

"I've had many dark times," she was saying. "But today has not been one of them, because I have been here. With you." As her words tumbled out, a pretty blush stained her cheeks.

"Are you attempting to flirt with me, Miss Thatcher?" he asked in a stern voice, but inside, his thoughts careened to and fro.

"No!" Her eyes widened, and her mouth opened in such a look of abject horror that he had to laugh.

"Lidgate accused me of such, and I did nothing—absolutely nothing to encourage his attention."

"I am not Lidgate," Nicholas said, feeling again the desire to strangle the man. "And if you had been flirting, it would not be a crime, you know." He caught her gaze and held it. "We are still—*betrothed*." The word that had felt like a shackle seemed suddenly ripe with possibility.

"Yes, but I've just told you my plans to leave." She did not sound at all worried.

"So you have." Maybe that was why he felt so free—free to care about her, to pursue her if he wished. "But the fact remains that, right now, today, we are still engaged to be married."

"But I was not flirting." Her blush was back. "I meant

only to give you a sincere compliment. Today has been . . ."

"Unexpectedly pleasant?" he suggested, for that was exactly how he felt about it.

She nodded.

"Perhaps your sunny disposition has spilled into my stormy one," he mused.

"Perhaps." She said nothing else but continued to look at him curiously until it was he who felt discomfort.

"Would you consider joining me again on another round of visits in the future?" He could have required it of her; it was well in his right to order her to do whatever he wished—no matter that their situation was temporary. He waited for her to answer, wanting to hear that she desired his company as much as he suddenly desired hers.

See what one compliment has done? He scolded himself. *Don't act the besotted fool.*

"I would very much like to accompany you again—if I am still here."

"If you are still here," he agreed.

CHAPTER 25

My Dearest Helen,

We have a new and surprising ally. Lord Sutherland has gone to London to meet with our solicitor . . .

Samuel rested his chin on his arms as he leaned forward against the fence. "Elizabeth died—in childbirth." He didn't elaborate, and Grace, facing him as she stood on the bench, did not press. She had asked about his daughter and how it was that the Sutherland family did not know of her existence. Samuel had just begun his story, yet Grace could see that the telling pained him already.

"Elizabeth was in fine health, right up to the day her labor began," he explained. "So well that I'd begged her to take care of herself. She was nothing if not the very beat of life—attentive and active, involved in everything around her. Being with child only seemed to intensify those traits." The wistful smile of memory touched Samuel's lips, making Grace yearn to know how it would feel to be loved and cherished as much as Samuel had loved and cherished Elizabeth.

"We had agreed—prior to our child's arrival—that I would attend her during the birth— as her physician."

This surprised Grace, but she remembered Samuel mentioning that he'd studied medicine.

"I'd had as much training—though not experience—" he said ruefully, "as any of the physicians in the area, and Elizabeth had told me all along that she wanted it to be me who brought our child from her womb into the world."

Grace looked away, feeling as if she were intruding upon a private moment not meant for her to see—or hear of even these years later. "Lord Sutherland held you responsible for Elizabeth's death," she guessed, hoping Samuel would be done with the telling. She'd only wanted to understand why Samuel kept his daughter hidden from her uncle.

"He blamed me for Elizabeth's death. He still does."

Grace met his anguished gaze. Samuel, too, held himself responsible. "But many women die in childbirth." Her words sounded feeble.

"Most who do are not as strong and healthy as Elizabeth. She shouldn't have died, and she probably wouldn't have . . ." He drew a shaking breath. "Had the child not been breech, or had I turned her with more care, or called a midwife as the others suggested."

"You don't know that." Grace hurried to his defense. "The same might have happened with a midwife or a physician."

"But I wouldn't have been the one who killed her." Samuel ran a hand over his face as if to wipe the memory away. "Elizabeth wanted me to do whatever it took to deliver the baby safely, and I did. I acquiesced when I knew she wasn't coherent enough to realize what she was saying."

"You did what she asked because she was *your wife*," Grace said.

"And *I* was her physician. It was my duty to remember that above all else." Samuel hung his head, and this time Grace found herself unable to resist reaching out to him. She placed a hand on his shoulder, and he reached up and took her hand in his own.

"You don't need to explain anything," Grace said.

"But I want to." He lifted his head to look at her. "You're involved in this now too. You need to know the truth if you're ever to understand Nicholas."

Or you, Grace thought.

She ached to heal the pain reflected in Samuel's eyes, understanding, at least a little, what it was to want someone to understand something about you. Something they might misconstrue if you weren't given the chance to explain. She'd finally had that chance and wanted Samuel to have the same. "Very well." She took a deep breath and braced herself for the telling.

Samuel gave her an appreciative smile, different from his usual lighthearted grins. His eyes were dark and shadowed, as if he'd struggled with many sleepless nights.

Has the thought of telling me worried him so much?

"The baby was in breech position and would not come," Samuel said. "I tried to turn her—Elizabeth hemorrhaged. Labor had taken hours, and then everything happened so quickly. Had I taken more care, had the midwife turned the child instead . . ."

The scene he described was too awful to contemplate, and Grace found she could not do so. Before he'd shared this burden, she never would have known he had a well of grief and guilt running so deep.

"But your daughter lived." Grace harbored only a vague hope that this was the right thing to say.

"She almost didn't." Samuel's faraway look returned. "When Beth was finally delivered, the cord was around her neck, and she was unmoving. But I hadn't a thought for her; I was doing all I could to stop Elizabeth's bleeding, and so I handed the baby off to the midwife Nicholas had fetched. A while later, she came to tell us that the baby had died too. Lord Sutherland—the elder—his wife, and Nicholas were leaving, so grief stricken that none could bear remaining to see the infant. I went into her alone."

An ache began in Grace's throat. She struggled to swallow as she imagined grief-stricken Samuel going in to hold his child, no longer living herself.

"Her skin was blue and cold. I hadn't even held her once, I'd been so focused on saving Elizabeth. I'd failed them both and wanted nothing more than to die myself." Samuel rested his head in his hands. Grace imagined him doing the same on that awful night.

"I had to hold our child at least once. The elder Lord Sutherland had come in to see Elizabeth after the birth. He'd held her hand while I tried to stop the bleeding—"

"Shhh." Grace said. Through the telling of the tale, he'd held her hand. Now she gave his a gentle squeeze. "It is enough, Samuel. I understand. You needn't say more."

As if he hadn't heard her or could not stop, he spoke again. "I was alone in a house that felt like a tomb. I picked up the baby and pressed my lips to her forehead, a farewell kiss."

Grace felt a tear fall and hurriedly wiped it away. *This was supposed to be a happy story. His daughter lives.*

"I held her tiny hand in mine and then detected a heartbeat so faint that I know it could only have been a miracle that I'd felt it," Samuel said. "My hands felt clumsy and trembling as I swaddled Beth. I pulled a chair as near the fire as I dared get, and I sat with her there, the long night through, my face close to hers, breathing life into her and begging her to stay."

"You saved her," Grace said, smiling encouragingly. "You saved your daughter's life."

"After depriving her of her mother," Samuel said.

"No." Grace shook her head. "It was a case of saving your child, of doing what Elizabeth wished."

Samuel's look of distress cut off her arguments. "You were not there," he said, his tone still kind, though firm. "I know what I did, and I must live with it every day for the rest of my life. Some day—" He drew in a shaky breath, then exhaled quickly. "I will have to tell Beth."

"When that time comes, I am certain she will be grateful for her life and realize that both of her parents acted out of pure love." With a last, gentle squeeze, Grace pulled her hand from his.

"Don't leave," Samuel said, a plea in his voice that made her heart ache.

"I'm not." It was fortunate Lord Sutherland was still away. He'd left for London the morning after their visit to the tenants. She'd often worried about being discovered conversing in the garden with his nemesis, but today there was little chance of that.

"Why did you never tell Elizabeth's family that the baby lived?" Grace asked.

"Because Nicholas threatened an inquiry. That was all he could do to me, having given his word to Elizabeth that he would never meet me in a duel."

"The two of you were not friends?"

"Quite the opposite," Samuel said, a bit of wry humor returned to his expression. "From the beginning—from the first day I conversed with Elizabeth in this very spot—Nicholas has seen me as an interloper. He holds me responsible not only for her death but for the death of his father—and for the destruction of their family."

"But—why?" Grace asked, a little unsettled, and a little stung, thinking of Samuel meeting in this same place with Elizabeth.

He shrugged. "For one, I do not meet his social requirements."

"Surely he's not that much of a snob," Grace said. She thought of the Lord Sutherland she'd come to know and could not see that he cared much for society and its many rules. His mother, however, was a different matter entirely.

"No," Samuel agreed. "It is less snobbery and more Nicholas's protective nature. He and his sister were very close—best friends, really. He had a difficult time believing anyone could be good enough for her. He found me far less than deserving."

"Apparently Elizabeth did not see it that way." Grace smiled, though inside she felt peculiar, as she imagined Samuel with his wife. *I have no right to feel anything*, she reminded herself. *I have no claim upon him beyond friendship.*

"'But love is blind,'" Samuel quipped. "'And lovers cannot see the pretty follies themselves commit; for if they could, Cupid himself would blush to see me thus transformed to a boy.'"

Grace sighed with pleasure. "*The Merchant of Venice.* I have not read that for a while. I shall have to search for it tonight."

Samuel nodded. "Wisdom from Shakespeare himself. Never truer than with Elizabeth. We fell madly in love, and she was blind to my faults—my lack of title and my less-than-pure bloodline.

"It sounds like she was sensible. What are bloodlines to—" Grace studied Samuel, truly looked at him as she had not since the night of his ball. His hair was mussed today—a sight she found endearing, though it was a sure sign of his worry. His eyes, usually merry, had proven equally striking when serious. Stubble grew along his jaw line, further attesting to his state of unrest. His cheeks were slightly pink from the cold, and his lips—

What am I thinking? Grace reined her thoughts to an abrupt halt. "What are bloodlines to a man as kind and good as you?"

Samuel's mouth turned down in a mock pout. "I had expected something a little more with the way you were appraising me."

There is more. Much, much, more. Grace turned away, though that did not lessen the attraction she felt toward him. "That is all that is proper for me to say."

"Oh, oh," he teased. "I'll not let you off so easily, Miss Thatcher." He reached for her, but Grace had already moved out of range to a safer distance at the far end of the bench.

"I am glad to see I have lifted you from your melancholy, at least," she said.

"It never lasts long." The smile that reached his eyes was back in place. "I have Beth to think of. She is already at a disadvantage, growing up without her mother, so I must do the best I can for her. I must bring as much joy and light into her life as possible."

Grace thought back to her first impressions upon entering Samuel's home. As she had walked through the doors, there had been an almost tangible feeling of joy. Every room had been filled with light, the air sweet with the scent of roses.

Elizabeth's roses.

"You are a good father," Grace said, wondering briefly what her life might have been like had her father taken half so much care with his children.

"It is the most esteemed title a man can have," Samuel said. "Beth is my reason for living. Loving her and the joy it brings has sustained me."

Grace thought she understood. *What would I have done without Helen and Christopher?* "Nothing ever came of the inquiry?" she asked.

"No, gratefully," Samuel said. "I went to London soon after Beth's birth, in part to hide her, and in part to obtain legal counsel. But the inquiry never went far. As you said, many women die in childbirth, and a large percentage of those involve infants with breech presentation. It was determined that nothing more could have been done to save Elizabeth."

Yet you have never stopped blaming yourself. "Lord

Sutherland and his family never came to see it that way," Grace said.

"No." Samuel's face clouded. "Nicholas has made it his life's mission to ruin me. He is determined to destroy me financially. I suppose he feels that would be the end of me."

"A common misconception of the upper class," Grace said. "That without money, one is . . ."

"Nothing," they both spoke at once.

Grace allowed her gaze to stray to Samuel's face and caught him looking at her with such longing, it made her breath catch.

We are perfect for each other in so many ways. We understand each other. She thought of his cheerful home and how she'd felt there during those brief seconds when he took her in his arms to dance.

"Lord Sutherland is certainly wrong in his assumption." She clasped her hands to keep them from reaching toward Samuel.

"He has no idea how wrong he is," Samuel agreed. "I have lost that which was most precious to me, yet survived. Losing wealth pales in comparison."

"And your daughter?" Grace asked. She was beginning to understand, to see the logic in keeping the girl hidden from Lord Sutherland and his mother.

"I always think of her first," Samuel said. "I must protect her from the world, and if that includes keeping her from her uncle and grandmother, then so be it."

I will not lose Beth too, he might have added. Grace read as much in the set of his jaw and in the determination in his eyes.

"Your secret is safe with me," she promised once more. "Though I cannot imagine how you keep it. The gossip that flows from your household to mine is quite impressive."

"Is it *your* household now?" Samuel sounded hurt.

"No," Grace said. "I meant Lord Sutherland's, of course. It is only that I live there."

For now. I am temporarily bound there. Now that she knew it was not to be forever—that she might truly get her wish to take Helen and Christopher away to live peacefully, leaving all this behind—Grace should have felt happy. Instead, to her great surprise, when Lord Sutherland had agreed to her release, she had felt the tiniest disappointment and loss.

Only because I have grown accustomed to my life here.

"Don't worry yourself over anything you've heard," Samuel said. "There are some things I want known to Nicholas, and those I arrange quite easily. As for Beth, the servants know her true identity—and they are sworn to secrecy. They are well compensated for their loyalty. Beth is rarely brought from the nursery when there are guests in the house, and if someone does happen to see her, she is explained as my niece. Though that is becoming more of a difficulty as she grows older and looks more and more like her mother."

Something he'd said troubled Grace. "Your servants are loyal at keeping your secret, but they are also adept at spreading gossip—that which you wish to have spread?"

"Ye-es," Samuel said, somewhat warily. "In a manner similar to that which you did with *your* servants."

It was the only way I could see to protect Helen. But what reason did Samuel have for spreading gossip? What would he possibly want Lord Sutherland to know? Grace pressed a hand to her stomach, suddenly ill with suspicion. "Did you—are you responsible for Lord Sutherland's knowledge of my servants' role in this? Is it because of you that he learned that I had planned for my reputation to be ruined?"

Samuel broke their gaze, but not before Grace caught a look of discomfort. "You did—you *are* responsible!" she accused. "How could you? Do you not realize that I might have been with Helen and Christopher all this time? I might have been—"

"With me?" Samuel finished, meeting her furious gaze. "Or at the least, free to choose whichever man you wished? Yes, Grace. I do. I think of it every time I meet you here. Every night when I retire to bed alone." He reached for her, taking her hand once more.

"But why?" Grace asked, pushing aside the image of Samuel sleeping alone. The last thing she wanted to feel for him right now was sympathy. He had incited Lord Sutherland's initial anger against her. He'd all but thrust her into her current role—temporary though it now might be. "Lord Sutherland wouldn't have known—or blamed me for our predicament." *We might not have started off so terribly. We might not have started off at* all.

She quickly dismissed the distress that possibility caused.

"I cannot explain my actions," Samuel said. His fingers stroked the back of her hand as if to make up for his words, but Grace would have none of that and pulled away.

Samuel's hand reached for her again, then dropped to his lap as if defeated. "Perhaps someday I can tell you, but not yet. Only know that I have questioned my actions—over a dozen times since. Beyond making clear to Nicholas what had occurred with your servants, sending that letter with your father, telling him I no longer wished to marry you was one of the most difficult things that I have ever done."

"Then why did you do it?" Grace demanded. Angry tears brimmed in her eyes as she looked to him for the answer he refused to give. "I do not wish to be some pawn in your game."

"You're not," Samuel said. "And this isn't a game."

Grace shook her head and removed herself from the bench.

"Please, Grace . . . Trust me awhile longer," he said. "Will you come again?"

She closed her heart against the tenderness of his

request. "I don't know," she answered honestly. She didn't feel as if she knew much of anything anymore. Lord Sutherland had proven that he could be agreeable, but Samuel had betrayed her in the worst way. She didn't know what to think. She started back on the path toward the house.

"You're not a pawn," Samuel called to her.

"You're wrong," Grace whispered. Somehow he was using her, and it didn't feel so different from the way Father had planned to use her. She was nothing but a game piece for men to move to and fro as they pleased.

If Lord Sutherland does not have success in London . . .

Then I will be nothing. I will have nothing. I will never be free.

CHAPTER 26

My Dearest Grace,

I am so glad to hear that Lord Sutherland is not as disagreeable as you first believed . . .

Grace plucked berries from an exceedingly overgrown bush near the back of the Sutherland gardens. Working with care, she managed to avoid most of the thorns and felt a sense of satisfaction as the berries dropped and the pail began to fill. The offering was sure to please Nicholas's mother, who just last night had requested a berry tart for today, only to have a message delivered from cook that there were no berries to be had.

Grace had begged to differ but held her tongue. This late in autumn, not many bushes still bore fruit, but she had seen one or two during her wanderings in the garden.

The berries on this bush alone are more than enough for a few pies. Grace worked quickly, pausing now and then to wipe her stained fingers across her skirt.

She wore her oldest, plainest frock, as the gown that had been ruined with mud had disappeared from her room after the gardening incident. She'd owned this dress for a dozen years and had kept it only because she'd refashioned it from a dress that had been her mother's.

Grace imagined the same fabric swishing about her mother's feet as she worked and felt a melancholy she did not often possess.

It is because I am away from Helen and Christopher. She had no ability to change their circumstance. Helen, in particular, had been on her mind of late, and though Grace had given another letter to Samuel to post, she had not visited him again to know if he had one for her in return.

If Father tries to arrange a marriage for her . . . after taking Lord Sutherland's money.

Grace wished she'd asked Lord Sutherland to inquire after her sister while he was in London. Based on their last afternoon together, she believed he might have taken the trouble to do such a favor. He'd been entirely pleasant company that day, and instead of feeling glad that he was gone, Grace had found that she missed him.

Especially since I've only his mother for company. And because I am no longer certain I can trust Samuel. The more she thought about what Mr. Preston had done, the more betrayed she felt. She was certain Miranda and Harrison would never have taken him into their confidence had they realized how he would reveal their involvement.

She missed Samuel's company but could not bring herself to seek him out again. She did not want to think about what missing Lord Sutherland might mean. And she missed her mother too. Grace forced herself to think on her previous resolution: to never fall in love with a man. Her mother was proof enough that doing so only led to misery.

I am miserable too, Grace realized. *And it is the fault of two men.* She glanced down at the near-full pail and questioned her motives for picking the berries. Was it only a way to pass the time or an opportunity to do something nice?

Or is it because I wish Lord Sutherland's mother to approve of me, because I am coming to care for him?

The thought was alarming—and distressful enough that Grace lost her concentration and pricked her finger on a particularly large thorn. Muttering an oath, she took up the pail and turned and fled the berry patch, intending to retreat to the safety of the library for the afternoon.

The only reason it is safe is because he is not here.

With a start, Grace realized the truth of the thought. Most afternoons that she spent in the library were with full knowledge—*hope?*—that Lord Sutherland would join her.

"Oh no, oh no, oh no."

This cannot be happening. I cannot come to care for him. Not now when I may soon be free. Not ever.

She marched past the bench at her meeting place with Samuel, not calling out to him or so much as glancing up to see if he was there.

"Grace!" His voice was hopeful as he popped up from the other side of the wall.

She slowed her steps, then stopped. Being rude would not help matters. "Hello, Samuel."

"You came." He was beaming.

"Not really." Grace held up the bucket. "I have been picking berries for the dowager and had to come by this way to return to the house."

One corner of his mouth lifted in a telltale smirk. "I know of another path. It is shorter and runs closer to the house. Though perhaps it has become overgrown in recent years."

"The most overgrown thing around here is your pride," Grace said, but her shoulders hung in defeat. "You have called my bluff," she admitted, having taken the shorter path to the house many times before. She set the pail on the bench and climbed up. She did not accept his hand for help.

"As you called mine last time we met," Samuel said,

looking into her eyes with open honesty. "Can you forgive me?"

"For ruining my life?" Grace said. "That is quite a lot to ask."

"Have I ruined your life?" Samuel asked. "Or just altered it?"

It was Grace who broke their gaze. "I don't know."

A sadness came to Samuel's face. "I suspected as much."

Grace doubted very much that he'd believed she might fall in love with Lord Sutherland, the man trying to destroy him. The bitter, revengeful side that Lord Sutherland presented to the world was hardly loveable. More likely, Samuel had assumed that she would come to accept her lot—one that he, at least partially, had cast upon her. She wished she understood why he had done it, but he'd already made it clear that he would not explain.

And so here we are again. She could remain angry at him and lose his friendship, or she could forgive him and trust that whatever his reasons, he had believed them to be best at the time. But not now, he had admitted. It seemed that Samuel faced the same dilemma she did: the continuous wondering of what if they had been able to be together? And what might be done so they could have that opportunity now?

Nothing.

For while Lord Sutherland might be willing to let her free to go far away with her siblings, it wasn't likely that he would allow her anywhere near Samuel.

Were I to choose Samuel over Lord Sutherland . . .

Grace could not do that to him—could not hurt Lord Sutherland in that manner when he had been kind to her.

But perhaps she could do something for both men.

Something before I leave them both. A daunting idea occurred to her, a seemingly impossible goal: reuniting the two families.

But how? Grace sighed with the heaviness of it.

"You are troubled today," Samuel said. With his usual patience, he had waited and watched as she attempted to sort out her muddled feelings.

"I am," Grace said. "I had imagined for myself a quiet life in the country with only Helen and Christopher as companions. In my dream of the future, the only man present aside from my brother would have been my grandfather, had he lived. I should have been content to push his chair along country lanes, with no more thought or care than which wildflowers to pick for the vase on the table."

Samuel's mouth twisted in amusement. He reached down, plucking a berry from her pail. "You wished for fields of flowers and an invalid man and instead find yourself with berries and a grumpy old woman."

"Lady Sutherland is not old," Grace said. "And had her son acquired his fiancée in the usual fashion, I doubt she would be so cross."

"Hmm." Samuel folded his arms and studied Grace as a doctor might study a troubled patient. "Defending one's mother-in-law is a serious indication of commitment."

"She's not my mother-in-law yet, and she may never be. Besides, I wasn't defending—" At his wicked grin, Grace broke off. "You are despicable."

"And you are no longer fretting over flowers or berries or whatever was bothering you. I've teased you from your mood."

"*Positively* despicable."

He laughed, and it warmed her heart to hear it. Their last meeting had no laughter, and she had missed it. She'd missed him. She needed his friendship and knew she must forgive him.

But I needn't make it easy for him.

"I will forgive you on one condition," Grace said. She pursed her lips and narrowed her eyes shrewdly, as if she had but a few coins and was about to bargain in the market for tonight's supper.

"All right," Samuel said. "Anything for the lady's favor."

"*Anything?*" Grace asked.

"Within reason," Samuel amended. He rolled his eyes and muttered, "Women. Always taking our statements literally."

"Your statement *was* literal," Grace said, turning from him to feign disgust. "Please be sure that you take my request the same way, for I want no substitutions."

"What is it you wish, milady?" Samuel asked with a gallant bow that had him disappearing behind the wall for a second.

"I would like to—no, I *need* to know if my sister Helen is well. Her letters say as much, but I should like to know what Father is up to and how Helen is really faring by herself at home with him."

Samuel reached into his coat and produced a letter. "Perhaps this will shed some light."

"Perhaps," Grace said, taking the envelope eagerly. "But I would feel better if someone had seen her. Miranda, my maid, will know how she is—if she'll still speak with you, that is."

"Oh, I am certain she will," Samuel said, with far more confidence than Grace thought he deserved. "And Harrison, will he be a reliable source as well?"

"Yes," Grace said. "Though he may be more difficult to locate. Miranda has likely returned to my father's house to be with Helen. With our carriage broken and the horses only borrowed, Harrison has probably been forced to seek other employment. He may have returned to my late grandfather's home, seeking a position with the new duke."

"Or it is possible that they are both nearby, worrying over their eldest charge and holding me accountable for her well-being?"

"What do you mean?"

"This time I mean what I said—literally." Samuel's

mouth widened in his mischievous grin. "Your maid and man have positions in my employ, for now. They ask after you daily and become rather testy when I have no news to give."

"This *entire* time they have been at your house, and you did not tell me?" Instead of being grateful, Grace flew at him, holding out her hands as if she meant to choke him.

Samuel leaned from her reach. "Such gratitude. I am paying them well."

Grace lowered her hands, but her ire did not dissipate. "I still hold you to your promise, and you be quick about it now. I must know that Helen is safe and that Father has not sold her off to some beast of a man."

Samuel chuckled. "That might depend upon your definition of a beast."

Grace felt her eyes widen. "You've more news, haven't you? What has he done?"

"Calm yourself," Samuel said, reaching for her and claiming her hand in his, then twining their fingers together. His expression grew serious as they stared at each other across the fence. "Your sister and brother are both well. They are safe. I assure you of this. I have seen them myself."

Grace willed her heart to stop pounding. *Helen is safe. Miranda and Harrison are near.*

"I did not mean to keep them from you," Samuel said. "This is not meant to be a game. When your servants explained the situation and shared their concern for both your welfare and your sister's, I had your father bring your siblings to my estate almost two months ago. They are currently residing in my guest house. Miranda and Harrison are seeing to their needs."

Grace opened her mouth, but no words came out. A knot of unexpected gratitude and overwhelming relief caught in her throat.

"After all that was settled, I wrote the letter and sent

your father to Nicholas—perhaps my only mistake in this whole ordeal—though I hope it is one that can yet be corrected." He paused, searching her face. "You need only request it."

Grace's heart continued its quickened beat, and she took deep breaths, trying to calm the tumult of emotions washing over her in waves. Her family was safe and close by. Samuel had seen to that and had been watching over her as well for weeks.

Why? Why had he proceeded this way? Why wasn't she at his house with the others?

Why have Helen's letters appeared to be sent from home and all but begged me to stay at Lord Sutherland's? None of it made any sense.

How much simpler things might have been if I had never left Samuel's house that fated night. How much simpler they might be now.

Grace could go with him while Lord Sutherland was away in London, and everything could be taken care of before his return.

Everything and nothing would be taken care of. I should rather have the difficulties I face now than repay his kindness in that way.

"Thank you for caring for my family," Grace said when finally she trusted herself to speak. "Thank you so very much, Samuel. I am forever in your debt."

As am I deeply hurt by your actions. Her eyes clouded with tears. It seemed all she could do lately was cry.

"You are welcome. It has been my great pleasure to care for a damsel in distress." He brushed a tear from her cheek, then trailed his fingers down her face with the gentlest touch. Grace reached up and took his hand, pressing it to her cheek. She closed her eyes, allowing herself to savor his touch, this moment.

That is all it can be. When she opened her eyes, his face was very near, his look searching.

He cleared his throat, as if to rid it of a constriction. “Those berries will grow mushy if they sit too long.”

Grace glanced at the forgotten pail. *The dowager’s tart.*

The temptation to make the request was great. *Take me with you. Today. Now.* She had only to utter the words but felt an undeniable force holding her back on this side of the fence.

“Do you think—” Her voice trembled. She withdrew her hands from Samuel’s. “That the dowager will like her pie?”

He nodded, and his smile—the sad, wistful one—returned.

“I daresay she will like it very much.”

CHAPTER 27

Rain fell in sheets as the landau rolled to a stop in front of the house. A moment later, the carriage door opened, and Nicholas stepped out, expecting the muddy mess he'd encountered the last time he'd returned home. Instead, his traveling boots landed on fresh-laid gravel, a welcome change. He'd forgotten he'd ordered it the week before.

His eyes left the weed-free drive and traveled up the front steps to the newly painted doors and iron rail. Even the knocker appeared to have a fresh shine to it, which glowed through the downpour, and Nicholas felt a moment of satisfaction at coming home to a place of order. His satisfaction grew as he made his way toward the entrance and a movement at the window above caught his eye. He tilted his head back and received a face full of rain for his effort.

He also caught sight of Miss Thatcher a split second before she disappeared and the curtains fell into place.

Eager to see me and hear news of her inheritance? Or avoiding me already? When she did not reappear, Nicholas assumed the latter. His coat nearly soaked through, he hurried toward the door. *Always raining when I come home. Maybe a sign I shouldn't come at all.* He stomped up the steps, feeling inexplicably upset.

Why should I care if she wishes to avoid me? A loud clap of thunder echoed his mood. *What reason have I given her to want my company?*

Save for the pleasant day they had spent visiting tenants a week earlier, he could think of none.

The door swung open, and Kingsley appeared, towel draped over one arm, the other extended to take his hat. "Lord Sutherland, your return is earlier than we expected."

"I trust you have not given my bed away this time." Nicholas stepped onto the rug, taking care with his boots so as not to make more work for Mrs. James.

"No, milord." Kingsley's mouth twitched. "One spirited young lady in residence is quite enough."

"Oh?" Nicholas arched a brow and removed his drenched hat. "What has she done now?"

"I think it best if she explains," Kingsley said. "Only if I may say—"

"Please do," Nicholas said. *What disaster awaits?*

"Be gentle with her," Kingsley said. "Cook has near had Miss Thatcher's head on a platter already, and—" He broke off again, as the subject of their conversation came bounding down the stairs.

Nicholas knew the second Grace caught sight of him, as her steps hesitated, then resumed at a slower pace. But she did not turn and flee. Instead, she looked directly at him as she descended. One of her rare smiles blossomed on her face, and Nicholas found himself returning it. This was the same sort of smile she'd worn the day they'd visited the estate; it meant she was pleased about something.

He'd seen a similar look before from Elizabeth when she, too, came racing down those stairs to greet Preston. Nicholas remembered the surge of jealousy he'd felt on those occasions, the way he'd resented Preston for breaking up their family. He'd not understood Elizabeth's fascination with the man—he still didn't.

But beneath Grace's warm smile and almost affectionate gaze, Nicholas suddenly understood what it was to feel welcomed by a beautiful young woman. He could no longer entirely fault Preston for being unable to resist his sister's enticements. A twinge of something close to understanding flickered to life deep in his soul as he and Grace stood there, gazing at each other as if truly seeing for the first time.

She was not avoiding me. He felt his grin broaden, and his mood buoyed, even though she was only interested likely in the results of his meeting with her solicitor. *She will not care to see me after I share them.*

He handed his hat to Kingsley, then crossed the hall, heedless of his dripping coat. Grace waited on the last stair, her hand curved over the newel post.

"You're home early." She sounded a little out of breath, and Nicholas wondered if her run down the stairs had winded her. She needed to take care with her health, fragile as it was since the pneumonia. It wouldn't do for her to be ill now—not when he'd discovered that she could be tolerable.

And with the news I bring from London.

"My business did not require as many days as I had anticipated." To his own ears, he sounded brusque, angry even, yet he was not. Again, Nicholas silently cursed Preston and the past three years of bitter living that seemed to have rendered him incapable of pleasant speech.

Grace did not inquire after his meeting but surprised him further. "I am glad you are returned."

"Have you been well?" he asked, attempting niceties while searching her face for any sign that she'd been ill. She looked healthy, her cheeks no longer pale, her eyes clear and bright.

Perhaps too bright, he thought, recalling Kingsley's twitching mouth. *What has been afoot while I was away?*

"I have been lonely," she said, a catch in her voice.

Her admission was unexpected and touched him deeply. He broke their gaze, feeling guilty for having left her to go to London.

Absurd. I went for her.

"My mother was not sufficient company?"

Grace's smile fled. "She will, at present, not speak with me at all. Nor will she allow my attendance at meals. I have been ordered these past two days to dine in my room."

What now, indeed. Nicholas crossed his arm in front of him and brought a hand up to pinch the bridge of his nose, only then remembering his dripping coat. There was a story here, and he wasn't at all certain he wished to hear it. Though no doubt he would—twice. He turned to find Kingsley directly behind him, towel still draped over his arm. Nicholas shrugged out of his coat and accepted the towel.

"Thank you, Kingsley. That is all. Actually, no. Please tell the kitchen staff that there will be three for dinner in the dining room this evening."

"At once." Kingsley gave a brief bow and left the foyer.

"I am not certain that is wise," Grace said, her eyes flickering downward to the puddle he'd dripped onto the floor.

"You assume you are to be one of those three?" Nicholas asked, annoyed with himself that he'd already made a move in her favor when he didn't yet know what her offense had been. He dried his face, and then his gaze returned to hers, and he noted with pleasure how fine she appeared this afternoon. He'd not seen this dress before—a pink creation that brought out the blush staining her cheeks and the highlights in her chestnut hair.

"I do assume you meant me." Her chin rose, and from the stair on which she stood, her eyes were nearly level with his. "Unless, of course, you have decided to invite your closest neighbor to dine with you."

Nicholas scowled, his mood taking yet another turn,

this one likely irrevocable for some hours. "If you think it amusing to bring Samuel Preston into our conversation—into *any* conversation in this house—you are sorely mistaken. Is that what you have done to upset my mother?"

"No." Grace remained where she was, but Nicholas noted the way her fingers clenched and unclenched. "I did nothing but pick berries and make a pie for her."

"A pie?" A burst of incredulous laughter escaped. He'd been wrong. Miss Thatcher's latest tale of mischief might yet save him from his temper. "You baked a pie? Downstairs in the kitchen?"

Grace nodded slowly. She gave a resigned little sigh. "You will say it was wrong too, I suppose. Your cook was most insistent that I should not even be below stairs. When I dared to light her oven, she acted as if I'd committed the gravest of sins." Her shoulders sagged, and with another sigh, some of her indomitable spirit seemed to seep away.

"I don't know about that," Nicholas said, wanting to rescue her from—what?

The feeling that she has disappointed me? From Mother? From this world so demanding and different from hers?

"I think, perhaps, that I shall have to reserve judgment until I have tasted a piece of your pie. Only then will I know if it was worth the cost."

"It didn't require much at all to make it," she said. "The berries were on your property, at the edge of the garden. The last of the season, to be sure. I was fortunate to discover them."

"It is not money I speak of," Nicholas said, wondering how long it would take for her to realize that he spoke the truth, that the Sutherland estate and holdings were well secured and financially fit. "You may eat pie every day if you wish. The monetary cost is of no consequence. It is the cost to you *socially* that I speak of."

He stepped closer, taking her hand and turning it over to look at her fingers. "These appear well now, but I am guessing they were—perhaps two days ago—stained with berry juice."

"A little," she confessed, a hint of her former smile returning. "But my hands do not appear well now either. They have not for many years, having spent too many seasons immersed in water and wrapped around a bar of lye. I have tried softening them, but the scarring and calluses will not leave."

She was right. Thin white lines crisscrossed her knuckles, where they had caught on a washboard, perhaps. The tips of her fingers were callused. But her slender fingers fit nicely in his, as they had on the night of the ball and on the day they visited tenants. Her touch both unnerved and comforted him. It was something he could get used to if he were not very careful. "Did you spoil a gown, as well?"

"Oh no." She shook her head. "I wore my very oldest dress—one I'd made over from one of Mother's years and years ago. The perfect dress for picking berries."

"Ah . . ." He was beginning to understand. His mother had always been a stickler about appearance. How he and Elizabeth had loathed her many rules as children. He had felt the sting of a switch a time or two after disregarding those rules. No doubt Mother's tongue had given Grace a similar lashing.

"Did you perchance wear this 'old gown' in the house around my mother?"

"Yes." Grace sighed again. "I hadn't time to change before tea. I didn't realize your mother had guests." She hurried on. "And once I'd entered, I had to say something, so I told them about the berries, thinking they would understand my appearance if I explained what I had been doing. But . . ." Her voice trailed off, and she looked away.

Nicholas touched her chin, turning her face to his. Her eyes sparkled with unshed tears. "But they *didn't* understand, did they?" he whispered, releasing her though he felt like pulling her close. "Instead they looked down their noses at you and said scornful, hateful things you were forced to endure."

She shook her head. "They said nothing, but your mother did. She said awful things to me—about me. That if I were to behave like an errant child, I should be punished like one. Then, in front of your guests, she banished me to my room as if I were a ten-year-old girl."

A new kind of anger burned inside Nicholas. What a mortifying experience for any woman, but especially hard on Grace, who was used to making her own decisions and had governed her own life from such a young age.

And she hadn't acted out on purpose. It had likely all seemed so innocent to her—picking berries to make a pie . . . But disgraceful from his mother's point of view, to be sure. He had to choose his words—and position—carefully. Grace's feelings were tender, but there was also Mother to consider. She hadn't had an easy time of things since Elizabeth's and then Father's passing.

"You're not a child." Nicholas looked into her clouded eyes and brushed a thumb across her quivering lip, suddenly more aware than he had ever been of the truth of that statement. She was a woman in need of comfort. A woman who was vulnerable and beautiful and—

Mine.

He stepped back abruptly, putting enough space between them that he could not touch her again. He sucked in a lungful of air, furious with the direction of his thoughts. Grace—Miss Thatcher—was *not* his. He didn't want to be saddled with her forever; Mother wanted it even less than he. Had he not just spent a week in London, exploring the options for escape from this entrapment?

"I apologize for Mother's behavior. I will speak to her about the situation before we dine tonight."

"Thank you." Miss Thatcher's eyes spoke of confusion—and new hurt he'd likely caused with his immediate withdrawal—but that could not be helped.

Any . . . *feelings* he developed for her would only complicate an already difficult situation.

"I will remain in my room until then." She turned away and began walking up the stairs. Nicholas followed her with his eyes, admiring all sorts of things he had no business noticing, much less appreciating. Her back, stiff with determination, earned a little more of his respect. Her hand on the rail begged to be held again. The swing of her curls tempted him to explore their softness as he had that night in the carriage.

He closed his eyes to all of it and turned to go into his study, intent on delving into paperwork once again neglected in his absence.

Kingsley met him at the doorway, a tray in his hands. "A bite to eat while you work?"

"Put it on the desk." Nicholas crossed to the window, looking out at the newly trimmed rosebushes. Next year they would bloom again, and he'd have no peace at all with the scent so reminiscent of Elizabeth filling the house.

Elizabeth—and Father. What would they have thought of the mess he found himself in? What would they have done in his place?

He heard the click of the door behind him but remained at the window, contemplating what he must say to his mother and how he was supposed to handle Miss Thatcher.

No doubt Elizabeth would have taken Grace under her wing, and they would have become great friends. But then, Elizabeth always had been his antithesis—friendly to a fault with everyone.

As was Father. Mother and I are cut from a different cloth. They were more reserved, more serious. It was Mother who had most disapproved of the match between Elizabeth and Preston. It had taken Father months to convince her that Elizabeth's happiness mattered most.

But had that fleeting happiness been worth the price? If Elizabeth had been denied her love, would she still be here?

Would their family now be as it had been?

Nicholas unfastened his cuffs and rolled up his shirtsleeves, eager to get to work and banish the uncomfortable, varied directions of his thoughts. As much as he'd disliked Preston, he couldn't deny that Elizabeth had been happy with him. Happier, even, than when she'd been growing up in their home. Preston had doted on her, encouraged her adventurous side, had been an eager participant in whatever schemes she concocted.

Elizabeth had been happier, certainly, than Miss Thatcher had ever been. *I have the opportunity to change that. To do something good for her. To be the one to stand up for her.*

And to stand against Mother.

Something he could not do. Neither, it seemed, could he be easily rid of Miss Thatcher.

Abandonment was not a pretty word, but that was what the solicitor had suggested their situation would be called were he to send her packing now—no matter that he'd pay her expenses, no matter that her inheritance might yet be settled so she could choose to go elsewhere.

Just not here with me.

And were something to happen to Miss Thatcher now—when she'd somewhat recovered her health, and the entire county had been made to know how he and Mother felt about his predicament—it would be very suspect.

I may have to marry her. The thought was not half as disturbing as it had been a month earlier. *But she cannot stay.*

Why not?

He was starting to feel that he wanted her to do just that.

But Miss Thatcher was distracting him from his purpose, upsetting his mother, and wreaking havoc in his life.

He moved to his desk and sat down, glancing at the packets that had arrived in his absence—only a few, as he'd been gone but a week. Beyond the letters stood a tray holding a plate with a generous slice of berry pie, which Kingsley had delivered.

With a furtive glance at the closed door, Nicholas leaned forward and picked up the fork. He cut himself a good-sized bite and brought it to his mouth, unprepared for the burst of flavor that followed.

Grace made this. Perhaps he should hire her as an assistant cook. The thought made him laugh, as did the realization that she must have gone downstairs to make pies *after* his mother had banished her to her room.

Backbone. Grace had one in spades. It was a quality he admired more than he cared to admit. He took another bite.

Unpredictability. In the past, he'd loathed the unexpected, but he couldn't deny that since Grace's arrival, life had been more interesting, at least. He took another bite, his eyes closed in bliss as he leaned back in his chair.

Delicious. A good description of Grace's cooking. *And everything else about her.* He found her far more than tolerable, and that fact had the potential to lead to the biggest disaster of all.

Miss Thatcher was causing his purpose to shift. *Back where it belongs. Here. At home.* She was a match for his mother in determination—as whomever he eventually married would have to be. But mostly she was wreaking havoc.

On my soul.

With the last bite, he admitted his folly. He had come to care for her. Miss Thatcher would have to go, though he didn't want her to.

"That will be all, Jenny. Thank you," Grace said, turning from the mirror to dismiss her maid.

"You look lovely tonight," Jenny said. "Lady Sutherland won't be able to take fault with you at all."

"Let us hope you are correct," Grace said, though she'd no doubt the dowager would find something in her dress or character to complain about.

Jenny curtsied, then left, closing the door behind her. Grace looked around the room she'd refused to stay in the past two days and felt a sudden longing to do just that. And not just to avoid confrontation with the dowager.

It was her son who had her worried.

Her son, whom I have dressed for tonight when I should be avoiding him.

She'd rushed to greet him earlier, telling herself it was because she had hoped for news from her solicitor, not because she had been lonely or had particularly missed Lord Sutherland or had ceased thinking of the day they had spent together.

He had rewarded her greeting with unexpected warmth—at first. Grace touched her hand where he'd held it, remembering the glorious feelings his simple gesture had caused.

But then he'd returned to himself—guarded, stern—and pulled away.

This way is best. It is what I want. There is no point in furthering this entanglement.

Grace turned to the long mirror once more, studying her reflection critically. *So why have I dressed with such care?*

The green brocade was perhaps a bit fancy for a dinner at home; it was certainly finer than anything she'd worn here yet. And her hairstyle was likely overdone as well, piled high with loose curls left to tumble about her face. Weeks ago, Lord Sutherland had instructed her to wear her hair up, but he'd said nothing about wearing it plain, and tonight she wished at least some of it free.

She'd taken pains with her jewelry and face powders as well, and the cumulative effect of the ensemble took her by surprise. She hadn't felt this pretty since Samuel's ball.

Yet that night, Lord Sutherland's only comment was that I looked ill.

Grace smiled at the memory, recalling how he had vexed her at the time, though likely she had looked ill, considering that she'd been about to faint. Her smile turned thoughtful as she wondered what had transpired during those moments she had not been herself. What had Lord Sutherland said to Samuel?

What had Lord Sutherland been thinking, *to bring me here again? Why had he done it?*

What am I to do about it now?

That single action had started a chain of events that thwarted her very purpose. She might have to marry.

If I marry, I will not be able to look after Helen. But for the moment, she is safe.

While I am very much in danger.

It was one thing to be forced into a betrothal, quite another to actually speak the vows—an eventuality Grace had all but convinced herself would never come to pass. But it was yet another problem entirely—

That I am starting to wish for that very occasion.

Grace studied the reflection in the mirror, so like her mother's. *I mustn't be like her. I must protect my heart against love, especially from a man like Lord Sutherland, who has so little regard for others—for me.*

She nodded resolutely; her reflection nodded back. But to Grace it seemed they only commiserated in their agreement that it was already too late.

"What did you learn in town, Nicholas?" the dowager asked as soon as their meal had been served by Kingsley and a newly hired servant and they had taken their proper places away from the table, against the far wall.

Lord Sutherland turned his head toward his mother, directing a look at her that Grace guessed she wasn't supposed to notice.

"I should prefer to discuss it later." His words were terse.

"Why?" Lady Sutherland asked. "All concerned are present, are they not?"

Grace sipped her drink and pretended disinterest. As Lord Sutherland seemed to be disinterested in her appearance. He'd hardly spared a glance for her when they'd walked into dinner together. Yet she was pleased that he'd escorted her as well as his mother to their seats. She'd at least earned that much respect.

I should be grateful they are ignoring me. But she wasn't. She wanted Lord Sutherland's attention as she'd had it on the stairs earlier. Of course, that was not likely to happen with his mother around.

"Have you or have you not found a way out of this disagreeable arrangement?" Lady Sutherland pressed.

Grace stared at her, affronted by the woman's continued

rudeness—no mistaking which *arrangement* she referred to—but she was determined not to show it.

"Do tell us, please," Grace said, turning her attention to Lord Sutherland, who sat between them.

A rather uncomfortable spot, no doubt.

Grace spoke in a voice of sweetest innocence. "Have you found another chaperone for me so your mother may be free to return to London?"

The dowager gasped, and Lord Sutherland appeared to have a sudden difficulty swallowing his food.

"What is this nonsense?" Lady Sutherland demanded, taking her eyes from her son long enough to shoot daggers at Grace. "I'll not be driven from my home by some impertinent chit."

Grace met her stare head on. "Nor will I any longer be bullied by a domineering woman in what may someday be *my* home." *Oh dear.*

"It will not be yours. Nicholas, set this woman straight. Tell her how you've been to London to find a way out of this entrapment."

Grace winced inwardly at the dowager's choice of words. From her point of view—and Lord Sutherland's—that is what this whole thing must seem. They were the unfortunate victims of a desperate female and her father.

Hearing that Nicholas had been to London to visit not only her solicitor but also seeking a release from their betrothal did not surprise her. But it stung.

He turned his gaze on her, and Grace was astonished at the tender, pleading expression in his eyes. "I took to heart what you asked of me on our drive last week," he said. "I met with Mr. Littleton and my own solicitors, as well."

"And?" The fluttery feelings she'd experienced this afternoon returned, along with a rush of gratitude at his kindness. "*Can* anything be done?" Unexpected hope buoyed her spirits at the same time a sense of dread rushed forth. She wanted to leave Sutherland Hall, didn't she?

Lord Sutherland shook his head. "Nothing that I have discovered. The new duke is using his position in an attempt to sway the court. Even if you were to get the money, and though you have professed to want to never marry, you must understand that scandal will follow you. You'd be unable to find respectable servants or a family willing to rent a decent home in which you may live. Were you to leave now, as a single woman, you would be shunned at every turn. It would make life excruciatingly difficult for you."

"A just punishment," the dowager huffed. "If that is the only thing holding you to this betrothal, Nicholas, think no more—"

"There is more." Lord Sutherland turned to her. "My name would be had for worse as well—and yours along with it, Mother. If I do not wed Miss Thatcher, the situation will be viewed as abandonment, and if *someone* was to be interested in pursuing the case, it could even be taken up in court."

"Someone" meaning Samuel?

A heavy sigh escaped the dowager, and her lips turned down even more. Grace did not care to ease her burden, but neither could she admit defeat so readily. She and Lord Sutherland had already danced around this subject for weeks. That it was finally upon the table for discussion could not be ignored. It might be the only chance she had to find a solution, to gain her freedom.

"What if I was to let it be known that I left you of my own accord?" Grace suggested. "If the fault was mine—"

"It would never be seen that way." Nicholas shook his head. "It would be determined that I drove you to desperate action. Indeed, Miss Thatcher, leaving would be desperate on your part. I cannot recommend it at all."

"What *do* you recommend?" Grace asked, feeling the flame of hope die as quickly as it had sparked. So did the dread at the thought of leaving.

"I suggest we carry on as we have," he said. "Neither

doing anything permanent, nor anything rash. Perhaps a solution will yet be uncovered."

"I fear I have lost my appetite," the dowager said, setting her napkin onto the table. Lord Sutherland jumped up to get her chair before Kingsley could come around the table. As Lord Sutherland assisted his mother, Grace witnessed a new side of both, one she'd not noticed before.

One I've not taken time to observe.

Lady Sutherland seemed to have deflated with news of her defeat. The creases lining her face appeared deeper, her arms more frail, as Lord Sutherland helped her stand. As she gazed up at him and patted his hand, there was a sadness in her expression.

Lord Sutherland sent an apologetic glance Grace's way, and she noted a new weight there, a responsibility he felt for his mother—for her happiness.

Which I have destroyed.

"Excuse us, please." He escorted the dowager from the room, leaving Grace alone save for the two, near-invisible servants somewhere behind her.

Grace looked at her food and found that her appetite had fled as well. A half hour ago, she would have felt incensed at the situation, certain that Lady Sutherland had contrived the whole thing to spirit her son away. But now . . .

Grace felt quite certain that was not the case. The sorrow and regret in both of their expressions had been real. She recalled her harsh words and wished she could take them back. She hadn't been clever at all, but ill-mannered. *The very impertinent chit Lady Sutherland described.*

Feeling ashamed, guilty, and overall wretched about everything, Grace stood quickly and was surprised at the ease with which her chair pushed back. She turned to find Kingsley behind her, his hands on her chair.

Grace gave him a sad smile. "You are extraordinarily good at anticipating everything, Kingsley. Would that I had that talent." She turned to go.

"You have others," he said, further surprising her with speech, and kindness at that. "A proverb my mother once taught, if I might?"

Grace nodded. "Please."

"'It takes more than a lovely gown a lady to make.'" He cleared his throat as if uncomfortable. "She used to tell that to my sister whenever she bemoaned the lack of fashion in our humble home."

Grace could see his point. *I might have looked the part tonight, but I did not act it.*

His implication hurt, but no worse than she already did.

"May I inquire what became of your sister?" Grace ventured, astonished that their conversation had gone this long already.

"She married well and has a passel of children," Kingsley said, a touch of pride in his voice.

"She is happy, then?" Grace asked.

"Very, miss," Kingsley said. "Lack of fine gowns, notwithstanding."

Grace smiled at him. "Some of my happiest days have been when I've been dressed the poorest. Thank you for sharing that tale with me." She walked toward the doorway.

Kingsley bowed. "If I might say one thing more?"

Grace stopped and waited upon him. He was certainly out of character tonight. *Probably taking the opportunity to pounce on my mistake.* Though she didn't quite think that was it. His comment had seemed sincere, not chastising.

He went ahead, holding the door for her. "Lady Sutherland may never admit it, and I don't know as Lord Sutherland will either, but they both enjoyed your pie. Ate every last crumb." The corners of his eyes crinkled, and a conspiratorial smile lit his face. "She even asked for seconds. Lady Sutherland has quite a fondness for sweets."

"Thank you for telling me," Grace said, feeling a little better and realizing that her efforts had not been entirely in vain. "Perhaps I would do better here as a baker."

Kingsley shook his head. "Now don't go getting any ideas, or cook will have *my* head next time."

Grace's eyes widened in mock horror. "Has she had many others?"

Kingsley chuckled. "I can see why Lord Sutherland appreciates your wit."

He does? "Thank you for the sincere compliments, Kingsley, particularly on a night when I am less than deserving. I shall take myself off to bed now, before I begin to think too highly of myself." Grace smiled once more, then took her leave.

"Just remember," Kingsley called after her. "Lady Sutherland has a strong preference for the sweet. You'll always get farther with her there than when serving up something tart."

CHAPTER 29

Nicholas finished admiring one of his tenant's newly dug wells, then went in search of Miss Thatcher. It was close to an hour since he'd last seen her, as she'd developed the habit of wandering off the moment they set foot out of the carriage.

Likely seeking better company than mine, Nicholas thought, somewhat irritated. The atmosphere between them had felt strained today, more so than that first outing together when he'd expected as much.

Last night's aborted dinner had cast a wall up between them. To Miss Thatcher, it must seem as if he'd chosen his mother's side. *And what of Miss Thatcher's actions?* He'd been surprised at her outburst at the table; she had crossed a forbidden line by speaking to his mother that way. *No woman wants to be reminded that she will no longer be mistress of her home.*

Especially when that woman did not approve of the one replacing her. Nicholas sighed. He couldn't entirely blame Miss Thatcher for her harsh words. Mother had seemed equally harsh over the berry incident, and while Miss Thatcher had been attempting to please.

She has been patient a long while. He was not angry with her but imagined she might think he was. He'd hoped his invitation to come visiting might have resolved their awkwardness, but instead, she had spent the day avoiding him.

Contrary to his usual inclination to be alone, he found he preferred her company. He enjoyed watching her in what appeared to be her element—everywhere they went, his tenants flocked to her, young and old, male and female. Meanwhile, he had stood on the outskirts, uncertain how to begin, yet she had seemed to know intuitively how to interact with them.

In the past few hours, he'd watched her help a busy mother take down her laundry, fawn over the size and beauty of a farmer's geese, sit on a porch step to visit and enjoy a piece of fresh-baked bread, and teach a child how to write his name with a stick in the dirt.

Before the day was out, Nicholas predicted that Miss Thatcher would singlehandedly win the affection of every Sutherland tenant. And all because she'd made them feel valued and important by showing interest in their lives and providing a listening ear.

Skills you would do well to develop, Nicholas's father had told him on more than one occasion when they'd made similar rounds. Nicholas recalled the respect with which his father had always treated those living on this land. For the first time in the two years he'd been in this position, Nicholas was striving to do the same. Having Miss Thatcher along made it easier. The people were starting to talk with him. They shared their concerns, successes, and ideas for how to make the land more profitable.

All because she is with me. So where the deuce is she now? He tromped through the long grass between two cottages, hoping to find her visiting in the back, perhaps helping another woman with her chores. But both yards were empty.

Nicholas turned to go up the road, thinking they might have just missed each other and that Miss Thatcher would be waiting at the carriage, when he noticed a crowd gathered around the entrance to one of his tenant's barns. A cry rang out across the yard, followed by shouting, then a minute later, silence.

What now? As his feet carried him swiftly toward the barn, Nicholas worried that whatever had gone wrong involved Miss Thatcher. The rose garden incident and pie-baking were still fresh in his mind. If she'd caused some sort of scene here, the tenants might spread the tale far and wide, and his mother would be furious beyond reasoning. About the only thing she had left was her reputation, and he—and Miss Thatcher—had done enough damage to that already.

He arrived at the barn out of breath and apprehensive. The crowd parted easily, allowing him to move to the front, just inside the open doors. A boy, probably around eleven or twelve years of age, sat on the floor by the wall, head in his hands, a cloth stained red with blood pressed against one side of his face.

"What happened?" Nicholas demanded and was answered by a chorus of shushing voices.

He ignored them. "Is the boy okay? Does he require—"

A hand on his shoulder silenced him. "Ben's fine. Quiet now. You don't want to spook her."

As his eyes adjusted to the dim light, Nicholas saw that the *her* in question was a mad cow, stomping and kicking on the far side of the barn just a few paces away from—

Grace!

He started toward her, but the hand on his shoulder tightened briefly in warning. "Begging pardon, milord. But I wouldn't do that." The farmer nodded respectfully and backed away.

Nicholas held his tongue, watching with everyone else as Miss Thatcher took a step closer to the distraught animal. The barn grew quiet once more, and he realized that she was singing. A soft, lyrical melody floated toward him. The words were nonsensical—something about how much better it would feel to be milked and how pretty the cow's eyes were and how important she was. The words didn't matter. Grace could have been repeating the word *mud* over and over again, and her voice would have had the same effect. The cow—along with the rest of the barn's inhabitants, including those human—stood transfixed, entranced . . . *enchanted.*

Nicholas wondered how it was that he hadn't known of her talent before. *How is it that we have lived weeks beneath the same roof, and until now I've not heard her sing?* He allowed his eyes to close briefly as he listened, relaxing, feeling the cares of life slip away beneath her spellbinding song. The animal began to calm and finally stood still.

Leave now. Move, Grace. When she did not heed his silent commands, Nicholas took a step forward, intent on removing her from danger. The cow's tale twitched, and she tossed her head back. Miss Thatcher turned looked over her shoulder and caught his eye, sending him a disapproving look. Nicholas motioned for her to back up, to come to him, to safety. She shook her head and returned to the cow and her song, edging closer until the animal was again calm and she was close enough to reach out and stroke its spotted back.

Nicholas held his breath, expecting imminent disaster. If the animal kicked, Grace would likely end up breaking a bone or worse.

Please don't. This time, his silent plea was answered. The cow did nothing save gently nudge Miss Thatcher's outstretched hand.

"There, girl, see? It's all right. We just want to help you." Miss Thatcher moved slowly as she spoke, retrieving an overturned stool and pail. These she set beside the cow, close to its hind legs, and gathered her skirts aside, as if to sit.

No! Nicholas felt like shouting but didn't dare. The barn had grown completely silent, as if the other animals were as awed by the performance as the people.

Miss Thatcher sat as delicately as if she were seating herself on a throne, and soon the sound of milk pinging into the empty pail made a sweet accompaniment to her continued melody.

"Well, I'll be," someone farther back said. Murmurs of agreement and admiration rippled around Nicholas. Some left the barn, likely returning to their own chores now that the excitement was over. Nicholas stayed until Miss Thatcher had finished milking, thanked the cow, and hauled the overflowing bucket far enough from the beast that another lad was brave enough to come close and take it from her.

Nicholas was right behind him and reached out, grabbing her wrist and pulling her toward him.

"What were you thinking?" He stared at her hard, expecting an apology for her lack of judgment. "You might have been kicked in the head or trampled or—"

"I am perfectly fine, thank you." Her voice was calm and unapologetic. With her free hand, she removed his fingers from her wrist. "I regret to say, however, that you do not look well at all." She brushed past him out to the yard, where Thom Wallace doffed his hat and thanked her profusely.

"I thought for certain we'd lost her," he said. "And without a cow this winter—well, let's just say it would have been terrible hard on the children."

"I know," Miss Thatcher said, and Nicholas suspected she very well did.

She squeezed Thom Wallace's outstretched hand as she smiled up at him. "Just treat her gently, and she'll take to you. The move to a new owner was a bit of a shock is all, I imagine. I think she'll do just fine now."

"If she doesn't, will you come back to milk her later?" someone called.

"No, she will not," Nicholas answered for her. He stepped up beside Miss Thatcher, placing his hand at her elbow. "It's time we were off."

"Of course." Her next smile was for him, and Nicholas detected no trace of anger in it, though he knew he'd likely upset her back there in the barn.

She tucked her hand in the crook of his arm and allowed him to escort her to the carriage, bidding farewell to those they left behind as if she'd had their acquaintance for years. He handed her up and went around to the other side, half wondering as he did if she might gather the reins and drive off without him.

Behind the curricle, a woman stopped him. "Oh Lord Sutherland, it's as I said it would be. Just as I told you. I'm so glad."

Nicholas stared at the woman, a short little thing with wisps of hair flying from her bun and a thin shawl gathered tight around hunched shoulders. It took him a moment to realize where he'd seen her before—and to what she was referring.

The not-so-timid washerwoman who tried to offer me advice. He felt a new respect for her profession, having learned the details, from Grace, of what it took to clean clothing. He glanced down at the woman's hands and saw that they were chapped and dry.

"There'll be happiness again at Sutherland Hall, mark my words," she said. "You'll see. It's her that's going to bring it." She inclined her head toward the carriage.

"Yes. Well, we'll see," Nicholas said stiffly. He wasn't used to conversing with his tenants like this—especially with the women. He bid her farewell, but she stared after him, her face folded into a look that was a mixture of disappointment and pity.

Nicholas sensed he'd done wrong, but he had no idea what he should have said or done differently. Instead he told himself that he'd double the woman's pay and see that Miss Thatcher had some new gowns made so there would be more clothing to launder.

She had not driven off without him, and she hadn't said

anything as they started down the lane toward the main road. In his mind, Nicholas reviewed the events in the barn, and his anger returned. He snapped the reins harder than necessary, and the carriage lurched forward.

"You shouldn't have done that. You might have been killed."

Miss Thatcher smiled as if he'd said something droll.

"What"—he demanded—"do you find so amusing about the situation?"

"It's not the situation," she explained. "There is nothing the least bit humorous about the possibility of losing one's cow just before winter. A good cow can be the difference between starvation and survival."

"Then what *are* you smiling about?" he asked, feeling more out of sorts by the minute.

"You scolded your mother in the same manner at breakfast once. You told her she shouldn't have chided me as she did."

"You heard that?" Nicholas's anger merged with unease, forming a heavy weight in his stomach.

Has Grace known Mother's intentions all along?

"What else have you overheard?" he asked.

"Nothing." She turned to face him, and he could see that she spoke the truth. He was starting to suspect that Grace was not capable of being anything but truthful.

"It is not my habit to eavesdrop," she said. "I happened to overhear what you said that day only because your tone was rather loud and—reprimanding."

Relief swept through Nicholas, followed swiftly by guilt. He *had* plotted with his mother for that day to be a dismal failure, for Grace to return home overwhelmed and defeated when she realized that no one would respect or accept her at Sutherland Hall. He'd never felt so grateful to be wrong.

I have been so wrong about many things.

"And my reprimand amuses you?"

"Merely the tone you used with me." Her mouth

quirked in a half-smile. "It was quite different from your kindness to me upon your homecoming yesterday. However, both sentiments indicate your concern and lead me to believe that you are not as unfeeling as I first judged you to be. Therefore—" Her lips curved upward. "I smile."

Nicholas had no reply. He sat stiff and straight on the seat and focused on guiding the horses, though they well knew the way. The things Miss Thatcher said and did were entirely untoward. No well-bred woman would have had the nerve to call him unfeeling to his face or to admit to overhearing a private conversation. Nicholas knew he *ought* to feel extremely put out, but for some odd reason, her behavior was having the opposite effect.

He'd never again doubt whether she spoke truth. He'd only need to be wary of what he asked, knowing that her answer—especially regarding his character—might prove unpleasant to hear. He realized suddenly what it was about her manner that he—and likely everyone else they'd encountered today—was attracted to.

Miss Thatcher is unaffected by the world and her position in it.

She'd come to the upper class too late in life to behave as selfishly as most ladies did. She didn't act as the privileged, spoiled woman he'd first assumed her to be. She didn't expect the world to pity her misfortunes, and she wasn't above trimming a rose bush that needed it or helping one of his tenants.

She is not cowed by Mother.

It was this startling contrast that Nicholas suspected he was beginning to admire. He'd never met a woman like Miss Thatcher—one who kept him on his toes and whose brilliant unpredictability was proving the perfect antidote for his grief. Grief, he realized, that had lessened in the past weeks.

When did my thoughts turn from Elizabeth—and Preston—to Miss Thatcher, to Grace? Nicholas wasn't certain, but he could not deny that it was she who had been most on his mind of late. Grace, who was slowly filling the void in his heart.

"You're terribly quiet," she ventured. "Have I offended you?"

Nicholas laughed. "Anyone else would be tripping over themselves apologizing."

"One need never apologize for helping someone or speaking the truth," Grace said. "But if I have worried you or hurt your feelings, I do regret it. If what I said was unpleasant to hear, may I suggest something Grandfather once told me?"

"Please do," Nicholas said, wondering what bit of sage wisdom she might impart.

"Grandfather said that whenever I felt that something in my character was lacking, it was my responsibility to change it."

No pity in that family. None. "So if I don't like being called *unfeeling*, it is up to me to do something about it?"

"Precisely," Grace said.

"What do you suggest?" Nicholas asked, eager for her response.

"Well." She considered a moment. "In your case, I think you may want to work on being the exact opposite. Try to become the most *feeling* man possible. Try kindness."

The suggestion hurt more than her original insult. *Try kindness.* He thought he had been.

"All right," he said at last.

"And now you must tell me something I am to work on," Grace said. Her hands were folded primly in her lap, though he noticed that her gloves had been off for quite some time—odd, as she typically wore them while driving.

"Where are your gloves?" Nicholas asked. "Have you left them somewhere?"

Her brow furrowed, and she tucked her hands in the folds of her dress. "You wish me to improve on wearing my gloves?"

He laughed again. "No. I do not wish you to hide your hands, either. You are far too conscious of them. I only wish to know if we need to return somewhere to retrieve the gloves. See? I am trying to be kind."

"In that case, well done." She clapped her gloveless hands. "No need to worry over going back. I gave the gloves to a little girl who admired them."

"What—why?" Nicholas looked over, appraising her. As mindful of her hands as she'd confessed to being—with their evidence of the hard life she'd endured—she'd given the gloves, something she valued, to another. He felt truly astonished. "What else have you given away?"

She paused a second too long for her answer to be quite believable, in spite of the fact that he'd already convinced himself that she was incapable of lying.

"Nothing. I have given nothing away." She looked at her lap. "But I thank you for your concern. It is touching. And I know you are kind, deep inside where it matters."

"Is that a *compliment* I hear from your lips?" he teased, worrying that he'd said something wrong, though he couldn't fathom what that might be. But her sudden switch to silence had him concerned.

"Indeed it was a compliment." Miss Thatcher took a deep breath and faced him once more, bestowing a tenuous smile on him. "You *are* kind. I've seen evidence of such all day. You arranged to have roofs patched before winter. Offered a higher price than is at market for livestock. Fetched a doctor for the little boy with the cough . . ." Her voice trailed off as their eyes met.

Nicholas leaned back, stunned by her revelation. And here he thought he'd been the only one doing the watching. He felt inexplicably warmed by the thought of her tracking his movements, being aware of his doings throughout the day.

"I fear that you are not at all the ogre I first believed

you to be." Her grin widened, and Nicholas caught a merry twinkle in her eye.

She is teasing me! Miss Thatcher—Grace—is flirting. With me. Nicholas had seen this sort of play between couples before, but never had he had such attentions directed at himself, at least not from one of whom he desired it.

And I do wish it from her, he realized with some consternation. He tried to steer their dialogue elsewhere, to a place where his thoughts might not be so focused on those long lashes or the pert lips awaiting his response.

"Have you feared me very much then?" he asked, knowing well enough what her answer would be. He'd read fear in her eyes a time or two, from that first night he'd railed at her in his room, to the afternoon in his study when he'd informed her of their betrothal, to the day of the flower garden incident, when he'd accused her of purposefully butchering his sister's roses.

"You know I have," she said.

Nicholas suspected she also knew that he felt uncomfortable with their banter. Her mischievous look had fled, bringing him both satisfaction and disappointment.

She let out a sigh that sounded rather discouraged. "But no longer. I will not fear you anymore. I've seen the true man you are inside, and though you may continue to try to hide him from me, I know he is still there. *You* are there."

"*I* fear that you are wrong," Nicholas said. He flicked the reins half-heartedly. During their conversation, he'd all but forgotten to drive, so the team plodded along at a snail's pace. "My soul is black. There is no hope for it. Whereas you . . ." He turned to her. "You are aptly named, Miss Thatcher—Grace. May I call you by your given name?"

Her smile was instantaneous. "I would like that very much."

Again such honesty. Why did it affect him so? Every word that fell from her mouth, from the simplest *yes* to her insults, drove him closer to . . . *madness*? He could think of no other term for the loss of clarity in his mind and the wrenching in his gut. *She has no idea . . .*

"Everything you do—even milking a cow—" He gave a half-hearted laugh. "Wherever did you learn to do that?" Nicholas allowed himself to be impressed with her skill—one he certainly did not possess.

"We owned a cow for a short while," Grace said. "Father won her."

Of course. How else would they have had a cow, if not through her father's *income*? "A short while? What happened to it?'

Grace scowled. "What do you think happened? Father gambled and lost. But oh, what a heavenly time while we had her! To have fresh milk every morn—how we all cried when they took her away."

Nicholas frowned at the image of three children huddled together, crying their hearts out over a cow. He felt like punching something, preferably her father. The man had best not set foot on Sutherland property again.

"You never finished your thought about everything I do," Grace reminded him. "Though I am somewhat fearful to hear its conclusion."

She worries over what I think of her? Yet another revelation.

"I was saying that everything about you, everything you do, bespeaks of *grace*."

This time her smile bloomed slowly and lovely, lighting up her entire face. Their eyes met, and she looked at him with an intensity she hadn't before. "Thank you . . . Nicholas."

Hearing his name from her lips pushed what was left of his sanity to the edge.

"I suppose," she continued, "that if we are betrothed, and if there is truly no way out of it—if we are to spend the rest of our lives together—it is good that we call each other by our Christian names."

The rest of our lives together . . . A month ago, the thought would have terrified him. It still did in a way, but he could not deny that the thought of Miss Thatcher's—Grace's—company for many years to come held a certain appeal.

As they approached the main road, the reins fell slack in his hands. He didn't want to return home just yet. This morning he'd dreaded the tasks of the day and supposed that the hours would drag on. Now he could scarce believe that the sun was already sinking low on the horizon.

Is this how it will be? Might every day with Grace be as delightful as this?

She was still looking at him. This time her face held no expectation of response but a look of patience, as if she understood that he needed time alone with his thoughts. He wouldn't have been surprised if she could read his mind, if she somehow knew of the conflict wrestling inside him.

He guided the team to a stop just before the main road.

"You are making me quite mad," he said, echoing the complete honesty she'd given him.

"Am I?" This seemed to please her, as another smile formed, melting away yet more of the hard shell around his heart.

Nicholas reached for her hands, and this time she did not pull away or hide them behind her in shame. He turned her palm over, tracing the lines, feeling the calluses left by years of gripping a washboard. "Your hands are lovely. Like the rest of you." He brought her fingers to his lips, wishing away all her sorrows with his kiss.

"That is the kindest thing anyone has ever said to me. I thank you, Nicholas."

His name again. How could one word bring such torture? Nicholas suppressed a groan. *What has happened to me since this morning? No, not just this morning—since that fated night I discovered her in my bed?*

As he looked at her face, he realized the change had

come about gradually. She'd been stirring feelings in him since that very first night.

At Preston's ball . . . during the carriage ride home . . . in the library . . . at meals—at dinner last night, when she looked as ravishing as any woman I've ever known.

Her brave words, in the way she'd stepped forward that first night to defend Kingsley, had left a lasting impression. Her defiance at the ball had been irritating, but intriguing, too. Their constant sparring, her wittiness, the way she stood up to his mother, the obvious love Grace felt for her siblings.

This woman, who was completely unaffected by the world, was affecting him greatly. She'd disturbed his existence to the point that he wasn't certain he could ever return to the way it had been before her most untimely arrival in his life.

He no longer wanted to.

Nicholas lifted his hand to her face, touching her cheek—something he'd longed to do again since that night in the carriage. Her skin was every bit as soft as he remembered, and when she leaned into his touch, he could no longer resist. He drew closer, intent on quenching this desire. Just one kiss, and he would be able to regain his sanity. Just once, and then he would be able to leave her alone.

His eyes never left hers as he lowered his face close, close, closer. Their lips touched briefly, then parted. He waited one heartbeat, and then another, half certain she would reject him. Instead she smiled, and in her eyes there seemed to be a desire that matched his own.

"Grace." He whispered her name with all the reverence it deserved, then kissed her hands again, holding his lips there, savoring her nearness. He was the luckiest man in the world.

One kiss is not nearly enough.

Behind him, Nicholas heard a carriage crest the hill, round the bend, and approach their crossing. Nicholas did not let go. He scooted closer, put one arm around her, and found holding her close to be nearly as sweet as kissing her had been.

He glanced up at the polished black carriage as the horses trotted past and glimpsed the Ellis crest on the side. A dark chuckle rose from his chest.

"What?" Grace lifted her face to his, and this time he was sure of her longing gaze, of the same burning desire he knew. She looked as overwhelmed as he felt. He kissed her once more, another light brush of his lips to hers, and then she pulled away, her breathing as ragged as his felt, though theirs had been the briefest touch.

Nicholas kept his arm around her. "We might be in a spot of trouble," he said, not the least worried.

"Oh?" Grace smoothed her dress and glanced at him shyly as a lovely blush stained her cheeks.

"That was the Ellis carriage just now. No doubt it carries Mrs. Ellis, the biggest gossip this side of the shire."

"Is that all?" Grace smiled, seemingly having recovered her composure rather quickly, he thought. It would be quite some time before *he* recovered.

"Is that *all*?" He shook his head in mock dismay. "By nine o'clock this evening, the entire county will know we were kissing at the crossroad."

"Then I suppose . . ." She took a deep breath, her words slowing. "The entire county will know that Miss Grace Thatcher cares for her betrothed, Lord Sutherland."

Something shattered inside him at her confession. "Does she, now?"

How can she possibly—

Nicholas reached for her, closing the space between them once more. "Perhaps Lord Sutherland is not aware of this affection." He used a teasing tone to be safe, lest she was doing the same.

"He'd best be aware," Grace muttered, her lips turning down in a most inviting fashion. "It's not as if I go around kissing—"

Another carriage came around the bend, and Grace broke off as she watched it approach. Nicholas turned to see who it might be, knowing that unless it was his mother, he had no care at all who saw them. The damage was done, and besides, he rather liked Grace's assessment of the situation.

But it was the one other person who did matter. Preston's carriage drew closer with its shiny, false crest—false because it hadn't been traveling these roads for generations; it didn't belong here.

Revenge flared to life inside of Nicholas, and for once, he knew he had the advantage. He had what Preston wanted and could make him suffer for it. Nicholas pulled Grace roughly to him, smothering her lips with his, kissing her—not gently as he had before, but in a way no one could mistake for anything but possession. She was his, and Preston would never have her.

She pushed against him, but he held her tightly until the carriage passed. Then he loosened his grip, and Grace pushed him away, her eyes blurred with tears.

"How dare you use me like that? I will not be a pawn between you." She stood and practically jumped from the carriage.

He leaned toward her. "Grace—"

She cringed as he spoke her name but drew herself taller and glared at him. "I stand by what I said earlier. Inside of you there is a noble man, a good and caring man desperate to come out, but he can't because you've locked him behind an iron cage of revenge." She shook her head as the first tear fell. "Only you have the key that will open the bars and set him free. Yet you refuse." She whirled away, stepped onto the main road, and hurried toward home.

And Preston's halted carriage.

Nicholas snapped the reins and hustled the team up the road. Just a short way ahead, Preston's carriage waited. The door had opened, and Preston was getting out, though both driver and footman remained in place.

He plans to rescue her. I cannot let Preston take her from me.

Yet is that not exactly what I did to him?

Nicholas's thoughts tumbled one upon one another, but none mattered except the possibility of losing Grace. He'd only just found her, and now she might leave him.

She walked briskly toward the open vehicle. Nicholas longed to call out to her again, but his pride kept him silent. *Not in front of Preston.*

Nicholas drove slowly, a hair behind her. She could rejoin him at any time. But she kept her pace—and did not stop when she reached Preston's landau.

Relief swept through Nicholas. He wasn't sure what he'd have done if she'd have gone with Preston. There might have been a duel right there, right then.

Preston shouted to his driver and pulled the door closed. His carriage rolled forward, and he leaned out the window, speaking to Grace. She glanced at him but shook her head and continued walking. A snub to Preston, to be sure, but Nicholas couldn't delight in it. He was too busy berating himself his rash decision and wishing Grace were still on the seat beside him.

She marched on, arms swinging resolutely, head held high, his carriage behind, and Preston's rolling slowly beside her. She left the road at the path that would take her through the gardens and on toward the house. Nicholas was first surprised she knew of it and then frustrated that he couldn't follow. But neither could Preston, who had withdrawn into his carriage while his driver was busy turning the vehicle around, as he'd passed his own drive some time ago.

Nicholas pulled up beside him. "Out of my way!" he shouted to the driver.

Preston's head appeared at the window. "Stop," he ordered his driver. The carriage door banged open. Preston unfolded himself from the seat and stood, leaning out, perilously close to Nicholas's team. "If you ever treat Grace like that again, I'll see that it's the last thing your lips ever do."

"Anytime you want to make good on your threat," Nicholas said, his hands clenched around the reins.

"At Miss Thatcher's word," Preston said. "And you can bet I'll find out if you've treated her poorly."

"You dare to speak. The man who killed my sister—his own wife!"

"I loved your sister—an emotion you wouldn't understand." Preston's chest heaved, and his fists clenched at his sides. "I honor Elizabeth's name by doing you no harm—today. But I swear on her grave, if you treat Grace ill ever again—"

"Empty threats," Nicholas spat. Preston needn't have uttered them. Nicholas felt enough self-loathing for his own actions.

I shouldn't have used Grace that way. I am the worst kind of rogue. He flicked the reins, intent on driving around Preston's skewed vehicle.

"You don't deserve her," Preston said.

I know. The truth of his enemy's words struck Nicholas at his core.

Preston's gaze followed him as he drove past. "You don't even realize what you have."

CHAPTER 30

Disaster was imminent. Grace dressed for dinner, dreading a confrontation with Lord Sutherland and knowing she likely wouldn't make it through the evening without some improper display of emotion.

"Any jewelry tonight, miss?" the girl who'd been sent up to help her asked.

Jenny had been reassigned to another task, leaving Grace without a lady's maid—an insult in itself and a good indication that neither Lord Sutherland—*Nicholas,* she thought with a pang—nor his mother expected her to remain at Sutherland Hall much longer. For all his noble words the night before, they were probably downstairs, deciding what to do with her.

"The pearls, please," Grace said as pleasantly as possible. *No use in taking my frustrations out on the servants, though that is what Lord Sutherland always does.*

She thought of the way he'd used her, how his antagonism toward Preston had been expressed in one passionate, overbearing kiss. Absently, she ran a finger over her lips. Instead of feeling bruised from the encounter, they seemed to ache, along with the rest of her, for the tender kisses that had come before.

Grace went to stand before the glass, staring at her reflection as Grandfather's last gift was fastened around her neck. Her fingers brushed the smooth pearls, remembering his words of praise when he'd given them to her.

You are as the pearl emerged from an oyster after a long period of refining—every bit as strong as when you were a grain of sand, now polished into something beautiful. Always remain so, Grace. Show the world your beauty and strength, both inside and out.

She closed her eyes, seeking fortitude from his words. She needed them tonight, for she didn't feel strong at all. She was weak, and it was her own fault. She'd brought this upon herself. In staying here so long, in searching for the good in Nicholas and seeing glimpses of it, she'd opened her heart to possibilities that were not safe.

Remember Mother, she silently admonished. *Falling in love will only break your heart.*

Studying her reflection in the mirror, she feared that the warning had come too late. When she thought of Nicholas and the way she'd left him, the things she'd said, she felt hollow inside. He was likely as furious as she.

He will not forget it easily. His long-standing anger with Preston was evidence of that.

Why should I care if he is angry with me? I am the one who was wronged. Grace told herself that she cared only because her reaction in front of Samuel had set back any progress she'd made in her attempts to convince him to introduce his daughter to Nicholas.

At this rate, Beth will be grown and married before she meets her uncle.

Grace let her fingers slide from the pearls to rest over her heart, heavy with sorrow. What she'd told Nicholas this afternoon was true. So long as revenge ruled his life, all else—all of the good she saw within him—could not come forth. He would not be capable of love.

Dinner proved as dreadful as Grace had predicted. Lady Sutherland criticized her throughout the meal, and Nicholas, in one of the worst brooding moods she'd yet seen, did not once come to her rescue. Grace caught each of them staring at her so many times she began to fear she had a spot on her chin or had made some terrible breach of etiquette.

She told herself that if that were the case, she did not particularly care. She kept her eyes averted to the far wall and kept her sentences clipped throughout the meal. Eventually even the dowager gave up taunting her and took to having a conversation with her son about matters of the past, which Grace knew nothing about. The exclusion did not hurt as it usually did—her feelings were already too mangled—but Nicholas would not engage with his mother, either, and the long, heavy silence that ensued proved exhausting and tense. Grace was only too happy to retire to the drawing room when the torturous meal was at last ended.

Choosing a settee near the window on the far side of the room, she settled herself and stared out at the dark night, watching for the moon to appear while stealing covert glances at Nicholas, who stood near the mantel, with his customary scowl in place. She intended to stay only a few minutes, long enough to give him the opportunity to say something to her, should he choose.

An apology from Lord Sutherland? She was mad to hope for it, when it was he, no doubt, who found her in the wrong.

"Perhaps you might favor us with a musical selection, Miss Thatcher," Lady Sutherland said, entering the room and seating herself on the sofa nearest Grace. "It has been so long since we've had music in the house. The pianoforte begs for attention."

Grace turned from the window and saw the shrewd, calculating look that had come into the dowager's eyes. She had a smile upon her lips, but it was not sincere, and instead, she seemed to be gloating as she looked at her son, then back at Grace.

She knows we are at odds, and she is happy about it.

"I am afraid I do not play much," Grace said, regretful that this was the case. She'd always loved music and envied those who'd had both the ability and means to develop it.

And it would have been wonderful to leave Lady Sutherland speechless, just this once.

The dowager looked taken aback by such a ready confession. "Your grandfather saw fit to give you riding lessons but did not see to your instruction in music?"

"I did have music lessons," Grace assured her. "But alas, it is not a talent I've been blessed with. I started too late in life and can play but the very simplest pieces." Were she to have seen the future and this very scene back then, Grace felt certain she would have tried harder and practiced longer. How it shamed her to acknowledge to Lady Sutherland all she lacked.

And Nicholas. What must he be thinking? Good riddance, most likely, to Miss Thatcher and her lack of refinement.

As if my rebuke this afternoon were not enough motivation for him to try again to figure a way out of our betrothal.

"What other talents are you lacking?" the dowager asked. "We have already established that you cannot sew a stitch."

"I sew many stitches," Grace said, unable to resist the urge to correct the woman. "I've made and mended many a dress. It's embroidery I've no experience with." Here, perhaps, Grandfather had neglected her education. But Grace would not have given up their evenings playing chess or reading together for the ability to sew even the most intricate of embroideries.

"As I said," the dowager returned sharply, her eyes narrowed on Grace, "you cannot sew a *proper* stitch, and now you admit that you cannot play the pianoforte. What a pity you have no talent with your hands."

"Grace has plenty of talent with her hands," Nicholas said.

The dowager directed her frown at him. Grace resumed looking out the window, pretending indifference. She dreaded what Nicholas might say next. She folded her hands in her lap, newly conscious of their scars. *Will he suggest to his mother that I become a laundress?*

She could think of nothing else he might say, for by society's standards, she *was* inferior. That he might disparage what she had done to survive hurt bitterly. In telling him of her childhood, she had made herself vulnerable.

I trusted him.

"Grace can milk a mad cow," Nicholas said, with what almost sounded like a touch of pride.

The dowager gasped, and both hands flew to her mouth.

How could you, Nicholas? Grace thought furiously, while at the same time relieved he had not chosen to make fun of her years spent doing others' laundry. *But why tell his mother of the cow? She will hate me even more.*

"A *cow*?" The dowager was only starting to recover. "Whatever do you mean?"

"Thom Wallace's new cow went a bit mad—wouldn't let anyone near her," Nicholas explained. "She kicked Thom's son in the head, and Thom was of a mind to shoot the animal when Grace stepped in. She calmed the cow and got a pail of milk for her efforts."

The dowager glanced from Grace to her son, her expression pained. "If word of this gets out, we shall be the laughingstock of the entire county." She brought a hand to her forehead and rubbed it as if trying to eradicate a terrible ache.

"You are missing the point." Nicholas shook his head. "Grace saved a valuable animal. She helped one of our tenants. She helped *us*."

His words surprised Grace and set her heart pounding. *One kindness is not a reason to forgive him for hurting me. Besides, it is about time he stood up for me.*

"But she *milked a cow.*" From the corner of her eye, Grace watched as the dowager retrieved a fan from the sofa table, snapped it open, and waved it in front of her face.

Grace waited for Nicholas to stand up for her again—yearned to hear more words of praise—but was not surprised when he remained silent. She glanced at him, wishing she knew what he was thinking as he stared into the fire with the same inscrutable expression, his face bathed in shadow.

She recalled her declaration that she would never again be afraid of him and realized that it was true. Nicholas had perfected his dark looks, but she'd glimpsed his heart. And it was not black, as he'd proclaimed.

Merely spotted and in need of a good cleaning. Which he will have to do himself.

She was not afraid of him, and she wasn't sympathetic to anything about his cause, either. *I am angry, and I have a right to be.*

Grace rose from her seat, intent on leaving the room. Her attempts at being polite company were finished, her patience stretched beyond its limit. "I fear all of that *cow milking* I did today has left me rather tired. I bid you both good night."

"The shame." Lady Sutherland moaned and brought a hand over her eyes as she leaned against the sofa.

As Grace started for the door, Nicholas removed himself from his place near the fire and walked so their paths would cross. Grace hurried her steps, intent on making her escape. He sped his pace as well, and they reached the door at the same moment. His hand covered hers on the knob.

"Forgive me," he whispered. "Please."

She felt certain he could hear her heart's traitorous beat, loud as it was, as it reacted to his touch. But fear did not cause her reaction as it had on that other occasion, weeks ago, when he'd trapped her at his bedroom door.

"It is customary for one to apologize before requesting forgiveness," she said with as much frost in her voice as she could muster.

"Did anyone see you milking?" Lady Sutherland called from the sofa. "Anyone besides the Wallace family? Where was this cow?"

"In a *barn*, Mother," Nicholas said. Then quieter, for only Grace's ears, "I *am* sorry." He leaned nearer, his head bent close to hers. "It was wrong of me to use you that way. I was rash and uncouth, and you've no idea how much I regret it. I would take the moment back if I could."

Grace could not look at him, but inside she trembled, and her heart longed to soar at his words. *An apology! From the man who guards his anger like buried treasure.*

Nicholas touched her chin, gently tipping it up, so she was forced to look at him. His eyes were sorrowful. "Can you forgive me? Will you? Please."

She turned her face away.

"But *who* was there in the barn?" Lady Sutherland called.

"Several dozen tenants witnessed the miraculous event," Nicholas said, openly exaggerating the facts. A sly grin curved his lips. With shock, Grace realized that he was enjoying discomfiting his mother. Were the situation different—were she not the center of the discussion—Grace might have found it amusing too.

As it was, she was enjoying his nearness altogether too much.

I am angry with him, she reminded herself. *He has used me ill.*

"You needn't torture her for my sake," Grace whispered, tugging her hand from beneath his on the knob. "If making her detest me even more is how you think to show remorse—"

"That was not my intention at all." Nicholas turned the knob and pushed the door open. He held his hand out, an invitation for her to leave.

Grace brushed quickly past him, out to the foyer. Nicholas followed her to the stairs, where, against her better judgment, she paused and looked back at him.

"Is there something I can do," he asked, "to prove that I am truly sorry for kissing you?"

I did not necessarily wish him to be sorry for that. Grace felt her pride inexplicably wounded. It must have shown in her expression, for Nicholas's had altered as well, as if he'd realized the implications of his admission.

"I am *not* sorry for it, in the manner you are thinking." Exasperation flared in his eyes.

Grace knew she needed to accept his apology, and quickly, or all between them might be lost. But she could not seem to bring herself to do so. The events of the afternoon were no longer holding her back—his first utterance of regret had melted that anger—but fear held her in its clutches. She'd overcome her apprehension of Nicholas only to realize a greater danger.

I fear myself. She'd crossed the one barrier she'd promised herself never to breach. This afternoon had been an awakening to the depth of her feelings—*my foolishness*—and she had this one chance to get herself in check, to restore the wall between them, before the damage to her heart became irrevocable.

"I am decidedly *not* sorry to have kissed you today." Nicholas placed his foot on the bottom stair. "It was my method and reasons that were lacking." His other foot gained the second stair. "I think perhaps the best way I might show my remorse would be to correct those actions, to right them, as it were . . ." His hand slid up the rail toward hers as he continued to advance. ". . . with a better kiss."

Though her lips tingled with yearning for that very

thing, Grace shook her head and began backing up the stairs. "No. Please don't."

Nicholas's hand dropped from the rail, and he stopped his climb. Grace read hurt and distress in his eyes and hated that she was the cause.

It cannot be helped. It is better this way. No doubt her mother had faced a similar moment but had been swayed by affection. *I must be stronger than she was. I will be. I shall guard my heart more carefully until such a time as I can make it free again.*

"Good night, Lord Sutherland," Grace said, shutting her heart against his wounded look at her use of his title. He might have given her permission to be informal, but as of tonight, she had revoked that privilege.

And all others that would only make it easier for me to love him.

CHAPTER 31

Nicholas sat at the table, unfolded his napkin, and placed it in his lap. He waited until breakfast had been served and both Grace and his mother had begun eating before making his announcement. "I have decided to host a Christmas ball."

His mother choked, and her hand flew to her mouth as she struggled with the drink she'd just taken. Grace's spoon went limp in her hand. Each woman turned to stare at him, her expression aggrieved. His mother's mouth puckered as if she'd just had a tooth pulled.

"What?" he asked calmly as he spooned marmalade on his toast. "Aren't women supposed to like balls? You both look as if I've grown a second head."

"I think you must have," his mother said. "And it is he that is speaking. The Nicholas I know would never suggest such a thing."

"And why not?" he asked. "Are we not approaching Christmastide, the season of goodwill and sharing? What better way to share than to invite our neighbors for a party?"

"Will the invitation include *all* of your neighbors, milord?" Grace asked demurely. She lifted her cup of chocolate, looking at him over the rim.

He read challenge in her eyes. His immediate instinct was to reply that, no, Preston would not be invited. *I'd sooner see him dead than in this house, near you.* But Nicholas held his tongue, considering carefully.

Grace no longer trusted him; that much had become painfully obvious when she'd rejected his advances on the stairs the previous night. He couldn't blame her, especially given her background and the lack of trustworthiness she'd seen in men like her father.

But along with that distrust, he'd seen a flicker of longing in the depths of her beautiful eyes. She had been a willing participant in their first kiss yesterday. She'd confessed to caring for him and had said words that led him to believe she might also be grappling with the attraction between them. And while at first that had seemed a terrible thing, his opinion on that matter had recently changed.

I want Grace for much more than a means of revenge upon Preston. I care for her.

It had taken several hours of soul-searching to come to that conclusion. He had wrestled with the problem before dinner, then proven the coward once again by letting his mother run roughshod over Grace during the meal. He'd thought it over as he stood by the fire last night, doing his best not to look at Grace, not to care that her heart was damaged, not to admire her fortitude in standing up to his mother time and again.

And then it had been too much. His mother's comment about Grace's hands had finally awakened him to a terribly belated sense of right and wrong. He could no longer tolerate the way his mother treated her. The Grace he'd come to know—the girl who'd grown up washing others' clothes to feed her siblings, the woman compassionate enough to help a worried farmer—had more dignity and *grace* than most gently bred women. She'd risen above her circumstances.

But has not stooped to acting as low as we have in ours.

It was high time he stood up for her, time he stopped

looking for a way to be rid of her and invested his energies into figuring out how to keep her.

It will take more than a few words before a priest. He wanted their relationship to be more than that—more than what had been forced upon them. *I want her to desire to be with me, as much as I desire to be with her.*

The greatest of the ironies was that he had to allow her to be with Preston if he had any hope of winning her hand. It was not lost on Nicholas that he'd treated Preston with the same disdain his mother had used with Grace, as if she were decidedly less a human because her father was not noble.

Did I ever give Preston a chance to prove himself—on merits of character alone—worthy of Elizabeth? Nicholas knew he had not. And he couldn't do so now after what Preston had done, after his lack of judgment that had proved fatal to Elizabeth.

But are we all not lacking in judgment at times? Nicholas knew he had been, for most of the last two years. *But what Preston did is unforgiveable—isn't it?*

"I seem to have rendered you speechless," Grace said. "Apparently you have not yet considered the guest list at great length."

"He has not considered anything," Lady Sutherland said. "Christmas is but three weeks away. One cannot arrange a ball on such short notice."

"Two weeks and six days, to be exact," Nicholas said. "I would like the ball to be held on Christmas Eve." He turned to Grace. "And I have considered the guest list. *All* of our neighbors will be invited. Whether they attend shall be up to them."

Up to him. *And if Preston has any sense at all, he will find something else to do that evening.*

If Grace was surprised by this—or pleased—she hid it well, giving him the barest nod before returning her attention to her meal.

"You cannot be serious," his mother said. "The house is

in no condition to have guests, and we haven't the staff to get it ready. Food will have to be ordered, an orchestra arranged. We'll have to get a dressmaker out from London; I didn't bring any of my formal gowns with me. And it's doubtful that she"—Lady Sutherland threw a disparaging look a Grace—"has anything proper to wear. Have you even looked at the ballroom floor in the last two years? What if it is no longer fit for dancing?"

"I am surprised at you, Mother," Nicholas said, wondering at the real reason she was protesting. "You have always been one to rise to any occasion of entertaining. I expected no less of you now. But if you're not able . . ." His gaze slid to Grace. "I shall ask Miss Thatcher to take charge of preparations. It will be good experience for her, as she will one day be mistress here."

His mother looked as if he had slapped her, and Nicholas felt a twinge of remorse at baiting her so. Perhaps he had gone too far; he needed her help if he was to pull this off. Men did not plan balls or parties; they funded and attended them with some reluctance on both parts. He wasn't at all certain Grace was up to the task, based on the slightly panicked look she'd just given him.

Nicholas could tell that his mother was torn between the temptation of foisting the responsibility onto Grace and sitting back to watch the ensuing disaster, or taking over the planning herself to save face and preserve what was left of the Sutherland reputation. When she stood suddenly and threw her napkin upon the table, he knew both that she had made her decision and which path she had chosen.

"I shall do it." Her eyes fixed upon Nicholas. "Meet me in your study at one o'clock. I will have a list of expenses and errands for you." She turned her attention on Grace. "I will meet you in your room at three o'clock to discuss what is to be done about finding something suitable for you to wear. If our neighbors are to come, we must ensure that you are not garbed in some berry-picking attire or other atrocity."

"Speaking of berries, Mother," Nicholas said, "did you ever thank Grace for the pie?" He casually leaned back in his chair.

"I—" Her mouth opened and closed in a fishlike manner. "No," she admitted, lips pressed into a smooth line of displeasure.

"Nor did I," Nicholas admitted. "A rather significant breach of etiquette on our part, don't you think?" His mother could only nod. Nicholas smiled at Grace, who looked stiff and uncomfortable in her chair. "It was the most delicious pie I have ever eaten," he said. "I thank you for going to the trouble of picking berries and making a pie for us."

"You're welcome," Grace said. Her eyes flitted about, as if expecting something to pop out at her, as if she were the center of a cruel jest.

Try kindness, she had suggested. *Was that only yesterday*? Nicholas hated that he had used so little kindness with her that she mistrusted it.

He cleared his throat and lifted a brow at his mother.

"Thank you," she mumbled.

"You are most welcome," Grace returned without a trace of malice in her voice.

With that fragile truce, Nicholas thought it best they all depart one another's company. Mother left to get started on one of many lists for the ball, and he took himself to his study to arrange the ledgers so they would be in readiness for all the expenses he would soon be incurring. Only Grace lingered at the table, with a curious look on her face Nicholas found to be promising.

For once, it seemed, it was he who had thrown her off balance.

CHAPTER 32

Grace removed the ivory gown from her wardrobe and laid it across the bed. "Please do not criticize it," she said, by way of warning Nicholas's mother, who stood in the doorway. "This gown and the pearls that go with it were the last gifts my grandfather gave me before he fell ill. I shall always cherish them."

"Your grandfather had exquisite taste," Lady Sutherland said, coming to stand near the bed. As she looked over the gown, her eyes flashed approval. "When and where have you worn this?"

"Once in London during the little season. And again at Mr. Preston's ball in September."

Lady Sutherland's face fell. "You'll need to have another made, then. You cannot wear the same gown to a party where the guests will likely remember you from last time."

Grace started to argue that she doubted anyone would recognize her, but then she remembered the scandal and ensuing scene that had taken place at Samuel's ball. *The neighbors will most assuredly remember me no matter what I wear,* she thought with no little amount of distress.

"What do you suggest?" Grace asked the dowager, deciding to place her trust in the older woman's hands. Not only would she know much more about the latest fashions, but she also had a vested interest in everything and everyone associated with her.

She'll help me look the best I can—even if she doesn't want to.

Lady Sutherland stood back, studying Grace critically. "Perhaps something green to bring out the color of your eyes, make them look less muddy." She brought a hand to her chin. "But should it be emerald or a shade or two paler?"

Muddy? Grace shrugged and held her tongue. "Whichever you think best."

"You don't care?" Lady Sutherland asked.

"Not really." *I would like to look nice for Nicholas—but I* shouldn't *want that.*

"You do realize why Nicholas is having this ball, don't you?" Lady Sutherland came closer, and Grace had to steel herself against backing away.

She shook her head. "I don't. Truly."

"It is for *you*," Lady Sutherland said, pointing her finger at Grace's chest. "He thinks that by hosting a ball and presenting you to our neighbors and acquaintances, they will accept you."

"Oh." *Oh dear. Oh no.* "Do you think it will succeed?" Grace asked in a small voice. *Do I want it to?*

Lady Sutherland's look turned shrewd and appraising. "It will be difficult. You have everything against you, of course—the scandal, your shameful upbringing."

Grace raised her chin. "We both know I have done nothing inappropriate. I have nothing to be ashamed of or embarrassed by, excepting the actions of my father."

"If you think what really happened matters more than what people believe to have occurred, then you are even more foolish than I thought," Lady Sutherland said.

"Truth is never foolish," Grace said. *It will set you free.*

It *had* set her free. Because of her honesty, Grandfather had found them. She well remembered that day, facing the stranger at their door and answering his questions honestly even when she feared he was a collector come to throw them all in debtor's prison. Instead he had whisked her and Helen and Christopher away to paradise.

"Aside from the matter of your disgrace, there are other obstacles. Your father is an impoverished gambler, and your mother had been disowned when she died. Your face is common, your manner lacking—"

"Enough," Grace said, cutting off her tirade. "I am acutely aware of my many shortcomings and flaws. You have been so kind as to point them out to me continuously. What I do not understand is why you hate me so much." She searched Lady Sutherland's eyes. "What have I done to earn your animosity?"

Lady Sutherland drew back, and her hand fluttered to her chest in a gesture of innocence. "I do not hate you. Whatever gave you such an idea?"

"What have you done to give me any other?" Grace gave a mirthless laugh and turned away so Lady Sutherland would not see the tears building in her eyes. "Since your arrival, I have done everything I could think of—caring for Elizabeth's gardens, picking berries and baking a pie, showing concern for your tenants—but everything I try seems to be wrong. Instead of earning your good favor, I have done nothing but incur your disdain."

"I see." Lady Sutherland let out a long breath. "And what of your little outbursts? Your threat to throw me out of my own house?"

"I have never threatened—"

"You *implied*," Lady Sutherland said. "And that is as good as a threat. It is what those in the upper class do."

"Forgive me for behaving as you would," Grace said sarcastically. She crossed to the window and looked out at the yard, where the lawn was swept free of leaves, the paths cleared, and the bushes had been trimmed in preparation for winter and a fresh bloom next spring.

I have done some good here. I know it. Because of me, Nicholas has seen to these things; he has begun to care for his home again. So why can his mother not care for me a little? Why can she not see beyond my faults?

"It would seem we are at an impasse," Lady Sutherland said. "Neither of us is likely to budge in our opinion of the other, so I will take my leave. The dressmaker will be here to measure you early next week. See that you are not gallivanting about somewhere when she arrives."

Grace closed her eyes, swallowing what little pride she'd managed to retain in Lady Sutherland's presence. *We cannot continue this way. If Nicholas has success with his ball, and we are eventually wed, life will be misery. He will be caught between us, and I'll ever be waiting for him to choose my side.*

Even were none of that to happen, were she somehow able to leave today to never return, Grace could not reconcile herself to taking her leave of Lady Sutherland on such a sour note.

"Wait." Grace turned from the window and quickly crossed the room.

"I am sorry," she said, facing Lady Sutherland. "I do have a temper. Grandfather was forever trying to tame my moods. He would be disappointed to know he was not successful."

Lady Sutherland's eyes narrowed with suspicion.

Grace twisted her hands. "For this ball, at least, I will do everything you ask of me. I will try to be less offensive and more like . . . a woman you would have chosen for your son."

Lady Sutherland looked at Grace a long moment. "That is the root of our problem, you realize. Neither Nicholas nor I was given any choice in this matter."

"Nor was I, in spite of what you believe," Grace said. "I am speaking the truth."

"Nicholas says that is all you speak," Lady Sutherland said. "He tells me he has never known a person so honest or trustworthy."

Something in Grace's stomach fluttered, and a surge of unexpected happiness filled her.

The dowager put her hand over Grace's, squeezing gently. "Perhaps I have been too hard on you." She inhaled deeply, then released a long breath. "I, too, apologize."

"Thank you," Grace said as their hands fell away. She felt tears stinging her eyes again, but for completely different reasons than moments before.

"It has been three years since I spent time with my daughter," Lady Sutherland said. "No doubt I have forgotten the tender sensibilities of young ladies."

"I have been even longer without a mother," Grace said. "I am the one lacking in proper speech."

Lady Sutherland smiled. "Now we are both disparaging ourselves. That will never do."

Grace returned her tentative smile. She could not quite believe her good fortune in gaining Lady Sutherland's sympathy, or at least that they were having a civil conversation.

Nicholas's mother made no move to leave but instead walked to the chairs near the fireplace and seated herself in the closest one. Grace followed, hoping against hope that this pleasantness might continue.

I will take care with my words, she vowed.

Lady Sutherland stared into the fire. "When Elizabeth married, I had no say in her choice of a husband. I had imagined many things for my daughter, and Samuel Preston promised none of them. I was against the match, of course, but her father had a soft spot for Elizabeth and was prone to letting her have her way. He gave his blessing, so there was naught I could do about it."

"Women have so few choices," Grace concurred. She'd never thought of that truth beyond her own hardships, but now she imagined having a daughter and not being allowed involvement in decisions regarding her future.

"It would seem you have had even fewer choices than some," Lady Sutherland said, turning kind eyes upon Grace. "I *have* been angry with you, because it appears I will also have no choice in seeing how my son is settled. I had thought to give him another year or two to recover from losing his sister and his father and to get over the infatuation with revenge he has so fixated upon since their deaths."

"I'm sorry—"

"Then I imagined that I would introduce Nicholas to the most beautiful, eligible young ladies in all of London. I imagined that one of them would capture his heart." Lady Sutherland had a faraway look in her eyes; Grace supposed she was imagining the very scenario she had dreamed of many times over.

I am not that beautiful young lady. I am not anything she hoped for.

"They would be married and reside here," Lady Sutherland continued. "And not many years hence, these halls would ring with the merry voices of little children as they once did."

Grace felt worse than she had all of the times Nicholas's mother had beleaguered her. *There is nothing I can do or say to make her like me, to give back her dreams.*

"I had planned my life differently too," Grace said, thinking that telling of her own, shattered plans might be the only thing to convince Lady Sutherland of the truth. "My grandfather left me a small inheritance. It is not much; the rest of his estate transferred almost immediately to the new duke."

Lady Sutherland nodded. "That is how these things work."

"We do not require much," Grace said. "Grandfather knew that we—my sister, brother, and I—could live on very little. He left us enough that I could rent a house somewhere in the country, and we could live simply, freely, without my father or his many debts."

"What happened?" Lady Sutherland asked, her full attention on Grace. "Why did you not do so?"

And leave your son free to live his own life, Grace thought. "The inheritance has not yet been settled, as we had believed. The new duke contested it. We had to return to our father's home." Grace looked down at her lap, ashamed to have to tell what came next. "Father was most delighted to have us back. His debts had multiplied, and his luck had turned for the worse. He was about to be thrown in prison."

"I do not understand how any of that relates to your being here," Lady Sutherland said, sounding somewhat less compassionate than before.

"I thought that Nicholas had told you what happened," Grace said.

"Perhaps he did. It is possible I have forgotten." Lady Sutherland waved her hand in the air. "I was so distraught, you see, that I did not listen to the particulars as I should have."

Grace told her all of them. The debt collectors knocking on Father's door, her going in Helen's place in search of a husband. She told of pompous Lord Crosby and of Sir Lidgate's scandalous offer. She told of falling from her horse on purpose and of the broken-down carriage, of her sickness and her plan to be ruined.

Throughout it all, Lady Sutherland listened with acute interest, leaving Grace no doubt that henceforth she would remember every detail.

When at last Grace had finished, Lady Sutherland sat back in her chair, a hand to her chin once more as she looked into the dying fire. The room had grown chilly during their conversation, but Grace felt that a new warmth—or an understanding at least—had sprung up between them.

At length, Lady Sutherland rose from her chair. "I have lingered too long. There are many more preparations to be made if we are to hold a ball Christmas Eve."

“Is there anything I can do to help?” Grace asked, standing as well.

Lady Sutherland considered her a long moment. “What needed to be done the most, you have already accomplished—quite probably without even realizing it.” She smiled wistfully. “I shall let you know if I require other assistance.”

She took her leave, and Grace was once more alone. She wrapped her arms around herself and went to stand near the fire, heartened that for the first time, the room felt cooler without Lady Sutherland’s presence.

CHAPTER 33

"Mrs. James," Grace called as she hurried down the stairs, silently blessing her good fortune at finding the housekeeper in the foyer with the newly hired army of servants assembled before her.

"Yes, miss?" The housekeeper's tone was slightly less frigid than usual, and Grace supposed she had the gathered servants to thank for that.

"I came to offer my services," Grace said. When Mrs. James stared at her blankly, Grace clarified, "To help you prepare for the ball. I know you've very little time and a great deal to do."

Mrs. James returned her attention to the new maids. "Go to your posts. Begin with the deep cleaning we just discussed, and I shall apprise you later of what else is to be done."

As one body, the uniformed women dispersed, disappearing quickly to the nether parts of the house. Mrs. James clasped her hands and looked at Grace. "Miss Thatcher, you must know that his lordship would have my head were I to give you work of any sort. I realize you've come from somewhat—different—circumstances, but here at

Sutherland Hall, as in any respectable household, guests do not *help* the staff."

Grace bristled internally at her choice of words. "I have lived here three months. I hardly consider myself a guest. Sutherland Hall is my home." The truth of the statement struck her.

When and how had that happened? When had the cold, uninviting stone transformed to a place she held dear? Was it during those cozy evenings spent in the library with Nicholas? Or during the many meals they'd taken together, during which her wit and willpower were at a constant challenge against his mother's? Perhaps it occurred that moment on the stairs when, heedless of his dripping clothes, Nicholas had spoken to her and had first taken her hand.

Probably it was the sum of all these events that had made her feel at home, even added upon by Lady Sutherland that afternoon two weeks earlier when they had first talked to each other civilly. Since then, during the many visits by the dressmaker and florist and caterer, Nicholas's mother had been cordial on almost every occasion they had met.

"Whether or not you are a guest is irrelevant," Mrs. James said, interrupting Grace's thoughts. "You do not see Lady Sutherland running around with a mop and bucket, do you? Of course not." Before Grace had the opportunity to reply, she continued. "It is not done. Now if you'll excuse me—"

"Please," Grace said. "It doesn't have to be a broom or mop—or anything so obvious as that—but there must be some small task I might help with. I am not used to so many idle hours, and I fear if I continue them, I shall go quite mad."

"Why don't you take one of your walks in the garden?" Mrs. James suggested. "You seem quite taken with wandering—much as Miss Sutherland was."

Does she know about my meetings with Samuel? Grace's heart pounded beneath her gown. "It has grown too cold to walk, and with the leaves fallen, the garden does not hold the same appeal."

She had not been walking, had not been to the wall to see Samuel, since that ill-fated afternoon when he had passed them on the road and caught Nicholas kissing her. Grace wasn't certain why she had not visited him.

I ought to, to tell him all is well, at least. But she could not seem to bring herself to meet him. Though they had never let their meetings go beyond friendship, she knew something of the depths of Nicholas's feelings concerning Samuel and that he would disapprove. And where at first she had not cared a fig whether Lord Sutherland was displeased with her, she found that she cared a great deal now.

"Why don't you visit the library, then?" Mrs. James said, sounding more exasperated by the minute.

Grace shook her head. "I adore Lord Sutherland's books, but there are only so many hours in the day one can read. Isn't there something I can do for you? And before you say no again, is it really so wrong that I want to help? Must you think ill of me because I wish to be of some use?"

"I do not think ill of you," Mrs. James said, but her words were stiff, her tone unconvincing. "It is only that . . . you do not treat the staff as the Sutherlands do. It is one of the reasons Jenny was taken from you. She'd never be trained as a proper lady's maid; you were too friendly with her."

"Are the Sutherlands not friendly—not kind?" Grace asked. She remembered Nicholas's temper those first weeks and how Kingsley seemed to take the brunt of it. But lately . . .

I have heard him speak words of appreciation. I cannot recall when last I saw him upset.

"Do Lady Sutherland and her son not care for those who serve them? Do they not have some tenderness of heart for their well-being?"

Mrs. James glanced around the foyer, clearly discomfited by the question. "It is not my place to say anything about my employer. Now if you'll excuse me—"

"I will not." Grace drew herself straight and folded her arms across her chest. "Whether either of us fully appreciates the situation, it is quite possible that I am here to stay, that I will be mistress of Sutherland Hall. And if that happens, I will not live like this. I cannot tiptoe around strangers in my own home, and I will not watch them slaving away while I sit idle. I do not care what society deems proper. It is *wrong*, and I will not have it. Now, put me to work."

Mrs. James opened and closed her mouth twice, then stared at Grace a good, long minute before she spoke. And when she did, it was in a voice Grace had not heard from her before, one that hinted at admiration and possibly even respect. "The holly was delivered today. It needs to be strung along the banisters. I suppose you might do that."

Grace beamed at her. "Thank you."

Mrs. James nodded toward the front door. "The crates are there. I'll ask Mr. Kingsley to find someone to open them for you."

"Thank you," Grace said again, filled with delight at the prospect of decorating the house with fragrant boughs.

"And the tree," Mrs. James continued, "is to arrive in the next few days. It will need to be trimmed."

"Of course," Grace said. *A Christmas tree.* They'd only ever had one at Grandfather's, and it had made the entire season more enchanting.

Mrs. James gave one of her curt nods of dismissal and turned to go, then seemed to think the better of it. She looked at Grace once more. "I do not think ill of you. Because of you, Sutherland Hall is returning to how it used to be. The master is returning to himself. If you never do any work again in your life, know that what you have done here is enough."

"Thank you," Grace said to Mrs. James's back as the woman took her starched dress and sensible shoes marching across the foyer.

Grace hummed contentedly as she worked, draping the heavy boughs down the curved banister. With Kingsley's help, she had festooned the upstairs rail with evergreens and ribbon and was now working her way down the stairs. With the holly already in place and held secure by Kingsley at the bottom of the stairs, Grace wove the ribbon carefully throughout, standing back frequently to scrutinize her work, to ensure Lady Sutherland would be pleased. Descending backwards, Grace concentrated on her task, intent on bending each bough just the right way and tying the red bows perfectly. Her heel bumped against something, and she turned, an apology upon her lips, meeting not Kingsley's startled gaze but Nicholas's purposeful one.

"Oh!" Grace exclaimed, bringing a hand to her heart. "You startled me." He was very near, only one stair away. *Far too close.*

"Kingsley had other duties to attend to," Nicholas said, a merry twinkle in his eyes. "I told him I would help you finish."

"Oh?" Grace said. She returned her attention to the ribbon and was irritated to discover her fingers shaking. "Could you move, please?" she asked, glancing at Nicholas, so close that she was practically in his arms.

"If I must," he said, sounding highly amused. "This is where Kingsley told me to stand, but if that is not of help . . ."

"It is not," Grace snapped. With a gallant bow, Nicholas stepped aside, and the remaining, unrestrained holly, slid from the banister.

Grace pursed her lips together. "That is not what I meant."

"Perhaps you should be clearer in explaining what you wish," Nicholas said. "It is rather infuriating to us men when we are left guessing."

Grace had no response to that other than the pulse

throbbing in her ears. *What I want,* she thought furiously, *is for him to be gone.* A lie if ever she'd told one. She gripped the banister, willing her emotions under control, but they would not be so easily heeled.

Nicholas restrung the holly and held it in place farther down the rail. Grace resumed her work with the ribbon and began humming a carol, attempting to bring to mind Christmases past. With no little sorrow, she realized this would be her first Christmas away from Helen and Christopher.

I shall have to visit Samuel, she realized. *It is the only way to discover how my siblings are getting on.*

While she decorated and hummed, another voice had joined in, singing the words of the carol soft and low. Grace paused, listening to the rich timbre, and her heartbeat escalated. She turned on the stair, leaning closer to better hear.

Nicholas stood on the bottom step, and he grinned when he noticed her watching him sing. "'Here we come a-wassailing among the leaves so green.'" He plucked a stray stem of holly and twirled it in his fingers.

Grace laughed. She'd never seen him like this, would never have imagined that he sang Christmas carols.

"'Here we come a-wassailing, so *fair* to be seen.'" He took the steps two at a time until he stood before her; then he tucked the bit of holly behind her ear. His eyes were full of intent, his gaze focused on her lips.

Grace licked them then realized what she had done, what she was doing. *What I must not do.*

"'Love and joy come to you —'" Their eyes met, and Grace found she could not look away. Nicholas's hand slid from her hair to caress her cheek.

She reached up, covering his hand with her own, pressing it to her face for just a few seconds. *Surely a few seconds won't hurt anything.*

"Love and joy," Nicholas repeated, no longer singing.

No, Grace thought. *They do not go together. You might have one for a brief time, but never the other.* She pulled his hand from her face and turned away.

"And God bless you," Nicholas said quietly. "And send you a happy new year."

Will it be happy? She did not see how it could be. *Will I be gone and thinking of Nicholas and missing him every day? Or will I be here and still living with this temptation?* She did not think she could endure it much longer. Sooner or later, if she stayed, she would give in to her yearnings for him. *I will give him my heart. I am weak as Mother was. And what consequences will I suffer for that weakness? What consequences I am already suffering.*

"And God send you a happy new year," Nicholas repeated.

"No more carols, please." Grace pushed past him and hurried down the stairs. "I am nearly out of ribbon," she said by way of an excuse. "I must find more." She sat near the bottom of the staircase and began rummaging through the open crate.

The heady smell of pine cleared her mind and steadied her heartbeat. *I must be strong. I must not get close to him again. Remember last time.*

"Let me help." Nicholas was suddenly behind her, his hands searching with hers through the packing. Grace pulled back, allowing him the task to himself, lest they touch accidentally.

After a moment, he withdrew a thinner, looped, red ribbon. "What is this?" He pulled the ribbon from the box. Hanging from it was a ball of green, a plant different from the holly, with small waxy leaves and white berries.

"It is a kissing ball." Lady Sutherland's voice rang across the foyer. She swept toward them, her skirts swishing across the polished floor. "I thought it might be fun to hang at the entrance to the ballroom. Everyone knows that any young lady standing beneath the mistletoe cannot refuse to be kissed. And everyone will pass beneath it."

Everyone, Grace thought feeling a little faint.

"It is said that if a couple in love exchanges a kiss under the mistletoe, it is a promise to marry and a prediction of happiness. You had best be careful, Nicholas," Lady Sutherland said, "that Beatrice Middleton does not find you there. She may take to kissing you on her own."

"Who is Beatrice Middleton?" Grace asked before she quite realized what she was doing. She quickly returned to searching the crate, pretending indifference.

"She is a neighbor of many years," Lady Sutherland said. "She and Nicholas grew up together, and she has had designs on him for some time now. Her mother confided in me that Beatrice and her sisters are all agog over our ball."

"And why might you be confiding that to us?" Nicholas asked, sending a pointed look at his mother. Grace continued to feign a lack of interest, when inside she was anything but disinterested. What did this Beatrice Middleton look like?

Does Nicholas care for her? That they had a history together long before Grace had arrived was obvious, and the fact stirred a feeling all too close to jealousy within her.

"Nicholas, will you hang the kissing ball for me?" Lady Sutherland asked. "The ladder is still in front of the doors from the dusting earlier."

"Of course." That he sounded a bit irritated about the whole thing did much to soothe Grace's mood. He carried the mistletoe off with him, walking toward the ballroom at the far end of the hall.

Grace located the remaining ribbon in the box, intent on finishing the banister alone.

"I'll do that," Lady Sutherland said, taking the ribbon from Grace's hands. "Go hold the ladder for Nicholas. He was always clumsy as a boy. It would be just like him to fall and break his leg before the ball."

This was the first negative thing Grace had ever heard the dowager say about her son, and it perplexed her greatly. She'd never seen any evidence that Nicholas was clumsy and imagined him quite capable of hanging a simple decoration of his own accord. But not wanting to strain the polite nature she and Lady Sutherland had arrived at in their interactions, Grace left the stairs and headed toward the ballroom, her steps dragging across the foyer; she hoped Nicholas might already be finished before she arrived.

Instead, it appeared that he was waiting for her.

"Will you hold this while I put the nail in?" He held the kissing ball out to her.

Grace took it and held the ball away from her, as if it were a dead rodent. She would have to take care to enter the ballroom quickly, either before or after Nicholas. And she would have to leave the same way.

Doubtful, at best, she concluded, as the ball was for him to present her to society.

He will want me at his side. And if I am not there . . . will Miss Middleton be? Grace wasn't certain which possibility concerned her more.

"I'm ready." Nicholas held his hand out. Grace gave the ball to him, then stepped quickly away.

"Are you so superstitious, then?" he asked, glancing at her.

"Only when kissing is involved," Grace said.

"Nothing bad will come of it, you know." Nicholas fastened the ball upon the nail above the doorway. "In spite of what Mother might have hinted at, I'll not be kissing any other young ladies on Christmas Eve."

Any *other*, he'd said.

Does he intend to kiss one? Me? She took another step away.

Nicholas jumped down from the ladder and stood back to admire his work. "It's festive, at least," he said, then cast a sly glance her direction. "Shall we try it out?"

“We shall not,” Grace said, whirling away from him. “You have had your kiss from me, Nicholas Sutherland, and I suggest you remember it well, because you are not likely to get another anytime soon.”

CHAPTER 34

"Another gingerbread man, please." Grace leaned away from the ladder, her hand outstretched.

Nicholas placed the homemade ornament in her hand then continued to hold onto her until she had righted herself and was balanced once more.

"I still say it ought to be me on that ladder," he said, feigning grumpiness. "The way you are leaning and stretching up there, you're likely to fall and break your pretty neck."

She looked over her shoulder at him. "I am trusting that you would catch me. Whereas if it were you who climbed to these heights and chanced to fall . . ." She shrugged. "I fear you would not be dancing at all tomorrow night. So you see, it is for your benefit that I am the one decorating and you are the one fetching the ornaments." Grace returned to her work, reaching far over the front of the ladder to hang the gingerbread man on one of the uppermost branches.

My benefit indeed, Nicholas thought with amusement as he admired the view she presented. *Go ahead and fall. I most certainly will catch you.* He was imagining such a scenario and Grace's show of gratitude at being thus saved when voices sounded from the front hall. If she heard, Grace paid them no heed, but after a couple of minutes, they grew louder, and a slight draft made its way into the room, indicating that the front doors were still open.

"Your gown must have arrived," Nicholas said. "Would you like to go see it?"

"Later," Grace said, squinting at the tree. "I think we can place a candle right here if we are very careful."

"You don't wish to see your dress?" Nicholas asked. "Mother tells me it is a sight to behold, that she has outdone herself in her selections this time."

"She has done that and more." Grace paused her observations long enough to look down at him. A new light shone in her eyes, and she smiled wistfully. "Lady Sutherland has been good to me these past few weeks—cordial and even kind. Would that we had reached this state some time ago. It is most pleasant. I have enjoyed her company."

"I am glad to hear it." Nicholas crossed the room and poked his head into the hall. "I imagine you shall enjoy *this* company even more," he proclaimed. "Come. Let me help you down." He crossed to the tree once more and held his hand out. Grace had barely taken it when the voices, clearer now, reached their ears.

"Where is she? What have you done with her? I've a need to see her with my own eyes before I'm about any other tasks."

"*Harrison?*" Grace's eyes grew wide, and she cast a horrified look at Nicholas, recalling, no doubt, the threat he'd made to her servants many weeks ago.

"All is well," he hastened to assure her. "I invited them myself."

"You did?" Her look of perplexity turned to surprise and delight as four people burst through the door, followed by Kingsley, looking rather concerned.

"It is quite all right," Nicholas called to him, over the heads of the four people rushing toward Grace. He stepped away, moving aside just as she sprang from the bottom step of the ladder, launching herself into the arms of the younger of their two female visitors.

"Helen!" Grace gathered her sister in a fierce hug then pulled away, staring at her as if to make certain she was real.

"And have you no thought for me?" the young man standing beside her asked glibly.

"Of course I do, Christopher." Grace extended one arm and pulled him close as well. The three of them huddled together, heads bent close, each speaking and laughing at once.

Nicholas knew a moment of longing as he watched the trio. He envied the young Christopher his sisters and again felt the acute sorrow of his loss in Elizabeth. *Never again in this life will we greet each other. Never will it be her voice I hear ringing through these halls.*

He glanced across the room at his mother. *Our loss,* he amended as he made his way toward her, feeling suddenly the intruder in his own home. As he passed Grace's servants lingering protectively near their charges, he felt only gratitude for them. He remembered the man's ready defense of Grace the night Nicholas had discovered her in his bedroom, and the way the woman had come forward and wrapped Grace in a blanket and steered her away from him. Their gossiping at Preston's had been at their lady's orders, and they had likely done it out of love—and desperation—to protect this little family.

"What have you done?" his mother whispered as Nicholas joined her in the doorway.

He glanced back at the three siblings, still embracing, dancing around with the joy of reunion. "I've given Grace something we cannot have."

His mother eyed him appraisingly. "You care for her a great deal." It was a statement rather than the question she'd posed more than a time or two.

"More than I should, probably." Nicholas recalled

Grace's parting words at the hanging of the kissing ball and hoped very much that they were not true, though he could not deny she'd every right to feel that way about him.

He'd been grateful this morning for the arrival of the tree and her enthusiasm for decorating, which seemed to have eased the awkwardness between them a little bit.

At last the siblings broke free of one another, and Grace turned her head, looking around the room.

For me? Nicholas dared not hope, but then she found him, and her eyes, radiating warmth and wet with tears, lingered upon his.

"Thank you."

He read, rather than heard, the words from her lips. Nicholas shrugged and leaned against the doorframe as he returned her smile.

"It took you all long enough," he said in a loud voice for all in the room to hear. Four heads turned toward him. "It has been nearly a month since I requested your company. Why did you not come sooner?" To his own ears, he sounded gruff and commanding—and unfamiliar.

A blessed thing. I have changed.

Grace's man servant and lady's maid exchanged uneasy glances, and Grace's younger sister paled and seemed to wither beneath his words. Grace put a protective arm around her and smiled encouragingly. Nicholas could tell why Grace had felt the need to protect such a fragile creature.

"Mr. Thatcher did not deliver your dispatch for some time," the man called Harrison said, stepping forward, hat in hand. "Believe me, your lordship, we would have come sooner had we known."

"Well, your timing today is perfect," Nicholas said, his tone considerably lighter. "This tree is in need of decorating—and Miss Thatcher seems determined to break her neck in the process of doing it. Perhaps you can assist in keeping her safe. It is proving almost too great a task for one man." He gave Grace a slow wink before turning his attention to her maid.

"There is to be a ball here tomorrow night. I trust you can help your lady accomplish something appropriate with her hair." Once more his gaze slid to Grace, who was blushing furiously as she felt her hair and likely realized the extent of its disarray, pulled from its once-neat bun by many tree branches.

"Of course, milord," the older woman said stiffly, as if affronted on Grace's behalf.

"Very good," Nicholas said, bowing slightly. "I will leave you to your reunion." With a last look at Grace's joyful smile and ever-tempting hair, he left them. Their timing *had* been fortuitous.

Being so near to Grace was torture.

CHAPTER 35

"How do I look?" Grace asked as Miranda finished helping her into the jade gown.

"Like you are rushing headlong into trouble," Miranda said, still fussing with the ruffles along the hem. "But then, you could have gone to the ball in a flour sack and found yourself in the same difficulty."

"You are imagining things," Grace said, trying to reassure herself as much as Miranda. "Mr. Preston and I are but friends, and Lord Sutherland has spent the better part of the last three months trying to find a way to be rid of me."

"Mr. Preston may be but a friend, but I daresay he desires much more than that," Miranda said. "The man was positively radiant each time he returned from meeting with you."

Someone knocked at her door, and Grace knew a moment of trepidation, wondering if whoever was outside had overheard Miranda. The door opened, and Helen, dressed in a pale pink gown, entered the room.

"Oh, but you look lovely," she said as her eyes cast upon Grace.

"I was thinking the same of you," Grace said, wondering how her sister would fare at the ball tonight. Two years ago, Grandfather had arranged a coming out for Helen. Gowns had been purchased, invitations extended and accepted. All was ready for a most glorious London season, but it had ended quickly and in utter disaster when Helen had fainted during her very first dance; then later, sometime after being revived, she had panicked and fled the dance floor—and her rather prestigious and sought-after partner—sobbing.

"How are you feeling?" Grace asked. "Have you sufficiently recovered from Lord Sutherland's greeting?"

Helen blushed prettily, her pale cheeks growing rosy, making her more beautiful than ever. She nodded, and her golden curls bobbed up and down. "I believe so. You do not think he will ask me to dance tonight, do you?"

"I should think he will," Grace said. "You are his guest, after all." For the first time in her life, she felt a moment of longing regarding Helen's good fortune in appearance. Helen had creamy skin and delicate features, while Grace felt keenly all she lacked. She hadn't as fair a complexion, and her hands were anything but delicate.

And my hair . . . How many times had Nicholas expressed displeasure with her unruly locks?

She shook off the feeling of envy and the worry over her inadequacies, telling herself to be glad of them, that they would make her less desirable.

"There." Having finished arranging the hem, Miranda stood, a satisfied smile on her face. "Your grandfather would be proud—of both of you," she added, turning to Helen.

Grace walked to her sister, looping her arm through Helen's. "Let us go down together, shall we?" She steered her toward the door, which Miranda hurried to open.

"There is something I must warn you of," Grace whispered as they walked. "Hanging above the ballroom entrance there is a ball . . ."

Nicholas waited at the bottom of the stairs. Several guests had arrived already, and he knew he ought to be in the ballroom to greet them, but for now he'd left the task to his mother, waiting instead to escort Grace in. This night was for her, and he wished her to know it from the very first. He intended to introduce her to everyone. He planned to dance with her three times and commandeer her evening so that few others could enjoy the same privilege.

He wanted to show her off and to show his neighbors just how fortunate he was. *How Grace has saved me from my path of self-destruction.*

A gasp came from the top of the stairs, and Nicholas looked up to see Grace and her frightened-looking sister arm in arm. This foiled his plan a bit. He'd wanted Grace to be with her siblings for Christmas; but tonight, he wanted her all to himself. He could see from the way her sister clung to her that this evening would not turn out as he'd hoped.

"It is all right, Helen," Grace coaxed, guiding her sister down the stairs. They reached the bottom, and Grace flashed an apologetic smile at Nicholas. "Helen did not realize there were to be so many guests. She is a little anxious."

Anxious seemed an understatement; Grace's sister looked to be on the verge of collapse. "Do you need to sit?" he asked, coming around to her other side and taking her free arm, lest she fall.

"Thank you," Grace said, answering for her sister. "I think that would be best. If we can get her inside the ballroom and find a chair . . ."

They walked across the foyer and down the hall, half-dragging Helen. Just before the entrance to the ballroom, Nicholas paused, glancing up at the kissing ball, then over at Grace, who he was pleased to see also had her gaze turned to the ceiling.

That will have to wait, he supposed, though it had not been in his plan to kiss Grace before the ball began. But later, after the festivities, when he hoped for a moment alone with her.

The three of them entered the ballroom, not at all the way Nicholas had imagined beginning the evening. He didn't even have the right lady on his arm, but there seemed no help for that.

He steered them toward the nearest set of chairs and deposited Helen in one of them, then scanned the crowd for his mother. She seemed able to read his cue of distress and began making her way toward them. Nicholas turned his attention to the musicians, giving a slight nod to indicate that he wished the dancing to begin.

"Will you do me the honor, Miss Thatcher?" He turned to Grace so there could be no confusion as to which Miss Thatcher he was requesting.

Grace bit her lip as she glanced at her sister, but to Nicholas's surprise, Helen smiled encouragingly.

"Oh please do dance, Grace. I should love to watch you."

His mother arrived at that moment, which seemed to further alleviate Grace's worry over her charge.

"I'll be back shortly," she said, taking Nicholas's arm and allowing him to lead her to the middle of the ballroom.

Though no other couples had taken the floor, the violinists started up the moment Grace turned to face him. Nicholas grinned in response to the perplexed look that crossed her face.

"Where is everyone else? We cannot dance a set by ourselves."

"This is not a set dance," Nicholas replied. "It is the first dance of the evening, and it is a waltz."

Her eyes grew large. She lowered her voice as if those along the sides of the room might somehow overhear. "Grandfather said the waltz is riotous and indecent."

"Your grandfather was very wise." Nicholas's grin widened as he stepped forward, taking one of her hands in his and placing his other hand at the small of her back.

"Whatever are you thinking?" Her whispering turned urgent. "Have I not caused scandal enough?"

"Precisely." Nicholas said, meeting her gaze, looking at her in such a way that she would be unable to mistake it for anything but desire. "At the last ball, *you* were the cause of scandal. Tonight . . . it is my turn."

"Your—"

"Follow my lead." He stepped forward, and she back, and it was started—an elegant gliding in time with the violins' music. Her hand rested lightly on his shoulder. He held her gaze as they turned about the floor.

"Why are you doing this?" Grace asked, her face scarlet.

"For the same reason you insisted upon ruining your reputation," Nicholas said, leading her from the center of the floor, toward the fringes. He wanted everyone present to see them, to witness what he felt for her.

"You think that by waltzing with me, you will not have to marry?" Grace asked, sounding even more confused and not a little hurt.

"That is not why you made the sacrifice that you did," Nicholas said. "It had very little to do with yourself—as is the case with most of what you do. Indeed, you are the most unselfish person I have ever known." He located the Ellises and turned toward them. "You sacrificed yourself because you love your sister. You were trying to protect her."

Grace gave no argument to that but lowered her gaze so he could not see her expression. Nicholas took his hand from her back for the briefest second and tilted her chin up so she had to look at him.

"I am dancing this waltz with you—not nearly such an act of danger and bravery as yours was—because I want to protect you. By the end of this night, everyone here will know that I have little use for scandal. They may think what they will of the Sutherland name. But they will think only one thing of *your* name, and it will be that you belong here, and that Mother and I hold you in the highest regard. After this dance, everyone will be talking, not of you, but of *us*."

The music slowed, and Nicholas raised his left hand above their heads. Grace followed his lead, her hand coming up in the same fashion to clasp his. Nicholas caught her waist and pulled her closer as they turned around in a tight circle.

Were more dances like this, men would not be so averse to attending balls.

She did not lower her gaze again, and she did not look away, either. He found he could not keep his eyes from her face, had he wanted to. The jade of her gown brought out the deepest green of her eyes, making them even more entrancing. They seemed full of emotion, and Nicholas watched as they changed from disbelief, to hope, to some other, unfathomable emotion—one she appeared to be fighting. Before the night was out, he intended to know what it was and to have her doubt removed.

His gaze slid to her lips, full and rosy with color and begging to be kissed.

"The way you are staring at me is—"

"Scandalous?" he suggested, with a raise of his brow.

The gesture earned him a smile, the first of many this evening, he hoped.

"Yes."

So close were they, he almost felt her whispered breath.

"I do hope so," Nicholas said. He forced his gaze from her mouth and glanced about the room. "And I hope everyone here notices the same. I have eyes only for you, Miss Thatcher."

Eyes and hands and my heart.

"Not for Beatrice—Meddlesome?"

Nicholas laughed. "Middleton. And no, most definitely not for her. Do I detect envy, Miss Thatcher?"

"Perhaps," Grace admitted in her characteristically honest way.

He pulled her closer, endeared by the confession.

The music changed, and with reluctance, he returned to holding her hand at his side and dancing farther apart. More couples—those brave enough to dance a waltz—joined them on the floor, and Nicholas swept Grace in and out among them, making sure they circled the room so all would see the beautiful woman in his arms and know how he felt about her.

When the dance ended, her face was still flushed, though Nicholas suspected, or rather hoped, that it was from more than embarrassment. He returned her to Helen and his mother.

"Well done," Lady Sutherland said, clapping. She bestowed a beaming smile upon them both.

"It was lovely," Helen agreed. "I could never dance like that."

"Nor should you," Grace said, with a sideways glance at Nicholas.

He answered with a wicked grin. "If you will excuse me a moment, ladies, I must greet our latest arrivals." He bowed and turned away only to see Samuel Preston coming toward them, just entering the ballroom.

Nicholas could not quite believe that Preston had the audacity to come. *And I didn't even have the pleasure of watching him suffer through the first dance.* Instead of leaving to greet other guests as he had planned, Nicholas stayed at Grace's side. He watched as Preston scanned the room and stopped when he'd spotted them. Without hesitation, he began making his way over.

Nicholas moved closer to Grace and placed his hand at her elbow. "Are you thirsty after our dance? Would you like some refreshment?"

Before Grace could answer, Helen exclaimed, "Mr. Preston!"

Helen rose to greet him, exhibiting more enthusiasm than Nicholas had seen from her yet. Grace, too, seemed to take notice and watched their exchange.

"Good evening, Miss Helen." Preston gave a brief bow, then turned to Grace. "Hello, Grace."

"Miss Thatcher to you," Nicholas snarled, stepping forward. He felt Grace's restraining hand upon his arm. He glanced at her and caught the pleading look she sent to Preston.

"My apologies," Preston said. "Miss Thatcher, Lord Sutherland. Lady Sutherland." He waited expectantly after addressing Nicholas's mother, but she did not return his greeting.

"It was good of you to invite me," Preston said. "It is good to be here again." He glanced round the room.

Do not count on it being a frequent invitation.

"Miss Thatcher," Preston asked. "May I request the pleasure of your company for the next set?"

Helen's face came alight, and a timid smile curved her lips, but it was to Grace that Preston held his hand, stepping in front of Nicholas to reach her.

"I—of course," she said, taking his hand and allowing him to lead her away.

Nicholas watched them go, feeling as stunned as her sister looked. "Would you care to dance?" he asked her in the softest tone he could muster. When she shrank back, he added, "I do not bite, you know."

"No, thank you, sir—milord. I am not a very good dancer."

Rather than press the issue, Nicholas gave her a curt nod. "Excuse me, Mother," he said, and left them. He made his way around the room, searching for another partner, and found one in Beatrice Middleton.

As quickly as she replied in the affirmative, he guided her to the center of the floor, practically pulling her along until they were standing near Grace and Preston already in formation for a quadrille.

This ought to be amusing, he thought, staring across the square at Grace and Preston. Grace had paled considerably since their last meeting, but Preston had his chest puffed out proudly, as if he were well aware that he had the most prized partner in the room.

The dance began, and they bowed to their partner and corners. Beatrice was grinning so, Nicholas thought he saw every one of her teeth. It was not pleasant.

They walked toward the center, exchanging places with Grace and Preston. As Nicholas passed Grace, he took her hand a little more firmly than required and gave it a squeeze as if to remind her: *You are mine.*

On their return pass, she whisked her hand away before he could grab it and shot him a look as if to say, *don't you dare.* Nicholas felt a need to rise to her silent challenge.

He escorted Miss Middleton around the circle, twice making eye contact with Preston, who appeared completely unaffected by their surroundings, completely unaware of anything or anyone but Grace.

How was it he came so easily to call her by her name? Unease stirred Nicholas's gut, his earlier suspicions slamming into him forcefully. He'd put his heart and reputation on the line with the first dance. *What is Preston up to?*

Grace and Miss Middleton met in the center, each with a rather tense smile in place. Nicholas reached out, eagerly taking Grace as his partner.

"You're glowering," she hissed. "Stop it." It was as much of a demand as he'd ever heard from her, and it surprised him.

He recalled her words on their drive weeks ago. *No longer will I be afraid of you.*

Tonight it wasn't Grace he was trying to scare, but Preston.

The dance continued—far too long and boring, as far as he was concerned. Each time he got close enough to touch Grace, she pulled away in as discreet a manner as possible, as if she feared he might pick her up and carry her off the dance floor.

A rather good idea.

As they sashayed around the circle, he faced her for more than a second or two. "If you want me to stop glowering, get him to leave." Nicholas inclined his head toward Preston, on the other side of the circle.

"You are frightening my sister," Grace said. "She looks about to cry."

They moved apart once more, and when he'd the opportunity, Nicholas looked over at Helen, who was still cowering in her chair. She did indeed look close to tears, but he suspected it had little to do with him and quite a bit to do with the fact that her sister was dancing with Preston.

Nicholas took Miss Middleton's hand and paraded her across the circle in the most ridiculous of steps. He'd forgotten how much he hated the quadrille.

The circle dissolved into two sets for the star. Nicholas put his hand into the center, joining Miss Middleton's, Grace's, and Preston's. As the star turned, his gaze found Preston's, and he issued another silent threat.

You cannot have her. You had Elizabeth, but you will not have Grace.

At last, the wretched dance ended. Preston escorted Grace from the dance floor, and Nicholas had no choice but to do the same for Miss Middleton, who was busily chatting away at his side. He returned her to her parents on the opposite side of the ballroom but was then delayed by her sisters and mother exclaiming over the house, the refreshments, and everything else he gave little care about.

By the time he was free of them, Grace was nowhere to be found.

Nor was Preston.

Nicholas returned to his mother, now alone, as the other Miss Thatcher was no longer in her chair.

"Have you seen Grace?"

"Out in the hall," his mother said. "Remember your promise to Elizabeth," she called, answering his next question before he could answer it.

Preston is with her. He strode toward the doors, thinking of the kissing ball hanging just outside them, of the possibility that this time he might not be able to honor his word.

CHAPTER 36

Grace wrapped her arms around herself to ward off the night's chill as she waited outside with Samuel for his carriage to arrive.

"I shouldn't have come," he said. "Nicholas is angry."

"He is only jealous," Grace said. "He has been ever so much better lately. I really think you ought to consider letting Beth—"

He pressed a finger to her lips, silencing her. "Kingsley is behind us," he whispered. "Standing guard on the step."

"I think he has grown rather fond of me," Grace said. "I do hope this will not sour his opinion."

"I am leaving in a moment," Samuel said, stamping his feet, as if to show that he, too, was not enjoying standing out in the cold. "I don't like to be away on Christmas Eve. I came only because I had to see for myself that you are well. You haven't been in the garden for weeks."

"It's winter," Grace said, knowing it was a meager excuse and that Samuel deserved better.

"That day on the road—"

"Please," Grace said. "I don't wish to speak of it. It is in the past. Nicholas has apologized, and there has not been another incident since."

Samuel searched her face. "Promise me that you will come if you need anything—anything at all."

"I've Helen and Christopher here now, and Miranda and Harrison."

"Promise me," Samuel said.

"I promise." Grace looked down at the gravel covered with a light dusting of snow. "What will you be doing tomorrow?"

Samuel smiled. "Having the grandest time." He lowered his voice to a whisper. "I've built Beth a dollhouse."

Grace imagined the little girl with Samuel and felt grateful that he would not be alone.

His carriage came into sight, and she felt both relief and regret. She did not know when she might see him again, but she did not want Nicholas to discover them out here together.

"I also have a Christmas present for you," Samuel said. "Will you come to the garden tomorrow so I can give it to you?"

"Oh, Samuel," Grace said, feeling terrible that he had gone to any trouble for her and that she had nothing to give him in return.

His carriage came to a stop in front of the house.

"Please," he said. "I will not ask you to come again after that."

The footman jumped down and opened the door. Samuel made no move to go.

Grace looked away, not wanting to give her word and feeling awful for it. "I will come," she said at last.

His answering smile nearly broke her heart. "Until then." He moved to the carriage and bounded up the step.

Grace turned away, not waiting to see if he would wave goodbye, not wanting to do so herself.

What have I done? Every second she had stood out there

felt disloyal to Nicholas. Yet rebuffing Samuel had felt wrong too.

He is at least partially responsible for my being here, she reminded herself. But somehow the thought did not make her feel much better.

She walked up the steps, past Kingsley's disapproving look, through the foyer, and down the hall. She paused before returning to the ballroom and stood still, just beneath the kissing ball.

She was not prone to superstition, involving kissing or otherwise, but just then, she wished she were. If allowing Nicholas to kiss her beneath the ball tonight would seal her fate as his wife, she would gladly welcome it. She thought she'd wanted to be free; she'd never thought to have to make this choice. Now that it was before her, she wished someone would decide for her. That someone were here to tell her what to do—which man to choose, if she should marry at all, or whether to take her original path: the quiet country cottage with Helen and Christopher.

Before, her life choices had always been apparent. Now they seemed anything but, and she felt desperate for clarity. The only thing certain was that she could not continue the way she had been. She could not be friends with Samuel, and she could not live under the same roof as Nicholas.

Unless . . .

He appeared in the doorway the very second she glanced up at the kissing ball again. But the look on his face was not the one of tender affection she had witnessed earlier. His eyes neither had the desire she'd read in them, nor the humor he'd used when teasing her. He was angry—truly angry, as she had not seen him since her first days at Sutherland Hall.

"Where is Preston?" he demanded.

"He has gone home," Grace said. "So you may stop glowering." She attempted to make her tone light, hoping to tease him out of his mood.

He stared at her, his expression unreadable. "Your sister has gone up to bed. She was not feeling well. You should see to her." He turned his back and entered the ballroom, immediately becoming lost in the crowd.

Bereft, Grace stood beneath the kissing ball alone, remembering the day they had hung it and how she had told Nicholas she would not kiss him again.

I did not mean it.

CHAPTER 37

"You came." Samuel sat on the fence, his thick coat around him, hair wet with falling snow.

"Did you doubt it?" Grace asked as she picked her way over the slippery path to the fence.

"Truthfully, yes. Last night I could tell that you did not wish to."

She had doubted too, both her ability to break away from the busy house and festivities and her capacity to continue feeling torn between two men any longer.

Today must be the last time.

"It is not that I did not want to see you. It is just that—"

"You feel disloyal to Nicholas," Samuel finished.

Grace nodded. "You know me well."

"We have become good friends," Samuel said. "I have enjoyed our time together immensely."

"As have I," Grace said. "When I felt the most hopeless, you were here to lift my spirits. When I was lonely, you were my comfort and friend." She reached the bench but did not attempt to stand on it. She didn't fear slipping on its icy surface but feared drawing any closer to Samuel.

"You make me sound rather like a close relative, like—a brother," Samuel said. "But that is not the place in your heart I hoped to achieve."

"What *did* you hope?" Grace asked. "What did you hope to accomplish by allowing Lord Sutherland to take me into his home and forcing him to keep me there after you sent that letter with my father?"

Samuel tapped his lip. "It is good you ask. The first gift I've come to give you today is answers to any question you wish to ask."

Grace smiled encouragingly. "Go on, then. Before both of us freeze." She stamped her feet to keep them warm.

"I could have kept you at my home the night of my ball," Samuel said. "I'd certainly planned on your staying. I wanted to hear from you a full explanation of the rumors before making any judgment for or against you. Then Nicholas showed up. I couldn't have been more astounded."

"Nor I," Grace said, recalling the startling moment when he'd joined her at the top of the staircase.

"I thought at first that he was only there to vex me. He had to have known that you'd fled to my house, and I thought he wanted to punish me, to brag, if you will, of his actions."

"There were no *actions*," Grace said, blushing over the implication and wondering how she'd managed to attend Samuel's ball when everyone already believed the worst of her.

"I know nothing happened," Samuel said. "And I suspected as much while watching Nicholas dance with you. I have seen him at other balls in London, and he does not dance. He does not converse with women. Yet he did both with you. All of that in addition to coming to my house—a place he swore never again to set foot in—to rescue you?"

He came to save me from myself. Grace tugged her cloak tighter, thinking how different her life might be had Nicholas not come. *How sad it would be.* To think that she might never have known him beyond that first awful encounter in his room . . .

"When Nicholas argued so strongly to take you home, I let him. You provided an opportunity to rid myself of an enemy. Nicholas had never been in love before, and I imagined that if he was to develop such feelings for you, it might be just the thing to turn his anger from me."

Grace shook her head. "I am sorry to say that I have not been successful in that regard. He does not love me. And he still—hates you."

Samuel gave her a wry grin. "I rather noticed the last at his ball."

Grace sighed. "So that is why I was sold off to Lord Sutherland."

"You were not sold off at all," Samuel contested. "I guarantee that Nicholas has realized from the beginning that he could send you back to me. I would have welcomed you wholeheartedly. Indeed, the longer I have known you, the more I have wished for that very thing, that I had not been quite so generous in my gift to Nicholas. After all," he added softly, "it was I who saw you first."

Grace turned away from Samuel, not wanting to see the pained expression upon his face. She heard a soft thump and whirled toward the wall again, only to see that he had gone. "Samuel!" she cried. "Are you all right? Did you fall?"

His hand shot up above the fence in a friendly wave. "Just fetching my second gift."

"Oh." Grace had hoped they were finished; she didn't want to ask more questions of him. The what-ifs were too painful to consider. Being with Samuel like this, she knew that being happy with him would not be difficult. She wouldn't have to suffer brooding and moodiness as she did with Nicholas. She would know that Samuel really cared for her; he'd said as much already, which was far more than Nicholas had ever told her. She could live in Preston's wonderful house with his little girl. Helen and Christopher would be welcome too. He could give her everything.

I could be so very happy.

A section of the fence beyond the bench began to tremble. Snow and soggy leaves from the ivy beneath broke free and fell in a shower beside the wall. As Grace stepped back, a hole opened before her—rectangular on the sides, domed on top and made of thick, weathered wood, different from the stone of the wall.

She came forward again, touching it, not quite believing what she was seeing. "A door? This whole time?" She looked at Samuel, who stood, for the first time, on her side of the wall.

He shrugged. "I was trying to be proper by keeping a respectable distance. Not to mention that Nicholas would murder me were he to find me here."

"You should go." Grace marched toward him, hands outstretched, to push him back where he belonged.

"Not so fast." He caught her hands and held them. "I have one gift more, remember?"

Grace bit her lip and nodded. She glanced over her shoulder. "Be quick about it—please."

"'Be quick,' she says." Samuel pouted, as if she had wounded his pride. "When a man is about to do one of the most important things in his life." Still holding her hands, he knelt in the snow before her.

"Oh, Samuel, no," Grace begged. "Please don't."

"Just listen." He would not release her.

Grace felt her eyes filling with tears.

Samuel cleared this throat. "Miss Grace Thatcher, it would please me more than anything if you would do me the honor of becoming my wife. I have come to love you, and I promise that I will continue to love you. I will spend the remainder of my life in the pursuit of your happiness."

"Oh, Samuel. I cannot." Grace fell to her knees and into his arms, holding him even as she rejected him. "I have never been more sorry in my life." She sobbed onto his shoulder, and he held her, saying nothing but crying a little himself.

Still shaking, she broke away and stood quickly. She turned her back and brought a hand to her face in an attempt to hold back a second wave of tears.

Behind her, she heard Samuel get to his feet and dust the snow from his trousers. "If it makes you feel any better, I thought you would say that."

"Then why did you ask it?" Grace whirled to face him. "Why torture me so—and yourself, too?"

"To give you the gift you have most wanted these months, the thing you have told me you most craved and have sought after your whole life."

Grace frowned. "Thanks to you, what I have most wanted, I have. Helen and Christopher are safe."

"All right, perhaps it is the second thing you most wanted." He smiled wistfully.

He will be all right. I have not broken his heart beyond repair.

Samuel stepped away from the doorway and held his hand out toward it. "I offer you a chance to go through, to marry me—or to go elsewhere, to have the freedom you have longed for."

"I have no funds—"

"As of December twenty-second at three o'clock in the afternoon, you do." He withdrew a sheaf of papers from his coat. "I asked Christopher to wait until today and to let me tell you the good news."

"Oh my." Grace brought a hand to her heart, but it was her head that was spinning.

"You may go wherever you like, whenever you like. I have already spoken with several landlords about properties available for rent. I know of some that are far enough from here that your reputation would not follow you."

"What of Nicholas's reputation?" she asked, feeling for all the world lost and completely stricken, as if what she wanted most had just been taken away instead of handed to her.

"It seemed to me last night—during that rather scandalous waltz—that he does not worry overly much about his reputation."

"You saw?" Grace asked. "I thought you came later."

"I was very much there," Samuel grumbled. "Only not standing in such an obvious place that Nicholas could flaunt you in front of me."

Grace wrapped her arms around herself, the cold long forgotten with the confusion of thoughts tumbling about in her mind.

"Well, what is it to be?" Samuel asked. "You can have anything you wish."

Grace closed her eyes, not wanting to see him, not wanting to look at the papers in his hand, not wanting to exist. It was too painful. "I don't know what to do," she said, feeling as utterly hopeless as she had upon their first meeting at the wall. "I don't know what I want."

"I think perhaps you do." Samuel slid the papers back inside his coat. "And I think it is what you already have, only you are too afraid to claim it—to claim *him* as your own."

Grace opened her eyes and stared at Samuel. *Is he suggesting—*

"Don't ever be afraid of love, Grace." Samuel stepped closer. He touched her cheek reverently. "Even if you lose it in the end, even if you pay the ultimate price, it is always worth the risk."

He leaned forward and kissed her cheek then walked back through the hidden door, closing it behind him.

CHAPTER 38

Grace stared at the door long minutes after Samuel had left. She needed only call out to him, and he would return. Or she could pull the latch herself and go to his side of the wall.

And be at his side. Instead, at last, she squeezed her eyes shut against the agony of her loss and spun away, determined forevermore to never walk this way again.

Tears tracked down her face as she opened her eyes and began walking the other garden paths. The afternoon was cold, but she could not yet return to the house, not until she had control of herself. As of late, Nicholas had become all too adept at reading her feelings, and she did not want him to discover the friendship she'd had with Samuel, nor the depth of her caring for him.

"I have made the right choice," Grace told herself as she walked. It was the *only* course she could have taken after spending months at Sutherland Hall and owing Nicholas for both her care and for the money he had paid her father. But there was more to it than that. As she moved farther from the garden and closer to the looming tower of brick and stone that had become her home, Grace felt a weight lift from her shoulders.

No more would she worry over Nicholas discovering her meetings with Samuel. No more would she feel torn between the two, her feelings pulled to and fro, from one to the other.

Most importantly, no longer will I deny what I feel for Nicholas.

Grace's heart beat faster with the realization and the freedom and possibility it brought. It had been increasingly difficult to protect her heart and remain at arm's distance from Nicholas. She had not always been entirely successful, and when she thought on the moments when her guard had been down and her resolve had slipped, she realized she'd been at her happiest. Nicholas had won, not because of the constraints of their situation—Samuel had offered her a way around those—but because Nicholas had won her heart.

A fresh set of tears gathered in her eyes. For all her efforts to try to protect herself from falling in love, she had done exactly that, and with a man she was not certain could or would ever return her affection.

Feeling somber in every way, Grace stopped before the front doors of Sutherland Hall. She tilted her head back, looking up at the enormous structure, which still appeared cold and uninviting on the outside. But on the inside, she'd seen its potential for warmth. Her evenings in the library with Nicholas, the day he'd returned from London and she'd greeted him on the stairs, that ridiculous night in the salon when he'd teased her from her anger.

Anger because he had kissed me.

The moments preceding that kiss had been glorious. A beautiful and almost sacred thing had sprung up between them—completely unexpected by either of them, she was sure. She had hated him for ruining it. And though she had granted forgiveness they had yet to regain the intimacy of that day. Several times they had been on the brink, but one or the other had retreated.

The time for retreating is past.

Suddenly she wanted very much to be close to Nicholas, to feel as she had—for him to feel as she believed he had—that afternoon in the carriage. She needed those feelings, a reaffirmation of her decision in the wake of losing Samuel.

With resolute steps, Grace mounted the stairs and pushed open the front doors. Closing them quietly behind her, she paused in the foyer, waiting for her eyes to adjust to the dim light. This morning the house had been filled with tenants come for their pudding and presents, and she, Nicholas, Lady Sutherland, and Helen and Christopher had all had a grand time greeting their guests and handing out gifts. The hall was now deserted—dark and silent, as it had been on that first stormy night.

"The hour is late. I have been worried about you."

Grace jumped and brought a hand to her heart. "You scared me." She glanced up to find Nicholas staring down at her, his face shrouded in the late afternoon shadows. "I have been walking—and thinking," she said.

"It is too cold to be out." His voice was harsh, but Grace had learned to detect his concern for her beneath his outward severity.

"I am warm enough." *More so now that you are here.* Her eyes had adjusted, so she could clearly see worry in the lines crinkling beside his eyes and in the downward slant of his mouth. "Fresh air is often best for clearing one's head and making decisions."

"You have been troubled." He raised his hand toward her, as if he meant to touch the side of her cheek where her tears had fallen. Grace stood still, anticipating his gentle touch—aching for it—but as before when she had given in to the longing between them, Nicholas retreated. His hand dropped at his side.

"You have the uncanny ability to know my thoughts,"

she said. *To know my heart.* For some reason, the admission filled her eyes anew, and Grace turned aside, blinking rapidly to hold back what was sure to be another flood of tears.

"Would that I did know them," Nicholas said, his words quiet, the edge gone from his voice. "I have oft wondered—as I do this very moment—what it is you are thinking."

Tell him.

"Hold me," Grace whispered, her face still turned from his. "I would like you to hold me. I could use some comforting."

"And you think I—"

She nodded. *Please,* she added silently. In answer, she felt his hands upon her arms, turning her to him.

"Your cloak is damp." Scolding words, but as their eyes met, she saw something completely different in his serious expression. An understanding passed between them, sending a shiver of anticipation down her spine. They were about to cross a barrier and were both committing to the journey.

With utmost care, Nicholas untied her cloak strings. As he pushed the garment back, his hands brushed her shoulders, sending a delightful tingling coursing through her. He whisked the cloak away, and Grace shivered and hugged her arms to herself. Nicholas crossed the foyer to the banister and draped the cloak over the post. His eyes again sought hers, and he retraced his steps, coming to stand before her.

Neither moved. Grace swallowed back both her nervous anticipation and any pride she might have had left. She stepped forward, closing the narrow distance between them, giving herself into his care, and laid her head against Nicholas's chest.

His shirt was soft, his heartbeat steady and reassuring, though faster than Grace would have supposed. He smelled faintly of expensive cologne but more so of the books in his study and of a fresh-laid fire. She found the combination dizzying in an utterly delightful way.

Nicholas's movements were stiff and awkward as first one arm and then the other came around her. Grace closed her eyes and sighed, then felt him relax as he pulled her more firmly to him. One of his hands circled her waist while the other moved up her back, beginning feather-light strokes, soothing away the last of her doubts about her decision and promising comfort and caring in a way she had only dreamed of.

"Is this what you had in mind?" His voice was gruff, yet tender.

"Yes," Grace said. "For quite some time, I have wished for you to hold me like this."

"I had no idea." His voice was full of wonder. "You see, I am not at all adept at reading your thoughts, after all." He broke off as Grace shyly wrapped her arms around his waist. She dared not move her hands as he did, but she wanted him to know that she, too, could give.

"Not that one, the *blue* one." The dowager's harping tones echoed from the hall above.

"Mother," Nicholas grumbled. "As always, her timing is impeccable." He released Grace, then stepped back, taking her hand in his own. He pulled her out of sight of the stairs a second before his mother appeared. Grace ran on tiptoe beside him to the study doors. Once inside, Nicholas closed the door behind them and turned the lock.

"Don't be frightened," he said, handing her the key. "You may leave any time you wish. I only wanted to provide a moment of privacy—if that is what you desire."

Desire . . . privacy. Dangerous words. Grace closed her fingers around the key, thinking that what she most feared had already happened. She had lost her heart to Nicholas, and she did not yet know if he would treat it with care. In this very room, he had demonstrated how little care he could have for her. She hoped he had changed, that his heart had softened, but she could not be certain.

"Again your thoughts are a mystery," Nicholas said.

"With the way they are flitting across your lovely face, they reveal much, yet nothing." He made no move toward her, did not attempt to resume the embrace they had shared in the foyer.

Grace wanted him to. She basked in the glow of his compliment but needed more than words. *Does he yearn for my touch as I yearn for his?* She wanted him to seek out her company and find value in it. Samuel had met her at the wall unfailingly; he had come several days when she had not. She wanted to see that kind of interest from Nicholas, to know he was not simply doing his duty or what was expected but that he, too, had come to care.

When she had not spoken but had only stared at him, lost in thought, Nicholas continued. "Were I to guess, I would say that you look as if you would like to be kissed. But then I have thought as much before and been wrong." He turned away and stepped toward his desk.

Do not separate us. The Nicholas she had oft found on the other side of that desk was not the one she wished for now. She moved in front of him, blocking his way. "I have wanted you to kiss me—I *do* want you to."

Her whispered confession stopped him. Once more he looked at her, his eyes searching for the truth. With a sudden lurch to her heart, Grace saw the same uncertainty she felt reflected in his eyes. *He does not know my heart any more than I know his.*

She stepped forward in the same moment he did and practically launched herself into his arms, which tightened around her at once. Grace buried her head in his chest as his chin came down upon her head.

"Grace." He whispered her name with the same reverence he'd used that day in the carriage. Awash in joy, she clung to him. "Do you have any idea—do you realize?" Nicholas said gruffly.

"What?" she asked, tilting her head back to look up at him.

His gaze locked upon hers. "How very much I've wanted to hold you, to kiss you. Denying myself has been agony. If I'd thought there was any possibility you felt the same, had I known—"

She placed a finger over his lips. "Now you do."

He kissed her fingertips then took her hand in his own and held it close to his heart.

But still he did not kiss her. He made no move to do anything but hold her tenderly. Confusion and hurt crowded her mind amidst the pleasure of being held by him.

Had she done something wrong? What more *could* she have done? She'd all but begged Nicholas to kiss her again. His finger stroked her cheek. Grace closed her eyes, reveling in his touch.

Perhaps he is only taking his time. Perhaps he is as nervous as I am.

"If we cross this line, there is no going back," Nicholas said in a tone of dire warning.

"What do you mean?" Grace asked without looking up to judge his expression. She could barely speak, entranced by his touch as she was.

"I have been investigating ways in which we may . . . end our contract," Nicholas explained. Grace stiffened in his arms. "Hear me out," he said, moving his hand to soothe her back as he had earlier.

Grace nodded, though she felt her throat constricting with fear and hurt.

"I have given my word and will not go back on it," Nicholas reassured her. "But some time ago, it came to my attention that it might be better for us both if I did. Of course, I would not just turn you out; there is another possibility. I have reason to believe that Mr. Preston may still have you."

He knows. Grace felt her breath catch.

"I have not spoken with him about it," Nicholas continued, and Grace held back a sigh of considerable relief.

"And I have not been blind to his attraction to you, either, at both his ball and our own." He had a hint of irritation in his voice.

Our ball. Grace clung to his choice of words, hoping he truly felt that it had been *their* ball, that he didn't really believe that ending their engagement was best.

"Preston is a forgiving man and would, I am certain, take you back were the situation properly explained. Both of you would have to move far, far away to get beyond the scandal, but I suspect Preston would not be averse to that." Nicholas drew in his breath slowly, as if pained. "I would be willing to speak to him, to explain—for you."

His stunning admission equally warmed and hurt her. Grace wasn't certain what to make of it. Was Nicholas so desperate to be free that he was willing to plead her case before his enemy?

Or does he care for me enough that he would do so to see me happy?

She wanted to believe the latter but could not. Though he held her tenderly now, she could not feel certain of his affection, not with the tumult of the previous weeks and the knowledge that he had been forced into his current position as her affianced. And not when he had just offered a means of escape.

As Samuel did.

She could neither accept Preston's offer then, nor would she accept Nicholas's plan now, unless it was truly what he wanted. Even then, it would not be to flee to Samuel. She had closed that door and would not reopen it. Her future lay either here with Nicholas or in the country with Helen and Christopher.

Grace pushed back from Nicholas, stepping from his embrace so she might think clearly—an impossibility when in his arms.

"Do you wish me to go?" She searched his face, knowing

she'd find the truth there. Nicholas was no better a liar than she.

"No." A sterner, swifter response she'd never heard from him. "At first, I did. But now . . ."

She understood. "What you believed you wanted is no longer true?" A reflection of her own feelings, if ever there was one.

Nicholas turned away and this time succeeded in reaching his chair behind the desk, effectively separating them. "What I wish is not under consideration. I am interested in what is *best.*"

"Might they not be the same?" Grace asked. Fear began to creep its way into her heart, as if the physical distance between them was suggestive of the final outcome of this meeting.

"Unlikely." Nicholas drummed his fingers on the desk in agitation.

"You think I would be better off with Mr. Preston?"

Nicholas grimaced. "I've no doubt that he would do everything in his power to make you happy."

Words so near to what Samuel had said. "What of *my* doubts and feelings?" Grace asked, angry at Nicholas's assumption—however true she'd feared it might once have been. "Would *you* be happier if I were gone? Have I been nothing but a distraction to you—a sore temptation to resist?" She whirled away and headed toward the door. With shaking fingers, she thrust the key into the lock and reached for the knob. Behind her, a chair crashed against the wall. A second later, Nicholas's hand over hers stopped her from opening the door.

He pulled her to him, but Grace refused to step into his embrace. Instead, they stood toe to toe. She tugged her hand from his and crossed her arms.

"You are maddening," Nicholas said.

Grace glared at him, further hurt and angered by the amusement in his voice.

"I've been mad with frustration and desire," Nicholas said. "Mad with laughter at your antics. I have been beside myself about what to do with you. It seemed entirely illogical for us to wed—a more ludicrous proposition I could not have invented just three months ago."

"I see." Grace looked at her shoes to hide her smarting eyes.

"You do not see at all." Nicholas gently lifted her chin so she would look at him. "I have found myself alternately irate over you and then frightened on your behalf. I've wanted to punish you, then wished with my entire soul that I might heal your hurts and ensure that you never suffered another. First I resented your presence in my home but then realized that it was your presence that made these walls a home again." He released her but held her gaze.

He continued in a softer voice. "I've known I must not touch you, yet I've longed for that touch nearly every waking—and of late, every sleeping—moment. I've been distracted and tempted by your lips to the point of insanity. Your voice, your movements, your hair and smile, your wit and wisdom have all combined to prove my entire undoing. And so I confess, Grace, that I cannot endure it any longer. To this point I have seen to your safety. Your innocence has been preserved for Preston or any other man you may someday choose. But if we cross this line, here, now—if I take you in my arms and kiss you behind a locked door—there is no returning. You will be mine irrevocably."

"The door is no longer locked," Grace said, unsuccessfully attempting humor as she tried to blink back the tears spilling from her eyes.

"Leave if you will." Nicholas stepped back and inclined his head toward the door.

Her heart pounded beneath her dress as she faced the door again. She stretched out her hand to the knob, then grasped the key and turned it swiftly, turning the lock. She pulled the key from the door and held it out to Nicholas, dropping it in his hand. "The key to my heart, milord."

Nicholas swept her into his arms and crushed her to him. "Don't cry, love."

Their lips met in a frenzy of desperation. The kiss was neither slow nor gentle, as Grace had imagined it would be. He held her close with a fierce possessiveness, his mouth on hers, testing the strength of her newly declared commitment, demanding more and more in a way that left her breathless and with no doubt that there was no going back from here.

I am his. A thrill of anticipation coursed through her. Nicholas's hands left her waist and cradled her face. She opened her eyes to look at him and witnessed his expression of awe.

"Grace," he whispered. "You have saved me." His lips found hers again, this time with the lightest touch. His lips lingered, tasting her, caressing.

He desires me. I am loved. Each kiss conveyed an entirely different message. The first had brought a rush of building desire; the second caused her heart to feel that it would burst.

Nicholas released her and pulled back, his breathing ragged. In a haze of desire and happiness, Grace crossed before him, seeking a chair for support.

"Don't even think about sitting," Nicholas teased, snatching her around the waist and pulling her close again. Grace slid her hands up to his shoulders. They kissed a third time, this one a combination of the first two—slow and sweet, hungry and possessive. Grace bent her head to his chest, her own heart thundering when at last they parted.

"I think," Nicholas began, his voice unsteady, "that it is time we obtain our wedding license." He pressed his lips to the top of her nose. "I could go to London tomorrow." He kissed her forehead. "While I am gone, you can have your gown made." He stroked her hair. "And then we can be married."

"Soon?" Grace asked, leaning into him so as to keep herself upright instead of melting to the floor as her limbs seemed wont to do.

"Soon," Nicholas reiterated and then kissed her again.

CHAPTER 39

Nicholas glanced at the crooked numbers hanging above the worn and filthy door. Grateful his hands were gloved, he pushed open the low gate—also filthy—and made his way up the uneven walk with care.

He rapped three times upon the door, then waited. It was mid-morning, the time—according to Grace—most likely to find George Thatcher at home.

When a minute had passed with no response, Nicholas knocked again and called out, guessing that Grace's father was more likely to make an appearance if he knew there was not a bill collector outside. Again there was no answer, so Nicholas went around the back to see if there was another door.

The yard was strewn with debris—mostly evidence of the tenant's drinking habits. Nicholas felt sickened as he thought of Grace and her siblings growing up in such a dismal place. When he saw the sagging clothesline and the old washtub propped near the back door, he felt even worse.

Never will she set foot here again, he vowed. *Neither will I.* He'd come only to tell Mr. Thatcher that he and Grace would be married within the week and to let the man know that Grace and her siblings were no longer his responsibility and that he was not to attempt contact with any of them ever again.

Nicholas raised his hand to knock on the back door and found it already ajar. He called out once more, pushing the door open as he did. The odor that met him sent him back out quickly, and not until he had a handkerchief firmly pressed to his face did he attempt to reenter.

The cottage was dark with the drapes drawn, the only light being from the door he'd just passed through. Nicholas stepped carefully over more bottles than had been in the yard. He felt certain the house had not looked this way when Grace and her siblings lived here, but neither could he imagine it to have been a happy place to grow up.

As he moved through a narrow hall toward the front of the house, the foul smell increased until he thought he could endure it no more. Clearly, George Thatcher was not at home, so there seemed no point in staying. Nicholas pressed on, intending to exit through the front door, quitting this place as quickly as possible.

As he emerged from the hall, with the front door in sight, another sight stopped him—scared him so that he dropped the handkerchief and gave a startled gasp. From across the room, George Thatcher stared at him, his limbs stiff and eyes wide.

Frozen in death.

CHAPTER 40

Nicholas sat at his desk, drumming his fingers, nervous about the news he must share with Grace and her siblings.

Christopher was first to arrive. "The girls are with the dressmaker," he explained. "Their gowns are full of pins at the moment, but they'll be down as soon as they can."

"Very good." Nicholas brought a hand to his mouth, considering how to delicately phrase what he must say. *Your father is dead,* seemed a little abrupt, though he very much doubted that tears would follow the news.

"You seem troubled, milord."

"I am," Nicholas said, then realized that the answer to his dilemma stood before him. *Why not tell their brother and let him break the news?* It seemed like a logical solution. Christopher was family, whereas he was not. *Yet.*

"I went to see your father on my return trip from London," Nicholas said.

Christopher's eyes darkened. "I hope you did not give him any money. He'll only waste it, you know."

"I gave him nothing," Nicholas said. "I did not speak with him, either, because I found him . . . dead."

It took a moment for his words to sink in. When they did, Christopher's face showed first shock and then relief. "Truly? You are in earnest?"

"Very much so. I would not jest about something so serious."

Christopher sank into the nearest chair, a look of incredulity on his face. Nicholas remembered collapsing in that same chair upon hearing of his own father's death. But in his case, it had been so he might weep in private. As he had suspected, no tears were forthcoming from the young Mr. Thatcher.

"Are you quite all right?" Nicholas asked. "Would you care for a drink?"

"I am well, thank you," Christopher said. "In truth, you could not have brought us happier news."

"That was my assessment as well," Nicholas confessed.

"First the settlement of Grandfather's estate, and now this," Christopher continued, wonder in his voice. "We shall finally be free."

"What about the settlement?" Nicholas asked. "Last I inquired, things were not looking good there."

"It finally came through," Christopher said. "Just before Christmas—a few days before we came here from Mr. Preston's. He still has the paperwork, in fact. Asked me to hold off on telling Grace so he could tell her him—" Christopher broke off suddenly, as if he'd realized what he'd revealed.

"You—and your sister Helen—were staying with Mr. Preston?" Nicholas tried to digest one piece of disturbing information at a time.

"Yes." Christopher looked toward the door with longing. "I'll go check the girls to see what's keeping—"

"Sit," Nicholas ordered, pointing to the chair Christopher was attempting to vacate. "Has Grace been in contact with Mr. Preston these past months?"

Christopher squirmed in his seat. "I think you should ask her yourself."

"I intend to," Nicholas said. "But I want your answer first."

"Yes," Christopher said with some reluctance. "They met in the garden. He brought us her letters and delivered ours to her."

"This went on for how long?" Nicholas asked. His stomach felt as though he'd been punched.

"October," Christopher answered quietly, his head down.

"Why did you not simply come see her yourself?" Nicholas asked, sobered to think of Grace walking in the garden—*Elizabeth's garden*—with Preston.

Christopher shrugged. "I don't know. I was away much of the time, working on the settlement, and Helen never goes out much."

So they were alone together. On how many occasions? "And this settlement from your grandfather—you have it now? It was awarded in your favor?"

"It was. I came to Yorkshire as soon as the ruling came down. The funds have been transferred. Mr. Preston was planning to tell Grace after Christmas, when he asked her—"

To marry him. Nicholas finished what Christopher, looking severely regretful, had not.

"I see," Nicholas said, cutting him off. He saw only too clearly that it was Preston, not himself, who held all of the cards in this game.

Except that it was no game. It was Grace—and her happiness.

This entire time, she has already had what she wanted—her means to freedom, Preston's loyalty, and most likely, affection. Nicholas brought a hand to his mouth once more, confused and distressed by this revelation. "What will you do with the money?" he asked.

"I don't know," Christopher admitted. "We always

planned to go to the north country—far from our father—though that isn't necessary now. Mr. Preston had found a few possibilities for us, far enough away for Grace to make a new start—had she wanted to," he added hastily.

"She will be here, of course," Nicholas said. "You and Helen are welcome to stay as well."

"Thank you." Christopher nodded, then looked toward the door once more.

"You may go," Nicholas said. "Will you give me your word not to mention our conversation to Grace?"

"Not a word," Christopher agreed. He left, closing the door behind him.

Nicholas stared at it, at the keyhole and the key that Grace had placed in his hand only days ago. *The key to my heart*, she had said.

If her heart had been given another choice, would she have chosen to stay behind his closed door? *When she learns of her father's death and the inheritance—and of Preston's feelings for her—will she want to leave?*

Her light knock came on his door—he recognized it—and anguish filled him at the thought of never hearing it after today. "Come in," Nicholas called in a harsh voice that no longer sounded like his own.

She pushed the door open slowly and peered inside. At the sight of him, her eyes brightened. "You *are* here. You did not sound like yourself at all." She entered and shut the door behind her. "Helen will be a few minutes more." She smiled as she stood there, hands clasped behind her back, eyes full of expectation.

Nicholas stood and came around the front of the desk, though not kiss her. "I have some news."

"Oh." The anticipation left her eyes, replaced by worry. "What is it, Nicholas?" She touched his arm.

He stood stiffly, doing his best to ignore her touch. "Your father is dead."

Her gasp proved his earlier concern true. He should

have found a more gentle way to tell her. "That is the bad news," he rushed on, sorry to have startled her. "The better news"—he could not bring himself to say *good*, for there was nothing good about it in his mind—"is that your inheritance has come through. The money your grandfather left you is finally yours. You may have your house in the country."

She had the benevolence to look confused. "Why should I need a house in the country?"

"Why not?" Nicholas asked, feigning indifference to her distress. It would not last long. If she stayed with him and denied her dream—or *dreams*, if Preston was now included in that list—her regrets would be final. Any sorrow she felt now would be temporary, soon wearing off in the joy of her independence. "You no longer require my protection from your father. The money is adequate for you to live wherever you should choose. I believe Mr. Preston knows of a few properties already."

"Mr. Preston?" Her shock was evident but closely followed by another, fleeting, emotion, which Nicholas wished with all his heart that he had missed—a flash of guilt, brief and intense in the second before she swept it away.

"You wish me to go?" Her voice shook.

"It is what you wanted. It is best." That word again. How he hated it.

"Best," she repeatedly numbly, then turned and fled the room, the sound of her steps echoing across the foyer and his heart.

CHAPTER 41

February, 1828

At the urgent knocking on his study door, Nicholas closed the volume of poetry he'd been reading and slid it discreetly in his desk drawer. Later tonight he would retrieve the book and spend some time alone, considering what opinions Grace might have had on the selection.

Rather pathetic that I spend my evenings thus engaged. But altogether, he had to admit it was an improvement over his previous, pre-Grace activities. His days—and nights—of revenge were over. He liked Preston no more than before. *If anything, I've more right than ever to loathe the man.* But hurting Preston would ultimately hurt Grace, and that Nicholas could not do.

"Come in," he called when the pounding came a second time. He couldn't imagine what could be so urgent as all that. Since Grace's departure nearly two months ago, the house had returned to a state of calm and quiet. Utter boredom.

Loneliness.

The door swung open, and Kingsley entered, a look of unusual trepidation creasing his brow and with what appeared to be a swathe of dripping wet velvet draped over his arm.

Nicholas was at once wary. The last time Kingsley had approached his study in any sort of state other than his usual placidness had been the day of Mr. Thatcher's visit.

Unless his ghost is haunting me . . .

Nicholas's eyes strayed to the wet fabric. "What have you got there?"

"A cloak, milord. Belonging to a little girl who says that she is here to see you."

"A child? How peculiar." Nicholas frowned in puzzlement. The garment Kingsley held appeared too valuable to belong to a tenant. Yet what other child could be visiting him? And why would a little girl come alone, on a cold, wet day like today, unless something was terribly amiss with her parents?

"Would you like me to show her in?" Kingsley asked.

"No." Nicholas rose from his desk. "I'll go to her." The past few weeks, he'd become particular about having visitors of any sort in his study. The room had become hallowed to him, rich with the memory of holding Grace in his arms on this very spot of rug his feet now trod. He feared creating any new memories here or doing anything that might disrupt the solace he derived almost nightly when he sat alone in his chair, remembering all that had transpired in this room.

The key to my heart . . .

Memory was not much for a man to live on; neither was it a particularly sane habit, but he was coping with his loss as best he could, and for now, it was only the daily reliving of their time together that allowed him to continue on without her.

They left the study, and Nicholas did his best to clear his head and focus on the matter at hand. "Is the girl quite alone? Did she give you her name?"

"She *is* alone, and she did," Kingsley said, then hesitated as if he did not wish to say more.

"Well?" Nicholas stopped and turned to him, struggling to keep his old habit of impatience in check. "Who is she?"

"Her name is Beth." Kingsley swallowed, and a look of unease flitted across his face. "Beth Preston. I believe she is—your niece."

"My—"

Lady Sutherland's scream rent the air, and Nicholas rushed toward the sound, nearly falling as he slid across the wet floor, then came to a stop directly in front of the open sitting room doors.

"I'm sorry, milord. The child's cloak was wet and dripping—"

"Never mind." Nicholas waved a hand, brushing Kingsley's apology aside. What did a little water on the floor matter compared with what the butler had said the moment before?

Beth Preston . . . your niece.

Nicholas entered the sitting room, his eyes flashing from his mother, who was deathly pale and clutching the back of the sofa as if for dear life, to the frightened and very young child, just peeking out from behind a chair. He caught a glimpse of her curls and guessed at once the shock his mother must have felt but a moment before.

"My *niece*?" Nicholas said in wonderment, repeating Kingsley's words and coming to that conclusion instead of the other, more illogical one that a ghost from his sister's childhood stood before him.

"Show yourself, child," he said, not unkindly, and stepped forward between his mother and the girl, then knelt so as to be closer to her height. "We won't hurt you."

She came out from behind the chair, a repentant look upon her face, her hands clasped behind her back. "I didn't mean to scare her. Well, I *did* mean to, but not that much. I thought it would be you coming into the room and that you wouldn't scare so easily. Papa never scares as easily as the maids do. He said you would be surprised to see me, but I couldn't see how unless I jumped out at you . . ." Her words trailed off, and she looked down at her feet.

And who might your Papa be? There could be only one answer to that, and it would anger Nicholas greatly were he to dwell on it and the secret Preston had been harboring until now. Instead, Nicholas forced his attention to the girl, reminding himself that her parentage was not her fault.

"You hid, then jumped out at your *grandmother—*" He threw a glance over his shoulder at his still-pale mother. "On purpose?"

The little girl nodded.

Nicholas felt his mouth twitch. He stood quickly, so she would not see. "That was very . . ." *Elizabeth-like.*

"Wrong?" the girl suggested.

He nodded and brought a fist to his mouth to hold back laughter. *It is the shock of it all,* he told himself. The shock of seeing this child, so like Elizabeth so many years ago.

"I think your grandmother will be able to forgive you," Nicholas said. He crossed to the sofa, pried his mother's fingers from it, and assisted her in sitting.

"How have you—" she began, staring at the girl.

"I've no doubt she will tell us how she's come to be here," Nicholas said, watching the precocious child. Already recovered from the trauma of the previous moment, she was busy studying the pendulum on the mantel clock.

No doubt trying to discover how to get her hands on it.

His memory stirred, taking him back to this room many years before, when he and Elizabeth were young and had similar designs on the tempting clock. They had built a tower from books and other objects, until it was tall enough for them to reach the mantel. Elizabeth had ascended first, having reminded him that gentlemen always allowed ladies that privilege, and had just reached the top and propped upon the mantel when their nanny was heard in the hall.

Self-preserving as he was, Nicholas had taken it upon himself to run and hide. But in the process, he'd knocked their makeshift ladder awry, leaving Elizabeth hanging in a rather unladylike fashion when their distraught nanny entered the room.

The previously forgotten memory brought a smile to his face. "Come here—Beth?" He looked to the doorway and Kingsley, who nodded.

The girl pulled her gaze from the clock with a reluctance Nicholas recognized all too well. Her eyes alone would have given her away as Elizabeth's child.

And what of Preston, does she have? He hoped against hope that it was not much.

Her steps were light as she hastened to stand in front of them, going so far as to curtsy. "It is a pleasure to make your acquaintance," she said quite properly.

"And yours," Nicholas assured her, surprised at how very much he meant it. He looked at his mother.

"Yes," she said. A bit of the color had returned to her face, but Nicholas could tell that she was still in shock.

"What is it that brought you to visit us this fine day?" he inquired, looking past her to the gloom outside. *Where has your father been hiding you for three years?*

"My father brought me here," she said. "But then he left."

"Aren't you a bit young to be calling on people by yourself?" his mother asked.

"I am coming up on four, but I think I'm ten," Beth said. "That is what Father says."

"Does he?" A surge of jealousy flared to life inside Nicholas when he thought of Preston having this delightful child to himself all this time. Nicholas recalled the night of Elizabeth's death—the night of her child's death too, they'd all been led to believe. It seemed the cruelest of tricks that Preston had let them continue thinking so all this time.

And why send her to us now? Nicholas did not have to

search far to find the answer. No doubt Grace had something to do with the child's being here. Honest to a fault, Grace would not be able to abide a lie such as this in Preston.

He thought of Grace's discovering his deceit—and taking him to task for it. The image brought a smile to Nicholas's face.

"So your father thinks you quite grown up?" Nicholas mused, studying the little girl.

Beth nodded. "He says Mother was like that too. She was very smart and very pretty—like me." She smiled.

"Such humility," Lady Sutherland muttered, rolling her eyes. But Nicholas caught her smile at the end.

"Why have you come to visit today?" Nicholas asked the child, whom he found more delightful by the minute. *What can be done to keep you here?*

"I came to give you an invitation." Her brow furrowed, and her lips pressed together, as if in deep concentration. "You are invited to come to dinner this eve. At our house. You'll be eating in the big people dining room," she added, as if that ought to be enticement enough.

"The big people." Nicholas let out a low whistle. "That does sound important. However—"

"Papa said you would say no, so I am to tell you something else," she added. "He would like to pick a new mother for me, and he would like your blessing. It is *most* important that you come."

Lady Sutherland clucked her disapproval. "I never—"

Nicholas held up a hand. "It's all right, Mother."

Don't shoot the messenger, his father would have said. Nicholas leaned forward, doing his best to fight the anger battling to erupt from within. *The nerve of Preston, first, to hide his daughter and then to send her to ask me* that. *A cowardly act if ever there was one. I've released Grace from our betrothal; what more does he expect? For me to be happy for him?*

"Your father was right," Nicholas said. "I do not wish to come. It is difficult for me to visit your house."

"Why?" Beth asked, tilting her head to the side and giving him such a look of wide-eyed innocence that he could not immediately answer.

Why? What could he say that she could understand and would be appropriate for her to hear? Certainly not that he loved the woman who was to become her new mother—the same woman her father loved. He couldn't very well tell Beth that he held her father responsible for her mother's death.

Nicholas realized that it would require a new cordiality with Preston if he were to have the opportunity to get to know his daughter.

If we are henceforth to have this miraculous child to be a part of our lives, I will have to be civil.

Preston had extended no small olive branch in sending his daughter. Perhaps it was not so much an act of cowardice as an attempt at reconciliation.

Something Grace had much to do with, no doubt.

If I go to dinner, I will see Grace again. All the more reason to refuse.

Nicholas leaned forward, elbows braced on his knees as he attempted an explanation. "It is difficult for me to visit your home because your mother died there. She was my sister, and I loved her very much."

"Oh," Beth said, her face crumpling with compassion far beyond her years. "It is not good to be sad. Mother would want you to be happy." She sighed. "That is what Father says, though sometimes I hear him being sad at night, when he thinks I am asleep."

"How is he sad?" Nicholas asked, already wary of her answer, imagining the child hearing someone crying out at odd times after dark. Was Preston engaging in illicit affairs during the night?

Has he been kissing Grace in his study, as I kissed her in mine? The possibility brought a sharp pain to his chest.

"Papa cries," Beth said. "He holds Mother's portrait, and he cries."

Nicholas sat back against the cushions, wanting distance from the child, from everyone in the room—Kingsley, still waiting by the door, his mother, eying him with a worried expression. Nicholas looked away, to the far corner, but he could not rid himself of the picture Beth had painted. He didn't want to think of Preston hurting that way. It was easier to imagine, instead, that his brother-in-law was no longer affected by his loss, that his carelessness that night had cost him nothing.

But it did gain him one thing. Nicholas forced his gaze back to the girl still standing before them, rocking from one foot to the other, eyes flitting about the room casually, completely unaware of the magnitude of her revelation.

Nicholas drew in a deep breath, reining in his emotions—something he would not have been able to do a few months ago. He glanced at his mother and noted apprehension on her face. Her opportunity to be a grandmother depended upon what he said.

"I will go," Nicholas said quietly. "And I will even play nicely."

Though it will only be play acting, it may kill me.

His mother sighed with apparent relief. She reached over, patting his knee. "Thank you, Nicholas. I know it will be difficult, but look at her." Their attention returned to Beth, who was hopping from flower to flower in the pattern on the rug.

"Beth," Nicholas called to her. She turned, stepping carefully across the rug until she stood before them again. "You may tell your father that I will come," Nicholas said.

Her face brightened. "Oh, I'm so glad. And now I am able to stay the afternoon and play. He said I might if you agreed to come home with me."

Clever of him, Nicholas thought begrudgingly. "And what if I'd said no?"

Her lips twisted as she thought on his question. She shrugged. "I don't know. He said you would come even though you wouldn't want to."

The devil take you, Preston, Nicholas thought as he stood. But as he looked down on the tow-headed child, he knew his mood was not nearly as dark as it might have been.

Elizabeth's child. My niece. I am an uncle. It might not be his children who filled these empty halls as he had imagined not long ago, but this unexpected gift felt like heaven's miracle. He held his hand out to his niece, intending to make the most of the afternoon at his home, as the evening was sure to be torture at Preston's.

Watching Grace and Preston together would not be as painful as the night had been when he'd waited in Preston's salon, listening for happy news but hearing of Elizabeth's death instead. But it would hurt.

And it will go on hurting beyond tonight. Seeing them together would put an end to his fantasy that Grace would someday return to him. No longer could he use that crutch to cope. It would mean an end to his pretended conversations with her, to the cherished memory of those moments in his study.

I'll not even have revenge to fill the emptiness, he realized. Not if he wished to know the child skipping along beside him.

She would force him to give up the demons of his past and face those of the future as best he could. Nicholas swallowed his doubts and fears in the hope that this miniature version of his sister was worth it.

"Come along," he said, voice gruff with too many emotions. "I'll show you your mother's old room, and then I'll teach you to slide on the banister the way she did."

CHAPTER 42

Nicholas allowed Beth to pull him up the steps to her house. "Papa, Papa. We're home." Her tiny voice echoed through the bright room—a room Elizabeth had loved, Nicholas remembered.

A moment later, Preston's study door opened, and he walked toward them, his arms opened wide for his daughter.

They had better be for her, Nicholas thought with dire humor. He might be here, but he was in no mood to hug Preston. *But where is Grace?*

Preston swept his daughter into his arms. "I missed you today. Did you have fun with your grandmother and uncle?" As he spoke, he looked over her shoulder at Nicholas.

Beth nodded. "I played with Mommy's old toys, and I learned how to slide a banister."

"Did you?" Preston's tone held a note of concern, but he smiled at her warmly. He looked at Nicholas. "Dinner is ready. Shall we join our other guests?"

Nicholas followed him to the dining room, though he could have walked there on his own. Elizabeth had invited them over frequently during her marriage. They had spent many a pleasant hour at this table.

Even with Preston. How could he have forgotten those times? Their laughter and sparring, the heated debates, which Elizabeth was often the center of, the constant competitions between him and Preston that, while not always friendly, had proven great entertainment.

The room was not empty, but the person he had been most looking forward to seeing, the one he had dreaded seeing as well, was not present. Grace's siblings stood near the door, waiting for them, but she was not with them.

When they took their seats, Nicholas noticed that no additional places had been set. "Is Grace ill again?"

I'll murder Preston right here if he's done her any harm.

"I hope not," Preston said. He glanced down the table at her siblings. "Was Grace well the last time you saw her?"

"It depends upon what you mean by the word *well*," Helen said, using more words than Nicholas had heard from her during the entire time she had resided at his house.

"What Helen means," Christopher said, "is that Grace is healthy in body, but her spirits are quite low."

"Why is that?" Nicholas leaned back so the servant could pour his drink. "Why is she not here with you?"

"She would not come," Helen said. "It is too painful for her to be so near you."

"So near me?" Nicholas stood and threw down his napkin. "That is absurd. She lived in my home for three months and endured my company quite well."

"No small miracle," Preston muttered.

"Whatever she has told you is not true," Nicholas said. "I treated her with the utmost respect, gave her every courtesy, let her go when the blasted inheritance came through and Christopher made it clear you intended to propose."

Christopher picked up his spoon and began sipping his soup. "*Letting her go* is the offense I believe she finds most painful."

The others began to eat as well, and Nicholas looked

from one to another, feeling both perplexed and angered at their lack of concern over Grace.

"If she does not wish to reside here, then why are you not with her?" he demanded of Preston. "If she were my fiancée, I would be with her instead of letting her go off alone to who knows where."

"She *was* your fiancée," Helen said quietly, head down as she buttered her bread. "And you did let her go off alone."

"I let her do what she'd wanted to do all along, what she had dreamed of and planned for years."

"Dreams can change, milord." Helen turned to look at Preston, her eyes softening. Preston reached for her, taking her hand in his on the table in plain sight.

"What is this?" Nicholas asked, gesturing at their joined hands.

"*This,*" Preston said, "is why I asked you here tonight. Helen and I have discovered that we have feelings for each other, and I should like your blessing in courting her with the intent that she shall become my wife."

Helen blushed prettily, reminding Nicholas so much of her sister that it physically hurt. He took a long drink of wine, feeling stunned beyond reasoning.

"Helen," he said. "It is *Helen* you wish to marry. Not Grace?"

"Grace would not have him," Christopher said, taking another bite of meat and rendering himself unable to speak for a moment or two.

Nicholas glanced at Helen to see if the frank assessment of the situation bothered her.

"It is true," she said, with only a slight wistfulness to her tone. "And I knew it would be so all along. Her letters were full of stories about you, Lord Sutherland. We could all tell, very early on, that it was you she was falling in love with. It was why we encouraged her to stay."

Nicholas looked to Preston for confirmation and received it in his slow nod.

"I did care for her," Preston admitted. "But my affection was never returned, and my feelings for Grace were never what they are for Helen. I only wish it had not taken me so long to come to a realization of what was right in front of me—what I had so near for so long yet failed to recognize or appreciate."

Nicholas knew exactly what he meant. What he didn't know was how to proceed from here. That Grace was not with Preston, and that she might still care for him, was enough that he wanted to run for his carriage.

After a minute of uncomfortable silence, during which all three stared at him, Nicholas asked, "Will you tell me where she is?"

"I'll do better than that," Preston said. "I'll take you to her."

CHAPTER 43

Helen came running down the stairs and rushed past Grace, her gathered skirts swishing. "He's here!"

"Goodness," Grace exclaimed. She set aside the book she'd been reading and glanced out the window in time to see a familiar carriage stop in front of the house. "*Who's* here?" she whispered. She brought a hand to her chest and leaned forward for a closer look at the Sutherland crest emblazoned on the side of the landau.

"Samuel is." Helen smoothed her skirt before opening the front door. "I saw him waving as they pulled up the drive."

"In Lord Sutherland's carriage?" Grace left her chair and followed Helen to the front door. Her usually demure, and always beautiful, sister stood on the stoop, bouncing on her toes and clasping and unclasping her hands. Behind her, Grace smiled.

It is good that one of us should be so happy.

"Restrain yourself, Helen. It has scarce been a week since you visited."

"A week is forever," Helen said. Silently, Grace agreed. A footman opened the carriage door, and Samuel stepped down, the look on his face as exuberant as Helen's. Grace's gaze traveled past him, hoping . . .

But the footman shut the door behind Samuel and put up the step, and a terrible surge of disappointment overtook her.

Even after all this time—nearly as long as I lived in his home. Will I never recover?

Samuel met them halfway down the walk. "Helen." He spoke her name with a joy that left no doubt as to his feelings. Grace felt her smile return, though shakier than it had been a moment before. She had kept her promise to Mother. Samuel would treat her sister well. Helen would be cared for and happy.

With an ache in her heart, Grace watched as Samuel took Helen's hands in his and leaned forward to kiss her cheek.

"Samuel!" Helen's rosy blush only heightened her beauty. "You mustn't kiss me in front of Grace."

Grace laughed. "On the contrary, I think he *must.*" She held her hand out to him.

He kissed the back of it, and the look in his eyes changed to a tender, brotherly concern. "How are you? How have you been?"

"Well," Grace said, withdrawing her hand. "The country is every bit as peaceful as we had hoped."

"I am glad to hear it," Samuel said. "Nicholas said to give you his regards. He hopes you are well and eagerly awaits news of your family."

"How is he?" Grace felt her own gaze softening to the point of unexpected tears building behind her eyes. She blinked and turned aside, pretending a sneeze. "And how is it you came to be driving in his coach today?"

"Ah," Samuel said and looked at her knowingly. Grace

knew she hadn't fooled him for a moment. He turned to the carriage. "You thought—"

"No." She shook her head. "I would never expect a visit." With a deep breath, she gathered her wits. "You two have much to discuss, I expect. And owing to the compact nature of our cottage, you do not have much place to do it. May I suggest a walk down the lane to the swing in the old oak?"

"Yes, let's. Please." Helen had linked her arm through Samuel's and was already turning him away.

"I'll search out Christopher, and we'll see you at tea," Grace called. "We can catch up then, and you can tell me all of your plans." She turned away, walking in the opposite direction. The thought of Samuel pushing Helen in the swing, of the two of them walking together, brought a smile to her heart. At the same time, it was a bitter reminder of what might have been had Father not died and their inheritance come through. If Nicholas had not released her from their betrothal.

And freed us all, she reminded herself. It was better this way, or so she'd been telling herself all winter.

She cut through the forest, heading for the steady sound of chopping in the distance. Seeing Christopher in his element would certainly help to clear her head. She'd chosen this life for him, as well, so that he might be free to live a life unencumbered by their father or anyone else.

Unless he chooses it. Not all marriages are as Mother's was. Nicholas would not have been an encumbrance.

Oh dear. Grace brought her hands to her face. Just when she'd believed her heart was finally mending, a little thing like seeing Nicholas's carriage had turned her upside down again.

This will never do. Will I ever forget?

She came upon the clearing. Christopher stood with his back to her, axe in hand, working over the latest tree he'd felled. It was hard work, she knew, yet he seemed to love it—

and this land. She'd be forever grateful to Samuel for helping them find it.

Grace walked around in front of him, where he might view her while she kept well away from the felled tree. After another minute of chopping, Christopher noticed her, buried his axe in a stump, and stood, greeting her with a grin.

"Is everything all right?" He studied her carefully as he wiped a towel across his face. "You look a bit pale." He offered her a dipper of water from a nearby bucket.

"I am fine, thank you." Grace waved the drink away until Christopher shrugged and drank the water himself.

"Mr. Preston has come to see Helen," Grace said. "Will you join us for tea?"

"Ah," Christopher said, much in the same way Samuel had a short while before.

Annoyed, Grace turned away and started for the house. Christopher threw aside the towel and joined her.

"Be honest with me," he said. "Do you have regrets?"

Grace looked at him askance. "About Samuel?" She shook her head. "No. Not a one. He is the perfect match for Helen, and she for him. They will be terribly happy together."

"Hmm," Christopher mused, his lips flattened in an unusually contemplative expression.

"Hmm, yourself," she replied and hurried ahead of him, not in the mood for a brotherly analysis of her life. "If you must know, I am not quite myself because Mr. Preston arrived in a Sutherland carriage, and for a moment I thought—"

"—that Nicholas had come to see you," Christopher finished.

"No," Grace said a little too quickly. "Well, perhaps." The admission pained her. "But why should I think that? I have everything I want here. A home of our own, plenty to eat. No one charging down our door demanding money. The only laundry to be done is our own."

"It sounds charming."

Grace drew in a sharp breath and stopped but did not dare to look back. "What did you say, *Christopher*?"

But it had not been Christopher's voice she had heard.

It is only my mind, playing tricks.

"I said your life here sounds charming. Samuel tells me you have everything you once described to him—freedom, fields of flowers . . ." Nicholas came from within the shadows of the trees into view beside her. "The only thing you lack, perhaps, is an invalid man?"

Grace pressed her hands to her heart. "Nicholas. You *are* here."

And there is nothing invalid about you.

He stood tall and straight before her, in dark breeches and boots, a cream-colored shirt just visible beneath his surcoat. His hair was longer than she remembered, and somewhat messy, as if it had been blown about by the wind. But it was his face she could not take her eyes from—his unsmiling mouth, the blue of his eyes, deep and ever serious.

Those eyes met hers, and neither he nor she moved or spoke. Grace hardly dared breathe.

At length, after glancing back at Christopher and seeing him returned to his task at the woodpile, she found the courage to speak. "Why did you not simply exit your carriage with Samuel? That was a cruel trick."

"As cruel as you visiting with him all those weeks without my knowledge?" Nicholas's gaze was steady, unrelenting.

Grace swallowed, reminding herself that inside his hard, outer shell there was a kind man whom she'd vowed to never fear again.

"No," she said. "Not as cruel as that. That was wrong of me."

The doubt and anger in his eyes dissolved instantly.

"I should have told you," she said. "Should have trusted you to understand."

He shook his head. "I wouldn't have. I was not yet ready to mend fences—or to have you meet him at ours. I shouldn't have driven you to seek out his company."

I do not seek it any longer. But Nicholas had to know that already; there was no point in telling him. She wondered how long he had known, and if that was why he had broken their engagement.

She dared to ask the question that had haunted her every day as she walked these fields and every night when she cried herself to sleep. "Why did you send me away?"

"I was afraid you would regret staying with me," Nicholas said. "You were finally free to go where you wished—to Preston, if that is what you desired."

I desired you. "It was not," Grace said. "It *is* not."

"I know that now. As I should have then, from the moment you offered me this." Nicholas held his hand out and opened it, revealing the silver key resting on his palm.

Grace trembled to see it and closed her eyes against the rush of memories from the most cherished afternoon of her life.

"I wonder," Nicholas said, "whether this key will still unlock your heart. Or have you done as I used to, locking it away behind chains and barriers?"

"It has been ill used." Her voice wavered. "And now I fear it is broken."

So broken. So frightened.

Nicholas nodded. "I was broken once. I did not ever think to be made whole again. But then I was blessed with grace, and my heart—my blackened heart—was mended."

"You did that," Grace said. "You were the only one who could, and you did."

"You showed me the way." He put the key into his pocket and took her hands in his. "I set out to save you, but it was you who saved me."

"I am so glad," Grace said, squeezing his hands then withdrawing hers. She meant it. He had changed—even more since she had last seen him. "You and Samuel traveled in the *same* carriage," she said, suddenly realizing the implications.

The beginnings of a smile curved his lips. "Seven hours together in the same small space—and we did not kill each other."

"I should hope not," Grace said, grateful for the change of subject and that she was beginning to feel that she could breathe once more. She started to walk toward the cottage, fearful he might touch her again and prove her complete undoing. "You had best not harm him. There is the matter of that promise you both made your sister."

"There is that," Nicholas drawled. "As well as a delightful child named Beth."

"What?" Grace turned to him, surprised, overjoyed. "He has shared her with you at last! Oh, Nicholas, I am so happy for you—for you both."

"As am I," Nicholas said. "And I thank you for your part in bringing Beth into my life."

"You are welcome," Grace said, feeling utterly pleased with this turn of events. *Nicholas will not be completely alone. He will have Beth now. And Lady Sutherland will too.* The thought of them all, even his mother, made her heart ache. How she longed to return to Sutherland Hall. How she missed everything about it—most especially the man beside her.

"But you bring up a good point," he continued. "I *always* keep my promises, even to the deceased. And I seem to recall promising your father that if you did not marry Samuel Preston, then I would marry you. And I must say, it appears that Preston is somewhat taken with your sister. She has surprised us all and overcome her shyness."

"He is beyond smitten," Grace agreed. "They are madly in love."

"And are therefore likely to marry," Nicholas said. "Which returns us to the promise I made to your father."

Grace tried to judge his mood but could not. His words were serious, yet his tone was teasing. She had no idea of the right thing to say or do. She had given herself to him once, and it had cost her dearly. He would have to declare his feelings first if that is what he had come for.

Dare I hope?

"Would you like release from your promise?" Grace asked, wondering as she spoke the words if today would be the last time she saw him.

"It is not so simple," Nicholas said. "The situation goes far beyond the promise. It goes back to this." He pulled the key from his pocket and held it out to her once again. "I find myself in possession of something that belongs to you. If you wish to break our agreement, you will have to take it back."

Grace looked at him, still unsure whether he was jesting. "That is the key to your study."

He shook his head. "It is the key to your heart. You told me so when you gave it to me. And I can only assume that since I have had it these long weeks, your heart has been locked."

He had no idea how close to the truth he spoke—or did he? Grace felt a sudden lump in her throat. Her eyes began to sting. She blinked to no avail. The tears came furiously and began to fall, one dropping on his outstretched hand when she looked down, attempting to hide her sorrow.

Nicholas tipped her chin up as he had done so many times before, ever impatient with her attempts at hiding from him. Grace didn't care that he was impatient. She cared nothing about his other flaws—his moodiness, his temper. *Which have all but disappeared and have made his tenderness all the more sweet.*

"My Grace," he whispered, brushing a tear from her face. His arms came around her. "My saving Grace." He pulled her so close that her cheek was against his heart, thundering loudly in his chest. Hers gave an answering leap, and after so many weeks of feeling bereft, a surge of joy coursed through her, bringing her the first glimpse of hope since the day she'd left his study.

"Forgive me for sending you away. Never leave me again," Nicholas begged. "Say you will marry me, and let me guard this key—your heart—so long as I live." He pulled back to look at her. "I cannot live without you, Grace. It is *my* heart that has been locked and cold since you left. Better you had taken it from me than to leave it as you did, painfully beating, making each moment of the day agony."

"It has been agony for me, too," she managed. Then, letting go of all her apprehensions, she threw her arms around him. "I will marry you, Nicholas. Tomorrow, if you'd like. Today!"

He let out a joyous shout, and she clung to him as he lifted her and spun in a circle.

"Stop!" she cried on the second turn. Laughter replaced her tears. "You are making me dizzy."

"That is my plan," Nicholas said. He lowered her to the ground then gently took her face in his hands. "I intend to make your head spin and your heart beat fast every day of your life." He brushed a kiss across her lips.

"Every day?" Grace asked.

He nodded. "So that you will never forget how very much I love you."

"I intend to hold you to that promise." Grace wrapped her fingers around the lapels of his coat and pulled him closer, kissing him until her head spun again and her heart beat loudly, and she knew without a doubt that Samuel was right.

Love was always worth the price.

About Michele Paige Holmes

Michele Paige Holmes spent her childhood and youth in Arizona and northern California, often curled up with a good book instead of out enjoying the sunshine. She graduated from Brigham Young University with a degree in elementary education and found it an excellent major with which to indulge her love of children's literature.

Her first novel, *Counting Stars*, won the 2007 Whitney Award for Best Romance. Its companion novel, a romantic suspense titled *All the Stars in Heaven*, was a Whitney Award finalist, as was her first historical romance, *Captive Heart*. *My Lucky Stars* completed the Stars series.

When not reading or writing romance, Michele is busy with her full-time job as a wife and mother. She and her husband live in Utah with their five high-maintenance children, and a Shitzu that resembles a teddy bear, in a house with a wonderful view of the mountains.

Visit Michele on-line: MichelePaigeHolmes.com
Facebook: Michele Holmes
Twitter: @MichelePHolmes

ACKNOWLEDGMENTS

Writing novels continues to be one of the joys in my life. Figuring out what to do with those stories, once they are complete, continues to be my challenge. To that end, I am thankful for an army of people who encourage, cajole, and otherwise motivate me to dust off the files on my hard drive and get them published. With this story in particular, there are several whose help made that possible.

I am grateful to Angela Eschler, whose insights often make my brain hurt and always make a story better. Her first look at early drafts changed my heroine from wimpy to one who took action and proved an equal to Lord Sutherland's temper.

I am grateful to Cherie Maclean for being particular about her romance reads and for her genuine and helpful comments.

I owe many thanks to Sarah M. Eden, who graciously pointed me in the direction of the best Regency Period research and then patiently explained the rules over and over again when I confused them.

Rob Wells is likely not aware of his contribution in getting this published, but during one of our rare critique group meetings, his comment, "This is good stuff," carried significant weight, since we all know Rob's first genre was romance.

J. Scott Savage and Jennifer Savage continue to be the best cheerleaders around. I am thankful for conversations around their kitchen table, especially those about painful, big-picture problems Jeff is so great at catching.

Lu Ann Staheli cleaned up my chapters at critique and set an enthusiastic example with her flurry of self-publishing last year. So much of what I know about writing has come from her, and I count myself fortunate to have learned from the best.

I am grateful to Annette Lyon for the most thorough edit I have *ever* received and for being a continually supportive friend the past fifteen years. Both our children and our writing have grown up during that time; Annette has always been there, offering support with each.

Heather Moore was more than instrumental in getting *Saving Grace* from my computer to Amazon. Heather is a generous and patient friend. She is also brilliant and always willing to share her knowledge with others. Thank you, Heather, for guiding me along, answering ridiculous questions, and otherwise hand-holding during the process of self-publication. I appreciate it more than you will ever know.

I am thankful for great children, who, at times, put up with a cranky mom and frequent leftovers. I hope you are each able to discover and pursue your dreams as I have mine.

And finally, it would simply not be possible to write without the support of my wonderful husband. Thank you, Dixon, for devoting your Fridays and Saturdays to being an awesome dad, giving me that time to finish manuscripts. Thank you for believing in me—even when I choose the more difficult path. I will always cherish our whirlwind East Coast trip—seven states and fifty thousand words make for a great vacation. I'm looking forward to a future that finds us walking the streets of Edinburgh.

Made in the USA
Lexington, KY
09 January 2015